RECOLLECTION

D1596580

JEREMIAH BECK

Print ISBN: 978-1-66789-913-8
eBook ISBN: 978-1-66789-914-5

Printed in the United States of America

for my Beez

RECOLLECTION

CHAPTER 1

The first mass shooting at a school in America happened at my high school in 1992. Everyone blames the shooter as the sole monster responsible, but the truth is deeper and darker: the murders are my fault.

Raw guilt eats holes through me but every effort to unburden my soul falls on deaf ears. People around me—a collection of acquaintances and strangers I force into the spaces where friends and family should be— take turns looking solemn, struggling uncomfortably to listen or find the right words. They nod knowingly, disagree gently, and console me out of ignorance.

It's not your fault, they say. You're wrong, I say back. I know I'm culpable. I was there. I caused it all.

Drug-induced stupors and drunken blackouts bring momentary relief, but I'm spiraling out of control. It's a manic cycle. The depression is darker, the descents steeper, the despair deeper, my recovery times are shorter. And everything's picking up speed. I'm barely functioning.

My therapist strives to convince me that it's survivor's guilt, post-traumatic stress, a martyr complex, and any number of other syndromes and illnesses that populate her textbooks and notepads. Dr. Darby Grover *is* wonderful. She listens carefully, talks patiently, and believes she can heal me. I love her too, but she has so much faith in her education and experience that she believes it's only a matter of time before I'll experience relief.

She's wrong.

I know it's hopeless; I'm hopeless, a lost cause. I've seen too much and done too much that can't be undone, and I'm too undisciplined to follow a treatment schedule of regimented medicine and ineffective advice. However, she doesn't patronize me, so I keep most of my appointments because she's smart and sexy and I have tiny moments of peace after talking with her. It's not her fault that she can't help me. I'm hiding secrets and I lie to her face. And the memories won't stay where they belong.

(blood's in my mouth and the smell of cordite is in my nose and everything is cold and wet and her dead eyes are pleading for me to help but she's already gone)

I'm guilty, but no one believes me, and I can't find forgiveness. My grief is a toxic, boiling cauldron of regret, helplessness, and rejected excuses. I don't want a pardon. I want to take responsibility. I don't want a pass. I want to pay the price. I don't want a coronation. I want condemnation. I want to fix the permanently broken parts. I want the impossible and I'll try anything. I want the relief that comes to a criminal when he's finally caught and collapses from exhaustion and sleeps because the chase is over.

I want someone to fucking *blame* me.

I dream about it. I've become myopically obsessed. I can barely think of anything else. I've been trying for years to bury images I can't forget, and shoulder a burden that everyone says isn't mine to carry.

Nothing I try is working. I can't keep it up.

My chest constricts with a suffocating heartache when I'm quiet. I hate to be alone and I'm terrified in crowds. I scream into whatever pillow I find in whatever bed I wake up in. I cry while I'm driving. People stare but I stopped caring. My stomach churns. I'm pitted against myself. I'm suicidal and feeble. I'm an addict and a drunk.

And I'm the host of the highest rated nighttime talk show in Washington DC.

I'm sick of living a lifetime of lies. It's why I set things up the way that I did.

Tonight's show is a two-hour long Hail Mary.

Because tonight…I'm going to interview Mason Reynolds, the man serving nineteen consecutive life sentences for murdering seven of my classmates and wounding twelve others.

I'll ask Mason to forgive me—live on my radio show—as a therapeutic stunt I've been promoting for weeks. A New Year's Eve show, from 10 p.m. to midnight, that is supposed to propel me out of the bleakness of my past and into a better future.

Hopefully. Probably not. But hopefully.

In the first hour, with the promise of anonymity and without judgment, I'll put anyone on air who wants to confess to anything: people who've cheated and stolen and lied for years and worse, and need to come clean. No sin is too big or too small. I'm here to listen, and if they hesitate I'll tug on the threads of their story and pull them toward clemency for the benefit of the show.

And then in the final hour, culminating at midnight, I'll confess that I'm the secret antagonist in the infamous Sugar River Shooting, and seek absolution from Mason. I perfectly recall each detail leading up to the murders and each second of that fateful day, unfailingly.

(*she's stretching out her hand, begging and pleading and crying, and the confusion and the violence and paralyzing panic is flooding my body with adrenaline and I'm shaking—*)

Afterward, no one can argue that I'm a victim, or my memories are confused by trauma and time. It's all going to be exactly validated because of a gift I was born with, a curse that I can never break.

My memory and my emotions are *perfectly* and *completely* autobiographical.

I remember and feel *every* moment of my life with painful, exacting precision.

Dates, times, events, meals, conversations, anything I've seen, said, heard or read, from the mundane to the dramatic, are stored in my mind for easy access or random, anxiety-inducing spontaneously triggered reappearances. I can't forget anything unless I'm in a stupor or unconscious. When I sleep—which is infrequent and comes in short bursts or extended disappearances—I have recurring nightmares. My dreams are vivid, terrifying, and incapacitating. I wake up disoriented and exhausted.

I talk to myself constantly, narrating the present to minimize confusion with the past.

I'm always reorienting. The past and present are permanently intertwined, the *Now* with the *Then*.

I'm lost in it.

Nothing fades. Time moves on and the world moves on, but I do not.

I cannot.

How can I be expected to heal when I can't forget anything?

Everyone else loses their acute pain, regret, and betrayal to The Great Forget. I don't.

I'm paralyzed by these unforgotten remnants. Of everything. Of her. Of Sarah.

How can I ever love someone else when I can't let go and there's a ghost who doesn't let go of me? I don't want to be alone anymore, but I don't want to share my life with anyone other than her. There are no words to say, no compelling argument to bring her back. I'm smothered by idealized memories and an imagined future that died when she did.

(my face is in her auburn hair and it smells like the purple and white lilacs blooming in her backyard and she laughs and I feel that she loves me—)

Every so often I need to look around, blink, and remember *when* I am. If I don't consciously bring myself into the current moment, I disappear into the undertow of memories and madness. Dr. Darby is helping me learn to will myself from *Then* into *Now*, to separate reverberating emotions from my current feelings. It's daunting and exhausting and feels impossible and unsustainable, but it's all I know. So just like Dr. Darby suggested, I focus on what's in front of me—the pictures on the wall, taken during my meteoric rise in radio.

Dozens of photos, none of my family. They're all of me with people more famous than me. I'm shaking hands with politicians, musicians, actors, and comedians. I'm swaggering on stage and in bars and at award shows. I'm behind a microphone, scowling or grinning smugly, from my early days in radio back in Madison, Wisconsin, up through these last several months in Washington, DC on Hot Talk 690 WTMI.

The sign on the door, now closed, simply reads, *The People's Talk Show*.

There's a stack of black-and-white, glossy photos of me dressed how I want the audience to picture me: smirking through beard stubble. My straight black hair isn't long enough to pull back and falls where it wants to. I slick it back, other than one spear that dangles above my left eye. I'm wearing a white V-neck t-shirt under a black leather blazer, which is what I'm wearing tonight, too. The camera caught the expression I get seconds before I wink, like I'm sharing a secret joke, but I'm exasperated that no one's figured it out yet. My green eyes are distant. I struggle to make eye contact because I know I'm guilty. The day of the photo shoot, it gave me the appearance of focusing on something off in the distance.

I've scribbled my signature across each glossy with a silver Sharpie so it pops. *Jeremy Peoples*. Big looping J, humps and stabs; big swooping P, loops and a flourish.

Jeremy *fucking* Peoples. *The People's Talk Show*. It's YOUR show, people. But it's MY show, too. I'm Jeremy Peoples. My audience calls themselves "The Little People." We love each other, mostly.

It's 9:47 p.m. on December 31, 1999. The biggest moment in my professional life is in minutes.

Radio personalities, and me especially, obsess over time. Our lives revolve around it. The clock never rests. Always advancing, never waiting. We're either ready or we're crashing and burning, the merciless, uncaring clock ticking away, completely apathetic to the plight of our personal lives. It doesn't care that I'm strung out and falling apart. Time's also vicious and slow when I least need it to be. I can't force it to move faster to escape the crushing embarrassment of public humiliation. Sometimes I get lucky and a segment or a show will come together, with preparation or spontaneously. Those moments are thrilling and rare. The only thing I love about time is that it keeps moving. When mistakes are made, more opportunities to win or lose rush toward me unrelentingly. I control none of it.

The clock's second hand is deafening, ticking faster that it should, speeding up, getting louder. Am I in an asylum? Have I gone completely insane, finally? Is this really happening or is it a delusion?

Oh my God. I need a drink.

Maybe Dr. Darby is right. She believes the interview is the worst decision I could make. She's repeatedly tried to talk me out of bringing Mason on the air, warning of an "irrevocable dissociative episode." Yet, her description of a worst-case scenario sounds identical to what I've been going through every day for more than seven years. Therapy is taking too long. I'm impatient and need a breakthrough. And if I pull this off, it should garner the publicity I need to get a radio show in New York City, a gig I'm supposed to covet. On the brink of even greater fame, I'm disgusted that my macabre celebrity past and talent have wealth-creating potential. I'm still driven to succeed as everything inside of me collapses.

There's no way I have the nerve to do this sober.

The office is usually desolate at night, and besides, it's New Year's Eve. I yank a bottle of Seagram's 7 out of my desk drawer, fumble with the lid, lift it to my eager mouth, hesitate for just a blip—should I, or shouldn't I?—and decide that I definitely should. The familiar burn hits my tongue, my lips, my throat, steaming warmly in my chest and stomach. I tilt the bottle back further, gulping compulsion taking over.

STOP, I tell myself. I catch my breath.

The bottle hits the top of my desk with a jarring thump, emptier but heavier. I even startle myself.

I cough, shake my head, blink my eyes several times, sigh, and instinctively retrieve the soft pack of Marlboro Lights crumpled in the right front pocket of my Levi's. Tobacco flakes fall from the cellophane on to my shirt. I pop a bent cigarette in my mouth and it sticks to my dried lower lip as I reach both hands to my chest, patting myself down in search of a light.

My Zippo is in the left pocket of my jeans.

I stretch out my legs, recline in the chair, and inspect it like I sometimes do. Remembering…

(It was early in the morning on June 3, 1994, and I'm lying face down on the ground, bleeding and laughing despite getting my ass kicked. My favorite pair of sunglasses crushed underneath me. My face, smashed. People literally stepping over me, no one asking if I need help. Why would they? They saw what happened. The must've thought I had it coming. They're probably right. I definitely overreacted.

Something in the gutter reflected a glint of streetlight and caught my attention through the semi-blindness that comes with a broken nose. I stretched and caught hold of it, noticing that two of my fingers were dislocated, the knuckles bulging unnaturally. I ignored the pain, rolling over on my back with a groan. Buzzed and busted up, I inspected my find.

A Zippo lighter.

The Jack of Clubs was engraved on one side, and on the other—inexplicably—was a cursive "J" and "P" over the date "3/16."

My initials.

My birthday.

Broken beer bottles and pea gravel poked into my back as I lay in the parking lot, holding the Zippo like a trophy in the soft moonlight and buzzing neon. I grinned but then grimaced as wet pain throbbed in my nose. I tilted my head to the side, gagged, hocked, and spit out a wad of blood and phlegm and—)

I shake my head. I'm back in the present. What startled me? Did someone knock on the door?

Management banned smoking in the building months before I arrived from Wisconsin. I flick open the Zippo anyway and light the crooked cigarette still stuck to my lip, take a deep drag, and blow a cloud of blue smoke toward the ceiling vent. Another quick inhale, then I drop the Marlboro, glowing tip down, into a cup with just enough stale coffee in it to hiss out the cigarette. I wave my hand at a lingering wisp of smoke as something catches in my throat and peels of wet coughing wrack my body, eventually settling into a wheeze after half a minute of near-choking. The headrush makes me dizzy, disoriented. My breath comes in tentative gasps as I try to get oxygen without sparking another spasm of hacking.

"Fuck me," I gasp.

Someone *is* knocking on my office door.

My producer, Wafer, is talking and lightly tapping to see if I want him to come in. Each tap is a nudge, creating enough space between the door and the jam to peek and see if I'm choking to death. He's talking work shit, hoping for an answer to confirm I'm all right, knowing that I hate being asked if everything is OK, especially when it never is. Nothing is fine. It's all fucked.

"… and the new bumper music is in, like you asked. Some really choice cuts, man. I got the Lauryn Hill stuff, Bittersweet Symphony, Gravity Kills, Cracker and Stabbing Westward. The show'll sound tight, Jeremy. There's already twelve callers on hold. They all want to confess. Anyway, man, can I come in? Or are you coming out? Are we cool?"

Wafer is a nervous bastard. He hasn't relaxed since the day we met on June 6, 1999, at 2:48 p.m.

Aaron van Waveren is a gaunt 6'5" and has a patch of the finest, blondest hair I've ever seen, like a newborn baby's. Tall, thin, and nearly albino white, I started calling him Wafer on the day we met. My boss sat us both down in the office after my last producer quit (she'd replaced the one who'd quit two months earlier) and said that he thought we'd make a great team and a bunch of other corporate bullshit. I couldn't decide what I thought of Wafer at first, but he made eye contact with me, smiled, and did *not* say, "It's going to be great working with you" (which I hate). Instead, he told me, "No one thinks I'll make it six months. There's a pool, so I bet on myself. You're stuck with me for six months and a day because I need that four hundred thirty-five bucks." I laughed and our boss relaxed.

We've been together ever since. He takes a lot of shit from me and always covers my ass.

I should treat him better. The oldest coping mechanisms are the hardest to change.

I clear my throat.

"Give me, like, two minutes, Wafer," I manage. "I can't find my phone. I forgot where I put it." Lies.

The familiar warmth of a Seagram's buzz is rushing into my chest and flashing heat across my face. I take one more pull from the bottle. Less burn. So I take one more sip.

My head is really swimming now.

Vaguely, I consider how little I've slept the past four weeks, and especially the last two days, fretting over the show. It wasn't a good idea to drink that much, that fast, without eating, now minutes before the most important show of my life. I get up slowly and kick the office chair backward. It skitters across the room before careening into the wall. I shove my lighter and cigarettes back into my pocket, grab my headphones, and take a few tentative, off-balance steps toward the door.

Dread settles in.

Anxiety rises into my chest, hammering away on my heart and again turning my mind to the memories that I have to confront again. Sheer willpower keeps me upright. I'm sick to my stomach, like I want to puke but know that I won't. How the hell am I going to do this? What the fuck was I thinking?

(the electrical ballasts are popping and arcing and exploding and I don't flinch and Mason keeps coming and points his gun at her and I watch it happen and why didn't I close my eyes so I couldn't remember?)

Calling it a memory is inaccurate. I relive the moments, feel the fear, see it like a fresh religious vision. An unhealed, festering wound. The memories come at me constantly, becoming more acute, more painful, more vivid, and more debilitating with each occasion. I'm in two places at once, two times at once, past moments confusingly fighting with the present for space in my today.

I feel myself walking toward the studio. Christmas decorations are still up, tired and useless. Red and green and tinsel and scotch tape. I hate Christmas. It's so fucking *happy* and *stupid*.

A salesperson, oddly out of place in the building after hours on New Year's Eve, appears in the hallway. She smiles and starts to talk, but my ears are ringing from alcohol and gunshots reverberating across time. I can't hear what she's saying. I watch her smile disappear as she averts her eyes and dodges past me. Do I look that bad? I mumble something; it's probably incoherent.

There are four radio stations in my building. One of the other studio doors is open, a Rock station, blaring sound into the hallway. I recognize a song. It's Metallica. "Nothing Else Matters."

I stop.

HOW the FUCK is it THIS song playing while I'm walking by to do THIS show? I want to run away, but I'm transfixed. I hate it and love it. It's the terribly perfect soundtrack for what's about to happen.

I'm transfixed, listening. Alcohol and this song and images of the day I keep reliving and the pressure I've placed on myself to make this a turning point are overwhelming me completely.

I've made a big mistake.

I cannot do this show tonight. It's going to be a disaster.

I feel a lump in my throat, telling me I won't be able to speak. I'm probably mute. The thought of talking to anyone, especially Mason Reynolds, causes an intense shiver to run up my spine.

My mouth is dry. My tongue is fat and lifeless in my mouth.

A piercing noise drowns out all other sound except Metallica and my thoughts. A brutal ringing.

My eyes are burning. They feel bloodshot. Every breath is labored.

I want to run to the elevator and escape. I want to smoke a cigarette. I have to get out of here. I'm about to commit career suicide and crater my life in front of hundreds of thousands of people and have a nervous breakdown live on the air and end up in an asylum scribbling confessions on the wall and I feel rivers of flop sweat running down my forehead and dripping off my nose and I wipe at them with my shirt and I really need something sweet to get the taste of Seagram's out of the back of my throat and—

There's a hand on my shoulder. I jump out of my skin.

Wafer's voice. "Whoa, man, hey. I got you a 7-Up. And there's coffee and water in the studio. You look like shit. I mean, I wouldn't say it if you didn't really look shitty but wow. You realize you're on in nine minutes,

11

right? We've got to do this, man. How much have you had to drink? When did you start drinking? Have you slept? Have you eaten? What can I do, man?" Wafer is rambling. Freaking out.

"I'm copacetic, bro." I'm not the least bit convincing. I'm a terrible liar when it matters. I'm a mess.

One second later, my mind explodes with living memories of my darkest day, helplessly watching life leave Sarah's body, failing to protect her, Mason's screams reverberating as the gunfire echoes dissipate. Adrenaline and anguish and regret and searing nerve pain. Gushing bullet wounds. My blood. I know it's *now*, December 31, 1999, at 9:57 p.m., but it feels exactly like it did *then*, on May 23, 1992, at 7:54 a.m.

Vertigo.

I turn to see Wafer's stunned face, then I'm looking up at the ceiling, as I topple over backward and crumple to the floor. Tunnel vision. Soft sounds in the distance, like people shouting in a soundproof room. Are they yelling at me, or for help? Doesn't matter. Darkness collapses the light into tunnel vision.

The past won't stay where it belongs. It bleeds over the present as I see and feel it all unfold again.

CHAPTER 2

I laid on my back in a pool of blood and water.

My blood.

Her blood. Her BLOOD. I was covered in her.

I screamed for an ambulance. I couldn't see or hear if anyone was helping.

I turned my head to look at her again, my right cheek on the floor.

I breathed water and viscera into my nose and mouth and then into my lungs and it choked me.

But still I looked again.

Her eyes were open, fixed, staring at me, devoid of the hope that had been there just seconds earlier. I couldn't tell if she was still breathing.

Her body didn't move. Her beautiful auburn hair was matted with the aftermath of terrible violence. Tears poured down my face. He shot me. Twice. It felt like I was bleeding out, but I felt no pain. The insanity of what I'd heard and seen—shock—and the enormity of the loss blocked out everything else. I saw her necklace, free of her neck, the chain broken but still attached to the pendant, inches from where she lay. The emotional anguish was more than I could take. It was my fault. She was dead. I had let her die.

No—I killed her!

There were other bodies, dark forms, scattered.

How many?

People moaned and screamed and someone else was crying and the sprinkler system had gone off.

Water poured down, only now finally stopping, dripping instead of flooding. Fluorescent light ballasts swung back and forth, sparking pops of blue-white brilliance.

Where was the ambulance? They needed to save her! She's not breathing! Forget about me! Forget everyone else. God, if you're real then keep her alive. Do a fucking miracle!

My clothes were completely soaked. I couldn't tell where the water ended and my sobbing began.

Why did it smell like metal? What was that taste in my mouth? I looked up, then back to Sarah.

Her favorite jeans, perfectly ripped how she wanted them, flecked with death. She's going to be pissed that they were ruined. I turned to fix my eyes on locker number 316, my locker, two bullet holes punched through the door, blood stains inside, the contents spattered along with the lockers next to it. Was it my blood? Did I just get shot? I again looked to Sarah, then squinted to look down the hallway through the chaos and darkness. My darting eyes met the face of Mason Reynolds. He glared at me, his hunting rifle at his hip, pointed at me. Mason pulled the trigger, but the gun was finally and mercifully empty.

CLICK.

I flinched. Nothing happened. Mason pulled the trigger, over and over.

Click. Click. Click. Click. Click. Click. Disappointed but resigned despite his failure, Mason persisted.

One more futile trigger pull.

CLICK.

I was alive. Why didn't he strangle me? Or stomp my face in? Had he'd gotten me good enough, content to wait it out as I bled to death in front of him? He tossed the gun aside and flopped down in the water next to me, his stringy, dishwater blonde mullet soaked and straggly. Mason leaned forward and pointed his left index finger at me. He showed no signs of remorse and howled, "Look what you made me do!"

I feel hands on me. Not Mason Reynolds. Someone else?

"Wake up, man. You passed out. What's happening? Somebody get some water. He's awake, he's awake, he's getting up. I don't know what happened. He just fell, you saw what I saw." Is that Wafer?

(CLICK. CLICK. CLICK. CLICK. CLICK. CLICK.)

"Whoa, hey, fuck, don't touch me!"

("Jeremy, help me," Sarah begged, screamed. "Please! Do something! Jeremy! Wake up!")

Three faces hover over me, bugging eyes, genuinely concerned. Someone's hand is on my shoulder, but they pull it away when I yell. How much time did I lose? Seconds? Minutes? Hours? Did I manage to completely fall apart and miss my show? I doubt I'm that lucky. I'd hate myself.

"What time is it?" I manage to croak.

"Shit, it's time to go. We are on in seven minutes. It's 9:59 right now." Wafer is trembling. The salesperson that avoided me in the hallway says something about calling 911, but Wafer is emphatically arguing with her, saying, "No way, he'll kill me" and twisting his head back and forth so vehemently I think he'll pass out next. The third floating head I saw when I returned to now is a fill-in DJ who works weekends and holidays and is getting his big shot on New Year's Eve. I don't know his name. I decide to unfairly blame him for being the asshole playing the Metallica song that pushed me over the edge.

"What the hell happened?" Weekend DJ asks. He wants to be part of something, anything.

"None of your fucking business, part-timer," I bark back, instantly regretting it, too numb and disoriented to apologize. I crane my head, lifting my shoulders and neck off the ground, then slump back again, resting my head on the floor and zoning at the ceiling. The vents need to be cleaned.

The Sales Rep is staring at me. I know her name now that I'm paying attention to her face. Jennifer. We met four months and 12 days ago. I recall thinking that while we spoke, if I made the right move, she'd sleep with me on the second date. I never made the move. I wonder how many Jennifers work in radio and get tired of *WKRP in Cincinnati* comments? I made one anyway, just to be a flirty irritant. Now, the look of concern in her eyes is more humanitarianism than attraction. Who could blame her? I smell like failure, alcohol, and body odor. I've sweat through my shirt and hadn't showered earlier today. It's probably a bad time to ask her out for drinks. I close my eyes again.

I'm in no condition to move. I try it anyway.

I'm up on my elbow, jerk on to my hip, roll over into a near push-up position, then maneuver myself into a kneeling stance that looks like I'm fearfully venerating some ruthless pagan god. Head down, palms up, eyes finally open again. I've never noticed the tile floor before. It's hideous; the grout is stained and filthy. I need to get up. One leg up, then another, I sway, I lurch, but I'm on my feet. I can't get my bearings. I know where I am, but it doesn't feel like I should be here now.

"Is he gonna try to go on the air like this?" Jenny asks Wafer. Wafer is now nodding "yes" just as emphatically as he was nodding "no" a moment ago when she asked about taking me to the hospital. Wafer has my back. I'll reward this moment. Eventually. Maybe.

"That's not smart. Either he's sick, or having some kind of episode or something. He's totally drunk. I'm calling…" I interrupt. Forcefully.

"Look. You. Are. NOT. Going to call anyone. There's no way you can stop this. So just get your shit, and go. This isn't your business. After tonight, this'll be a story you can tell when you want to impress people with how well you know me. But I swear to God. If you call someone and get me pulled off the air tonight, I will fucking ruin you."

Every word I say is calm but fierce. I'm not drunk. Not completely. I'm having a nervous breakdown.

The color drains from Jenny's face; she blinks away a frustration cry, backs up, and, without saying another word, turns and high-heel jogs down the hallway. I turn my ire to Weekend DJ but he's already retreating to his studio like a scolded coward, glancing over his shoulder to ensure I'm not following him. He has to be aware that he can't alienate me. My photo hangs in the corporate lobby.

"Jeremy. We gotta go. Right now." Wafer hands me a Styrofoam cup of ice-cold water. I slurp it. His hand is in my armpit, guiding me to the Hot Talk 690 WTMI studio. I can walk on my own, but it's strangely comforting with Wafer's arm around me. He's running his mouth and I'm ignoring him.

I'm trying to get my shit together, my thoughts together, a show together.

I can't clear my head. I can't prioritize information. Give me the god-damn coffee. It's almost time.

I lean into the heavy studio door, force it open with what feels like my last remaining strength, and sit down in front of the mic. Even drunk or disoriented or whatever-the-fuck I am, I easily pop my headphones on, putting one can on my left ear and placing the right one just behind my other ear.

I adjust my blazer, pull at my damp shirt, smooth the front. I reseat myself, settle in. My routine.

Breathe.

I clear my throat. And keep clearing it. It is a weird little glitch with me. I have to clear my throat in a certain way, otherwise I get the hiccups. It's all throat action, a sort of cluck-cough noise. Then, a sip of 7-Up. Sniff. Cough again. I wish I knew some trick like this to clear my head. I'm still hazy.

I look to see Wafer behind the glass directly across from me, along with Sammie, my call screener. She's the absolute best. An intern. Smacks her gum, but shows up on time, no drama, little chit chat. Perfect.

When the national news wraps, it's two minutes of local headlines, and two minutes of commercials, and two hours of me. I'm drinking coffee out of my stained, dirty, DC101 coffee cup, promoting Howard Stern before he left for WNBC. I put my lips to it. Radio station coffee is notoriously terrible. Stale, strong, burnt, lukewarm. This sample is all of that and worse, but it's doctored with just enough cream and sugar to gag down a couple of swallows.

At 10:06 p.m. *The People's Talk Show* presents: my reckoning.

"Two minutes, Jeremy," Wafer deadpans into my headphones, as though it's my first day.

"Yeah, no shit. I'm good. I'm ready. Aircheck tapes ready? This is history tonight, dude." I'm getting into my headspace. Finally. Did I manage to get perfectly drunk in order to do this the way I want? Am I in that "loose and relaxed" phase that allows people to walk away from a car accident without a scratch? The stars have aligned. Or I'm convincing myself. Does it matter?

"Aircheck deck is loaded. Callers are still on. Been holding for almost twenty minutes. Sammie tells me to take Line Three first. It's John from Silver Spring. He's calling from his cellular phone, says he's a drunk driver. The others are all straightforward, but he sounds like a killer way to start this thing. But, hey, bro, do it your way. We got you," Wafer chirps, clearly feeling more at ease. He seems to sense that something big could happen tonight. Terrible or wonderful. Either way, the atmosphere in the room is electric. Nothing will be the same after this (hopefully). My heart is drumming behind my ribcage. I finish the coffee. I finish the 7-Up. I gesture at my empty cups and Sammie scurries in to fill all three again.

It's time.

The phone box is flashing red lights, racked full, LED names assigned to blinking blips, each a story. It's only me at the round counter-top table, alone with my microphone and The Little People.

It's only me.

I take in the room and the moment. The studio is circular. Tan walls, logos and soundproofing, more photos, curtains to cover the glass when the room sounds hollow, carpeting and a low ceiling. It's a chapped-lips-sore-throat blast furnace when the heater's running. My eyes are dried out. I pull a plastic squeeze bottle of Visine from the inside pocket of my blazer, squirt two, cool drops of relief into each eye and toss it on the table. There's air moving but not enough to make noise. I should take off my blazer, but I like I how I look when I wear it. I need to feel cool. I'd stand up if I wasn't buzzed. Why can't I smoke? I need to smoke. The show would be better if I smoked. It's bullshit I can't smoke in here.

I hit the mic button, silencing the overhead speakers to kill the feedback loop.

A full-throated radio station voiceover talent touts my greatness, and the greatness of my show, as the intro music for my opening segment begins. It's Marilyn Manson, "The Beautiful People."

Reaching down for as much bluster and bravado as I can possibly muster, believing my confidence will catch up to the image I want to portray, I take a deep breath.

CHAPTER 3

"This is *The People's Talk Show*, on Hot Talk 690 WTMI. Your voice, your freedoms, your calls and faxes, your host, me, Jeremy Peoples. The Libertarian, Gen X perspective, where the people rise up, because the institutions—the government, the church, corporations—are *all* corrupt. Liberals, conservatives, Democrats and Republicans *all* want to take away the parts of you that make you *YOU*. But we won't be bought, we're not silent, it's our time, the Baby Boomers have gone bust…and tonight, on the eve of destruction, on the last night of the millennium, on the cusp of a Y2K computer meltdown, we're living like the End is Near. The End is *Here*! We only have two hours before society could completely crash, before nuclear weapons launch accidentally, power plants shut down, criminals run rampant as blackouts roll from coast to coast, before it comes down to you protecting yours with your Second Amendment rights, we're going to exercise our First Amendment rights.

"Tonight, we're *coming clean*, you and I.

"We're going to take responsibility for the things we've done, for the things we're doing right now. If we're all going to face death and destruction, we need to do it with a clean conscience. If the Information Superhighway and the World Wide Web come crashing down and access to money and information goes with it, we have to trust one another on the other side of this.

"Tonight…anything goes. You all get a free pass.

"Tell me your secrets, Little People. Tell me your name or disguise your voice and give me an alias. The only thing I ask? Be honest. Whatever stories you plan to tell had better be true and had better be *you*. I can tell when you lie. But if you're telling the truth, and you need to come clean, and you need me to help you unburden your soul…or find the person you need to confess to…I'm here for you. I'm on your side. I'm not going to judge you. I'm not going to tell you you're wrong, that you shouldn't have done this or that or you should have done this instead. I'm going to listen, I'm going to ask questions. I promise I'll be gentle—"

I am on fucking fire.

"—and I promise to lead by example. I, too, am going to confess something that none of you knows. I'm going to shock you. Some of you will be disgusted by what I've done. Many of you will try to call and defend me from myself. You'll think I've lost my mind, that I'm taking responsibility for something that isn't my fault. Each of you will be wrong. Of course you're free to think as you want. You can call and plead your case. But I'm right, and you're wrong. In fact, for those of you who know a bit about my life before I came to be your voice in our Nation's Capital…you'll know that what I'm going to confess to has already been discussed in a court of law, and ad nauseum in the court of public opinion. I've been under oath in one of the highest profile cases our country has ever suffered through. O.J. Simpson, the Clinton Impeachment, and the Sugar River Shooting trial of Mason Reynolds. The biggest trials of the past 50 years. I lived through the Sugar River Shooting. I was shot twice. It's part of the public record, but what I'm about to share, tonight…what I'm going to confess to you…is not common knowledge. It's not something people know. And I have a special guest in the final hour of the show—maybe the final hour of our lives—to make *my* confession *to*. None other than Mason Reynolds, on the phone

21

from Waupun Prison in Wisconsin, to talk with me, one of the people who survived the 1992 killing spree that left seven of our classmates dead. You know nearly all the details that our national news media *chose* to present to you, based on their agenda and their bias and their desire to sell papers or grab ratings. You may even know the inspiring stories…how several of my friends overcame their wounds to walk again, or despite traumatic brain injuries pressed on to achieve greater things like completing college and starting a foundation. But this part of the story has not been told to many people, and those who've heard it still don't believe it. So tonight…as we face the uncertainty of the end…I'm going to share with you the unbelievable true story, and my part in it, and I'm going to confess my guilt to Mason Reynolds, live on the air, for each of you to hear. If we're gonna go out…we're going out with a frigging bang."

(Sarah is smiling her perfect dimpled smile as she comes around the corner.)

I shake my head. Blink my eyes. Stay in the moment.

"Don't ask me how my team and the lawyers managed to make this happen. I'm still not sure. Don't ask why the warden agreed. Don't ask why Mason Reynolds said yes. The effort to put this together must have been guided by some higher power. The universe *wants* this to happen. This is cosmic, kismet, fate, serendipity, bashert, fortuitous, magic, predestination, whatever word you want to use. But I can assure you, it's happening. And before we get to all that, the microphones are yours, first. Porn addiction? Tell us. Drug binges and drunk driving? You're safe with us. Hedonism, adultery, stealing, assault, harassment, stalking, corruption, secret abortions? You want to come out of the closet, admit to cheating in college, tell your parents you hate them, tell your children they're adopted, tell your boss to screw himself—it doesn't matter what it is. None of it matters tonight. In less than two hours, we could all be dead or locked in a dystopian struggle for water, gas and survival while Western civilization's grip on power, always tenuous, slips away and we descend into anarchy. Y2K might take it all away from us, in less than a second. But one thing it cannot take away from us is our capacity to confess, to seek forgiveness, to unburden ourselves before it all comes to an end. Armageddon? The Apocalypse? Ragnarök? Or just a bump in the road that's been hyped to the hilt by fear merchants and swallowed up by the ignorant gullible masses? That's the insanity of it all. No. One. Knows. But even if we're wrong, and tonight is just another wild party with Dick Clark and the Ball Drop and "Auld Lang Syne" and champagne kisses at midnight…we've still come clean. They can't take that away from us. We've still lightened our mental load, our emotional baggage. We've restored relationships, gotten right with our gods, made ourselves feel better, and maybe we'll all sleep just a little better tonight, rested and ready for all the Bowl Games tomorrow. And then again…if we're right…and this is the end…we'll meet our makers together, free of sin, confessing secrets, forgiven and ready for whatever's next…"

I don't believe any of this end of the world bullshit, but it makes for great radio theatrics.

"So, here's the phone number. If you get a busy signal, keep hitting redial. Find a phone booth, dig around in your car for spare change. Spend the minutes on your cellular. It *will* be worth it. Are you ready? I'm about to open the phone lines for the next hour and ANYTHING GOES. In fact…"

I pause here for eight seconds; Wafer, always nervous, is used to my pauses but still hates them. He points at the mic light, and just as he reaches for the in-studio intercom, I start talking again. Wafer throws his hands up in mock annoyance. Sammie snaps her gum, silent behind the glass. I'm feeling it now. I needed a strong start and I'm rolling and I'm ready to be honest with the audience. With everyone.

"I started drinking heavily before the show, I haven't eaten in two days and haven't slept much this year, and I'm pretty sure I'd get a DUI right now if I was on the road. But my thoughts are clear, I mean everything I'm saying, and you all know I'm totally uninhibited by social pressure, manners, or the internal filter that tells us we should keep our secrets, not show anyone who we are, be afraid, be inauthentic, lie to protect the soft underbelly. It's gone. Seagram's killed it."

Wafer's face freezes. He grinned at me throughout the entire monologue. But the second I confessed that I was drinking, his smile remained as his eyes filled with surprise, creating a grotesque, pale-white opera mask of dread in the window. His hand goes first to his forehead, then pulls at his hair. I literally see Sammie's gum drop from her mouth. I see two more faces appear in the producer's room. I'm drawing an audience from inside the building. I am walking the tightrope. I've never been this amazing.

"My producer, Wafer, is already freaking out that I'm telling you that I'm buzzed, drunk, right now. The government could fine us, hundreds of thousands of dollars. This is now, technically, an illegal broadcast, according to the FCC standards and practices—who, by the way, have their home office right here in DC. Hot Talk 690 WTMI could lose their broadcast license for what I've just told you—"

I'm wildly exaggerating.

"—but honesty, confession, truth…is all that matters to me. I've lied for too long. I passed out just minutes before coming on the air with you. I was out cold, suffering from a panic attack or vertigo. They had to crack smelling salts and literally carry me to the microphone—tonight's show is *that* important…"

More bullshit. I often embellish when it's completely unnecessary. I need the story to be bigger than it is, even when it's already huge. The persona is protection; the bigger the façade, the deeper I can hide.

"That's the burden I'm carrying. I couldn't do this sober. It's that big. I'm putting my career and my life on the line with you tonight. You're not alone in your confessions. We're going to go down in flames together, or find redemption on the other side together. Are you ready for the number? It's 1-800-696-WTMI. That's 1-800-696-9864. You're going to get a busy signal. All the phone lines are taken. Keep redialing. Over and over and over until you get through. Or fax your secrets to the WTMI Fax Line at 1-800-696-6900 and I'll read your confession on the air. Your friends, your family, your neighbors, your co-workers, are already calling. Maybe they want to reveal something they did to you. Wouldn't you like to know the truth? If you don't want to call, you still *need* to listen. You may hear about something that's happened to *you*. You may be the co-star in someone's confession. Hundreds of thousands, millions, are listening. You may hear someone asking you for your forgiveness. You will NOT. WANT. TO. MISS. A. SECOND. OF. THIS. We're back in three minutes, on a special New Year's Eve edition, of *The People's Talk Show* on Hot Talk 690 WTMI."

Bumper music. Wafer chose "Guilty" by Gravity Kills.

I'm clear.

Opening monologue, totally ad-libbed.

Commercial break. Microphone off.

I wrench my headphones off and they get tangled in my hair. Pulling them loose from the snarl and tossing them on the table. I rub my face, starting at my forehead, down across my eyes, pinching the bridge of my nose, wiping the stickiness from my lips and on to my jeans. My eyes remain closed, but I hit the intercom button without looking and calmly ask, "Who the fuck is in the producer's studio other than my people?"

I open my eyes to glare through the window.

A crack of light turns into an open door as the interlopers scatter. Wafer shrugs. Sammie cradles the phone receiver between her ear and shoulder, filing her nails with certainty. She's undoubtedly asking the right questions as she guides the callers who've gotten through to replace the others who've grown impatient and hung up. I can't believe how raw and suspenseful this all feels.

"Jeremy, man—" Wafer's voice echoes in the room over the intercom.

"I know. Don't say it. The audience needs me to be real."

Wafer is rarely firm with me, but he says, "Dude, this isn't *just* about *you*. This is my life too. If you get fired, I get fired. Then what? You've got a shot at another gig somewhere, even if it isn't New York. I'm a nobody. I'm trying to make this happen for myself. This show isn't just your dream, man. I have a dream too." There's an air of desperation and expectancy surrounding Wafer. He's counting on me not to blow it. But I'm the last person he should put his faith in. Wafer thinks—needs—me to make my future happen, so he can have the one he's fantasizing about.

I'm the meal ticket to his celebrity. He needs to know I'm taking this seriously.

"OK, Reverend Doctor Martin Luther King Junior." I'm sarcastic when people need me to empathize. I'm at arms' length when they need a shoulder to lean on. I'm a terrible friend. It's not that I don't recognize what's happening. Is it a wall? Probably. I'm safe behind the borders I've built to keep pain and intimacy at bay. Compartmentalize and perform. Fake authenticity masking doubt, powerlessness, and fear.

"Hey, yeah, whatever, Jeremy. You're a comedic genius." The intercom pops off with a click. The only thing I hear in the room is the faint sound of advertising jingles playing through the speakers. I light a cigarette. Exasperated, Wafter shakes his head again, and points at the (massive) sign that reads, "ABSOLUTELY NO SMOKING." I blow a smoke ring at the glass and give him the finger. He smiles back, sort of. Now I need a fucking ashtray.

The commercial break is over.

I want to get back into the show quickly. Callers are stacked twenty deep, and I have to jam as many in as I can before the end of the first hour. I've got to create a show that the audience will remember and talk about for years, and a tape demo that will take me to stardom…or infamy.

I go to the phones.

After the drunk driver, who I quickly discover is faking, The Little People don't let me down.

Call after call is absolute awkward, uncomfortable broadcast brilliance. People are eager to confess their deepest, darkest secrets to me, in front of an audience that *has to be* enthralled, even on the New Year's Eve at the start of a new millennium. If they're in the nation's capital, they're listening to me. I'm completely caught up in salacious secrecy and emotional unburdening. Porn. Drugs. Embezzlement. Adultery. I'm sweating, pushing coffee into my body and pushing callers on and off the air. It's visceral ugliness, it's moments of pain, it's eager authenticity and the freedom that comes with it.

Amidst all this, I focus on a name on the phone box that's stayed there for nearly the entire hour. One call after another either went on air with me and blabbed or hung up and had their name replaced by another. I imagine people hitting redial on their phones as they drive, people at payphones pumping in quarters, getting a busy signal, hanging up, collecting their change and starting again. People at parties, the radio loud, dialing again and again, ready to talk about a date rape or some other secret shame. Through the turnover, there is one person that remains stubbornly and persistently on hold.

Stacy.

Twice now Sammie has picked up the line to see if they're still there, and both times she looks up at me and nods. Stacy is mysterious; they won't tell Sammie what their confession is. I'm also feeling dread about seeing that name for the first time in year.

While another caller prattles on, I hit the intercom and ask, "What exactly is Stacy wanting to talk about?" and Sammie and Wafer shrug. Normally, I'd bail on a caller like this. Talk show hosts are like attorneys: I never ask a question I don't already know the answer to. Taking a caller on the air live, unprepared, is the quickest way to sound like an idiot in front of hundreds of thousands of listeners.

I punch the intercom again.

"Well, what the fuck *did* he say?" I demand.

"Wait," Sammie pauses. "How'd you know this is a he?" She puts at the phone box, inquisitively.

"I've known men and women with that name." My heart races. Is it really him? Tonight?

Wafer looks down, then back at me. "He says he knows you, dude. Needs to talk. We should do it off-air. I don't know what this is all about, the guy won't say. It doesn't feel right to me. I can—"

I click the intercom off, and the rambling confession of the current caller again fills the room. I reach for my microphone again, then stop. Could it actually be him? After almost four years? If it is…why now?

Stacy fucking Ramone.

It feels sinister, but I also have this gnawing need to put Stacy on the air and see what happens. I'm down to the final five minutes in my first hour, prison officials confirming with Wafter that they've moved Mason Reynolds, he and his attorney are on the phone as planned. Everything's working out perfectly. Brilliance has unfolded. Can my shaky mental state hold together for one more hour?

Maybe.

But I know I have to talk to Stacy, and it has to be live on the air.

I'm so fixated that I didn't notice the caller I have on has finished. "Hello? Jeremy? Are you there?"

"I was. Good luck," I retort and hang up on her. "Got time for one more confession before 11 o'clock, when I'll face the man who shot me at point blank range on May 23, 1992, at Sugar River High School—Mason Reynolds. One final caller. I have no idea what he wants to say, but he's been on hold for the entire hour, so it must be something big. Special. Dark. Secretive. And here's the best part: he says he knows me. So let's find out together. They say you should always save the best for last. Stacy, you're on with Jeremy Peoples and *The People's Talk Show*. It's your turn…to confess and make amends."

"Hey, Jeremy Peoples. What's it been, hoss? *Four years?*"

I recognize the voice.

It's him.

My heart thuds in my chest and ears.

Fresh sweat forms at my hairline and under my arms.

Hard swallow. I reach for the coffee, but the cup's empty. The 7-Up can is crumpled at the bottom of the garbage can. My water's gone too. I open my mouth, close it, open it again, and blurt out, "Three years, ten months, five days. If you give me a second to think, I could get you the exact time. It was a pretty big day for all of us. I'll never forget it."

"Yeah, you and that crazy memory. You don't forget anything, do you?" the voice rasps.

"Not if I'm sober," I joke, but I have this sinking feeling that I know where this is going. I cannot believe that of all nights, when I'm confronting the part of my past I want to confront, another part I've tried to bury has appeared without warning. How did Stacy know where I am? Why did Stacy call the studio line? How did he manage to get through? Why is it happening tonight? Why am I doing this to myself?

I should hang up, but I can't.

"Always a smart mouth too. I'm not surprised that this is what you're doing," the voice continues.

"Stacy, I need to tell The Little People who you are. We're down to the final three minutes of the show, and I don't want anyone left out. Are you cool if I explain our...*friendship?*"

I am on dangerous ground, and this *might be* messier than I can control. Yet at the same time I have a show to do and time isn't favoring me any longer. The hour *had* flown by as I got absorbed in revealing secrets. Things begin to move in slow motion. Stacy and I have a long and sordid history, and I have no idea what he's going to say, live on the radio, about me. Or his wife, Michelle. Or *that day.*

"Yeah. Sure. Tell everyone," the voice agrees. He doesn't sound hostile. He's…stoic? Somber?

"Stacy Ramone and I were roommates for about a year. We partied. A lot. Had a falling out four years ago and Stacy kicked me out of his place. Threw all my stuff out in his backyard. In January. In Wisconsin. We haven't spoken since, and I don't have the slightest clue why he's calling now, of all nights, to talk to me on the air." I regain my confidence as I tell these half-truths.

"No idea why I'm calling?" Stacy scoffs. "I've been listening on hold, hoss. I had no idea the number I found was a studio number. I just called it. And waited, and listened to the confession show you've been doing tonight. And now you're going to talk to Mason Reynolds too. No, I imagine you don't know why I'm calling, but I guess you might be thinking very hard about what I *could* say—or what I *might* say." The voice is measured, neither foreboding nor friendly, and it's making me nervous. "I think your audience would actually understand why I did everything I've did. You deserved worse. I used restraint."

"Tell us, Stacy. We've got less than a minute left in the hour. Otherwise, like the number of licks it takes to get to the center of a Tootsie Pop, the world will never know." It's too cute for the moment, but I still have to be the Jeremy Peoples my listeners expect me to be.

"You slept with my wife when you were living with us," the voice begins. "I caught you, but the two of you stayed close even after we had— what'd you call it, hoss?—our 'falling out.' It's about all that."

(she asks me for a cigarette, and I know she doesn't smoke but she's been drinking and I've been drinking and we're home alone together again and—)

The yearning rushes back. I'm acutely aware of how the empty spaces she had filled are vacant again. Timelines in my mind intermingle between Mason Reynolds and Michelle Ramone. I shake my head. I can't disappear into my recollections right now. I need to be sharp, emotionally detached.

But now I'm spinning. I've been caught completely off guard.

"Not a secret," I interject. "At least, it wasn't between us. Then. And we broke it off when you caught us. And it stayed broken off. We only talked once more. We were friends, Stacy. Michelle is a beautiful person. But nothing else happened after you threw me out. You're still together, right?" Wafer and Sammie have both stopped; each are pressing their headphones tight over their ears to listen. Wafer notices I'm looking at him, panic in his eyes, makes the throat-slashing motion with his finger and mouths "DUMP OUT OF THIS!" Sammie can't make eye contact but is chomping furiously on a fresh piece of Big Red. At some point, four other people have crowded back into the producer's room despite my orders. There's a studio audience in here. The voice doesn't answer my question. It proceeds.

"*You* called it a falling out that led to me throwing your stuff in the yard. I wanted to kill you. And yeah, we worked it out because I loved her. But I don't need our dirty laundry aired like this. I called because you need to come home. I didn't want to go on air, but I was sure you'd blow me off if I just left my number. Jeremy, I need you to come back to Wisconsin. *Tomorrow.*" There's an indiscernible emotion in his voice, his cadence quickening. Urgency. Not anger. What is he feeling right now? I'm off-balance.

"Tomorrow?" I'm incredulous. There are sixteen seconds left in this hour of my show before I have to get to the news. "On New Year's Day?" Suddenly, I'm paranoid. Shaking. "Why now? What happened?"

"Michelle. She's gone. She's...she died. I have no one else to call. She had secrets. I found things she wrote. A diary. I have questions I think only you can answer...and *you owe me,*" the voice is expectant, morose, and accusatory.

Breathing. Silence. Waiting.

I glance at the clock. Four seconds left in the hour.

Sammie is shaking her head "yes" with a look of disbelief.

"Will you come to Michelle's funeral Jeremy?" Stacy presses. Two beats of dead air. The hour is up.

I blurt out, "Yes. I'll leave in the morning," right before Wafer cuts my mic and Stacy's phone line, pressing buttons with a flurry of jabbing fingers and consternation, perfectly joining the national news update. He runs his fingers through his wispy, white hair and flops down into his chair, slowly swiveling in a circle as he closes his eyes, head tilted backward. Sammie mouths the words "fucking whoa" at me.

It's precisely 11 o'clock. In six minutes, I'm confessing secret sins on the radio and interviewing Mason Reynolds, but I can't stop myself from daydreaming about the last time I saw Michelle Ramone.

CHAPTER 4

On April 2, 1996, I was dead to the world, clutching a pillow under a sleeping bag in the backseat of my car—a red 1986 Dodge Charger with a five-speed manual transmission and a turbo kit. It had been a decent ride when it was new, but eleven years of Wisconsin winters, road salt, and neglect had turned it into a rusty rattle trap. The windshield wipers had turned into black licorice weeks ago, when I was too drunk or lazy to pry them free from the ice before turning them on. The Charger needed new brakes, a muffler, a tune-up, and gas...but I was broke. I bought the car a few months ago from my friend Soda (I learned his real name was Brandon Bollinger on the day he signed the title over).

A piece of notebook paper taped to the back window was my makeshift license plate. I'd outlined "LAF" (License Applied For) with a ballpoint pen and darkened it with scribbles until the ink ran out. It was amusing to me that my car was boldly—in ALL CAPS—ordering people to LAF at ME.

It was funnier still that I had never actually applied for the license at all.

I was sleeping in this fucking Charger because Stacy had thrown me out. In January. Homeless in the middle of a winter in goddamn Wisconsin. I had deserved my eviction, but had escaped even worse.

All my clothes and music were in the hatchback. The rest of my belongings were in the passenger seat. Although it was early April, it had dropped into the twenties the night before and the windows had frosted over. Wisconsin winters hang on like the nagging cough.

I couldn't figure out why I was awake this early when I'd only passed out a few hours earlier.

I scowled and rubbed my eyes and the upholstery lines on my face. I was groggy, still high.

A silhouette loomed near the passenger side door, indistinguishable through the foggy frost and predawn darkness. "Jeremy, it's me. Open the door." A woman's voice.

Barely awake, I scraped away the frost, scratching a few dirty lines in the icing that coated my back window. I blew warm air into my fist, smoothed my hands together, back and forth, and put the side of my palm on the window to melt a clear spot so I could see out.

"C'mon, Jeremy. Unlock the door. It's Michelle. It's cold."

"How...how'd you find me?" I shouted. I wasn't angry. I was thrilled. I was scared.

She should not have been looking for me. I was momentarily, wonderfully, happy.

"I thought I saw your car the other night. Now please, open the door. I'm freezing. I need to talk to you. I don't have anyone else to talk to other than you." She sounded worried. "Please, Jer, just...I don't care what you look like. It's OK. I'm...I came alone. Stacy doesn't know I'm here."

I yawned and unlocked the doors. "You'll need to get in back with me. The passenger seat is full of my shit. I can't turn the car on because I'm almost out of gas, but there's a sleeping bag in back to bundle up in. It's sort of romantic, right?" I was smiling.

I could still smile.

Michelle stifled a laugh, opened the passenger door, and climbed in the back next to me. It had been a little more than two months since I'd seen her but she looked the same as always. Maybe better.

It caught me off guard. I'd imagined maybe she was just as lost as me, that we were spiraling together.

If she was, she was hiding it. If she wasn't…the thought of it came with an unexpected stab of disappointment. I didn't want her to struggle. But I didn't really want her to thrive, not without me.

Her strawberry blond hair was messy, unbrushed tangles, and old hairspray. Michelle's face was puffy and her eyes bloodshot. Without any makeup on, a constellation of freckles stood out across her dimpled cheeks flushed pink from the frigid morning air. Her emerald-green eyes sparkled. I reflected on how our eyes were almost magically the exact same color.

Michelle had pulled on a heavy men's black leather jacket.

Stacy's coat. A couple of dangly silver chains, pockets, and zippers, a refugee from the hair metal style of the mid-1980s. It was hard to tell how many layers she'd piled on underneath the coat. Her turtleneck ended at her jawline, protruding from the collar of an inside-out sweatshirt. She had on jeans and a pair of fur-lined snow boots. Michelle was dressed to be out in the cold for a while.

She pulled her scarf away from her mouth, cinching it to keep her neck warm, took off her teal stretch gloves, one at a time, touched my face and asked gently, "Are you going to make it, Jer?"

I had a slight spasm that I couldn't control, a sort of full body shiver. I started to pull away, but then leaned into her touch. Was this a dream? It felt real. I placed my hands over hers. She flinched and pulled away. It WAS real. She WAS here. Michelle was careful to only reveal her thoughts and emotions at the right moment. This morning she seemed barely in control of her feelings.

"Yeah, I'm OK." I touched my hair, which was standing at attention in four different directions. I had crusty eyes and nostrils, and hadn't shaved in weeks.

"Are you eating?" she asked. Her compassion was one of the things I adored about her the most.

"I do eat. Sometimes. I got this great thing going. I go into a restaurant, order coffee, and sit and watch for tables of people with kids. Kids never finish their food. When they leave, I slide past the table before the busboy comes and shove a half-eaten toasted cheese sandwich or chicken nuggets into my pocket. It's pretty smooth." I felt the need to overexplain myself to her. I was rambling.

"Are you...bathing?" she pried. Her persistent spirit was one of the things I adored about her the most.

"When I feel especially gross, I sneak into the hospital through the emergency entrance. I look for an empty room with a shower. I get a good clean-up about once a week, which is really all I need since the weather is still cold. But summer's coming. I may get ripe faster." I smiled. Michelle wasn't smiling back. Almost five years older than me, her line of questioning felt prying and parental.

I pulled off the old, brown work glove that I had found in the hatchback of the Charger. It was soft, threadbare, and smelled like stale gasoline. I opened an old Marlboro Reds box; inside were the ingredients needed to roll my own cigarettes: a pack of Zig Zag papers, and a sandwich bag with a crumble of mixed tobacco varieties. The baggy was rolled into a neat tube that I unfurled like a tiny, clear plastic bedsheet. Michelle wrinkled her nose and narrowed her eyes. "Where'd you get that?" She pointed, and spun her finger in a circle two or three times. Of all the things to be judgmental about, it was my fucking tobacco? "That...looks nasty. And it stinks."

"I pick cigarette butts out of public ashtrays, pinch off the filters and the burnt ends, tear apart what's left, and roll my own. It's a bunch of different brands, some are menthol. And papers are cheap, so it's saving me like

$2 a day. It's not that bad. You get used it." Michelle shook her head. "You really do."

"That is absolutely disgusting." She gagged. Her brutal honesty was one of the things I adored about her the most. "I can't believe you're smoking those. Jesus, Jer. It's so gross. I can buy you some smokes."

I pulled out a paper, creased it, sprinkled in a pinch, flicked out my tongue to dab at the glue, roll-twisted it into a tobacco-joint but stopped short of lighting it. I clinked open my Jack of Clubs Zippo, then closed it again. No way I could smoke this in front of her. It smelled dirty, like hot cat piss, stale and smoky.

Michelle looked at me again, penetrating my heart.

I felt deeply, painfully for her, but I couldn't allow myself to call it love. My capacity to feel that way for someone had died years earlier in a school hallway. I was desperately in love with a phantom, an ideal, a dead future that was more zombie than daydream. I was forever in love with Sarah.

Yet our lives were connected; we meant something to each other, and those emotions were still so horribly and sweetly close to the surface. Dangerously close. She didn't look away. I didn't either. There were miles of loneliness between us, begging for an end to this awkward dance.

I'm terrible at guessing people's motives. Why can't they just tell me what they want or need? I'm constantly in my head with nonstop memories and emotions and confusion and drugs and exhaustion, so I miss social cues, misunderstand body language and don't internalize what people were saying until hours, or days, later. I was always off-balance, but never this badly with her. It was incredibly obvious that she had something crucial to tell me. I suddenly wanted to scream.

"Hey...Shell...Just...why are you here? You can tell me. It's OK."

Michelle rarely lost her composure; she seemed surprisingly vulnerable. She clutched a ball of Kleenex. Puffs of steam clouded from her mouth. Her nose was running. She sniffled and wiped at it.

"Jeremy, I don't know what to do. I'm so sorry. I shouldn't have come. I need to go. I don't have anyone else. I can't say anything to Stacy and I don't want my mom and dad to know. Yet." Michelle looked down at her feet and shifted in her seat. A single tear traced down her cheek and disappeared into the corner of her mouth. She licked her lips. She frowned.

Her entire countenance darkened.

Michelle reached up between the seat and the door to find the handle and run away. The seatbelt slowed her down. She was tangled in her escape attempt, upset and scrambling to flee but couldn't. When I put my arm between Michelle and the front seat to stop her, she paused and peered over her shoulder, hunched and defeated, tense and coiled.

"Just. Goddammit, Shell. Hold on a minute! What the fuck is going on?"

Whatever was going on, it had shaken a woman that was unflappable; she was brilliant and perfect even at gunpoint. God, she was brave in every way I was a coward, strong in every way I was broken.

She was better than me.

Michelle slumped back, her shoulders sagged, her neck relaxed, and her head fell to her chest, but only for a second. She looked up, took a deep breath, and confessed, "I'm going to have a baby, Jeremy."

I need to wake the fuck up, I tell myself. Come back to today. Now. The past doesn't want to stay where it belongs. Wafer is saying, "Earth to Jeremy. Bro," into the intercom as I realize what is happening.

How long have I been lost, reliving the distant replay of crossroads intimacy in the backseat of my car? A minute? Two? Longer? I reach for the in-studio phone and grab the handset to see if Stacy's still on the line. Dial tone. He's gone. I point at Sammie and don't even bother reaching for the intercom.

She knows what I'm going to say.

"Get him back on the fucking phone! God. DAMN. It."

Wafer frantically punches the intercom and starts unloading on me. "Mason FUCKING Reynolds is on the Hotline! Right now. With his lawyer. And the prison warden. And instead you want us to get the guy who just called you out for sleeping with his wife BACK ON THE PHONE? For what? We don't have time for Jerry Springer shit, bro! This interview with Mason is the whole fucking deal, man." Wafer throws both hands in the air, turning the intercom off when he does, but keeps yelling. Sammie points this out, so he cuts it back on. "...insane. I respect you, man. I really do. But this is totally out of control. Call this Stacy dude back tomorrow. This interview took weeks to work out. We can't just flame out on it, and I swear to GOD if we do you'll blame me for this somehow..."

I'm paralyzed. Maybe tomorrow *is* the end of the world, and it has nothing to do with Y2K.

"I don't even know if he lives in the same place," I mumble. "I need his address."

"Jeremy. Wake. THE FUCK. Up." The intercom clicks off again. Dazed, I realize I'm holding the phone and staring at it. Wafer pushes through the crowd in his claustrophobic producer's box, yanking open the door, running to the studio. I think about throwing my body weight in front of the door. My social anxiety is reaching a climax. I can't focus amidst this intermingled mess of memories.

"Sammie." I look up at her. "Sam, was he on the caller ID? Can we star-69 from our system? Did you jot the number down anywhere? Tell me you got it. Tell me someone got the fucking number."

Then I stop myself.

I *had* looked at the screen. Take a deep breath and remember. I saw it. The number is 608-855-0316.

I sigh.

Wafer barges into the room.

I'm going to save myself, just in time for the next hour. I'm focusing. I sit up in my chair, adjust my shirt under my blazer, slick my sweaty hair back into place. I'm smirking. Wafer's face is red. He's panting.

"You really need to get laid, bro," I tell him. "You're seriously uptight. A real buzzkill sometimes. Find yourself a Little-Miss-Right-Now and get that tension out with someone other than me."

"I hate you, Jeremy." Wafer glances at Sammie, but I don't bother looking.

"You love me." My face softens to feigned indifference, but my eyes are smiling.

"No, I hate you." Wafer takes his wirerimmed glasses off. They're the type that loop around his ears, so he has to pull one stem up and around with his thumb and forefinger, then move the entire pair of glasses across his face to the right and unloop the other ear. It seems like a lot of work. He loosens one of his shirt buttons, and starts rubbing his lenses, cleaning them.

"You...hate that you love me?" I poke.

"I just hate you," he immediately replies.

"You love that you hate me, then?" I'm chiding him. He has to know we're cool again.

"No, man. I fucking hate you. OK? You're the worst person in the history of humanity."

"And you, Wafer, are the daughter I've always wanted." He finally cracks a real smile. "Let's go into the first break with the mixdown edit you did of Stabbing Westward's 'Save Yourself.' If this goes like it could, commercial breaks will be tricky, so prep to bunch them at the end of the show. It's already a shitshow with Jennifer watching me pass out in the hallway. I can't blow off a bunch of spots too."

"You take care of you. I've already thought all this through. Just nail this interview, man."

"It's not an interview, Wafer," I say sternly. "It's a *confession*. I'm confessing to him."

Wafer nods, slowly at first, agreeing, understanding, and finishes with a couple of quick, final, affirmative jerks of his head up and down. "I get it. Just be ready. There's no room for error here."

CHAPTER 5

"Just give me…one goddamn minute." I am on the verge of exploding.

I'm in the radio station parking lot with Wafer and Sammie and an assortment of other people that I recognize but don't know. They're lingering, probably waiting to hear if I have anything else to say. Who are these people? Why don't they have something better to do on New Year's Eve at the start of the year 2000? I look at my watch. It's 12:11 a.m. It's actually New Year's Day now.

I'm filled with confusion. I feel emasculated. I'm raging inside.

"Why are you still here?" I ask them. "Don't you have some place else to be? The show's over." No one seems to know what to do, except look at me, Wafer, Sammie, and each other. They're not leaving.

I'm trying to process what's transpired over the last two hours, but can't make sense of any of it. I've never lost control of a situation like that before. I've been out of control, but have never lost control of *my show* to someone else. Until now.

Fucking Mason Reynolds.

He stole something from me, again. No, he *murdered* something I needed in my life, again. But how? I had been ready. I confessed. I asked for forgiveness and then he….

"Why would he say that?" I ask no one in particular. Wafer holds his hand up to the group of people nearby, directing them to keep quiet. Sammie gazes across the parking lot, stomping her feet to stay warm, glancing at me out of the corner of her eye. "How could Mason know those... things? Do you think the fucking lawyer set me up? There's just no way. Right after Stacy called. And Michelle. She's..." I can't say it. I don't even want to think it. My mind wrestles feverishly, the effects of my drinking binge mostly worn off. I'm trying to bring order to chaos, trying to find a rational explanation for the metaphysical. I'm trying to believe what I don't want to believe, terrible truths that are real but shouldn't be.

"There's just no way he could know that," I hear myself say. "THERE'S NO FUCKING WAY!" I scream, startling the group still hovering around me.

I can tell from Wafer's face he wants to leave. So does Sammie. Our small group of co-workers finally disperses. I twist into my black wool trench overcoat and button it up. From our vantage, I can see the Washington Monument silhouetted against the skyline. President Clinton set up a special millennium celebration to culminate in the illumination of the iconic obelisk on the Potomac. Y2K was a bust.

"Jeremy, I...I don't really know what to say. I don't think I understand what that was, and I don't know that any of us ever will." Wafer cautiously sizes me up after watching me swing wildly from blacking out to performing, from hopeful and genuine contrition to stark confusion, from volcanic rage denial. He's trying his best to settle me down. "Bro, I got a call from Michael."

"What did he want?" I whisper. Michael Hess is my General Manager. I'm not surprised that he was aware of what happened on air tonight. "Am I fired?"

Would it really be that terrible to get fired? The embarrassment would undoubtedly sting. This job—this career, this fame—was someone else's idea for me. I hardly love it even though I get paid (well) to sit behind a mic and run my mouth. It actually feels gross tonight. Do I really want any of this now that the show is on the verge of turning into something big?

Or am I just giving up?

A weak, forgotten nobody? A quitter? A loser? Maybe. Probably.

Wafer answers me. "Fired? Dude. Mike said he had the office manager check the voicemail system because when he tried to dial into his own messages, he was getting an all circuits are busy notification. So when she finally got through, there were literally dozens and dozens of voicemails. Hundreds of missed calls. When people couldn't get through on the studio lines, they started calling the business line. They left voicemails on *Michael's* account! I got three other calls from people in the building, asking me what was going on because they got pages about messages at the office with an emergency call back request. Sammie changed the fax paper *twice* while the show was on! And I know you're not an AOL guy, but the chat rooms and message boards were going *nuts* talking about what just happened. Bro, this thing was…I don't know what it was…but the whole thing…the end-of-the-world-confess-your-sins-thing…and then this Mason Reynolds 'prediction.' You did it, man! We're going to New York! I've never in my life seen anything like this. Fuck, I've never even *heard* of anything like this. I know Mason wasn't what you wanted, but man, this… this was something else altogether." Wafer laughs. "No, we're not fired. This wasn't the end. This is the *beginning*!" He's grinning and simultaneously trying to provide the right amount of empathy for all he's watched me go through. I guess he's being…encouraging.

"It was pretty fucking trippy," Sammie agrees.

I guess I should be happy. How can I be? I don't give a fuck about New York. Not really. Maybe tomorrow the thought of even greater success and more money will prove an effective substitute for redemption.

But I know I'm wrong.

I have to go to Wisconsin, and bury my lover, my last friend.

"You pulled it off, man. I have no idea how you did it. They might try and burn you for what happened in the first hour. I mean, you were drunk and two people saw you pass out in the hall. Especially if you leave for another station and void your contract. But *so-fucking-what*! I wish there was some way to know the ratings just for tonight. Dude, we've been number one in our timeslot for the past three books, and now people are talking about this show on New Year's Eve at the start of the fucking *millennium*! This Y2K thing only helped you. The theater of the mind you built and knowing that the tinfoil hat people would be listening to a talk station for the first signs of the end of the world, and then talk about it on their computers, it was just…genius! How did you know it would work? How did you do it? Just you and a microphone. No computer. No notebooks. The way you worked all those callers, playing off them. The way you hit the news to the *second* after that Stacy guy called. I don't. I can't. I'm just …" Wafer's finally run out of words. It was one of his better rants, and I may have stopped it sooner were it not so specifically tailored around how incredible I am. "It was awesome. That's all I can say. Fuck Mason Reynolds. You're going to New York. It was awesome, bro."

I smile wanly. "I don't really know why it worked. I just felt it when I started talking."

"It was fucking awesome," Sammie nods, blows a bubble, and snaps her gum. "So weird."

The adrenaline is draining from my body. I'm completely exhausted, but I know I'll never sleep. I'm in desperate need of numbness. I want to forget, to go down to where new memories can't be made. Relief from my swirling mind. A blank canvass in the darkness. I'm mentally building my wish list now. If I can't find forgiveness, then I'll go looking for oblivion.

I need to find The Floyd Chicks.

"I'm gonna go get fucked up. Wanna come?" Wafer and Sammie look at each other, then back at me without saying anything.

It dawns on me.

Sammie's not waiting around for a ride. She's waiting for Wafer. Sammie and Wafter are together, now.

I'm suddenly lonely.

"No man, thanks, we're gonna…we're gonna go out to eat. Just…be careful. Don't drive. Take the Metro. It's amateur night and cops are everywhere. I don't want to bail you out or ID your body." Does he care about me, or does he care about what will happen to him if I'm gone? "And bro, eat something. OK?"

"Goodnight, Jeremy," is all Sammie says.

They head off toward Wafer's car, parked on the far side of the lot, in the back. I'm embarrassed that I have my own spot close to the building, and people who are working harder than me are relegated to the outlying areas. I watch them grow smaller and further away as they approach one of the only cars still here. Sammie's a foot shorter than Wafer, yet somehow they fit together. Wafer, it turns out, is a gentleman. He opens the passenger door for Sammi, and she jumps in. He scurries around the back of the car, almost giddy, and tries to open the driver's side. Apparently, Sammie pranked him, locking the door. He playfully yells, "Hey, c'mon!" and "I'm serious, it's cold out here!" before she relents.

Wafer lets the car warm up for a few seconds.

I watch them leave.

"Wafer and Sammie," I say. "Well, OK then." Everyone has someone. Except me. My someones are gone.

I turn to my car, a black, 1999 Mitsubishi Eclipse 3000GT. It's the first new car I've ever owned. I love the tan leather interior contrasting against the black exterior, the vented doors, the spoiler, the aftermarket window tinting…the *speed*. When I turn the key, the engine roars to life. It wants to be driven. I look up.

Dots of frost on the windshield immediately bring me back to my recollections of Michelle.

(nose running, hand clutching a damp ball of Kleenex, puffs of steam coming from her mouth as she struggles to find the words, her cheeks pink from the cold, emerald eyes flashing, tearful and angry)

"I can't believe you're gone now too, Shell." I compartmentalized my feelings while I was on the air in order to get ready for Mason. Performance over, disappointment and despair have begun to swallow me into darkness. "How are you gone? Why are you gone? Why does everyone have to fuck-ing *die*?"

Tears well up in my eyes. I look to see if I'm alone.

I am.

I crack.

My shoulders heave and I'm sobbing for Michelle and for Sarah, but mostly I'm crying for me. I'm alone. I'm in trouble. I've got to face something and I'm not ready. I'm haunted, mocked by personal demons, suffocated in a suffering worse than hell. I'd rather be dead, but I can't pull the trigger.

(Sarah's wide eyes look into me, no, through me, lips pursed and word-less, auburn hair matted with gore)

Suddenly, I'm done crying. It's been less than a minute. I'm either in shock or all my emotional exhaustion has drained away, and there's nothing left. My head is pounding. I need to escape myself.

I wipe my face on my gloves and blow my nose into a Burger King napkin.

I have an Alice in Chains CD in my car stereo. "Rooster" is playing. I turn it up, then turn it up more.

Louder. I can't hear myself think anymore.

Clenching a freshly lit cigarette between my teeth, I angle the stick shift into reverse and pop the clutch. The Eclipse squalls backward out of my parking spot. I crank the steering wheel to the left, find first, turn the wheel sharply back to the right and punch it. I hit second gear, then third.

I careen out of the parking lot and onto the street, picking up speed. I'm through the first red light without stopping. Someone honks. I roll the window down and a blast of ice-cold air rips through the car.

How fast am I going? I glance at the speedometer: 80 mph in a 35 mph. I accelerate.

I fly through another red light. This intersection is deserted. Then another. I'm in fifth gear. I'm screaming. Over and over. Anger, confusion, frustration, hopelessness, all coming out at once. I slam my fist on the steering wheel. If I keep driving, faster and farther, maybe I can escape. I force the accelerator to the floor and lock my knee. "Why her too?! WHY!!?"

I hear Michelle's voice again, like it was moments ago, not years. I close my eyes. *"I'm going to have a baby, Jeremy."*

I opened my eyes. It took a few seconds for the words to register after she said them. Michelle carefully took in my hesitation, my body language, my averted eyes. I tried to find the perfect thing to say.

"Are you sure?" I asked.

"Of course I'm sure! I took three pregnancy tests. And my period is late. Like, really, really late. And I'm never late, Jeremy. So yeah, I'm pretty sure." *Michelle folded her arms with a huff.*

"You took the test yesterday? On April Fool's Day?" I either think too much and won't share what I'm feeling or I blurt out cutting comments or quips as a deflection. "Are you playing a prank on me...?"

Michelle punched me in the mouth. "You fucking ASSHOLE!" she yelled. "You're not funny, Jeremy. This isn't funny. Not everything is a joke. Not everything is a set-up for you to make fun of it. Out of anyone in the world, you should know that you can't just keeping pushing people...." She stopped, gasped, put her hand to her mouth, and instantly pleaded, "Oh my God, Jeremy, I'm SO SORRY! I didn't mean that..."

I think the utter hostility in the implication of what she said would have hurt more if not for the shock and pain of getting hit in the face. I deserved it.

I never even tried to duck—I was too stunned. She hit harder than I would've guessed she could. I dabbed at my lip. Michelle rubbed her left hand. There was a nick of blood on her knuckle. I saw only compassion and contrition in her eyes.

My mouth brought unexpected violence out of people my entire life, from friends, family, and enemies alike. It wasn't always what I said, but how and when I said it. My reactions created overreactions.

"I cannot believe you just punched me in the face. What the hell?" I exclaimed as Michelle giggled uncomfortably. "I've been punched by more than a few people, but you're the first woman."

She was fierce and emotional, with perfect timing. It was one of the things I adored about her the most.

"You deserved it. I'm sorry for what I said, but I don't take back the punch," Michelle said. "This isn't a practical joke, Jer. I'm pregnant. And I needed to tell somebody. I needed to tell you, actually. I thought about telling my mom, but I can't because…I just can't. Not if I decide to…not ever. She won't—"

"Shell, why aren't you telling Stacy?" I interrupted. I dreaded the truth of it, regretting our carelessness.

"You know why."

Michelle unzipped Stacy's jacket, wiggled out of it, and flopped it over the back of the passenger seat. She fidgeted with her hair. She picked at the seatbelt, pulling it out from underneath her.

"Will you hold my hand?" she finally asked.

We interlocked fingers and she squeezed. Gently at first, then harder. Her painted nails dug into my palm. Our faces were closer now. Her gaze shifted to my mouth. I leaned forward. She pressed toward me, then abruptly stopped and pressed her fingers gently—but firmly—against my chin.

"Jeremy. Don't. I'm not going to kiss you."

"What? Why? Is it because of Stacy still?"

"I don't know how else to say this, so I'm just doing to say it. I'm sorry. Your breath. When's the last time you brushed your teeth? If you think I'm going to kiss that mouth..." Michelle grimaced.

"Wow," I protested. "You just came out and said that. Rude. Probably true, but rude."

And then she just blurted it out.

"I think this baby is yours. Probably. I know it is. It has to be. I thought about not telling you, but I feel like that would make me a terrible person. I thought you'd want to know, but now I'm not sure. I know you've already been through too much. But I can't hide this from you because I'm afraid of what it might do to you. What if I didn't tell you and you somehow found out anyway? What would that do to you? I can't...I don't think I can do this without you, Jer. I don't know what else to do, who else to tell. We did this. You, me, and...this. We can't ignore this and we can't wish it away. We have to deal with it."

CHAPTER 6

How long have I been here?

The music is deafening. Painfully loud. It sounds like Prodigy, "Firestarter."

I'm holding a drink. I taste it. Judging by the how easily the Seagram's overpowers the 7-Up, I probably ordered a double. How many drinks have I had? I don't feel drunk but I can't remember how I got here.

I'm at a bar.

It's packed, too small for a club, but a rave is climaxing around me. There are high tops situated throughout the room, although no one is seated, and no one is eating. Not tonight. Not on New Year's Eve—now New Year's Day—at the start of a new millennium. The entire place, other than the bar itself, has turned into a dance floor. It's dimly lit.

Several attractive female bartenders in tight, low-cut shirts are serving drinks, collecting tips, and pretending to flirt. They're smiling and chatty, but it's impossible to hear what they're saying over the music. Three men with gelled hair, whitened teeth, and spray tans also work the bar. It all feels fake.

I can't stand crowds. I feel claustrophobic when I'm in large groups. I'm on the verge of panicking.

Each breath is a shuddering necessity, my hands tremble. Too many people.

I spy a sign behind the bar above the rows of bottles and tap beer handles that reads: "By Order of the Fire Marshall, Maximum Capacity Shall Be Considered Reached at 316 Persons." There must be nearly double that amount crammed in here, nearly touching me, hundreds of unwashed, inebriated, grinding, and cheering strangers. It smells like fresh sweat, a drunken organism with a sexual hivemind objective.

Alcohol and hormones.

There's a House DJ on an elevated platform, behind a wall of sound equipment and plexiglass, in the furthest corner behind me and to the left. Bass reverberates in my chest and skull. Smoke, swirling color, dim overhead lighting, and strobes obscure the rest.

Whatever is happening deeper in the darkness belongs where it is.

I'd never choose a place like this. I usually sit in taverns and play a jukebox and drink until someone calls me a cab out or I start a debate over politics and sports until I've exasperated all of the regulars or there's a fight. Why am I here? I hate clubs. I need a quieter space to get wasted. This is too much.

I pull out a cigarette, but leave my lighter in my pocket. I lean in to ask the nearest bartender a question.

Where the fuck am I?

"Got any matches?" I yell instead.

She reaches under the bar, grabs a glass bowl filled with matchbooks, and holds it over the bar. I take one from the jumble and see that I'm somewhere named "Club Insomnia." Still totally confused.

"Crazy question," I shout.

My bartender settles her chin on the palm of her hand, elbow and breasts resting on the bar.

"Where am I?"

"Sixth Street Northwest." How did I get Downtown?

"Another crazy question," I yell.

She's slyly smiling now, enjoying a break from the normal bar bullshit.

"How long have I been here?"

She points at my watch. I shrug and refuse to look it. Are we flirting now?

"You came in about 30 minutes ago. You been sitting here staring into space, drinking your drink and then ordering more. That one—" she points at my glass "—is your third. You been tipping well, too." She seems unconcerned that I'm clearly confused and moves on to the guy next to me who's waiving a $20 bill and asking for a Cosmopolitan and a Bud Light.

I finally look at my watch. It says 1:07 a.m. I snatch my glass and down my (third?) Seven and Seven. I'm suddenly self-conscious; essentially I'm at a rave and I have no idea what I look like. I catch the eye of my bartender; I assume she's talking about me with her co-workers because it shouldn't be that easy to get her attention through deafening music and strobe lights. She whisks over with gliding strides.

"Got a normal question this time," I shout.

"Boring," she says. Why can she speak normally, but I keep shouting? Maybe I don't need to yell.

"Where's the men's room?" I say.

"What?" she asks, cupping her hand to her ear.

"Bathroom!" I yell.

She turns slightly to her left, and points at an angle to the corner opposite from the DJ booth. It's dark. I can't actually see where she's sending me, but I act like I get it. "Thanks."

"Crazy question," she says. Now I know she's flirting with me. For tips, or for real, it doesn't matter. I arch my eyebrow so she knows she has my attention, and make eye contact for the first time.

"Are you that radio guy? Jeremy Peoples? The talk show host?"

"Why do you ask?" I shout, far too loudly as the music transitions into Nine Inch Nails, "Closer." The pulse of Trent Reznor's degrading sexual passion rage builds behind the background noise of clinking glasses and dozens of indistinguishable conversations.

"That guy," she waves at one of the male bartenders," said he met you at a car dealership. You were there doing something on the radio and gave him a signed picture. He said he listens to you every night, and on his way here tonight he listened and said you had a meltdown on the air or something. Are you, like, some kind of celebrity or something?" She says the word "something" a lot.

"Or something." I shrug.

She loves that answer.

"Are you saying you're truly something?" she teases. I pause. Things have moved from "I'm pretty sure she's flirting for tips," to "She's making a move" now that she's learned I'm semi-famous. I run through some responses to what she's said, but instead I smile and ask her to save my seat.

"I'm coming back," I promise.

Lights pulse brighter as I try to find the alleged men's room, pressing through the crowd and their conversations, disoriented. The momentary euphoria that came with the thought of opportunistic sex vanishes. Someone spills their drink on me. I brush it off and no one apologizes. I'm jostled. Someone steps on my foot. The music is again a deafening and throbbing roar. I'm trying to navigate the path of least resistance, but the dancing and drinking creates an unpredictable maelstrom. I take shuffling steps. Someone grabs my jacket. Mistaken identity. She doesn't know me and I'm both relieved and disappointed. I turn away, anxiety mounting as I weave and nudge my way out of the mob. I don't want strange sweat on me. I push myself to keep going.

I need to stop being touched.

I'm finally at the door to the men's room.

The door swings inward with a forceful shove and I step inside.

The bathroom is bigger and cleaner than I expected. The door closes behind me, muffling the music but incapable of blocking it out completely. I'm relieved to be away from everyone, even as my body shivers with nervous energy. I hate crowds, but I love that the sensory overload overwhelms all of my shattering memories and the debilitating apprehension about what I'm about to face in Wisconsin.

The bathroom is completely empty. Four urinals, three stalls, and me. I kick open each door, confirming there's no one hiding in any of the stalls, standing on a toilet, waiting to attack me or eavesdrop as I talk to myself. Since I was a child, as long as I can remember, I've had a fear of my privacy being violated or being randomly and viciously victimized without warning. I always check bathrooms. Always.

"What the fuck am I doing here? I need to get out of here."

I walk over to one of four sinks and turn the faucet on. The water is instantly scalding hot. I put my hands together, splash the water on my face. The pain feels cleansing. I should've checked for paper towels before soaking myself. What if there are only air dryers? I'm in luck, sort of. It's a cloth dispenser, hanging loosely. I hate these things, but I need to do something, so I pull at the cloth a half-dozen times to ensure I've found what I tell myself is a clean spot, and wipe my face and hands. I take a deep breath, hold it in, and turn back toward the sink. I must have closed my eyes, instinctively, to avoid seeing myself in the mirror. I make myself open my eyes. I don't want to see.

I look anyway.

I look like shit.

I'm older than I remember, thinner too, and pasty pale. I've lost about 15 pounds in the last month. My cheeks are hollow behind two-days' stubble. Bloodshot eyes. Forehead lines. Crow's feet. My pupils are dilated.

I spread my fingers and run both hands through my hair from front to back. Did I sweat through my shirt? It's still damp under my blazer. I stink. Where's my overcoat?

The mirror shows I'm on the verge of defeat. I'm a spent reflection.

I barely recognize myself, but I'm sure it's still me because I'm here. Right? I'm not dead. I'm me, I'm in here somewhere. My inner voice sounds familiar, but the thoughts are foreign. Who am I?

The two necklaces I bought when I got out of the hospital after the Sugar River Shooting hang free, dangling outside of my shirt. A crucifix and a St. Jude medal. I tuck them back in, near my heart and my scars, where they make me feel safer, and pat them through the fabric. For a moment, I feel better.

I'm having déjà vu, which I never experience with my perfect recollection, and that makes me unsettled again. I can't figure out how I ended up here without remembering—now self-isolated and feeling trapped inside this fucking bathroom—and I cannot understand how it seems like I've been here before when I haven't. Reality is a tunnel closing in around me, vertigo collapsing my vision.

Dread overtakes me in a dizzying swarm of demented doubts, enough to send me flailing through the bathroom door, back out onto the dance floor and into the crowd of strangers I fear and hate.

CHAPTER 7

Pink, Syd, and Piper are standing right in front of me. The Floyd Chicks are here?

"Jeremy? Oh-my-fucking-God you came! We've been looking for you! Don't you check your phone?"

Suddenly, Syd and Pink are talking at the same time, rushing up to me so fast I recoil. Piper hasn't moved and isn't saying anything. She's intentionally looking at everything but me and her friends.

I call them Floyd Chicks because they're 1970s' music-obsessed Pink Floyd fans. There's no way they're using their real names with me, but I think I figured out their street names. Pink is obvious. Syd has to be named for Syd Barrett, one of the original members of the band who had schizophrenia and went insane; the album "Wish You Were Here" was about him. Piper took me longer because I'm not a huge Floyd fan, but I put it together at a vinyl shop when I found a copy of "Piper at the Gates of Dawn" for sale. I've never asked them if any of this is true, but in my mind it is and that's good enough.

They're super cool and I desperately want them to like me.

I get my drugs from these cream-colored roommates. Weed, pills, acid, shrooms, opium, mescaline, or heroin. Dirty and alluring. Trashy and sexy. They exude a dark vulgarity that seduces me.

Piper is tall, too thin, probably 6'2", with shoulder-length, silky-smooth blonde hair. She's wearing a t-shirt from "The Wall Tour, 1979," a pair of skintight jeans and Army-Navy surplus boots. Her makeup was an assault on her face, dark stabs and smears and a bloody streak across her mouth, more punk than Pink Floyd. She's pierced up and down her ears; so is her nose, her eyebrows, her nipples, and her lip. Piper seems perpetually disinterested. Enigmatic. I don't know anything about her.

Syd can't be any taller than 5'2". Her clothes are baggier, nondescript, probably stolen. A compulsive thief, Syd told me she thinks shoplifting is hilarious. Her hair was California blonde when I first met her, although lately it's been dyed blue-green with a combination of Kool-Aid flavors. Syd's a bit overweight, but confident with a sharp tongue. She's the closest to a friend out of the three, alternately sweet and tough, guarding their business interests but seemingly concerned about my well-being.

Pink is the most attractive to me. She's about 5'7" with a great body, incredible ass, perfect breasts. Pink's a brunette; her hair is chopped short in a jagged bob. Tonight, she's wearing a pair of leather pants, ankle boots, a "Dark Side of the Moon" prism t-shirt that's so ripped, stretched, and old it's fallen off her shoulder, exposing her black bra strap. Pink has count-less earrings, but only one other piecing ("in my clit," she whispered to me once) and is wearing a pair of red plastic sunglasses. Her fingernails are painted black. In the dark, with spotty illumination from the strobes, I faintly see her neck is scratched and covered in love bites. Pink turns me on.

The artwork they've inked on their arms, necks, legs, and (presum-ably) the rest of their bodies is exquisite and complex, creative combina-tions of 1960s and 1970s album covers and imagery.

Syd and Pink have stopped talking. I have no idea what they were saying. I'm still shocked to see them, still staggered from the vertigo in the bathroom, still jumpy with anxiety in this too-small club.

Why are they here?

That's almost as confusing as I how I got here, and why we're here at the same time. Club Insomnia doesn't seem like their type of spot, either. And Syd seems to have expected me.

I open my mouth to ask, but Pink interrupts me and I let her. I'll always let her do what she wants, I decided not long ago, even when it hurts—especially if it stabs deep and is wrong for me. I want her to violate me. "Baby, we heard your show tonight. Most of it," Pink says. Syd nods. "Are you all fucked up?"

"They heard it," Piper points out, yawning. "I don't listen to the radio. But I heard *about* it."

"Did any of you see my car outside?" I ask. "Or my coat? I don't remember parking. Or driving here. Or coming in. Or when I got here. I'm not sure why I came here. When did you get here?" I'm stammering. "I just found out where *here* is a few minutes ago. I don't remember much of the last hour. At all."

"You *are* all fucked up," Pink affirms. She slides her sunglasses on top of her head, using them to push her hair back from her face. Pink has dark circles under her eyes, heavy mascara, thick lashes, and guile. She smiles coyly and cunningly. I can't stop looking at her. I have no idea what she's thinking. I hope it's terrible and I really want to know. I'm instantly vulnerable with her. She could kill me and I'd kiss her while I was dying. I want her to care about me, and I want it to ruin me.

"You don't forget anything," Syd states matter-of-factly, finally drawing my attention away from Pink.

"I saw your car when we got here," Piper says. "You're a block away. I think you have a ticket. Why do you drive everywhere? Take the Metro.

There's no place to park in this fucking city. I hate it." Of the three, she's the one giving me something useful. My car isn't wrecked. My coat must be in the car.

Syd hugs me.

She's short, so she extends her arms like a toddler demanding to be picked up, wraps them around my neck, and pulls me lower into an embrace. Her face nestles into my neck. I feel her eyelashes blinking against my skin, and flicks of moisture. Is she crying? I pull her tight and she welcomes it, squeezing me back. It lasts only five seconds, but in that time I experience warmth and peace, the music disappears, the fear of the crowd loosens its grip. Syd doesn't seem to care that I reek of body odor. She gently kisses my ear, which feels delightful and awkward, and sighs, "We'll take care of you. It's OK."

I shudder and nod. "Thank you," is all I can muster. "A lot keeps happening." I sniff. I blink. I tense. I feel this sudden need to talk about everything and want to tell her more, but don't. This compulsion to share wells up inside of me at the wrong times, with the wrong people, so I swallow it. For a fleeting moment, I think about calling Dr. Darby and immediately remember it's almost 1:30 in the morning on a holiday.

Syd lets go, but not before she studies me. I'm sure she's going to ask me something. She doesn't.

Pink is talking to some guy who is making a mistake trying to get her to dance, and Piper is talking to some other guy who is making an even bigger mistake doing the same. Resistance D's "Feel High" starts. The entire club takes on an even more ominous tone. I'm eyeing people with an air of suspicion. Syd's hand finds my lower back. It's not sexual, more sibling-like. Steadying and reassuring. Déjà vu returns.

Did I lose something?

Set something down somewhere and leave it?

Meet someone?

Was I supposed to get something from someone?

I start patting myself down, wondering what it could be. Pink notices. Syd is bemused.

"I think I left something at the bar," I shout.

"Do you want us to come with you?" Syd asks, and looks over at Pink, who is toying with Guy #1. Piper is blatantly ignoring Guy #2, who is desperately trying every line possible to get her to engage. The lights are strobing again. My eyes can't focus. Is this what it feels like to have a seizure?

Clubgoers have become manic, dancing shadow puppets, jerking and evil marionettes in my peripheral vision. Why does everything feel like this? It's just a club, it's just people dancing, it's just music and alcohol and cigarettes and sex, but it's like a deaf person trying to learn a foreign language by lip-reading from across the room. I feel ostracized, excluded, and watched. Are they all starting at me?

No one is looking at me.

"Do you want me to come with you?" Syd asks again.

Piper and Pink toy with Guy #1 and Guy #2. "I'm into chicks," I hear Pink say. "Me too," Guy #1 tries.

My head's a black hole.

"What?" Syd shouts. "Your what is a what?"

I'm startled. "Did I say that out loud?" What did I lose? I can't let the thought go. What am I missing?

Syd points at her ear and laughs uncomfortably. "Can't hear. I hate loud techno."

I battle the urge to start blurting out my inner thoughts and fail. "I said 'my head is a black hole.' I'm…I'm really…I feel like I'm lost in space, like that dude in the David Bowie song."

"Major Tom. Space Oddity." Syd knows everything about music. "Well, you look like hammered shit."

"I feel like I left something at the bar." I don't know why I keep repeating this. It seems desperately important. Was I supposed to get something from someone? I'm obsessed. It's on the tip of my tongue, just out of reach. How do other people function, not remembering perfectly?

I HATE THIS FEELING.

"What'd you lose?" Syd asks. "Want me to help look for it?"

"I don't know."

"You don't know what? You don't know what you lost or you don't know if you want me to help you?"

I don't know.

Syd gestures, a wordless and irritated "Hello?! Anybody home?!" She snaps her fingers at my face.

"I can't tell you what I'm looking for. I don't know. I just need to go back to the bar for a minute."

Syd is sweet, but she's also frustrated with me. Justifiably. I wish she'd let me be for a minute and stop being so insistent. I feel stupid explaining to her that I've lost something I never had.

"Do. You. Want. Me. To. Come. With. You?"

I jut my chin at her. She bugs her eyes, stiffens her neck, bewildered. "Is that a yes? Look man, you don't have to take me over there. I'm ready to go anyway. If you've got something going you don't want to talk about, you know our deal. We're cool, as long as you're cool."

Then it clicks. Syd definitely seems to care, but she doesn't want to let me out of her sight for another, more selfish and pragmatic reason. They're here, dressed the way they are, because they're dealing.

I'm a friend, but I'm still a customer.

Syd thinks I'm going to score at the bar and I don't want to tell her.

I laugh joylessly at finally picking up on a social cue. It took me for-ever, but I got it.

"I'll be right back. Will you and Pink and Piper wait for me?" I shoot her a crooked smirk.

Syd relaxes. "Pink could stay all night, and Piper will leave any time. We'll wait. But if you decide to leave without us, don't just leave. You can do what you want, Jeremy, but…just let me know, OK?"

"I will," I reply. And then I don't know why, but I turn to her and say, "No one knew whether or not it was the end of the world before mid-night. What if it was? What if we're all dead and this is the last moment of our lives, extended out into eternity as our minds die? What if…our final, forever second is just superficiality and pointlessness? What if this is our hell, doomed to spend the rest of our existence as the universe collapses in on itself, living in the decision to be here, doing this…this bullshit made infinite, dying a torturously slow, painful death at entropy's end and leaving only emptiness and nothing behind, erasing our lives and meaning? What if we're our own demonic tormentors?"

Syd focuses, listens, and then nods. "You got bad acid. You buy from someone else?"

Confirmation of my suspicion. "No. And I'm not high."

"Well, that's seriously weird and dark. Did the guy who tried to shoot you at your high school get in your head tonight? I heard what he said to you on your show. Is that what's fucking wrong with you?"

I shrug. "Probably. But I left something at the bar. I'll be right back. Wait here."

I dive back into the dance floor. The bar is farther away than I remem-ber. How much time went by since I asked the bartender to hold my seat? Is that why I'm going back? Do I think I'm going to take her home with me? I haven't even asked for her name, let alone her number. I fish around in my jacket pockets, inside pocket, and pants pocket as I push through a fresh crowd of unfamiliar faces and bodies. Keys, wallet, cellular phone, Zippo lighter. More people arrive. I'm shoved and jostled and squeezed as I force my way through a heaving mass of hormones and flesh. It's bedlam. Fatboy Slim's "Right Here, Right Now" drops and the crowd cheers. Someone flings a full cup of beer in the air, soaking dozens of others, inspiring copycats. I duck and flinch. No one else seems to mind.

When I get back to the bar, I have an erection from thinking about Pink.

My seat is still empty.

My bartender gestures for approval. "I saved your spot. Didn't think you were coming back."

"I ran into someone I know. Thanks for holding it." I slump onto the stool, and swivel off to the side. I pull out my cigarettes, grab my Jack of Clubs Zippo, snap-strike the flint, and touch the open flame to the tip of a Marlboro. I take a long pull on the cigarette. My exhale is an expression of surrender. The bartender is stalking my every move. I squint. I think.

"So, crazy question," I say through pursed lips.

"Oh, we're going to do this again?" she asks, leaning both elbows on the bar, resting her chin on her palms, tapping her fingers rhythmically on her cheeks. She smiles slyly. "Ask away."

I look down the front of her shirt. She notices and purposely holds her pose. I make eye contact again.

"This one is really crazy. You might even need to ask somebody for the answer."

"You've piqued my curiosity. This one sounds like it might really be crazy." She's fun.

"Did I leave something at the bar? I have this feeling that I did and can't get over it. I checked all my pockets and have my phone, keys, wallet, lighter, cigarettes, everything. But I swear to God—" I am really into this conversation, "—I think I'm going to walk out of here without something important."

The bartender laughs delightedly. "Not bad, Jeremy Peoples, radio DJ."

This is not the response I expected. She's…flattered? I watch her skip a few steps down the bar, grab a pen and a cocktail napkin, and start scribbling on it. The napkin tears, so she presses it flat to finish writing, folds it, and hands it to me. A sly smile emerges as she holds tight to the napkin, not releasing it to me right away. I'm gripping the corner, a gentle game of tug-of-war.

"I never do this at work. I'm making an exception. This is my number. Call me. I hope you can now leave tonight knowing you got that important thing you were missing at the bar." She lets go. I cram it inside my blazer pocket, and then spectacularly destroy any opportunity I might have with her in the future.

"Thank you, but I'm serious. Did I leave something here? I can't shake this feeling and it's driving me nuts. Did you or any of the others see me sit something down, drop something, anything?"

My bartender's demeanor changes dramatically. Her posture stiffens, her eyes narrow. "Are you fucking kidding me right now?" she exclaims.

"No. Could you please check? I'm not trying to be a jerk. Could you just ask?" I can't get this idea out of my head. I know I'm going to find what I'm looking for. It's certainty. Belief. Conviction.

Faith.

I need to leave with whatever I've forgotten I have here. Everything is riding on it and I don't know why.

"If you're not trying to be a jerk, then it must come naturally," my bartender spits out, stalking off. For a second, I think she's going to blow me off, but she huddles up with a few of her co-workers, points at me, and says a few things that are probably unkind because they all look up at me simultaneously. Her hands go up in the air, and then come down with a flourish to rest on her hips.

"Dammit," I mutter dejectedly.

But then something happens.

One of the guys reaches into his apron and pulls out a white stationery envelope and hands it to my bartender. She pinches it reluctantly between her thumb and index finger, dangling it. Over the music I barely hear her demanding, "Are you sure it's for him!?" but I can't make out the other bartender's response. She trudges reluctantly back toward me, holding the envelope like it might bite.

She shows it to me, defiantly.

My name is written on it in perfectly scripted purple cursive.

Time has chosen to slow down, the music and mayhem are a distant distraction now.

I stand up, take a step backward, and then totter two steps toward the bar and lean on it for balance.

I'm going to throw up.

This doesn't make sense. I've never been here before. It's not one of my regular spots. I've never even heard of it, have I? How...why...would someone leave me a letter *here*? How did I know I had something here? Who left it? Should I take it? What does it say? What does it mean? How is this possible?

"Are you going to take it or not?" the bartender is demanding emphatically.

I try to say yes, but no words come out. I try again. Still nothing. I nod, and she shoves it at me and whirls around on her heels. She's done with me. I twirl the letter over and over in my hands.

I recognize the handwriting. It looks like Michelle's. This doesn't make sense. Why can't I open it? The idea paralyzes me. I need to find another way to satisfy my craven anger and morbid curiosity.

White Zombie's "More Human That Human" explodes like techno-rock pornography across the club.

"Hey!" I yell at the guy who had my totem in his apron, waving the letter at him. "Hey!" He notices me shouting and, with an irritated eyeroll, reluctantly starts in my direction.

I'm face to face with the bartender, and I realize how much bigger he is than I am. I don't care.

I hold up the envelope as though he's never seen it before and thrust it into his face. "Where did you get this? Who left it for me? When did they leave it here? How did you get this? Why do you have it?" My voice is escalating in pitch, volume, and rage as I shotgun blast him with questions, one after another.

"You need to chill the fuck out, bro, or I'm calling security." He doesn't look like he needs to call anyone. The way his clothes fit I can tell this guy spends as much time in a gym as I do behind a microphone. He points when he talks. I notice he has acne and a receding hairline.

I'm pissing him off but I am not about to chill the fuck out.

"Where did you get this fucking letter?!" I'm mishandling things, but I don't care.

The bartender sighs. I watch him struggle to remember, something I never do, and prepare what he's going to say. I tighten my grip on the envelope and can barely keep my mouth shut while I wait for him.

"It was three days ago. Maybe four? I was picking up my check in the afternoon. I guess I forgot to lock the door behind me because this chick walks in, looks around, asks if anyone had been here waiting for her, then hands me this envelope. No explanation. I told her we were closed. She didn't care. Real direct. Said it was important so I took it. She said someone was supposed to be here to meet her. I told her no one would be here in the afternoon. I forgot about it until Dani—"

The flirty bartender's name, finally. I wonder if she wrote her name on the napkin?

"—came over and asked if anyone had anything for the asshole radio guy. You." He jabs a finger at me.

I'm hanging on every word. When he finishes, it was so anticlimactic I explode again. "That's it? What did she look like? Did she say anything else? Do you remember *anything* else? Her fucking name?"

"Why don't you just read the thing, bro?"

That's a fair question.

"Look," I try to calm down a bit. I have to get what I want and if I keep yelling at this guy, I'm going to lose the moment. I take a deep, shuddering breath and start over. "Sorry. I'm cool. What did she look like? Do you remember? Did she leave anything else? A business card, a phone number, anything? Did she say why she was leaving this for me here? I've never even heard of this place before today."

I know it's her. I keep asking questions that I know won't bring me any more information or satisfaction.

The bartender is giving this way more thought and attention than he should, considering what I dick I'm being right now. I should be cool. I'm not. "She was hot. I remember that. She had this thick, reddish-blonde hair. Like, she was Irish or something but no accent or anything. A lot of freckles—"

(she's in the backseat of my car, a single tear streaking down her cheek toward the corner of her mouth)

"—I'm not into freckles, but they didn't look bad on her. She was hot—"

Yes, she was hot. I got that. Was she crying? Did she say anything else? Why can't people *remember*?

"—with nice tits. Oh…one other thing. Right before she gave me the letter, she must have remembered there wasn't a name on it. She got this weird pen out of her purse, wrote on it, and *then* gave it to me."

"What do you mean 'a weird pen'? What was so weird about it? Come on, man. Help me out here."

"It was one of those rainbow pens. You know what I mean, the ones that we had back in the day? The clear pen with the clicker thing on the top that you'd push, and a different ink thing would come down and you could write in all different colors? Red, blue, black, green, purple—like a little kid's pen. I thought it was weird that she had that but didn't think much about it, just figured she had kids. She put your name on the envelope and then gave it back to me." He shrugs. "That's all I remember. Sorry, bro. Just read the thing," he says again and turns to walk away, but I reach out and grab his arm.

"Wait—"

This pisses him off. He jerks his arm free of my grip, easily. "Hey! Don't fucking touch me, bro."

"What was her name? You just took the letter like a dumb shit and didn't ask her name, get a phone number, ask her who I was, or when I was coming to get it? None of this is fucking weird to you?!" I'm raging again. The music has stopped. A crowd is gathering around me in a semi-circle. It's all peripheral. Why can't anyone ever remember anything clearly, or accurately, or completely? What's so fucking hard about it? "You stupid fucking asshole!" I shout at him across the bar.

The bartender smooths his shirt and points at me again. "Wait. I do remember one more thing. She wanted me to tell you something when you got here."

He's talking much quieter now that the music has stopped, so I get closer. "What? What did she say?"

It's a ruse.

The moment I'm within arm's reach, he grabs me by the lapels of my black leather blazer.

I try to headbutt him.

And fail.

One second later, without any attempt to block it or shrug to the side, the bartender—still holding my jacket with his right hand—smashes his left fist into my right eye. My knees buckle. Sparkles of light explode across my field of vision. Searing pain. My legs wobble and give out completely. I go down.

I'm on my back, my head bouncing off the dance floor with a crack. The bar disappears into swirling white obscurity. The sounds of the club become a high-pitched ringing inside my skull. I try to touch my face but I can't, my hand waving gingerly in front of me like a sorcerer, reaching toward my pulverized eye, once, twice, multiple times before finally finding its destination. I wince.

My stomach flip-flops. I'm going to puke.

Yet there's also the unwelcome familiarity that comes when I get my ass beat. I feel myself smiling.

"Hit me again, fucker," I hear myself say, and I giggle like a small boy. "I don't care what you do."

"Get the fuck out of here before I call the cops. You think because you're some fucking DJ you can just do whatever the hell you want in here? You're gone, bro. Do NOT come back. I see you again, I'll fuck you up worse." The bartender looks down on me and points while he yells. I'm sprawled out, staring at the ceiling, both knees tented, feet flat on the ground, right palm clasped over my eye.

My left hand clutches the letter.

I need to get out of here. Now.

CHAPTER 8

I'm not sure I can move.

I try.

I don't want to get arrested. The bartender is mercifully giving me a few seconds to gather myself.

I can't.

Everything. Spinning.

It's Syd who saves me.

She's suddenly there, picking me off the floor. "Come on, we gotta go. Get up." Pink helps her. Piper only watches the crowd of people watching us. Pink and Syd are talking to me, but I can't hear. Blips of words I can't comprehend. Pain. Ringing. My face is throbbing. Syd is yelling and gesturing at the bartender. "—you can't just hit people in the face, motherfucker!"

Pink is holding me up. "Come on, baby. Cops. Time to get your shit together."

Piper heads for the door. Syd stands between us and the bar, yelling as the rest of us make our way out. Pink keeps chastising me with "You can't do shit like this, baby. You just can't do shit like this" over and over as she escorts me to the street. As soon as the cold air hits me, I puke. Pink lets go and I crumple to the sidewalk. Piper deftly sidesteps out of the way as I vomit up Seagram's, 7-Up, coffee, and stomach acid. Bile burns in my mouth, I spit, I try to hold it back, but I can't stop retching.

Syd gets the last word as the door closes, thrusting both middle fingers up and holding her post, but when the door fully shuts, she turns her anger on me. "What the fuck was that all about, *Jeremy*?" She puts a weird emphasis on my name. "Since when do you start fights with people?"

I'm still on my knees, wiping my mouth.

Piper shivers. "Can we, like, get out of here?" she asks. "It's fucking freezing."

"Am I bleeding?" I wonder. I touch my eye again. It's tender, but I don't see any blood on my fingers. I'm sure it's already bruising into shades of blue, green, yellow, and purple. "Man, he really got me. I had it coming. It was my fault. I deserved it." My eye is swelling closed. I can barely see out of it already.

I laugh. My head rings.

Pink starts barking orders. "There's no way he can drive." She thinks I'm drunk. I'm not. I don't know what I am, but somehow, after four drinks, and all that I drank before the show, I feel sober. "I'll take him home. Follow me, we'll drop him off, and then we can hit the spots we need to hit later. Where's his car?" Pink turns to Piper, who points down the street without turning around, just bends her elbow and lazily foists her finger over her shoulder. Syd grabs Piper and they saunter up the middle of the street, leaning on each other comedically and laughing uproariously as they recount the ignominious end to my night at Club Insomnia.

"You done puking?" Pink asks, bemused.

"Yeah, pretty sure." I have no idea if I'm done puking.

"Let's get out of here. Where are your keys?"

It takes nearly a full minute to get up. When I'm finally on my feet, I sway from side to side. The cold air feels good on my face. I'm stunned but feeling better. The adrenaline is subsiding.

I'm grinning. Violence is nostalgic.

I pat myself down. My keys are in my left jeans pocket. I hand them to her, when I notice her eyes have lingered at my pocket. Is she contemplating a delicious secret? I want to know what it is.

"C'mon, let's go."

I'm horny, even with a broken face, and the lingering humiliation of four hundred people watching it happen…after getting a letter from the mother of my child.

I never think of Michelle that way. The mother of my child. My last true friend. Gone, like Sarah.

Shamefully, I look down at the ground and realize I'm still clutching the stationary envelope in my clenched left fist. I slide it discretely into the inside pocket of my blazer and tell Pink, "The Mitsubishi's a stick." I don't let anyone drive my car, but tonight I'm letting Pink. I want to be alone with her.

She snorts. "I learned to drive in a 1966 Pontiac GTO. Three speed on the column." She rolls her eyes. "So yeah, baby, I can drive your little bitch car." Her ass looks amazing in leather pants.

We're a short walk to my car. Nothing looks familiar. I have no memory of this street, parking the car, getting out, walking in. Even now, nothing jogs my memory. It's a blank wall of suppression.

Pink unlocks my car and opens the driver's side door. "Want to lie down in the back seat?"

"No FUCKING way. I've slept in the backseat of a car enough for a thousand lifetimes." Pink has no idea that only a few years ago, I was homeless and vowed I would never live that life again. She holds up one hand, rolls her eyes, and sits down. I get in the passenger seat, and lean back into the headrest.

"Your eye is all kinds of fucked up," she laughs. "Why'd he hit you?"

"I tried to headbutt him," I say, and it strikes me as ridiculous. Laughter starts in my soul, moves through my chest, and boils out in a snarling chortle.

Pink laughs with me as she starts the car and pulls out. "You head-butted him?"

"No. I *tried* to headbutt him. I didn't even come close. It was not my finest moment." The formality of that comment only amplifies the absurdity, sending both of us into peals of hilarity. I'm laughing and Pink is laughing at me laughing. Taking a beating in a bar makes me miss Michelle even more.

(she was pissed, disapproving and exhausted, demanding we eat pop-sicles while sizing up my injuries)

"I have no idea where you live." I give her my address, but I'm not sure how to get to my apartment from here. Pink knows the city better than I do. I'm an imposter in DC, a transient poser from Wisconsin. This is Pink's domain. "We're 15 minutes away," she informs me, and creeps for a few blocks until she pulls up next to Piper and Syd, then pops the clutch and guns it, accelerating quickly while working her way deftly through the gears. I notice headlights in the side mirror as the other Floyd Chicks fall in behind us.

There's a Burger King cup in the cupholder, about a third filled with melted ice and flat Diet Pepsi. I grab the cup, put my lips on the straw, and drink the ice cold, watered down, stale liquid. Anything to get rid of the taste of bile, stomach acid and Seagram's 7. I swish some around in my mouth. Swallow. Sigh.

"How long has that been in here?" Pink asks me as I finish it and toss the cup on the floor.

"Two-and-a-half days," I answer.

"Gross," is all she says, but she doesn't seem all that grossed out by it.

"Anything to get rid of puke mouth." Pink's facial expression indicates agreement.

We've been driving for about 10 minutes, and the whole time my mind races with questions. At the same time, this is the first I've been alone with Pink. I'm intimidated. I'm turned on. It's all mixed up, thinking of Michelle. I just got my face smashed in, publicly humiliated, but Pink is sexier than usual, dangerous and dirty and desirable. She has to feel me looking at her. I'm aroused. I need her. Fuck it.

Why would Shell write me a letter?

I put my hand on Pink's leg. She doesn't say anything. Doesn't move. Doesn't look at me. Drives.

What was she doing in DC? Why didn't she call?

I slide my hand up her thigh. She still doesn't stop me. I'm going for it.

How did she decide to leave me a letter at Club Insomnia? Why didn't she just come to the radio station?

My hand is between her legs now. Pink shifts, slightly. Warmth.

Why don't I just open the letter and read it? What's holding me back?

"Jeremy." Pink says my name. It's a seductive warning.

Seduce me. I don't care. Use me. I want you to.

She's gone now. I keep saying "gone." She's dead. How did she die? Was she killed? Did Stacy kill her?

"Yeah." She has perfect eyelashes. Her brown eyes should warn me off. They don't.

"Are you sure this is where you want to take this?" She adjusted herself in the seat, spreading her legs. Pink looks at the road, back to me, back to the road. She's going to let me do whatever I want to do.

What if it wasn't Michelle? What if it was someone else? No. It couldn't be. She wrote my name on it. It's her handwriting. She had that stupid pen. The description matches. I'm terrified of that letter.

I nod.

"This isn't the start of something between us."

"I don't care," I lie. I'm desperate for meaning but always willing to accept less.

"We've got a pretty good arrangement. I don't want it to get weird. Can you do *this* and not have it fuck *that* all up?" She's so serious about casual sex.

I don't say anything right away. I stare out the window at the other cars, clouds of exhaust in the cold night air and blinding headlights cutting beams back and forth. Strangers going somewhere together.

"I don't know," I finally answer. "I just wanna do it. I don't care. And I think you do too."

Pink scoots up in the seat, unbuttons her pants, and unzips them with her right hand, her left hand never leaving the steering wheel as she navigates the early morning New Year's Day traffic.

I've wanted her for months, since the first time I saw her. I'm obsessed with the idea of sleeping with her. I've fantasized and masturbated. She's raw and cunning and carnal and filthy.

Why didn't you come see me when you were in DC, Shell? What the fuck happened?

Pink looks at me again, expressionless.

I turn in the seat, switching out my left hand for my right. I tug her shirt loose, touching smooth skin, noticing tattoos, her belly button, goose-bumps, black panties. I explore, slowly finding wet softness. Pink gasps. I slide my finger inside her to see if what she'd whispered to me—

(in my clit)

75

—was true. Pink has no trouble concentrating, driving, eyes wide. She's breathless when we pull up in front of my apartment. The moment she turns the car off, I pull my hand free and kiss her. She forces her tongue in my mouth. My hands are in her hair, down her neck, past the hickeys she earned in an earlier escapade. I pull away from her mouth. She bites my lower lip when I do. I kiss her neck, fingertips on her breasts. They're perfect. Pink whimpers at my touch, my mouth, smiling wickedly.

I'm hard. Her hand is on me.

Everything that's happened since 9:47 p.m. last night vanishes, replaced with lust and desire.

"You wanna fuck me, Jeremy?" Pink sneers. "You think you can fuck me? Use my body and cum on me? Put your cock in my mouth?" She's aggressive, like my fantasies. "What do you want to do to me?"

I nod. "I'll do whatever I want with you." She laughs, joylessly. Dark and loveless.

There's sudden, LOUD knocking on the car window. Startled, I whip my head to the right and see Syd and Piper's faces both pressed against the glass. Syd's nose is squished flat. Piper is bent over, hands on her knees, eager for us to continue. "Jesus Christ!" I hear myself yelp.

Pink giggles and wipes her mouth. "I'm going inside," she tells them. I'm out of the car faster than she is. Piper and Syd find this hysterical. They must've gotten high while I've grown more intoxicated with Pink.

"We're coming too," Syd declares, and howls with laughter.

"Yeah. I'm not a dog. I'm not waiting in the car while you and he fuck," Piper says, starting into space and taking a drag off a Newport 100. She blows out a plume of smoke and steam into the night air.

Syd doubles over, laughing harder.

CHAPTER 9

I keep calling my place an apartment, but it's actually a condo. I have neighbors, but we keep to ourselves. This is the first time I've had anyone at my place other than movers, cleaners, or decorators, in the seventeen months and twenty-eight days I've lived in DC. I'm impeccably careful to avoid arousing suspicion about my drug use. I don't know my neighbors, and want to believe that no one knows me.

Tonight I'm violating all my rules.

It's 2:07 a.m. We cannot continue to stand outside. It's a bad idea to let all three come in, but Pink has locked on me with her dark eyes, not even bothering to zip her pants back up. Those few moments in the car didn't satisfy either of us, and she is coming inside no matter what Syd or Piper want to do.

"It's cool," I agree, shrug my shoulders, and lead the way.

I'm at the entrance to my building in a few jogging steps, and fumble to punch in my security code.

It takes me three tries. Syd and Piper whisper and Syd laughs again but quieter now. Thank God.

We're in and out of the elevator and at my front door in minutes. Syd has the giggles. Piper is annoyed. Pink is dead serious. When I unlock the door, she prowls inside like an owner, nudging me to the side.

I flick on the lights.

"Holy shit, Jeremy, how much money do you make?" Pink exclaims.

Piper flops down on my couch. Pink goes directly to the bar that separates my kitchen and dining room and grabs the first bottle of red wine she sees without even looking at the label. She yanks open drawers until she finds a corkscrew, pops open the bottle, tosses the cork in the sink, and fills a water glass with what I can now see is a Mascota Cabernet Sauvignon. She gulps it down and pours another glass. Syd is looking for the remote to my 55" rear projection TV. Piper is rolling a joint.

"I don't know how much money I make," I finally admit.

Syd, Piper, and Pink all stop and look at me. "What do you mean you don't know?" Syd demands.

"I make enough. I can't remember all the details. Salary and ratings bonuses and endorsements. My agent cares. I don't do radio for money. I really don't know how much I'm making right now. So what?"

It's off-putting to me to say it out loud. I'm conflicted about my status. At times I brag and showboat. Other times, I'm coy. The money is gross to me, a reminder that other people's opinion of me is more important than my own self-worth. Possessions and fame are what I'm supposed to want. I don't.

Michelle would probably think the persona and the apartment doesn't suit me.

I wonder what Sarah would say. Would she be surprised, proud that despite my listless ambivalence in high school, I'd made something of myself? Would she be embarrassed, seeing through the phoniness of it all, and saddened that I've succumbed to building a life like this just to prove certain people wrong?

Piper is paying attention to me for the first time. Pink's eyes narrow. Syd shakes her head. "That's the kind of shit people with money say," she judges. Piper nods. Pink finishes her second glass of wine.

I'm still in the narrow foyer that leads to the main living space: an open floor plan, vaulted ceilings, skylights. In the center of the living room are two couches facing each other, a massive glass coffee table between them. Across the room there's a floor-to-ceiling tinted glass wall with a patio door opening onto my third-floor balcony. The kitchen and dining area is off to my left, separated from the rest of the room by a bar. There's a guest bathroom at the far end of the kitchen. To the right, past my media center, is a hallway that leads to my bedroom, a guest room, and another bathroom. The floors are covered in thick, soft carpeting and the walls are the same off-white color they were when I moved in.

I guess it's fashionably furnished. Modern. Stark. I gave my decorator my checkbook and my trust.

Basquiat and Rauschenberg prints are prominently displayed, among other prints from my artistic fascination, and a variety of Peter Lindbergh's iconic noir photography and trendy local art that my decorator discovered. I rarely objected to his suggestions. I didn't want cheap. I hate clutter.

It was brilliantly put together but sterile.

No family photos. Just things I paid other people to buy for me that no one else will see.

The kitchen has a tile floor, the counters are spotless, the refrigerator is mostly empty. I never cook.

The dining room table, matte black and glass, with seating for six, has never been used.

The ashtrays are empty. The maid comes on Thursdays. I'm sure my bed is made, the bathrooms are perfect, there's no dust anywhere. I never have to compromise about what I buy, what I display, what I like. It's 1,600 square feet of what I wish I was.

It's beautiful and I hate it. I feel phony and pretentious when I'm home. It's why I'm never here.

It's lonely.

Sarah should be here. This should be our place. She should have decorated it. I want a home with her, one that we've built together, not this superficial shrine. It feels even more disgusting with guests seeing it. I'm ashamed of myself, esteeming accomplishments and this inventory of what I think rich people are supposed to decorate their homes with. It's all wrong.

"I have to take a piss," I announce. "Make yourselves at home," I say, wondering if they'll catch the irony. Pink finds it amusing. Syd found the remote and is looking through my inventory of VHS movies. Piper is rolling another joint. "I'll be right back. Listen to music. Watch TV. Get fucking drunk."

I'm in the bathroom. I lock the door. I'm desperate to see how fucked up my eye is, but there's no way I'm looking at myself in the mirror again. I hate myself. What the fuck am I doing to myself? To my life?

Alone with my recollections and regret, I'm again overwhelmed by the image of Michelle in the back seat of my car, losing hope and the little bit of misplaced faith she'd had in me. I've imagined hundreds of times what she must've wished I said, instead of the callous selfishness I demonstrated as her life was changing unexpectedly, forever. I hear the words come out of my mouth before I can stop them.

"Are you gonna get an abortion?" It was the first thing I thought to say. Why was I so terrible?

"Jesus, Jeremy. That's what you want? 'Are you going to get rid of it before Stacy finds out?' You're always avoiding things, feeling sorry for yourself, getting fucked up and never EVER doing the right thing. I don't know why I expected anything different. It's kind of pathetic, really." Michelle again tried to get out of the frost-covered Dodge. I again managed to stop her. If she had really wanted to go, she could.

80

She was testing me.

I was failing. She was giving me second chances and I kept wasting them.

"Is that what you want? You want me to..." she didn't finish.

"I'm processing some out-of-the-fucking-blue MAJOR news here, Shell. I'm just asking the question."

Michelle noticed that we were still holding hands. She let go. It was the last time we ever touched.

"Let's think this through, OK?" I asked. It's a statement and a question. I didn't know what to do. It's fucking complicated. She didn't want to be with me. I didn't have a place to live, job, or a future. I wondered what Michelle wanted. It was weird thinking of her as a mom. She'd be great, probably. But what would Stacy do when he found out I got his wife pregnant?

He'd kill me this time. Or her. Or both of us. All three of us, actually, since....

That idea stopped my racing mind.

All three of us.

There's another person whose life was going to be impacted forever by the choices made in the backseat of this car. Some little boy or little girl....

No. Not "some little boy or little girl." My son. My daughter. No. Our child.

Our child would come into this world and have to deal with the life we were building before they arrived. We were inept gods, creating life without regard for consequences, incapable of knowing the outcome of infinite possibilities, blindly and foolishly plotting. Did this thought weigh heavy on Michelle already? Was it more important to her than what could undoubtedly happen to her, or me, when Stacy found out?

"I don't know what to do either," Michelle said, reading my mind.

I spun a hand-rolled cigarette in my fingers. "I need a smoke."

Michelle nodded.

"I don't want to smoke around you anymore." I grimaced. The irony wasn't lost on either of us. Seconds ago, I was asking if she was getting an abortion, and now I'm so protective of her baby's health that I wouldn't smoke a cigarette around her. "I'm getting out. We can keep talking. I just really, really need to smoke this cigarette right now." I deftly finagled my way out of the backseat of my two-door jalopy.

The freezing cold air on my face was fleeing relief. Arguing had made it stuffy inside the Charger.

But now, neither one of us knew what to say. Michelle was sullen. A terrible silence settled in. I'd betrayed her hopes. Worse, neither of us knew what to do. Every possible future seemed impossible.

Who would be the one to bear the largest burden? Would we be alone, or together? I was a coward, seeking the path of least resistance, heartbroken over my inadequacy but unwilling to change.

What was Michelle capable of, if she thought it was best for her baby?

I smoked my entire cigarette before Michelle spoke again. What she said set into motion a series of events that no one could have foreseen. "What if I just let Stacy think the baby is his?"

CHAPTER 10

How long have I been in the bathroom? Minutes? An hour? More?

I look at my watch. Not long.

"Jeremy, you have seriously good taste in movies," Syd yells from my living room, not realizing I've already made my way back down the hall and I'm just about to rejoin the group. I have 800 tapes—I never made the jump to laser disk—and she's right: I have great taste in movies. Syd is holding four films. *American Pop* and *True Romance* in one hand, *Taxi Driver* and *The Doors* in the other.

Piper looks through my music collection, hundreds of CDs filling matte black metal racks hung on the wall above my stereo. In the cabinet under the components I have another 700 cassettes. My vinyl collection is equally vast, although I rarely use my record player. It's mostly so I can tell people I have albums, a shrine of status for no one to see but me. The bookshelf contains novels by Salinger, Hemingway, Palahniuk, and Kinsella, along with biographies and conspiracy theories.

"If it's worth watching or listening to, I have it. If I don't have it, then it's not worth watching or listening to." Piper regards this as the most philosophical things she's ever heard. She and Syd are both stoned.

The energy in the room changed while I was in the bathroom. The crass interrogation about my money and Syd's silliness are behind us.

There's no mention of their plans for later tonight (this morning) about the spots that they needed to hit after the bars and clubs closed down. I'm the center of their attention.

Syd has put the movies down and holds something else in her hand.

An eyedropper.

Pink is sitting on the bar that separates the kitchen from the dining room; her bare feet swaying back and forth. Her toenails are painted black. The bottle of wine is empty. I look away and look back; she's still staring. She doesn't need to read my mind; she doesn't need to hear any more words. Pink knows.

She owns me.

I want her. I'll do anything to have her. Anything.

I want to tear her clothes, pull her hair. I want to put my mouth on her, bite her neck, draw blood. I want her to beg me to do it. I want to take back control. I want to forget Sarah's pleading dead eyes and Michelle's disappointed tears. Blood rushes inside me. I want Pink to scream my name, making a replacement memory for lost love. I want her to know I'm settling for her. I want us to violate each other. I want to stop remembering the pain of my past. I want a new punishment. I want to force my way inside of her. I want it to last for hours, distract my racing mind and dull my broken heart.

Fuck the letter. Fuck Mason Reynolds. Fuck the radio show. Fuck Stacy Ramone.

Pink's sizing me up. This atmosphere is suddenly electric. The Floyd Chicks are positioning themselves.

Syd speaks first.

"Ever tried Liquid?" she asks.

Ecstasy. I've tried everything else.

"No. Not yet. I want to."

Piper speaks next. "It's, like, fucking amazing."

"Fucking amazing," Pink agrees. "It's unlike anything you've ever had."

Syd nods. "Fucking. Amazing."

"My brother's heavy into the club scene on South Beach," Pink continues, "and this is all anyone's doing down there. It's like the euphoria of LSD, but you can fuck for hours on it. The ravers all take it. They're tweaked out with painter's masks and trance music and Vick's VapoRub which kind of just ruins the whole point. Imagine cocaine sex in a Peter Max painting." I can't imagine that. "GHB is the shit."

Pink is drunk, walking toward me in bare feet and leather pants like an assassin. As she stalks by, Syd hands her the eyedropper and a small glass bottle. She dips the eyedropper in the bottle and squeezes the rubber tip. "A couple drops on your tongue. Sometimes you feel like everything that happens next is a dream. Like it's not real. Sometimes you can't remember anything you did. You can go out past your limits. No remorse about doing things you wouldn't normally do when you forget it ever happened."

There's nothing in me that says I shouldn't do it.

I stare as Pink drips three or four tiny drops on her tongue, and then does something I don't expect. She refills the eyedropper and turns to Syd. Piper is on her way over, closer to us. She's put in Uriah Heep's "Demons and Wizards" and starts the song "Rainbow Demon." Piper turns the volume up loud, louder, and tosses the stereo remote on the couch. My walls are soundproofed. It was a selling point when I moved in. Pink holds up the eyedropper and drips several drops on to Syd's tongue. Piper is next. She rolls her eyes, tilts her head back, and lets Pink dose her.

Pink is a hedonistic High Priestess. She slides her red plastic sunglasses down from her hair, setting them on the tip of her nose, and looking at me over their rims through bloodshot eyes. She's quoting Jim Morrison now, as she refills the eyedropper. "I believe in a long, prolonged derangement of the senses to obtain the unknown. Do you believe that too, Jeremy?" What the fuck am I supposed to say to that?

"I'm living it," I answer.

She laughs. Piper and Syd, laughing at everything earlier, are quieter now. I'm surrounded by the daughters of the Sirens who tried to lure Odysseus to his death. Piper slips in behind me. Syd closes her eyes, dancing as the driving organ and bass of Uriah Heep builds. This is what I need. Disrupt my senses. Compel me to stay in the present. Overrule my conscience. Push past my boundaries. Take me to the edge and throw me off. Is this really happening?

Pink pulls me closer.

I open my mouth, and two, three, four drops of cold liquid touch my tongue. There's a hint of salt. The moment I swallow, Pink puts her hand behind my head and forces her mouth on mine. I push back, kissing her openly in front of the others, my tongue in her mouth. Piper embraces me from behind, hands spread across my chest, digging in her nails through my shirt. Eyes closed, Syd's now by my side.

Pink has something more.

"We heard what that psycho who shot up your school said to you on the radio. We see how fucked up you are over all of this. That guy calling about his dead wife you were sleeping with. Who wouldn't be?" Syd opens her eyes, plaintively looking into mine, nodding. Piper is pressed against me.

"We talk about you, Jeremy. Your freaky memory. We see how you get lost in your head, that darkness. Your sadness, your memories. Baby, it's terrible what happened to you in that school. You can't hide it from anyone. You're a good person, but your soul is sick. You don't feel alive anymore, all numb inside. Like you're dead, right? A fucking vampire. You're lost. We'll bring you back, baby. You need to feel something good again. I want you to feel good, Jeremy. Make us feel good. Give yourself to us tonight."

Pink's talking like she's reciting a mantra, a ritualistic passage of ancient pagan text. Her cadence is convincing and hypnotic. I'll do anything she says. I'm enchanted. I'm euphoric. Not that I need to be manipulated into doing what looks like is about to happen. It's a dark fantasy.

Liquid ecstasy doesn't take long to soften my awareness of reality, a fuzzy warmth that casts my apartment in a dreamlike state, pushing memories and my pounding headache to the periphery.

It feels wrong, like sin, but so good. I can't think of a better word. I'm not stopping them. I won't stop.

Syd tugs my blazer off. Piper pulls her shirt off, up and over her head. I can't help but stare at her tattoos; she's adorned with incredible imagery. Her sleeve extends across her ribcage and her lower back, dragons and talons and daggers and runes. Pink watches me look her over, but only for a second, and then she extends her arms up, taking off her "Dark Side of the Moon" t-shirt and unfastening her bra, shifting from foot to foot, hip to hip. She kisses me like an assault. Piper bites my ear, then my neck. She bruises me. Viciously sexual. I flinch but press into it. Syd touches my necklaces, holding them between two fingers, replacing them, gently touching my chest with her palm. Pink pulls away just long enough to unwrap the rest of her body from her leather pants and panties; she's completely nude, uninhibited, yanking open the button fly on my Levi's, reaching in, touching me. I stretch my arms out, eyes closed, and lean my head back as Piper strips my shirt off.

Suddenly, they stop.

All three of them are gaping at the two bullet holes in my torso. Syd gasps. Pink's eyes light up.

One of the scars is just below my heart; the other is in my stomach. I pirouette, holding my arms above my head in surrender so they can see the exit wounds in my back. My tattoos are simple blue ink, just dates. Above one scar is my birthday, and below it, the date of the shooting. The other, nearest my heart, is inscribed with Sarah's birthday, and "May 23, 1992." My body is our obituary. Our memorial.

I'm a human cemetery.

(Sarah reaches out for me, sprinklers pouring down and Mason is advancing and reloading and shooting and Sarah is begging me and then she's silenced and her head snaps back as Mason takes her from me)

"I died that day, and then I lived on. She didn't. I wish I was dead with her. I want to be dead too."

"Jesus Christ," Syd says. Piper is wearing only her panties and piercings. Pink kisses my scars.

"Stop," I tell her. "Just, fucking, stop! They're not for you. They're hers. These are mine."

Piper stares at my shirtless body. Syd has tears in her eyes. All three of them reach for me at the same moment, descend on me, pulling me toward my bedroom, turning us into a tangle of nudity.

CHAPTER 11

Kurt Cobain's voice rouses me from a nightmare.

I wake up feeling empty.

No, that's not exactly right.

More like numb. Depressed. Exhausted. Used. Discarded. Gross. Disappointed. Culpable. Empty.

The shades are drawn. Strands of light spear the room.

My alarm clock reads 3:16 p.m. What day is it?

I don't know exactly what time I finally fell into a restless sleep dominated by nightmares. Sometime after 5:00 a.m. Is it still New Year's Day? Things are rushing back to me as my mind wakes up.

Michelle.

Stacy calling in during the show.

The letter.

Mason's prediction.

My head is throbbing. Pain pulses with each heartbeat.

That bartender with the letter. My fucking eye. Jesus Christ.

Ecstasy. It's…blurry after that. The Floyd Chicks. Did I really….? With all of them?

There are people in my bed. I have no sheets or blankets on me. I'm not wearing any clothes.

Piper and Pink are sprawled out together next to me. Pink is on her back, a sheet covering her from the waist down, mouth open slightly, hair and makeup a mess, fresh bite marks. Piper's on her stomach, face turned toward Pink, left arm draped over Pink's chest, my sheet mostly hiding her body. Both are breathing softly and rhythmically, almost in sync. Blankets and pillows are on the floor. I sit up on my elbows. There's a mirror on my nightstand, powder residue, a twenty-dollar bill partially unfurled.

Where's Syd?

I slept for…ten hours?

Am I supposed to leave for Wisconsin? I said I'd come home for Michelle's funeral. When is it?

Wait.

I rub my face, and immediately my eye explodes in pain.

"Ah. Shit!" I snatch the coke mirror and tilt it so I can see my eye. My eyebrow has swollen and distended, turning a shade of green-yellow-purple and has pushed my blackened eyelid completely shut. A crescent bruise extends around the eye socket and dissolves into a red blotch on my cheekbone.

"He really fucking got me," I hiss. I touch my face again, recoil again. I grimace, but keep touching it.

I'm supposed to be on my way to Wisconsin and I slept the entire day away.

Where are my clothes?

My tongue sticks to the roof of my mouth. My nose burns; there's cocaine in my sinuses and in the back of my throat. The drains should've ended hours ago. How much coke did we do? There are dabs of blood on the sheets. Am I cut? When I stand up, the room heaves suddenly and I can barely maintain my balance. I feel sick. Do I have a concussion? I find a pair of black boxer-briefs lying on the floor, bend down apprehensively, snatch them, and pull them on. I nearly topple over but manage it.

I stumble out into the living room. My shirt, shoes, and jeans are strewn on the floor, mixed up with other clothes that don't belong to me. An empty wine bottle. A broken glass. Used ashtrays. I'm not used to my apartment being in disarray. I'm uncomfortable with it. I'll call the maid when I get back.

Syd is sitting on one of my couches watching a VHS recording of "Nirvana: Unplugged In New York." Kurt is chatting with the audience and encouraging them to applaud the Meat Puppets after finishing up "Lake of Fire." Stargazer lilies, black candles, a cardigan, and a set list that feels perfect in retrospect.

A wave of self-awareness hits as I stand in front of Syd in my underwear. My face feels flush. Her eyes dart from the TV to my bullet wounds and back again. She won't look me in the eye. Still dizzy, I gingerly pick up my t-shirt and wrestle it back on. I'm not feeling coordinated enough to try and pull on my jeans.

Syd's eating Cap'n Crunch with Crunch Berries out of a bowl from a set of dishes I rarely use.

"I have milk?" I ask her. She's just put a spoonful into her mouth and giggles out some milk and nearly snuffles a mouthful of cereal onto the couch but catches herself in time. "Uh huh," she says, yellow-pink milk dribbling down her chin, which she catches with a scape of her spoon just under her lower lip.

"Did you check the expiration date? It can't be good."

"I sniffed it. It passed the smell test," she explains. I'm oddly concerned about Syd and salmonella.

"When did you get up? I never sleep that much."

"I couldn't sleep…afterward," Syd says, shifting uneasily and placing the bowl on my coffee table. "I've been up watching movies. I'd never leave your house if I had the movie collection you have. Where did you get *American Pop*? I didn't think you could buy it anymore because of music rights or some shit."

"They sorted it all out last year. I found it at Circuit City. I can watch it over and over. Never gets old."

I shuffle over to the kitchen sink, turn the cold water on, slurp from the faucet for a few seconds, then open the fridge and crack open a can of Diet Pepsi, guzzling it gone. "I wish I had some black cherry Kool-Aid. That sounds awesome right now. It's the hangover cure." I feel like shit. My. Whole. Body. Hurts.

"I have all kinds of Kool-Aid, but I use it for hair dye. I don't know if I've ever drank any. Drunken any? Have ever drunk any? What's the right way to say that?" Syd looks over at me, a tight smile on her lips.

"Fuck if I know," I answer.

"But you're the *professional communicator*," she teases. "The *wordsmith*. The *radio broadcaster*. Isn't it your job to know proper English and grammar and all that other stuff?"

"Then I say it's 'ever never have drunken' and since I'm the expert you can't challenge me."

Syd turns back to the TV to watch Dave, Krist, and Kurt perform "All Apologies." Neither one of us wants to interrupt this moment. It still feels powerful, years later, watching what I've come to believe was Kurt Cobain's suicide note put to music. "I love this song," we both say at the same time. Nirvana is finished. The studio audience cheers. There's an encore coming, but I can't keep watching. Staring at the screen is making my head pound again. I need something. Aspirin. A beer. A joint. Pills. Anything.

I slug down another Diet Pepsi. My stomach churns.

"Is it still Saturday?"

Syd finds this funny. "Yeah. New Year's Day. Longest day ever. Maybe what you said to me when you were at the club was closer to reality than you realize." I wince at the memory. "What was it, something like we're all dead and this is our last moment extended forever in hell or some crazy shit like that?"

"Maybe. If we're still doing this on Monday, I'd call that confirmation." Instinctively I touch my chest. "Have you seen my smokes?"

"No, but you can have one of mine," she replies, tossing me a box of Newport's. Ugh, menthol.

"Thanks." A nicotine fix is a nicotine fix. The first inhale nearly gives me an asthma attack. It takes me a full minute to stop hacking and wheezing. My thumping head feels like it's exploding in slow motion.

"Your eye. It's fucking nasty. Does it hurt? It looks like a *Rocky* movie."

"Not really." I don't know why I compulsively lie about little things and I'm brutally honest about the stuff most people would understandably hide. "I forgot about it until you said something."

Syd looks like she doesn't believe me but accepts my answer. "What happened with that asshole bartender? I've never seen anyone do anything like that to anybody before. What'd you say?"

I can't figure out how to explain it all to Syd in a way that makes sense. I can't comprehend it either. My thoughts shift to the letter in my blazer. Was Michelle really in DC just a few days before she died? Did she really write a letter and give it to a bartender at a club—while it was closed—that I happened to go to just a few days later? What's stopping me from reading it? And why were the Floyd Chicks being at the same random club at the same time I was?

The missing time. The missing memories.

Syd is staring at me.

"It was a misunderstanding," I finally answer.

Syd snorts. "I'd say." She shoots a quick glance down the hallway.

"I called him a motherfucker. Then I tried to headbutt him." I'm almost finished with the Newport, thank God. I blow out a cloud of smoke. "I'm a tough guy, now," I wheeze.

Syds face brightens, her mouth gapes open. "Shut UP. You did NOT. We all thought you were a lover and not a fighter." She's laughing and sits up on her knees. I wink at her with my good eye.

"Judging by the results of my fight and the way the night ended, you were right."

"What started it? What'd you forget at the bar that you had to go back and get so bad?" She's not letting it go. I don't want to tell her, but she's pushing me and I'll give in.

"If I told you, you wouldn't believe me. Swear to Christ, I don't even believe it myself," I start. "Nothing that happened yesterday makes sense. Have you ever had the feeling like you're living someone else's life? I've felt that way—"

Since May 23, 1992

"—for a long time. Years. But last night it was like I snapped back into the life I was supposed to be living, but, like, the timing was wrong. I was in some parallel universe and the real me shows up, but the alternate me thinks *he's* the real me and everything is all confused and I have to work my way back into control of my life so this other me will go away."

"That's crazy fucking weird," Syd interjects.

"I know. It is. Something happened last night I can't explain. I showed up at that club and I don't remember driving there. I knew I needed to get something at the bar before I knew there was anything for me. It was like the 'fake me' was supposed to show up and get it, but instead the 'real me' arrived and got it before the 'fake me' could get it. And then you guys were there, and everything was just…all fucked up," I say, in fits and starts. I feel stupid saying it out loud. "It was a letter. A letter from a friend that I haven't talked to in forever. And I have the letter and I can't open it. I *want* to read

94

it and can't. I tried to get that fucking gorilla at the bar to tell me how he got it and I got pissed off and freaked out."

Syd looks toward my bedroom out of the corner of her eye. "You haven't opened it? Why not?"

"I don't know. I'm…." I pause for a second. I'm being too vulnerable with her. "I'm afraid of it." It pisses me off that I can't keep some of my secrets to myself. People push me and I share more than I want to.

"Isn't it driving you apeshit wondering what it says? You know who it's from? Are you sure?"

"Hundred percent. I recognize the handwriting. And the strangest thing. The bartender told me he *saw* her write my name on it using a weird pen. One of those multi-colored pens like we used to get as kids. So you could switch from red to purple or whatever. Remember those?" Syd nods, and lights a cigarette. "She loved those pens. Always had one. Told me using them kept her 'young at heart.' Sometimes she'd write her name in one color and dot the 'i' with a heart using a different color. It was her. I know it. I just don't know *how* it was her. I don't know why she was in DC—and just a few days before she died."

Syd is really into the story now. "HOLY fucking SHIT. The letter at the bar was from the wife of the dude who called your show last night? Jeremy. What the FUCK, man?! I mean…how have you not read that letter yet? What if this guy was trying to kill her, and he did, and now he wants you to come back to Wisconsin, and he's set a trap for you too, and is going to, like, kill you too?"

I roll my eye at her.

"You're a paranoid stoner with an active imagination. I don't think it's some revenge fantasy, three years in the making, done on my radio show so that he's the prime suspect. Doesn't make any sense, Syd."

"You have a point," Syd agrees, and settles down. "Are you really going to Wisconsin today?"

"I don't know. I definitely thought so, but after last night I don't know now." I want another cigarette.

"Jeremy," Syd again looks to the bedroom door, gathering her courage. "I think you should go. And if you can somehow not come back, you should try to, like, stay gone. For real. Like, stay in Wisconsin."

I'm suddenly angry. Syd can see it. "I don't understand. What the hell do you mean?"

"Just, shut up and listen. Last night wasn't…last night was different than you think it was. OK? We took you home. We were being nice but we're also protecting our interests. You're one of our good ones. Never trouble. We didn't want you to go to jail and fuck that up. But then we get to your place and we see how you live, and when you went to the bathroom Pink and Piper just fucking *decided*. They want you on a hook, Jeremy. Pink knows you want her. You're, like, so obvious. They said we should get you to do Liquid so we could…just…we didn't all just fuck you because you're irresistible, OK?"

I open my mouth again to speak but Syd keeps going. "You're not very strong. All that shit Pink said last night? She didn't just make that shit up. *I* said most of that to her while we were listening to your show. *I* think it's true. But she doesn't care. *I'm* worried about you. She's not. I think we're gonna suck what's left of the life out of you and burn through all your money and use you. And if I'm totally honest? I'm worried that this will blow up in our faces. You're not some average dude. You're, like, half-a-celebrity. People know who you are. Like, the President can't even get a blow job and get away with it anymore. They don't even have a plan. It's, like, the start of a plan. But they wanted last night to happen. Not to help you. *We wanted last night to happen for the three of us.* Not you." Syd's done. She'd been sitting up on her knees, but now unfolds her legs and slumps back into the couch cushions. The weight is off her.

"You're the one who brought up trying Liquid," I remind her.

"Because Pink thinks you trust me the most."

I don't have any other accusations. "Why are you telling me?"

"Remember how you told me you feel like you just appeared in an alternate timeline or something out of *Back to the Future II*, and you're the second Marty McFly? Well, I've been sitting here for hours, can't sleep, trying to decide whether I should tell you or keep my mouth shut. And then you just fucking TOLD ME about the letter and the pen and how you can't even read it, and you're all honest and shit and I can see it on your face, Jeremy...."

Syd has tears in her eyes, but she seems more angry than sad. Her voice cracks, she clears her throat.

"You're a good person. Bad things are happening. More bad things might happen in Wisconsin, but worse shit is gonna happen if you don't get out of DC. I guess it's my fucking conscience or God or the universe or whatever the fuck, but I just had to tell you. I couldn't help myself. I'm sorry. Just, go home. Stay away. Don't come back. I fucking mean it," Syd orders me, in a whispered voice.

Go home. Even Syd knows I don't think of DC as my home. *Go back home. To Wisconsin.*

"What worse shit will happen if I stay here? How can I just leave town and never come back? What could be so fucking bad? What do you think will happen? What if I don't care what Pink does?"

"Yeah, all that stuff you said about wishing you were dead. I know you *think* you mean it. I've been around a lot of junkies and crazies. You wish you'd died in that school shooting. You want to die, but you don't have the balls to kill yourself. You want someone else to do it because you can't. You fucking *coward*! You want *us* to kill you so you don't have to do it. You don't give a fuck about what that would do to me, do you? I gotta live with that, for, like, ever."

"I can fuck myself up in Wisconsin just as well as I can here," I try to argue.

"Try to figure out what happened to that girl instead. Read. The. Letter. Go to the funeral. Make shit right. But if you fuck yourself up in Wisconsin, at least it's not my fault." Syd's remarkably intuitive. For the first time, I see how she could be doing so much more with her life. "We'll get you strung out. Suck away all your money. Get at your friends. Destroy your career. You might make it out with only jail or rehab. But you have to *leave* because if you stay here, you won't stay away from us. You won't get help. You'll let us do it. You *want* us to do it. But I don't want to do it to *you*. I've seen it over and over. Lawyers. Doctors. Corporate assholes. I don't really like it, but I didn't really care that much about them. I don't want to do it to you, Jeremy. I don't think you'll live through it and I can't live with myself."

"I've tried to kill myself before," I confess. "I guess if I'd really wanted to do it, I'd have put a shotgun in my mouth, but I just did this." I show her my scars. They're faded but unmistakable.

Syd looks at the faint white lines on my wrist and forearm. "Jesus. I never noticed those before."

"Maybe being with Pink for a while sounds good. If I live through it, fine. If I don't, better." It feels good to say these things to someone other than my therapist. Fuck! Dr. Darby. Maybe I should call her. Wait, it's a holiday. Does this count as an emergency? I can't differentiate between my normal life and these ongoing series of tragedies. What's normal for me? What's an emergency?

"You're not gonna be with Pink, dude," Syd corrects. "You guys are not gonna fall in love. Pink isn't wired like that. You're not gonna be, like, a couple. You're not taking her to the prom."

I wince.

"Why are you telling me about it? Why fuck over your friends?" I demand.

"I shouldn't have told you. I should've just let it happen," Syd responds. I've noticed that I can push her in an argument for just a short amount of time and then she'll give in to her feigned indifference.

"But you did."

"Yeah, I gave my power to half-a-famous person who's suicidal and mentally ill and self-destructive and can't make decisions and is dealing with trauma and is basically an addict and an alcoholic and is horny for my friend who's sort of a sociopath when it comes to men. I'm fucking stupid. I don't know."

"But why?" Impishly, it feels good to push her the way she pushed me to tell her about the letter.

Syd's arms are folded, her legs pulled together and off to the side, postured unapproachability. "Because. Because my stepsister killed herself, Jeremy. And you remind me of her, like she's been reincarnated as you. She was a good person too, but just..." Syd searches for the right words. "She couldn't handle life. Shit bothered her *so* much that she was always thinking and obsessing. She'd replay conversations back in her mind and worry about what she should have said instead. She was fun, and kind. And caring. When my dad left and my mom hooked up with her new man, she was the only good thing that came of it. But normal life killed her, Jeremy. Shit that all of us struggle with took her from me. You're just like her, but she was braver than you. She did it herself. You're going to make us do it, and I don't want to be responsible. I can't be."

Syd's trying to save me for the second time. The last person who risked themselves for me was Michelle.

I genuinely don't know what to say.

"I wish I would have told my sister to leave and start something new, healthy, at least try, before she...did what she did. I found her. Before anyone else. After she did it. I can't...I don't want to see you like that, Jeremy."

She's doing it because she feels guilty.

She's doing it because she's afraid of blowback, that I'll get busted or die and they'll all go down too.

But she's really doing it because she cares about me. She's trying to save me because she wasn't able to save her stepsister. I'm *her* second chance. Syd needs to experience forgiveness like I do.

"Jeremy. Just do what I told you to do. Leave. Don't come back to DC. I don't know how it works in radio but just tell them you have, like, a family emergency or some shit and then get another job somewhere. Disappear. Go into rehab. Move back in with your parents—"

"FUCK my parents," I interrupt.

Syd shrugs. "Fine. Fuck your parents. Whatever. But I'm serious. This isn't going to go the way you think it's going to go, and I don't know why I'm so sure, but you need to go back home. Today."

Syd lights another Newport.

"It's your funeral." Last word.

She exhales menthol smoke and smiles ruefully. "I won't bring it up again. But if you stay? You will NEVER sleep with all three of us again. That's a fucking promise."

"How many last words do you want? Do you know how hard it is for a talk show host to keep his fucking mouth shut? Have mercy." I need to break the tension.

"You're sick, Jeremy. Sick." She's holding her cigarette between her fingers and spinning a circle around her ear. "Coocoo for Cocoa-Puffs. Like that lady in *Misery*. What did she call it? The booby-hatch."

"Please," I wave my hand. "Speak your mind. Tell me all your secret thoughts. It feels so good to hear."

Syd stab-swipes her half-smoked cigarette back and forth in the ashtray. Instead of leaving it there, she stares me down, holds the cigarette butt out in front of her, and tosses it in the bowl with the last of her milk and cereal. "Sarcasm is the lowest form of wit," she lectures and turns defiantly back to the TV.

"But the highest form of intelligence," I finish. "You forgot the best part. Props to you for knowing some Oscar Wilde." Smirking at her, I feel the same uneasy exhilaration when I realize a caller on my radio show is smarter than me. Syd gives me the finger without looking at me. A tiny smile appears at the corner of her mouth, and then disappears.

The bedroom door opens.

Piper and Pink are awake.

Pink is wearing my black and gold silk Japanese robe. It's billowing mostly open, the belt sashed loosely across her waist, exposing skin from her neck to navel, her flat stomach and the supple curve of her barely covered breasts draw my eye. Her legs go on forever; she's wearing a toe ring. Even knowing what I now know, I still want her. I'm hopeless.

Syd notices me noticing.

Piper has wrapped my sheet around her, tucking it under her arms, leaving her shoulders exposed. It trails behind her like a disheveled bride walking to the altar after a one-night stand. Individual strands of her hair stand on end. Piper looks confused but determined to be unimpressed. She yawns.

"How long have you been up?" Pink asks with a hoarse voice.

"Not long," Syd replies, fidgeting with her hair and ejecting "Nirvana: Unplugged" from the VCR. "I was hungry. And his bed is big but not big enough to sleep all of us. It's cold in here, too."

Pink looks me over and smiles.

Piper flops on the couch next to Syd, looks at the Cap'n Crunch ashtray, and fakes putting her finger down her throat. "The shit you eat," she tells Syd. "Fucking gag me."

"What about you?" Pink asks me. "How are you this morning? Feeling…" she narrows her eyes, her lip pulling into a seductive sneer. "…

better than you were before? Or at least…good enough?" Pink knows she's sexy. She doesn't have to try, but when she tries, goddammit, it's even sexier.

"You're a rock star," Piper offers. I know she's flattering me and lying. Still, I want to believe her. I do.

(surrounded and swallowed by three bodies, three mouths, ashamed and incapable of stopping)

"I've done a lot of things in my life. A lot. I've never done…that. Yeah. I'm better. I'm good. I'm great," I lie. Pink and Piper exchange a quick glance, and Pink nods. Syd is staring off into space. "It was…yeah. Wow. Didn't expect that." A spontaneous and sheepish grin appears. I reach to rub my face again, but remember my eye just in time and catch myself in mid motion.

"Damn, your fucking eye is fucked up," Piper says.

"Fucked," Pink agrees.

"It's not that bad," I argue.

"Have you looked at it, man?" Piper persists. "It's like, green and purple and gross. Can you even see?"

"Yeah, I can fucking see," I snap. I'm defensive about it, probably more than I need to be, but I'm tired of talking about it. "I need to take a shower." I turn to Pink. "Can you wait?" I look at all of them. "Can you hang a bit longer? If I'm going to go to Wisconsin, I need to decide, and I just need to—" not a lie "—clear my head for a second and think through what I'm gonna do. Don't leave. Just eat. Or get what you want from the bar. Watch some TV. Give me 15 minutes. Cool?"

If I'm going to Wisconsin, I'll need drugs.

If I'm staying in DC, I'll need drugs until I see them again.

Either way, I need drugs. I don't trust Pink and Piper, but I need them to stay so I can get what I want. I'm slightly less offended that they'd use me and lie. I'm doing the same thing to them right now.

"Want me to join you," Pink purrs, "for that shower?"

"No," I'm surprised to hear myself answer. "Thanks. I just need time. Just…I need to be alone."

"OK. Be alone." She's offended, not used to being rebuffed, or she's faking and wants me to believe it. Thanks to Syd, I know they're capable of convincingly lying to my face.

I grab my pants and leather blazer, mainly because I cannot stand the thought of leaving the letter unattended around Pink and Piper. It's still tucked carefully away in the inside jacket pocket, next to a folded cocktail napkin with Dani's (now) useless phone number on it. Pink watches me casually, and sits down on the couch, strategically placing Syd between her and Piper.

Syd can't hide her discomfort.

"You're quiet," I hear Pink say.

"I think I'm still fucked up," Syd replies. She has more street smarts than I ever will.

On the way down the hall, I toss my clothes on the bedroom floor, but take the letter with me to the bathroom. I'm not going to let it out of my sight until I figure what I'm going to do next.

"Hey," I volunteer, "there's a guest bathroom with a shower just off the kitchen. You can freshen up—" I've never heard people say that in real life, but women always say that in the movies I've seen "—if you want to. Seriously, ten minutes and I'll be done." I slam the door.

I pull my necklaces off, up and over my head, and sit them on the sink next to Michelle's letter.

Moments later, the hot water hits my face, steam billowing around me, and stings my eye. Face down, the water soaks my hair and washes over the rest of me. I feel guilty about leaving Syd alone with Piper and Pink. I feel gullible, never considering that last night was a scam.

I'm so fucking stupid.

The pull to go home feels stronger.

How can I just *leave town*? I have a show.

A career. After last night, there's an opportunity on the horizon to take the show to New York. To the top—fame, more money, syndication, television. Everything everyone has told me should take ten years or more is coming to me in less than five. All thanks to Mason Reynolds.

Each time I think about Mason and his peaceful insistence that he had something he needed to tell me, and how it harmonized impossibly with Stacy's call, dreadfully points me to a destiny back in Wisconsin.

And I said I'd go back.

I told Stacy I would. Even after everything that happened years ago, I feel loyal to him. Mason's prediction only added a tantalizing promise of something more if I go. *When* I go.

Yet, my audience—*the Little People*—and Wafer and Sammie...I can't just walk away from them. Can I?

Michelle was right. I leave messes for others to clean up. I want forgiveness, but do nothing to earn my redemption. Now, for whatever reason, events are converging and forcing an impossible decision.

If I stay, I'm fucked. I can't live like this anymore.

If I go home, I'm fucked. I have no idea what is waiting for me there.

"Fuck it," I say out loud. I'm going back to Wisconsin. I don't know if I'll stay, like Syd thinks I should. But I'm going. Because for the first time, it's at Stacy's invitation, and I'll finally be able to meet my son.

CHAPTER 12

I was at a pay phone on State Street in Madison, Wisconsin.

Masses of people slipped in and out of shops on both sides of the street, others were walking, talking, riding bikes, or skateboarding. There were students and beggars, yuppies and freaks. It was 3:16 p.m. and the bars were busy. A few blocks up the hill, on the Square around the State Capitol Building, the farmer's market was wrapping up. The University of Wisconsin campus was only a stroll away, as were Lakes Mendota and Monona.

I dialed from memory.

One ring. Two. Three.

Four rings.

I wasn't sure what I'd say if anyone picked up.

Five rings.

Six rings.

I slammed the phone into the cradle and collected my quarter.

It was 95 degrees on June 27, 1998, and I had sweat through my shirt. Mostly due to the sweltering heat and humidity, but partly because of the phone call I was trying to make. Waves of heat rose from the asphalt, cooking me through my shoes. I finished a lukewarm Mountain Dew and set the can down.

I was in the middle of State Street because it was the site of my final, live radio show in Madison, and I was obsessively scouting the location once more (and would again three more times) when I gave into a foolish urge to call Michelle and invite her and Stacy (and our child) to the show.

It was idiotic, but I was desperate to see her, and my son, and wanted to make some type of peace offering to Stacy, in public, where I wouldn't get shot. I wanted his forgiveness, and I needed Michelle's. Their absence had created a void in my life I couldn't fill.

I also wanted Michelle to see me in action. I was in radio because of her.

It turned out I was a natural. She had been right. I wanted her to know that the off-handed comment she'd made on our first night together had led to something…positive.

Shortly after I'd last seen her on a freezing April morning over two years ago, I began to pull myself together. I took a job as a waiter in a Madison restaurant. Three months after that, I visited a radio station to see if my big mouth and love of music could actually amount to a job as a DJ. It didn't— not at first. But they did hire me to run the console and play local commercials during the Green Bay Packers games. My first day on the air, as a DJ, was the day Michelle had her (their? Our?) baby.

That was the second worst day of my life.

I tried to shake that memory, but everywhere I looked I saw families, seemingly so loving and dedicated. I was alone, without a family to go home to, without a family of my own, without a childhood of my own.

I was desperate to be attached to anything that felt like a real family.

I pumped my quarter back into the phone and stabbed in Stacy and Michelle Ramone's home phone number once more.

It started ringing again.

And rang. And rang. And rang.

I lost my nerve again. I tried to hang up again.

This time the answering machine picked up. The pay phone would keep the last of my money.

Michelle's voice. "Hi, you've reached Shell, Stacy and…" I could tell she'd handed the phone to someone else. Another voice came in after an awkward pause. A small boy. "Stevie!" he shouted. Those two voices took my breath away. Michelle took the phone back and continued: "We can't come to the phone right now but leave a message at the beep"—Stevie yelled "BEEP!" in the background and Michelle apparently thought it was cute because she'd left it in—"and we'll call you back if we feel like it."

What message could I leave?

"Oh, uh, hey, Shell. And Stacy. You guys. How are you? It's Jeremy. I'm good. Um, so I hate leaving fucking messages, but I wanted you to know that I'm getting ready to move soon. I got an offer at a radio station in Washington DC and it looks really good, so I'm going to take it. My last show in Madison is going to be on Friday on State Street with a studio audience. I don't know why I called. I guess, I just wondered if you want to come. Maybe? All three of you. It's cool if you can't. Short notice. But I've got some cool guests. Chris Farley is coming up from Chicago, Shirley Manson from Garbage, Michael Finley is in town with Dallas to play the Bucks, so we got him, Butch Vig with Nirvana stories. Lot of stars. Anyway, I miss you. I miss you guys and I'm sorry and please forgive me for everything. Stacy, for sleeping with Michelle and betraying you and lying to your face, and Shell, for abandoning you and leaving you to lie to Stacy about who Stevie's real father is and Stevie, for not being in your life—"

The machine beeped, and a robotic female voice announced, "MESSAGE COMPLETE." Then a dial tone.

I never said any of those things. I stayed silent.

Angrily, I started to slam the phone down but I hesitated, and instead gently set the handset in place.

Maybe it was finally time to leave Madison behind. It was the right move for my career. Washington DC was an unbelievable market to break into. Howard Stern launched from DC101 to WNBC in New York City. A Gen-X talk show in the Nation's Capital would be unique. I capitalized on my narrative as a school shooting survivor despite the self-loathing it fueled. However, that wasn't the only reason I got a Late Night time slot in DC. I was undeniably exceptional on the air: dogged in booking guests, constantly listening to other talk show hosts—and airchecks of my own show—to improve. I had a natural rapport with callers. I was honest with the audience and the ratings had been fantastic. I had fucking earned it.

But while radio brought me pleasure, it offered no satisfaction.

My career was drawing me away, with so much still unresolved here.

Taking the job in DC also felt like I was running away from home.

Could I put this buried mess with Stacy, Shell, and Stevie behind me? So many secrets. Guilt.

Sarah's death still seemed surreal. I'd been in a coma when she was buried. She's never been laid to rest in my mind, endlessly living and dying in perfect, haunted recollections that never, ever stopped.

I was leaving Madison, our city.

Another betrayal.

I was leaving a part of us behind to pursue another woman's idea for my career. I wanted to run from the past, the tragedy of this place. The job in DC allowed me to run, and point to something in my mind that contradicted what I'd heard and believed my entire life—that I was worthless and would never be anything and would never do anything. It should have felt right. It felt wrong. Tangled.

Understandable doubts hit me. Was I good enough? Would my Madison show translate into DC ratings?

Irrational fears followed. I was a nobody and a phony and people hated me and wanted me to fail.

I was a chickenshit. I was a coward when Sarah died. I was a coward when Michelle needed me.

I'm always afraid. I couldn't remember a time when I wasn't terrified. I was afraid to stay, and afraid to leave. My new career was the best thing that happened for me in years and I hated myself for it. Decisions paralyzed me, because the consequences of a wrong decision had always meant reprisal.

I wanted someone to tell me I deserved good things. Someone who mattered to me. There was no one.

I drew my arm back, balled a fist, reflexively and finally defending myself, and punched the pay phone.

My fist shattered the shower door glass, sending shards in all directions and bringing me back to now. A thousand pieces of glass crash into the tub and scatter across the bathroom floor. Larger pieces fall in a cascading clatter. I reach for the faucet. Blood swirls in the drain. Crimson drips down the wall.

The cuts are deep. There are two large gashes on my right hand and forearm.

My first suicide attempt, complete with fresh desperation and regret, waves over me as I look away.

(adrenaline fueling my despondency, I turn the music up louder and grip the utility knife and cut and cut deeper and pull against the skin and veins and blood is pouring from my wrist terribly and wonderfully)

Unrelenting memories from unhealed places, like sacred sadness.

It's been months since I've had an involuntary violent reaction during a memory. Dr. Darby calls it "dissociating"—when a memory feels so real, emotions sharp and urgent, that what I remember seems more real than what I'm seeing. This is the first time I've accidentally fucked myself up this badly.

I turn the cold water back on in the shower and rinse the cuts to see if I need stitches. It could go either way. I'm not going to a hospital. Fuck it, I'll bandage it myself. I'm fine.

Syd and Pink pound on the door, rattling the handle and yelling. Syd's freaking out. "Jeremy?! What happened?! Why is the door locked? Are you OK?"

"Yes, I'm fine. I'm OK. I just…I slipped and broke my shower door. You don't want to come in. You'll get cut. I'm serious. There's fucking glass everywhere."

"Are you *cut*?" Syd shouts. "Do we need to get you to a doctor—?"

"No! I'm good. I mean, yes, I'm cut, but I don't need a doctor. It's cool. The shower is trashed, but it's fine. I'm fine. It's just a big ass mess in here, glass everywhere. I don't want to step on any, but I can't figure out how to get out of the shower without tearing my feet up like Bruce Willis in *Die Hard*."

I step cautiously out of the tub, tiptoe across a minefield of partially visible glass, snatch a clean towel from the vanity and dry off. Blood runs down my arm and drips on the floor. I pull open a drawer and fish around until I find some gauze, band-aids, and an ace bandage.

It's all too familiar. This bandage came home with me, wrapped around my left wrist after I'd tried to end the pain, and I kept it, a memento of my desire to die and my fear of letting go. I unfurled it, finally, tossing it in a box of bathroom supplies, wondering if I'd ever look at it again, or need it again.

Using my teeth—and patience I didn't know I have—I pinch the cuts closed with tape and band-aids. Next, I bind gauze around the larger gashes like a trainer wrapping a boxer, covering the dressing with an ace bandage. The dressing is bulky, like a cast, making the injury look worse than it is.

I admire my handiwork, recalling previous damage in a similar spot that was grievous, deeper, and intentional. I wipe the mirror free of fog and slick my hair back with five practiced flicks of my wrist.

Gingerly, I poke at my eye, forcing open the eyelid. My eye isn't just swollen shut and bruised. A broken blood vessel has turned the sclera from white to a grotesque maroon. It's going to be nasty for a while.

Little splotches of blood have already speckled through my bandage. I probably need stitches.

I untangle my necklaces from each other and slip them back on. Wrapping a towel around my waist, I make certain I have Michelle's unopened letter, now damp and wrinkly from shower steam, purple ink smudged. I yank open the bathroom door, leaving behind a glass covered floor, blood, and wet towels.

Syd is *right there* in the doorway. Pink is further down the hall. I can't see Piper; presumably she's still in the living room, disinterested. When Pink sees me step out of the bathroom, she moves in. She's gotten dressed. Syd eyes my makeshift first aid attempt suspiciously.

I talk before they can. "I'm good." Syd starts to say something, and I hold up my hand. "Nope. See?"

Pink is more assertive. "You slipped?" She arches her eyebrow. "And only cut your hand?"

I brush past her, heading straight for my bedroom closet and throw on a black V-neck t-shirt and an old pair of Guess blue jeans with torn back pockets. I find my suitcase and fill it haphazardly with the clothes I'll need for a few days in Wisconsin. I toss my handheld recorder and microphone into the same bag.

I fold my precious envelope in half and poke it into my back pocket behind my wallet.

I'm going home. I've decided. I want to leave—*now*. I feel like a caged animal, anxious.

"Pink," I yell from my room. "Pink!" She's at the door, then sits on the bed.

"Yeah, baby, what's up?"

"I'm going to need some shit for the road."

"So, you're going? To Wisconsin? Now?" Pink questions. I'm shaking with nervous energy.

"Yeah, and I'm going to need some shit for the trip. I don't have a connection in Wisconsin anymore."

"Hey, will you slow down for a second, baby?" I yank the last loop tight on my Chuck Taylor Converse All-Stars and when I try to stand up she puts her hand firmly on my shoulder. "Stop. You're flailing around here and rushing out the door. Twenty minutes ago, you were all like, 'Hey have some fucking lunch and freshen up and I'll be right out.' Now you're just leaving? You're not even going to sweep up the glass in your bathroom? You're just throwing clothes in a bag and demanding shit for the road? You're leaving now? When are you coming back?" Piper materializes in the doorway, eyes cold and probing.

I know now for sure that everything Syd told me was true.

Last night Pink said that I shouldn't expect a relationship. Now, she's talking to me like a concerned wife. Piper is never interested in anything, but now she's watching me pack?

I never would have picked up on these shifts in behavior if Syd hadn't warned me.

I want to leave. I don't know that I care *where* I ride the downward spiral, or *who* might be complicit when I hit bottom. But I don't want to be used, knowingly. If they blow up my life and the radio show here in DC, then I'll take out Wafer and Sammie and others at the station. I need to stop intentionally ruining lives and turning people into collateral damage. I'll take a minute, get sorted out, talk to Dr. Darby, figure out how to walk away

112

responsibly. And I have to know what happened to Michelle, and maybe, possibly, get time with Stevie, if only as his "daddy's friend."

Pink kisses my neck. She puts her hand on my upper thigh, and even with everything I'm now aware of, even with the pain in my eye and my hand, even with the anxiety of knowing I'm leaving for Wisconsin, my body responds to her touch. I turn toward her and she kisses me lightly on the lips. Her dark eyes absorb everything, suspicious and searching. Syd's right. I'm weak.

"I'll only be there a few days."

Pink's breast brushes against my arm. The manipulation is obvious. Even though it's a lie, the façade of being wanted feels better than emptiness. Pink bites my ear, touching me with the tip of her tongue and whispers, "How much do you need? What do you...want?" I can be comfortable with the theater of this arrangement for a few more minutes. We can use each other to get what we want and pretend that the other doesn't know what is happening.

Just seconds ago, I was contemplating a responsible exit strategy.

Now, the addict and coward rise up inside of me. I'm leaving, but I can't leave sober. It's inconceivable that I'd try to face Michelle's funeral, Stacy's erratic emotional state, and Stevie, without what I need. I rationalize it by telling myself I'm more likely to come back if I don't have any drugs.

"Everything. Give me everything." I need to be ready to avoid what I need to face.

"What do you mean everything?" She's still whispering, but has stopped kissing my ear.

"All of it." I can't run the risk of needing what I need and not being able to get it.

"You can't buy all of it. What are you talking about?" Pink cocks her head to one side, pulling away.

"I need enough of everything I normally get," I explain, condescension creeping into my voice. "OK?"

Piper is still wearing only my sheet, leaning against the door jam. Syd is behind her and off to the side.

All three of the Floyd Chicks are staring at me, each undoubtedly for different reasons.

"What are you, Raoul Duke and Doctor Gonzo heading to Vegas?" Pink is always ready with a 1970s reference, and I've proven often enough that I get them when she uses them with me.

I look at Pink once again. She's beautiful. Smart. Dangerous. Should I stay and orbit her toxic heart of darkness to the end? There are worse ways to die. I could ride a crashing wave of drugs, sex, and betrayal, overdosing into the abyss, my circle of vision growing smaller and tighter until maybe I'll see Sarah waiting for me before the light goes completely dark.

No, I have to leave.

"Yes. Exactly like that." I laugh and it feels fake. Can they tell? "Fear and Loathing in Wisconsin."

Piper lets the sheet fall to the ground. "If he's leaving, I'm getting dressed." Stepping out of the pool of linens, she pads off toward the living room to scoop up her clothes from last night. Syd follows her. Pink gets up from the bed, leans in close, and says, "I can't wait for you come back, baby. No one has *ever* eaten my pussy the way you do. No man, anyway." With that, she joins Piper in the living room. They'll have to get their supply out of their car and divide my order into baggies or balloons.

I know they'll have everything I need.

Syd comes back into the room, sees that I'm aroused again.

"Problems?" she giggles. I give her the finger, stand up, adjust myself.

I open my mouth to say something smartass, but her demeanor has already shifted. She puts her finger on my lips, shushing me, and gives me another warm, comforting, sister-like embrace. It's a near-duplicate of the one from the club. She kisses me on the cheek, like a parent comforting a child. "Get into rehab. Or therapy. Or a psych ward. Something. Anything. You're not gonna see your next birthday if you keep pushing it this hard. And for fuck's sake, eat something. You can clearly afford a nice hotel. Stay in the room, get room service," she orders. "I mean it. Be careful. Funeral. Rehab. Start over."

I agree to none of this, but I don't disagree either.

Syd pauses. "And remember. Don't fucking come back."

CHAPTER 13

Twenty minutes later, I'm in my car and Washington DC is receding in the rearview mirror. Flying would've been easier than driving 900 miles through the night with a fucked-up hand, a swollen right eye and a splitting headache, but I can't fly to Wisconsin with $2,000 worth of drugs in my suitcase.

It's only thirteen hours to Wisconsin. It won't be that bad. Besides, I need time to think.

But first I need to get out of DC. Traffic is terrible in this city, and even though it's early evening on a national holiday, today is no exception. After an hour of indulging my impatience and screaming at everyone around me, I'm finally in rural Maryland. Scanning the radio, I find the 86th Annual Rose Bowl. The Wisconsin Badgers are playing the Stanford Cardinal. Sarah and I had planned to go to the University of Wisconsin together. It was one of the last things we talked about.

I put miles behind me. Cigarettes, amphetamines, and cans of pop. I just want to get there.

I squint into the setting sun, contemplating the ancient ruins of my personal history and obsessing over what happened during the second hour of my show last night. I allow myself to recall—no, feel and relive—every detail of the broadcast, hoping to grasp what Mason Reynolds had meant....

"Tonight, we have a special guest. I told you I wasn't asking you to do anything that I wasn't willing to do myself. I told you last hour that if you were going to confess, I would also confess my deepest, darkest secret. I can't live with the shame...the regret. This secret cost me everything, so tonight, you'll learn the truth. My secret lead to the death of seven people and the devastating injury of twelve more, myself included. My secret put me in intensive care for months. And my secret cost me the love of my life."

As I spoke, I saw rivers of blood running down my high school hallway, I smelled gunpowder, heard the wailing of students and teachers and sirens. I felt water from sprinklers soaking my skin and was overwhelmed as Sarah again—for the 10,000th replay—screamed and cried and begged me to do something, to run, to save her, anything. Mason Reynolds reloaded, fired. My scars ached with shattering explosiveness, like fresh wounds, only deadened next to the memory of my beloved Sarah, collapsed, hair soaked in blood, eyes darkening forever.

"Tonight, it's time to share my secret with you and ask the person who unfairly bore sole and complete responsibility for this tragedy if he can forgive me. I'll let you decide if I'm responsible. I can't stop you from excusing me—like so many others have—but it's up to Mason Reynolds, serving 22 consecutive life sentences in a maximum security prison in Wisconsin, to accept what I say or throw it back in my face.

"The Sugar River Shooting was the worst school shooting in U.S. history until Columbine. On May 23, 1992, Mason Reynolds, part of my senior class at Sugar River High School in rural Wisconsin, about an hour Southwest of Madison, walked into the building at 7:54 a.m., right before the start of the school day carrying a rifle, wearing a hunting vest with pockets filled with .30-30 shells. Sugar River is a farm town, so no one apparently thought much about it, until he started firing on students first, then on the teachers

who bravely, and selflessly, tried to stop him. The hallway was a kill zone. He fired on classmates trapped in the cafeteria, killing my best friend. He came upstairs, shooting wildly, but took aim and—"

I had to stop for a second.

Two.

Three seconds.

Four.

Five seconds.

I had to battle to get the words out. Wafer's hands were clamped over his headphones, listening intently to my monologue. Sammie chomped her gum and stared.

I found my words again and continued.

"—and he killed my girlfriend. She was only 17. We'd gone to prom together two nights earlier."

My voice cracked. That sentence was barely audible through the mic, a mournful whisper.

I had to keep talking. There were no allowances for dead air, for crying, for gathering myself. I sighed and purposely cleared my throat into the mic without pressing the cough button.

"By the time Mason Reynolds turned his weapon on me, he was down to his last two shots. My locker door swung open just as he fired from about 10 feet away. The locker metal was too thin to stop the bullets, but it slowed them enough so that even though I took one in the chest and one in the stomach, I didn't die instantly. Doctors, cops, the media, called it a miracle. There's no scientific explanation beyond that. I got lucky. I took two .30-30 slugs from less than 10 feet and I'm here today to tell you about it. Then, for reasons no one but Mason knows, he sat down next to me and waited for the cops. I think he thought he got me. I was the reason he came to the school with a gun. Everyone else was collateral damage. I still don't know why I lived, when seven others didn't. I didn't deserve to."

I blinked away a fleeting moment of recall, this time it was Stacy holding a revolver as Michelle calmly revealed, "He wants to die. Letting him live is torture. He's in love with his dead girlfriend."

"Those are the facts. But the facts are incomplete. They don't tell the whole story. I'm here tonight to tell you the full truth. Fill in the blanks. So much more happened in the hours leading up to the shooting, terrible things. Mason pulled the trigger, over and over and over and over and over and over. But something pushed him to do it. I know what it was. Mason never took the stand in his own defense. I testified but didn't say what I knew. What I had done. I was ashamed, and confused, and back from the dead and I wanted revenge on Mason for killing my girlfriend, killing my best friend, for shooting me. If Wisconsin had the death penalty, I thought he deserved it. So I never, once, told under oath. No one else told either. Not about what they knew about the post-prom party, nothing. Mason himself has never spoken publicly or granted an interview until tonight. Until now. Only on the People's Talk Show. Hot Talk 690, WTMI, and the biggest thing that has happened in the history of broadcast radio."

I was on fucking fire.

No one had ever been as good as I was at that moment. I was the best in the radio industry that night.

Wafer indicated the conference line was ready. Sammie nodded. Others in the room stood still, waiting.

"Mason Reynolds—LIVE and uncensored—is on the hotline and joins us from Waupun Men's Correctional Facility in Wisconsin, where his attorney will also be conferenced in. You, the Little People, Mason, me."

I took a deep breath.

"Mason, it's Jeremy. You're on the air with The People's Talk Show. Are you there?"

I heard shuffling, someone said, "Go ahead," and the next voice I heard was Mason Reynolds.

"Hey, Jeremy." A shockwave hit me through the headphones, a jolt to the head and heart. I hadn't heard Mason's voice since he screamed "LOOK WHAT YOU MADE ME DO!" as I lay dying in front of him. Mason never said a word to anyone on the day I testified during his trial.

I swallowed and continued.

"Quick ground rules, Mason. Business talk, OK?"

"Sure." Mason Reynold's voice was gruffer than I remembered. He rasped heavily into the phone. Exhale. Exhale. Exhale. Directly into the mouthpiece. I couldn't hear the attorney, but I knew he was on, as was the warden. Wafer had lined it up seamlessly. No technical problems. All parties were ready.

I could barely keep the tremor out of my voice.

"I know you and your lawyers have seen this, but the Hot Talk 690 WTMI Legal Division needs me to do this before we get started." Mason mumbled something that I couldn't understand, and I pressed ahead with the paper Wafer had left for me in the studio. "Please refrain from using profanity. You cannot reference any of our classmates, teachers or their family members, victims, or otherwise, by name. Please do not provide any personal information like phone numbers, fax numbers, or addresses while on air. Any references that could be perceived as being delivered in a threatening manner to anyone at the prison, or a public official, or anyone who served on either of your juries, members of the media, any of the victims or victims' families, radio station employees, or anyone not specifically mentioned in this list will result in the immediate termination of the interview and could result in charges being brought by Hot Talk 690 WTMI, or any of the parties that were threatened. Don't discuss the judges in your case, or your appeal. No references to any inmates at Waupun or any other correctional facility. Court documents that have been sealed or redacted cannot be read on the air. Do not put anyone on the phone, other than your attorney, without permission. Do you understand? You have to answer audibly for us to proceed."

"I got it. And I have all the stuff you skipped over, too. We're good." Mason was steady. I was not.

"Excellent. To those listening in, we have to take a commercial break. When we come back, we'll dive into the conversation between me—a survivor of the Sugar River Shooting in 1992—and the shooter himself, Mason Reynolds—" I was interrupted by a voice on the line I didn't immediately recognize.

"Alleged shooter," was all the voice had said.

"Excuse me?" I barked. "Who is this, exactly? Just want to make sure I know who I'm arguing with."

The interloper had an unmistakable, thick Northern Wisconsin Upper Peninsula accent. "I'm Mr. Reynold's attorney, Roger Sandusky. Want it on duh record, there. He's dee alleged shooter."

"Look, Mr. Roger Sandusky, how about we meet in the middle and agree to 'convicted murderer' which I believe, after two trials, and the subsequent convictions, and the convictions being upheld, I can safely say without fear of legal repercussion? I mean, Mason agreed to the interview, and I've got some things I'm going to say to him, but I'm not going to let you rewrite history with semantic gymnastics."

Roger Sandusky tried to rebut me like an effective courtroom litigator should, and Mason stopped him.

"It's OK, Roger. This ain't important to me. Jeremy has things to say, and I have things to say too. I ain't gonna derail all of this because a little detail that don't matter to me or nobody else. Sound good?"

Sandusky sniffed.

I immediately started back in. "As I was saying before LA Law cut me off, we're gonna take a break. You're not gonna want to miss a single moment of what comes next. Mason Reynolds, convicted murderer in the mass shooting at Sugar River High School, is my guest tonight on The People's

121

Talk Show, on Hot Talk 690, WTMI. Back in three minutes. Don't touch your radio dial...."

Wafer played me into the spot block with "Mouth (The Stingray Mix)" by Bush.

My mic was barely off and I exploded at Wafer over the intercom.

"Tell the fucking attorney to stay off the air unless I invite him on! I don't want some Johnny Cochran wannabe interjecting every six fucking seconds because of some tiny little characterization he may have a problem with! Fucking Mason didn't even care that I said it, and this guy is jumping on the air like he's my fucking co-host?! Sammie, pick up the hotline, put Wafer on with him, and Wafer? Tell Matlock to stay off the fucking phone unless there's some egregious legal wrong being committed, or I ask him back on, by name. Got it?" I needed the show—the confession—to go exactly according to plan. Desperately. I hated how I let Mason's stupid fucking attorney throw me off my rhythm.

Wafer gave me the thumbs up and I knew he'd communicate the point in a far more tactful manner than I could. Sammie handed him the phone, the commercials were running, and despite the fact that we weren't taking phone calls, every line coming into the studio was flashing red with people trying to get through. On New Year's Eve, 1999, with less than an hour left until a new millennium. Amazing.

"I need more coffee!" I barked into the intercom. "And another water. Before the rejoin," I added.

I saw someone leave the producer booth and 30 seconds later he ducked his head cautiously through the door and held out the coffee and water like a shield against my insults. "Just bringing you the coffee. And water. Wafer and Sammie are busy. This is incredible radio, Jeremy. I can't believe you got—"

I interrupted him. "Set it down there." I pointed to the table when I could have just taken it from him.

"Thank you," he said as I grabbed the Styrofoam cup and swallowed the water with hard, fast gulps.

Wafer was back on the intercom. "Sandusky had a lot of legal shit to say, Jeremy, I think maybe you should get on with him for a second and the two of you talk directly. He's not listening to me, bro."

"Didn't the goddamn lawyers sort out all of this shit weeks ago? What's with lawyers? No wonder everyone fucking hates them. Always picking picking picking. Loopholes and bullshit. I'm over it, man!"

"I thought so, dude." Wafer shrugged and again held the phone toward me, gesturing through the glass for me to pick up my extension and talk to him. "Try your charm on him. The two of you seem to have a good rapport. Maybe if you just sit and discuss his concerns like rational—"

"Fuck him. I'm done with him. I'll deal with him on the air if I have to."

I clicked the intercom off. Wafer said something I couldn't hear and everyone in the producer's room laughed. Fucking Wafer, probably being a smartass, partly about Sandusky, mostly about me. I leaned back in my chair and closed my eyes again. My thoughts were jumbled. I strained to focus on what I wanted to say to Mason, and how to express it the right way to get what I needed. Stacy's call had knocked the wind out of me, and despite my efforts at recovery, I was incapable of compartmentalizing Michelle's death separately from what I was attempting with Mason Reynolds.

It had gotten totally fucked up.

The intercom clicked on. Wafer popped out a quick, "Thirty seconds, dude," and clicked it off again.

There had been so much sadness. Pain. Irreparable damage. Death. Destroyed families. I was at the center of it. I've been the cause of it. I was the black hole that sucked in good people and corrupted others. So much damage in such a short amount of time. It seemed like there was nothing that could satisfy the immeasurable injustice I left in my wake. It demanded a counterbalance. A reckoning.

The universe wasn't putting things in order, wasn't making all things right. My apologies were meaningless. I had to act. People needed to see what I was, what I had done, and acknowledge the horrors so I could finally take the blame. The full truth had to come out. I was prepared to rip open my chest and then they'd finally turn on me. Hate me. But in that hatred, there was honesty, and in that honesty, a path to forgiveness. If they blamed me, deservedly, maybe I could have some hope again.

The intercom again. "Dude. You're up."

Wafer. He always had my back. I should treat him better.

Headphones on, eyes open, mic open.

Fuck it. This is what I wanted.

CHAPTER 14

"Thirty-nine minutes until the End of the World. Or not. You're right where you're supposed to be, with the Little People you love the most, The People's Talk Show, on Hot Talk 690 WTMI. Reports from across the world, where the new millennium has already arrived, indicate Y2K is going down as a hilarious historical footnote of man's hubris and overreaction...but no country on Earth is as reliant on technology as we are, and it only takes one event to cascade the country into a downward spiral of madness.

"While we wait, we're unburdening our souls to one another, and I can say with certainty I've wronged my guest as badly as any other person on the face of the Earth has ever been wronged. Mason Reynolds, and his attorney... Mr. Roger 'Chatty Cathy' Sandusky...are on the line from Wisconsin, but not to be interviewed. To listen. If he wants, Mason, the shooter...ahem—the alleged shooter who allegedly put two alleged bullet holes in my alleged body that I can see right now when I pull up my alleged shirt—can ask me any questions he wants, and I'll answer them. I hope he can find it within himself to forgive me."

Mason cleared his throat. He had to sit through the broadcasting bombast. It was still a show, after all.

"Hey. Before all that happens, can I say something first? I come on your show and agreed to do this interview 'cause I wanted to tell you something that I know you need to know. I can't explain how I know you need to know it or even how I know it, but I got something important to say too. I need to make sure we have time for me to say it 'cause it's the only reason I said yes to doing this," Mason interjected.

I wanted to be in control of how I things would go, but I was intrigued. I mulled it over for a couple of seconds. Wafer held up his hand to silence the people talking in the producer booth and put his headphones back on. He needed to know what my decision would be, so he could adjust any plans.

"Let's save your little speech for the end. Best for last. I swear to God, I'll make sure we have time before the end of the show and the End of the World. Work for you, Mason?"

I bullied Mason. My contrition was sincere, yet at the same time, I forced him to submit to me. I still thought of him as a punk kid, all these years later. This instinct came from a hidden, ugly place, to treat Mason like he was my bitch. For the briefest of moments, students no longer, he in prison and me a radio star, I'd slipped back into the role I played in high school. Mason wasn't so eager to turn back the clock.

"Sure. As long as you're swearing to God," Mason agreed. "That way the deal's between you and Him."

Clever comeback.

He wasn't at all like I remembered, aside from his flat Midwestern non-accent and terrible grammar. Mason wasn't just a convicted murderer. He was a victim who no longer sounded like one. Mason had been cast as the boogeyman after his killing spree. He wasn't that either. On the phone, he was in possession of a cool confidence. I never would have tolerated him mouthing off to me in high school. When were teenagers I wanted to rob him of his dignity. He was the human shield that I put between any threat to my vulnerabilities. Mason had gone from victim, to monster, to this current version. This idea that I'd imagined, that I'd apologize and Mason would sob his *forgiveness, suddenly seemed remote and unrealistic. In my self-centeredness, I hadn't taken into consideration that Mason Reynolds wouldn't be the person I remembered. I didn't have a secondary plan. I pressed ahead, uncertain. I had no choice.*

"Mason, I need to confess something that you and I know, but my audience doesn't. You never took the stand and you seemingly never told your lawyers what I'm about to reveal. At least, they never used it in court during cross-examination, never asked about our Post Prom Party. Before I share what happened, I have to know: why didn't you tell anyone what I did?" This question had gnawed at me. I pictured Roger Sandusky putting pen to legal pad, wanting details more than my audience did.

"I guess, I didn't see how what you did somehow undid what I did," was all Mason said.

Roger Sandusky snapped at Mason, but it was muffled and indecipherable. However, Mason could clearly be heard retorting, "I already said I don't want another appeal. I'll say what I wanna say."

I persisted. "You're telling me that you don't feel like you were pushed into doing what you did?"

"Yeah, you and…your friends were like wolves in school, Jeremy. You were the worst. But I can't say that I think what you did to me was a good excuse for what I did on Skip Day. 'Cause it wasn't."

My face flushed with fast anger and frustration.

"Your personal responsibility is admirable but unwise if you ever plan on getting out of prison," I said.

"I don't. I'm right where I need to be. But say what you wanna say so I can say what I wanna say," Mason replied. He had an agenda and was patiently biding his time, waiting for me to finish. Each time he spoke I felt the relief I was hoping for slip further from my grasp.

In 10 minutes, Mason Reynolds had wrestled control away from me.

Still, I had to continue. Time was again my enemy, slowing to a crawl on the digital display in front of me.

"There wasn't a lot to do in Sugar River, Wisconsin. There's less than 2,000 people in the whole town, and less than 300 people in our school. That was junior high and high school, both in one building. Our senior prom was on a Saturday night, May 21, 1992. I don't know why it was so late in the year, only a couple of weeks before graduation, but it was. Tradition at Sugar River High School was anyone who was a Senior could skip the Monday after prom and not get in trouble. It was supposed be one of the best weekends of our lives. Prom, after prom, Skip Day, then a few meaningless class days, another week for the faculty to set up the gymnasium for commencement, and then we graduate."

Mason didn't try to add anything. He let me set the scene for The Little People without disruption, breathing into the phone. EXHALE. EXHALE. EXHALE. I wanted to shout at him to "stop breathing."

"Nothing especially important happened at prom," *I lied. My heart fluttered as I recalled with vivid clarity the dinner Sarah and I shared before the dance, blowing off plans my Senior Class had made, showing up late, and buzzed. It was at the dance that I told Sarah for the first time—*

"I didn't go to the dance," *Mason interjected.* "I didn't ask no one. No one woulda went with me."

"Afterward, a bunch of us had planned a massive party. We'd spent about two weeks gathering branches and logs and a couple of old telephone poles and made a huge bonfire out in the country, on one of our friends' parents' farms. It was way, way out. No cops were going to come. We managed to get my hands on four bottles of tequila and three bottles of cheap whiskey. Am I missing anything?"

"Nope," *Mason stopped exhaling to answer.* "You remember it right."

Of course I did. When the thought of that night came to mind, it's less that I remembered what happened. I re-witnessed it. I felt it. Somehow it was new each time, and also a memory.

"After prom, we all rolled out there. Bunch of cars, farm trucks, a few dirt bikes and four wheelers. We lit that bonfire up with cans of gasoline and a road flare. It was pretty damn impressive. It was 11:48 p.m. when you arrived. We..." I swallowed. "We just got there too. You came alone."

"I didn't go to the dance, but I wanted to go to that bonfire," Mason added.

"You want to tell what happened next, Mason? So the audience knows I'm not lying?" I asked.

"Yeah, I'll tell it. I said something that pissed you off. I don't remember what it was, but you always got mad real easy. I said something, and you started talking real loud and you pushed me and told me to shut up and that you'd kick my...butt. I was trying to get away from you, but your friends were all there too, everyone was laughing and telling you to do it, that you should do it," Mason recounted.

"Do what?" I prodded.

"Fight me. Beat me up. I thought I'd get hit a few times or something. I didn't know you were gonna do what you did. I figured it'd just be like all the other times during high school with you or someone else."

Wafer pantomimed "breaking a stick," meaning we had to play our commercials. The timing was perfect. I'd built the drama to keep the audience for another few minutes, through another slate of advertisers.

"Mason, I'm being told I have to take a commercial break now. Gotta do it. But after the break, we'll pick the story back up." I metaphorically turned to the audience. "My confession is next. Then Mason's special message he says he prepared just for me. This is The People's Talk Show, with an exclusive New Year's Eve interview with Sugar River Shooter Mason Reynolds, only on Hot Talk 690 WTMI." I closed the mic.

I knew we had to get to the point of this or the audience was going to tune out. I wasn't competing with other radio stations tonight. I was going to head-to-head with the biggest party in decades, if not ever.

More importantly, I needed Mason to hear me accept the blame, and I needed him to forgive me for driving him to kill Sarah and six others. I needed him to agree that the shooting was my fault, let me take my share of the responsibility and the burden, and then let me promise to try and earn his forgiveness.

I had to deliver in the next segment.

Wafer was talking to me through the intercom. "Jeremy? You with me, dude?"

"What?" I was so lost in thought I hadn't heard anything he'd been saying.

"Bro. Tell us what you did to him," Wafer repeated.

Sammie nodded. "Yeah, Jeremy, tell us before you go back on," she demanded. "What did you do?"

"No fucking way," was all I could find to say. I waved my hand at the window and closed my eyes again. There was nothing left to do but finish it, but I didn't have it in me to finish it twice.

When the commercial break ended, I recapped what had happened, bringing late arrivals up to speed, and reintroduced Mason. Anyone listening was now standing with us, next to the bonfire in May of 1992.

"Mason, what happened next must have been incredibly personal and embarrassing for you. I feel like I need your permission to tell everyone what I did, with a few dozen teenagers looking on. Can I share this? It's the most important part of the story, but I'm not doing it without your OK." I held my breath.

"Tell it. You did it. I couldn't stop you. Three of you held me down. I fought back. I wasn't a—" He stopped. I assumed he was looking for a word aside from "pussy" that he could say on the radio. "I wasn't a baby. I tried to stop you. Go ahead. Tell everyone who you are. At least, who you was then."

I had a violent streak that came out of nowhere when I felt threatened, even in seemingly inconsequential ways. My instinct was to defend myself

130

at all costs. It never felt like I was attacking anyone when I put them in my sights. It felt like revenge.

I was a bully.

"I taunted him with every name I could think of. Nothing I can say on the radio. I lost my mind, and at the same time I knew exactly what I was doing. When I couldn't get him to throw the first punch, three of us tackled him, and slapped him around, kicked him, spit on him, smashed his face in the dirt. I ripped his pants off. He was crying, screaming for us to stop, but I stripped everything off, down to his underwear. Everyone watching, no one stopping us, everyone uncomfortable. But it wasn't enough. I got ahold of him again and yanked his underwear off. He was on the ground, trying to cover himself, bloodied and dirty, and people were telling me to stop. So I threw all of his clothes into the fire."

Wafer, Sammie, and everyone in the producer's room stood silent staring at me through the glass.

"But I wasn't done, was I, Mason?" I prompted him.

"Tell it all. You wanted to do this," Mason urged. "You know what you done next, Jeremy."

"I took a bottle of tequila and I made him stand up and I poured the whole thing over his head. I'm yelling at him to spin and dance and by now people are heading to their cars but I didn't stop. No one was laughing anymore, except me. You remember, Mason? What set me off? What you said?"

"I don't. Does it matter?" EXHALE EXHALE EXHALE EXHALE. The humiliation, while never as fresh for Mason as a memory would be for me, was still painfully embarrassing. "You remember. I know you remember. We all talked about how you could remember stuff so good, Jeremy. Perfect. Probably never failed a test. Tell me what I said that made you so angry with me."

"I do remember it perfectly, and will forever. You said, 'I brought the trig book you left at my house.' That was it. You'd thought to bring my math

book and I was so worried about what people would think if they knew I was hanging out at your house sometimes, and it sent me over the edge. And I was drunk." My face burned with shame. This part of the confession was the hardest. It sounded so...

Inconsequential. Ridiculous. Impossibly small. I was such a fucking asshole. There was literally no excuse. No justification. Mason had done nothing wrong. He had just been nice to me at the wrong time.

I didn't want anyone to know I went to his house after school so I wouldn't have to go...

Home. Anywhere but home.

A textbook. And kindness. And then seven dead classmates, worst of all Sarah. I destroyed people.

"I never knew that until today," Mason whispered.

It took me eight seconds before I made myself continue. Wafer mouthed "DEAD AIR," but even he was subdued, caught up in what he heard. Sammie swiveled her head "no" back and forth, slowly.

"After I poured the bottle of tequila over you, I grabbed one of the burning branches out of the fire and pretended like I was going to set you on fire. I was drunk, careless, and with you soaked in tequila I easily could have done it. I was reckless out of control, but I swear to God I wasn't actually trying to burn you. But by that point you were crying and screaming and begging for your life, and I was poking the burning branch at your face and...other spots... and then I just...stopped."

I had to keep going.

The truth and contrition weren't enough.

There was penance due.

"You didn't 'just stop.' She made you stop. She yelled at you and you stopped."

Mason was right. It was Sarah's objection, her shocked voice that stopped the exploitation and humiliation from going further. I couldn't allow myself to acknowledge Mason's correction.

"And then we all just left. Left you there. Naked. Your clothes and keys burning up in the fire. Miles from anywhere. I have no idea how you got home. Your car was open, I know that, because I took that math book on the way to my car. I never even looked back. I just left. We all left you there, soaked with tequila, naked and scared to death that I had almost burned you alive. I didn't see you again until Monday morning when you...How'd you get home?" Overdue compassion, born within me.

"I walked. I had a jacket in my car. Wrapped it around myself an' walked to the road, then walked as far as I could until a farmer picked me up and took me to my mom and stepdad's house. It was the middle of the night, so I guess I thank God that there was anyone out there at all," Mason explained.

I sighed directly into the microphone and addressed the audience. "It's up to you—The Little People—to decide whether or not what happened at the bonfire was the reason Mason went to school 32 hours later and started shooting. I believe, beyond a shadow of a doubt, that Mason Reynolds came to Sugar River High School on Monday looking for me because he was scared that what happened at that bonfire was going to happen again, only the next time there wasn't going to be someone there to stop me."

I turned my verbal attention back to Mason.

"Mason, I've told everything that matters. This will undoubtedly be national news over the next few days. Now comes the part that I don't know how to handle. An apology is inappropriate, although I am sorry. I'm deeply, deeply sorry for what I did to you and for what it caused. But what I really need to know is this: what can I do to earn your forgiveness? How can I begin to take the first, tiny steps toward fixing this somehow? Can I help your attorneys? Can I go to court and swear under oath that I terrorized you and that you acted in a kind of proactive self-defense? What can I do, right now,

to hope to have you forgive me for what I've done?" Tears brimmed in my eyelids. I struggled to get the words out.

It was genuine remorse.

Mason's voice, in my headphones, was calm. Resolute. I turned the volume louder. I waited. I listened.

"Jeremy, there ain't nothing you can do to fix what's happened. You done what you done, but I did what I did. Those two things ain't the same. I can forgive you for what you did at the fire but I can't forgive you for what happened at the school because you ain't the one who done that. I did. That's me. I did go to the school on Monday to find you. I forgot all about the Skip Day, but I saw your car out front and my stepdad's gun was in the truck and his hunting vest, and I was driving his truck because my car was still out in the woods. When the teachers saw me coming in with the gun, they tried to stop me and I just started shooting to stop them from stopping me. You didn't make me do that. I can't forgive you for something you didn't do. It ain't my place. I'm guilty. Not you. Not for the shooting."

I wasn't about to let it go. "But I started it! If everything at the bonfire hadn't happened, you wouldn't have come to the school looking for me. You wouldn't have seen my car at the school—even on Skip Day—and you wouldn't have gone in. You wouldn't have had your dad's truck, his gun, and his vest full of ammo if I hadn't thrown your car keys into the bonfire with your clothes! Can't you put two and two together here? I set the events into motion. I did that! The shooting is my fault! Her death—everyone's death! You brought the gun to school that day, but I was the trigger, Mason! Can't you see that?"

I was screaming into the mic, pegging the needles, distorting the audio.

Wafer waved his arms, frantic to remind me that there's one last commercial break. I'd forgotten I was doing a live radio show. It was just me and Mason, on the phone. I saw what I needed, just out of grasp, and Mason was dangling it out of reach. His next words were familiar, and they pissed me off.

"It's not your fault, Jeremy. And I don't want your help to get out of prison. I'm staying here. It's where I belong for what I done. I don't want you to go to court. I don't want you to help my lawyers or talk to anyone or use your radio contacts to try and make yourself feel better. I'm where I'm supposed to be. I should be the one asking for your forgiveness. I shot you. I shot...her. I shot everyone. I need to be begging and apologizing and not you. You have a guilty conscience. I'm just guilty."

I sensed the moment was slipping away. "Mason, I don't know if I can forgive you for what you did, even though I know I caused it. I'm willing to try, if that's what it would take for you to forgive me."

Wafer held up a piece of paper and clapped it against the glass. He'd written one word on it. "SPOTS!!" He pointed at it, grimaced, shrugged, and then pointed at it again. Sammie looked worried. I gave him the finger and jerked my head back and forth, mouthing "NO" and glared at him. Fuck the commercials.

This was my only chance.

"Look," I barked but Mason again wrestled control away from me.

"No, you look. Even though it's an hour earlier where I am, I know your radio show is almost over. And you swore to God that you'd let me tell you what I needed to tell you. Before you said all the stuff you just said to me, and how you wanna make things better and fix things, I didn't really understand much about why I had to say the stuff I was supposed to say, but now I know for sure that you need what I got for you. I'm guessing this is as close to a message from God you're ever gonna get," Mason lectured me.

He'd gotten enthusiastic, his voice had gone up an octave and he was talking faster.

What was he talking about?

"What the hell are you talking about, Mason?" I challenged him. "I'm trying to get back to what happened and you've got messages from God and some kind of epiphany you've just experienced?"

135

Mason sounded like he was in a trance. *"Have you been invited to come home to Wisconsin, Jeremy?"*

My memory spontaneously accessed Stacy Ramone's phone call: ("I need you to come home. To Wisconsin. It's why I called…will you come, Jeremy?")

There's no way Mason could have known that. Right?

"How do you know that? How were you listening to the show in prison? Who told you? Did my producer tell you? Or did he tell your lawyer? Sandusky, what did you tell Mason about what happened last hour?"

Wafer has gone white, even paler than usual, undoubtedly assuming I believed he'd told Mason about Stacy's phone call for some reason. He hit the intercom button, something he rarely did while my mic was hot, and yelped, "Didn't do it. No one heard that phone call," and snapped the intercom back off. The intercom, when on, cuts my mic. In that moment of silence, Sandusky had come back on the phone.

"Mr. Peoples, Mr. Reynolds is not privy to anything that has been said on your radio station prior to his coming on the air at your request. He was placed in your telephone system just moments before the broadcast began. We have not been provided with any audio feeds or recordings of your program and thus have no knowledge of what you are alleging."

"Say what you came to say," I spat. *I almost cursed when I said it. My show was over in two minutes.*

Everything had gone according to plan and nothing had worked out the way it was supposed to.

It was humiliating. I was powerless. Emasculated. Anger and frustration came to a boiling point.

"You're gonna have to go home soon, Jeremy. 'Cause God wants you to. He has something for you to do. You're the only person that can do it. I know now it's the reason I didn't get to kill you in 1992. I shoulda got you. I was right there, there's no way a locker door was enough to stop them shots.

It wasn't bad luck. God spared your life 'cause you got a job to do. You need to accept that invitation and come back home. I'm also sure that I need to tell you this part perfect; I need to get it exactly right. I wrote it down the night before your interview request came in. I swear that's true. More than a month ago. It's why I fought so hard from the inside to be on the show. God told me I was His messenger and needed to go on the radio. I heard His voice tell me to say it as clear as I hear you on the phone."

Paper crinkled faintly in the background.

EXHALE.

EXHALE.

I heard Mason smooth out his notes. I almost jumped in and started talking again, but he finally began.

"This is what I heard the voice tell me to tell you. It said, 'Because you hate yourself, I know you'll do what is required when the time is right. And if you do, you'll give up everything you don't want in order to get the thing you can't seem to acquire.' I know you want to die. I can hear it in your voice when you talk. Tonight's like one of them deathbed confessions for you. Spill your guts so you can let go. Well, I think you're gonna die soon, Jeremy. I just don't know how. But you're gonna have to come home to do it."

CHAPTER 15

I'm somewhere in Pennsylvania. Cigarette after cigarette, stopping only for gas, I've just been driving. I'm not hungry. Turnpikes and rest stops and 18-wheelers. Dingy snow. Yellow dividing lines on blacktop. I try to listen to music and hate everything I have with me. State Troopers setting speed traps. The dark smudges of rolling hills surround me in the night. Headlights glare. Road noise.

UW beats Stanford in the Rose Bowl. I miss most of it. Lost in thought, trying to decipher Mason's message, the radio station finally fizzles into static as DC slips further into the distance. I barely notice.

More than once, I have the unsettling feeling that someone is in the backseat of the car with me. I keep checking the rearview mirror, turning around. I'm paranoid. It's the circumstances. And the cocaine.

The memories are vivid.

Sweet and painful and jumbled.

Sarah. I see her now, alive.

(auburn hair fanned out on the picnic table, brown eyes an invitation, my mouth on her mouth, kissing deeply, deeper. Sarah hummed and murmured. Knees apart, eyes closing, "I want you to...")

And Michelle. Her letter. I still haven't read it.

I'm afraid of the outcome. I don't know what she wants me to know, and I don't want to know. Not knowing drives me insane. Not knowing is better than finding out something I'll wish I hadn't. I almost pull over and rip it open. I can't. There's no way this letter is good news. I tuck it away.

I'm brokenhearted that we missed each other, again, and now Michelle *(like Sarah)* is gone, too.

(strawberry blonde hair fanned out on my bed, green eyes guilty, exactly the same as mine, warning me and wanting me, touching me, she gave herself over to me, healing me)

I skirt past Pittsburgh, heading Northwest toward Cleveland. I stop at a gas station, eat a Snicker's bar, and do another line of cocaine off the toilet tank cover in a filthy bathroom. A vending machine bolted to the wall advertises condoms and aphrodisiacs making dubious claims. I again see Pink in my bed. Phone numbers and crude comments are scratched silver into the paint. Vile stench. I do another line.

Sarah would be shocked. Michelle would be disappointed. No one else matters.

I look at my watch. January 1 is the longest day of my life. The last twenty-four hours weigh on me. I struggle to separate "then" from "now." Suddenly, Mason's with me now, haunting and taunting me.

(inviting me to his house, scuffing at the ground, hoping for a friend. I'm relieved to have a place to go, anywhere but home, anywhere, secretly accepting, afraid someone will find out, embarrassed, ashamed)

I blink my eyes. He's still here.

(bonfire hot on my face, bright against Mason's pale skin as I humiliate him, power flooding through me, thrilling and overriding any compassion, sparks and cinders from burning branches, terrifying him)

Blinking repeatedly now. More images. And again the lasting one.

(I can't move, can't stop him, powerless to move, a coward, she reached out her hand as a shot rang out)

Exhausted. Chain smoking. My throat and eyes burn.

I grasp the steering wheel tighter as I get closer to home. Home.

(flinching when the door swings open it's not punishment it's violence and insults and I can't stop it please GOD please send somebody to make it stop)

Outside of Toledo, the clock passes midnight and I'm momentarily relieved that New Year's Day is finally over. I take a deep breath. Mile after mile. Bad radio stations. I critique song selections and DJs.

I run out of cigarettes and get a carton of Marlboro Lights. Indiana. Get my toll ticket. I still have over six hours left but it feels closer now that I'm in a state that borders the state I'm going to.

Snow-covered, harvested cropland. Green signs indicating upcoming towns and exits. It's all the same.

Mileage to Chicago. Blue signs enticing me to stop for this fast food restaurant or that motel. Attractions, meaningless at this time of the morning. Any time I see the State Police, my heart races as I imagine I'll be pulled over, searched, and arrested. Minutes drag on like hours. I'll never get home.

(the barrel of Stacy's revolver touches my forehead, cold steel. It mercifully feels like the end; it's not)

What's in the letter? How did she get it to me? Why didn't she call me? Why didn't we meet?

I repeatedly check to make sure the letter is in my back pocket. It always is, now smeared with my blood, my purple name blurred by steam and sweat. The envelope is creased at the fold, glue weakening, the flap peeling open, showing tantalizing contents, but I still can't read it.

I can't do it.

More coffee. I bump another gram of coke. I don't want to sleep. I just want to get there.

It's colder in the Midwest than it was in DC. I'm underdressed. I catch a chill when I stop to dump my ashtray on an offramp and take a piss along the side of the road. I'm shivering in my t-shirt and blazer.

Another cigarette. My mouth tastes like dirt. I find a truck stop, stamping my feet to stay warm while pumping gas, and buy an Orange Crush. I haven't had one since high school. It always went perfectly with a dip of wintergreen Kodiak chewing tobacco. The microwave burgers and burritos actually look tempting; gross roller dogs and coagulated pizza—ageless under the heat lamps—smell delicious.

I bump more coke in the bathroom and tell myself I'll stop for breakfast if I make it to Chicago.

If I'm going to eat, it sure as hell isn't going to be some botulism-infested hotdog or congealed pizza at a 7-Eleven in Gary, Indiana. Sitting down and eating a traditional breakfast sounds amazing. Egg yolks oozing across the plate, chewy bacon, sausage, white bread toast, maybe a pancake—no, waffles—and orange juice. Hashbrowns smeared with ketchup. Syrup and jelly. Coffee with sugar and cream.

I'm starving. When was the last time I had a decent meal?

I know precisely. Eight days.

I merge onto the Chicago Skyway. It's just after 3:00 a.m., Sunday morning. I toss my 1998 Rand McNally Road Atlas into the backseat. I bought it at a gas station when I moved to DC on July 5, 1998, realizing I had to no idea how to get there.

A lifetime ago. So much has changed. Nothing is different. Moving to DC fixed nothing.

I have money, a place to live, drug connections, a career. I don't care.

I need an exit so I can stop and get some food. Not a chain place.

A diner.

The type of spot that I worked at in Madison before I got into radio.

I find one without trying. "Kay's South Side Cafe." The dashboard clock in my car reads 3:16 a.m. when I pull up and park. The after-bar crowd has thinned out. I'll get my breakfast in relative privacy.

A damp and bitter Chicago wind whips through my thin leather blazer and sweaty t-shirt when I open the car door. My teeth chatter as I trot toward the entrance. "Why didn't I wear warmer clothes?" I ask.

A set of jingle bells clanging against the glass announces my arrival. Some of the tackiest Christmas decorations I've ever seen adorn the dining room. Cardboard letters spelling "NOEL" and plastic garland and pictures of Rudolph and Frosty and the Grinch and Santa Claus and The Chipmunks and a Nativity Scene with a manger, the baby Jesus, Mary and Joseph, some animals, the Three Wisemen, and a star. None of it looks like it was purchased at the same time; none of it could have been purchased by the same person.

"Sit anywhere," a pleasant voice yells from somewhere.

I look around, spinning a full 360 degrees, but, seeing no one, I flop down in a booth in the smoking section. A circular plastic ashtray is positioned like a small brown ashy island in the center of the table; the booth is damp from a recent wipe down. My menu has a glob of grape jelly fossilized to it. I pick at it and it pops free, scooting across the table and onto a carpeted floor that hasn't been vacuumed.

"Give me one second," the same pleasant voice yells, from the same somewhere that I can't see.

There are three grizzled patrons eating plates of food and slurping coffee in between occasional spates of drunken laughter. Forks and knives clink. Activity in the window between the kitchen and dining room catches my attention, a heat lamp glaring off the stainless-steel surface. Harry-knuckled-hands push three orders of food forward and ding a bell four times in rapid succession. One of the hands yanks the lone ticket from the

142

wheel and slides it under one of the plates. A gruff voice—different from the pleasant one that greeted me—hollers, "Order up!"

I reach for my cigarettes and, realizing I've left them in the car, I jump up and breeze toward the exit.

"I said I'd be right there!" the pleasant voice is less pleasant this time, anxious, but still coming from somewhere I can't discern. I look around, again turning a full circle. Where is she at?

"No, it's cool. I forgot my smokes in the car. I'll be right back. I'm not leaving. I'm ready to order."

When I come back in, I finally spot the source of the voice. She's standing at the cash register, ringing up three guys who look like red-eyed truck drivers or Calumet City factory workers. "Welcome back," she says, fingers darting around the register with the same precision Wafer's fingers exhibit when navigating my radio console. Next, she's tearing receipts free, handing them to each customer, nodding and giggling. She seems happy. Does she actually like being awake at 3:30 in the morning, waitressing for a bunch of losers by herself? On the Sunday of a holiday weekend?

"Sit anywhere. Oops, I already said that. Habit," she chuckles. "I'm a silly goose sometimes."

"I think I'll just sit where I was sitting. But maybe I'll change my mind and move, since I can sit anywhere. I might sit in several different spots for the length of my stay, and then vote on which one I like the best." It feels playful while I'm saying it, but then I remember: she doesn't know me, my face is bashed in, I don't think I'm smiling, my hand is wrapped in a blood-spotted bandage, and it's the South Side of Chicago. I'm acting like a creep. I try to clean it up; normally I wouldn't but she's just so *fucking nice.*

"Hey, I'm just teasing," I offer self-consciously.

"I know, silly goose," she says. I glimpse her name tag. It reads "WENDY." She flashes another smile.

I collapse in the booth, leg bouncing.

My cigarette is halfway gone by the time she finally gets to me, splashing coffee into a cup and digging around in her pocket for a pen. "Whatchya gonna have?" she chirps. Wendy gives no indication that she is concerned with my appearance. I look at her closely for the first time.

She's maybe 5'5" with dishwater blonde hair pulled back into a ponytail. I'm guessing she's in her mid-30s, but I'm terrible at estimating ages. Wendy's put on a little makeup, not much, some blush, lipstick and eyeliner. She's got on a "uniform" consisting of a white button-up short-sleeved shirt, lightly stained from a past food or coffee spill, and a knee-length navy-blue polyester skirt. Her white nylons disappear into the type of sensible shoes that women choose when they're on their feet all day. Or night. Her face lights up when she smiles, which she does frequently, but her teeth are crooked enough to be noticeable. No wedding ring. A tattoo on her wrist.

What's it say?

"Are you ready to order?" Wendy asks. "Or do you need a few more minutes?"

I realize I'm staring awkwardly at her. "No. Don't leave. I'm ready." I slap my good hand on the table, startling Wendy, who smiles nervously. I'm coked out and riddled with cravings. I'm eating the whole menu.

"Two eggs, over easy. Toast..."

"White or whole wheat?" Wendy interjects.

"White toast. Sausage..."

"Links or patties?" Her ability to time it out during my pauses is impeccable.

"Which is better?" I ask. "I don't want bland sausage. I like it a little spicy."

"Then you want the patties."

"Do that. I also want some bacon, but not crisp. Chewy. And get me some hashbrowns..."

"You want those crisp?" she interrupts again, but she's just so eager to please, I'm not exasperated.

"Yep. And I want a waffle."

Wendy is writing furiously, trying to keep up. "A waffle, too? Wow. OK."

"Tell me about your biscuits and gravy. Fresh? Or have they been sitting around for a while?"

"I think you're good. If not, I won't charge you."

"Cool. Give me a half-order. And I want a glass of milk, and a glass of orange juice."

Wendy stops, looks over what she's written. "Is that it?"

"Isn't that enough?" I'm in the mood to joke around a little, but Wendy hasn't totally caught on to my sense of humor. It's not that she's slow. She's so sincere she seems oblivious to sarcasm. I've ordered a ridiculous amount of food.

"Sir, are you expecting someone else? Do you want me to get another glass of water or a cup of coffee over here for them?" I have never met anyone this genuinely positive and engaging. She's great.

"No, why?" I ask with a straight face. Wendy thinks I have a date arriving. I get it, but play dumb.

"Oh my gosh, I'm so sorry. It's just, you...you have four different drinks and I thought maybe you were ordering for a friend or something. I'm SO sorry!" Wendy is falling all over herself trying to make up for calling me a gluttonous pig in the nicest way anyone could. But she owned it. I respect that.

"You're good. It *is* a lot of food. I've been driving all night." I use my nearly finished cigarette to light a fresh one, then poke and twist it to death in the ashtray. "I'll finish this and see about seconds. Or dessert." Why am I in such a good mood? Being around Wendy has inspired joy from somewhere. She's just...friendly? Uplifting, maybe? She definitely doesn't respond to me how I expect her to. When I'm off-balance, I try to make everyone else uncomfortable too.

My face and hand are a battered mess. Maybe she's just being sweet.

"Seconds? After all of what you're already getting? Dessert, too? Wow. You *are* hungry. That sounds like a good plan," Wendy nods, still smiling. "Let me put this order in first, and if you want more just let me know. Did you want all your drinks right now or with your food?"

"Fill up the coffee again, bring the OJ now, bring the milk with the food."

"Aye, aye captain!" Wendy salutes, rips the order from her ticket book, literally skips to the window, clips my breakfast order to the wheel, and spins it like she's on *Wheel of Fortune*. It whips around about three times before a hand reaches up and stops it. Wendy's laugh fills the restaurant. A gruff someone barks an order to "stop doing that! I've told you time and again to stop spinning the ticket wheel..."

She's a great waitress.

I can't help it; she makes me smile. When I do, throbbing pressure in my eye turns the grin into a cringe.

The gashes under my ace bandage sting and itch. My smile fades.

I check to make sure the letter is still in my back pocket. It is. I still can't bring myself to open it.

CHAPTER 16

"What if I let Stacy think the baby is his?"

Michelle's words hung in the air as relief and dread washed over me simultaneously. I hadn't considered this as a possibility. My mind was moving slowly—I was barely awake, still high, and hungover—and Michelle had taken more time to think through her options. I fidgeted with my dirty fingernails and picked a crusty from my eye with my pinky.

I was the worst at hard conversations.

Stacy was my best friend—more than a friend: a big brother, a father figure who looked out for me. I betrayed his trust. Michelle had been more than my lover. In the short time I'd lived with them, she became a savior of sorts, and then she stabbed me in the heart so she could save me for real.

I could feel myself getting ready to betray Michelle.

We'd gotten out of the backseat of my Dodge Charger and into the frigid Wisconsin air. Why hadn't I put on my shoes? Michelle zipped up Stacy's coat and pulled her hat and gloves back on, her freckled cheeks and nose again growing pink. She stamped her feet and tucked her face down inside her collar.

I finally broke the silence. "I don't know," I mumbled, my breath steaming into the brightening sky.

"You're so helpful." Michelle wasn't often sarcastic, but her fear and frustration continued to bubble out into the open. She rolled her eyes, then narrowed them and looked at me with a pouty scowl.

"I mean, I guess you could. What if...?" my voice trailed off to a mumble as I lost my nerve.

"What if what?" Michelle glowered. "God, Jeremy, just be an adult and say what you're thinking."

"What if Stacy suspects something is weird? Like, what if he wants to do a paternity test or something? Do you guys even...you know...since he found out about us?" The conversation was so uncomfortable.

"Recently enough that if this is what we do, he'll believe me. He wouldn't have a reason to think so. We're in counseling, I'm planning to stay married, and we talked about having a baby anyway."

"You're staying? After what happened between us? After what Stacy did? He pointed a gun in your face! Normal people get divorces, they don't take hostages. You're trying to work it out with him?"

"What can I do, Jeremy? I love him."

I shook my head and snorted.

Michelle persisted. "I did. I do. Still. All of us made mistakes."

I wanted to ask her if she still loved me, too. I didn't. "We all made mistakes," I agreed. "But you're making another one by staying. He's too suspicious. He'd never believe you. You know that, right?"

Michelle spoke, barely a whisper. "He'd accept it. He would."

"Look." I was incredulous. "He'd have at least one big fucking reason to question whether this baby was his. You cheated on him with me and got caught. Whether or not the two of you had make-up sex wouldn't wipe out his suspicions. You know how he thinks. He never leaves shit alone. Your doctor would say when you got pregnant and that date is too close to...us."

"Jeremy, I'm a nurse. There are ways I could put some distance between when you left and when Stacy would believe the baby had been conceived.

Not much, but enough. He might think it would be born premature, but it's not impossible. I've gotten away with bigger things than this at the hospital."

"Do you think Stacy would be a good father? I can't see it." I asked heartless questions and passed judgment on her decisions without offering any help.

"You can't ask that. How can you ask that? How can you say that?!"

"Do I have to spell it out? We sell drugs. You stole tens of thousands of dollars in pills from the hospital. Sooner or later everyone gets busted, or gets sideways with people who will fuck your shit up. Would he put that behind him if he knew he was having a kid? Does he want to? Can you get all the way clear of the hospital? You said once you got the money right, you were out. Did you mean it? You want out but Stacy likes it. He won't give it up. You can't have a kid around with all we're up to. I know the plan was to get out and buy the tavern before he found out. But still. It's bullshit. You'd buy the fucking Brew Haus and keep running weed and pills and who-the-fuck-knows what else through there once you owned it."

Another tear traced a fresh line of sadness down Michelle's cheek. "You don't want this baby at all, do you, Jeremy?" She turned her back to me, her right hand moving to wipe the tears away from her face.

"Why would you want to have a kid with me?" I tried to redirect and deflect. It was a hard question to answer truthfully, because the honest answer was painful, ugly, and selfish. We both knew that it would be messy. I lived in my car; I didn't have any money. Or a job. Stacy would probably try to kill me again. I didn't know what he'd do to Michelle. Neither of us knew what he'd do after learning the truth.

Yet, it wouldn't be impossible. We'd have to leave, together. Immediately. But it could be done.

"Don't play the 'I'm so worthless why would anyone want to have any-thing to do with me' card, Jeremy. Don't avoid the question. Just answer me. You don't want to have this baby at all, do you? There's nothing in you that says you could love this child and be a dad and do the right thing, is there?"

Back still turned, Michelle's tone of voice was one of resignation and sadness. She could see the future.

"Sort of true, I guess. I don't not want you to have the baby," I tried, but she quickly cut me off again.

"That's not what I asked. You don't want this baby, do you? Not, do you think I want the baby. Not, you aren't good enough of a person to have a baby. Do you want this baby? Could you love it?" She turned around to confront me. Michelle's face flushed red, no longer pink in the brisk dawn. She was livid. Her eyes flashed defiantly, her jaw set. "Answer. The goddamn. Question. Jeremy."

"No."

"No, what? No, you won't answer the question? Or no, you don't want the baby?" I was in a chokehold.

Horribly guilty, I knew what I should say. I prepared a heroic answer, one that would show Michelle I was a good person, that I'd be there for her—and our child. The words were on the tip of my tongue. I would commit to provide the support that both Michelle and our baby would need, no matter the cost.

"No, I don't want this baby."

"I knew it." Michelle burst out crying. I tried to reach out to her. "Don't you fucking dare touch me!" Michelle shouted. "I'm so stupid." Then, she just stopped crying. "You're such a coward."

"There's just no way it can work," I began, hoping to justify my immaturity—my reckless disregard for anyone other than myself, my lack of personal responsibility, my selfishness—with pragmatism.

But there was more. A terrible truth. A secret only Sarah had known. I was unfit to be a parent. I knew it. Things had broken inside of me. I should never be a father. To anyone. Ever. A part of me wanted to tell Michelle, hoping she would see and understand, but I wilted under the pressure of the moment and fell silent again as Michelle interrupted me and passed judgment with a string of accusations.

"Wrong. You don't want to make it work. It's not impossible. You just won't do the right thing. And honest to God, right now, I hate you, and I hate that I kind of understand. The shooting and everything—how could you be OK? I just hoped. I had this idea that you'd find something in you, somehow, and do what's right," Michelle admitted. "And I was totally wrong about you."

I wrestled with my thoughts, trying to decide what I could say without revealing authentic vulnerability.

"I'm so stupid," she said again.

"What do you want me to do?" She knew I wasn't going to do anything. It was a pathetic effort. "I don't understand what you want! One minute you're telling me you love Stacy and you're going to make it work with him somehow and the next minute you're asking me if I want the baby and it's like you want to be with me instead. What do you want me to say? What do you want from me?"

Michelle brushed aside my attempt to appear offended.

"Nothing. I don't want ANYTHING from you. I'm going to tell Stacy this baby is his. He'll never know because it wouldn't change anything and you're a mess and always will be. What the hell was I thinking, coming here, expecting anything from you? You can't get your life together. I'm so stupid."

It was a dagger of truth. Again. Her insight was a gift and a weapon.

She was right. I knew she was right.

It made sense. It was the secret lie that felt better to me than the truth.

In that moment, it felt like the only decision that could work.

CHAPTER 17

Wendy the Waitress is depositing plate after clattering plate of food in front of me. She drops a handful of jelly packets onto the table in one of the few vacant spots, and bangs a trio of syrup dispensers in between the eggs and the biscuits and gravy. I'd been lost in time, thinking of Michelle, for ten minutes.

"Ketchup's right there," she points to where it sits, three inches from my bandaged hand. "I'll be right back with your milk. And a coffee refill." Wendy gets about two feet away, stops, turns, touches her finger to her temple, and says, "Oh no! I can be such a silly goose sometimes. I forgot your orange juice. You wanted it with your meal. I'm so sorry! I'll get that too." She scoots off toward the kitchen again.

"I'm not gonna eat all of this," I mutter under my breath. I've lost my appetite.

Wendy is back in seconds. "Is there anything else I can get for you?"

I let out one loud, scoffing cackle. "I think you've done enough damage, thank you very much."

"Oh, you're welcome!" she chirps. "You just holler if you change your mind. Enjoy." Off she goes.

I stab at the eggs with a corner of toast. Yolk spreads across the plate like a yellow oil spill. I nibble the toast, chew a piece of bacon, and fork at the sausage. Gross. I grab the glass ketchup bottle and try to pour some on my hashbrowns, but it's freshly opened and nothing comes out. Spinning it back and forth and slapping the bottom of the bottle finally releases a smothering torrent of ketchup on the potatoes. One bite. Yuck. I swirl boysenberry syrup in a circle atop the waffle; it's the only thing that tastes good, even though everything's perfect. I'm not interested in the biscuits and gravy. I continue to carve up the waffle and make short work of the bacon. I don't want the milk anymore. The orange juice tastes weird with the syrup, bitter and tart. I try to eat the eggs again. They're already cold, and I gag. The dried yolk matches the wet floor sign in the hallway. A bite of sausage; it's not bad, but I'm done eating out of obligation. I light a cigarette and survey the uneaten breakfast wasteland that my lack of impulse control has wrought. The hashbrowns look like a murder. I take a slug of diner coffee.

Wendy's back.

"Oh no," she says. "Is something wrong? With your order? Did I do something wrong?"

"No." I blow double plumes of smoke through my nostrils. "It's perfect. I'm not hungry anymore."

"Are *you* OK?" Wendy asks. I don't think she's nosy. She's what? Compassionate, I guess? Kind? Before I can come up with a believable lie, she's jabbering away, breaking the uncomfortable silence.

"Did you know that my name, Wendy, is a totally made-up name?" I wasn't expecting her to say that.

"Uh, what's that now?" is all I can muster, and I grin in spite of myself. She's nice, which makes me want to return her kindness, but I'm mildly annoyed. I just want to sit and not eat my food and smoke my cigarette. I'm the only customer and she's lingering.

"Wendy," she continues. "I never told you my name earlier when I took your order. I usually do, but tonight's been a crazy night. It's so busy." The diner is empty. "I mean, my name tag says my name, obviously—" Wendy laughs, shrugs, and looks at the ceiling "—but that doesn't count." She points at the tag affixed to her white, coffee-stained shirt. Wendy the Waitress curtsies.

I sit back in the booth. I'm going to hear her story whether I want to or not.

"My name is an invented name. It's only been around for a very short time. It was invented by the man who wrote *Peter Pan* in 1936. His name was J.M. Barrie, and he came up with the name Wendy when he heard a child try to say the word 'friendly' and it came out 'fwendy.' He thought it was perfect for the main character in his play, and so TADA! He turned 'fwendy' into 'Wendy.' Pretty neat, right?"

This story doesn't feel true to me at all; she shares it like someone who read it somewhere, memorized it, rehearsed it in a mirror, and tells it the exact same way every single time.

I decide to burst her bubble. "All names are made up. That's how names become names."

Wendy's spirit is indomitable. "But not everyone knows *how* their name is made up. I know the story!"

"I always thought Wendy was short for Gwendolyn."

My comment deflates her, but only for a second, as she considers my stubborn disbelief over the history of her name. Wendy quickly recovers and brightens again. "That could be, but the name on my birth certificate is Wendy, not Gwendolyn, although if I were a Gwendolyn, I'd prefer to be called Gwen."

She's unshakably positive.

"Well, then, it's nice to meet you, Wendy from *Peter Pan*. I'm one of the Lost Boys." I wave with my bandaged hand, fingers poking through the top of the blood-speckled ace bandage.

"It looks like you had a run-in with Captain Hook." She gestures at my injuries.

"Long week, and all my pixie dust is in the car," I continue. She doesn't realize I'm only half-kidding.

I glance at her wrist tattoo. It reads "FORGIVEN."

"Do you want to sit down? Can you sit down?" I invite her. "Does that break the waitress-customer restaurant code?" I point at the table. "Hungry? I ordered enough for both of us." She laughs, loudly, and snorts. There's an intangible quality about Wendy the Waitress. She's...pleasant. Five minutes ago, I just wanted to eat alone. Now I *have to* talk to her.

She seems genuine. I pause to recall when someone was nice to me, but also didn't want anything.

It's been years.

I'm certain she's being friendly because I'm her only customer and she wants a good tip.

"Oh, I don't know if I should sit down. I'm supposed to be working. Even if the restaurant isn't busy I have to mop the floors and clean the bathrooms and do condiments for the dayshift. We're supposed to be nice to the customers, but I don't think we're allowed to sit down and visit."

"Why? Is it because all of the other customers would get jealous of our special relationship?"

Wendy reflexively looks around at the empty diner and laughs again. She hesitates. "I'm not sure."

"Come on. Five minutes." Still bullying people, years later, now passive aggressively instead of violently.

"OK," but she corrects me. "*Two minutes.*" She holds up two fingers, like a toddler sharing their age. "Coach is in back, his name is Mike; he's

155

the cook but also sort of the night manager, and he doesn't really want us to talk to the customers because he thinks it's unprofessional. We call him Da Coach, because of Mike Ditka. But they don't look anything alike. I could use a break. It's been so busy."

I offer her a cigarette.

"No, thank you. I quit six months ago. It was soooooo hard."

"Quitting is easy. Not starting again, that's the hard part." She smiles wanly.

"You know my name. I'm Wendy," she reminds me. "But you didn't tell me who you are."

"I'm Jeremy Peoples." I put a cigarette in my mouth, squint, and reach my left hand across the table. We shake hands, which Wendy finds curious, but social pressure is powerful. "Nice to meet you. Officially."

It's become a habit to use my first and last name. The notoriety that comes with radio has its perks, so dropping my name often leads to free drinks and special attention. Few people outside of Southern Wisconsin would still remember me as a victim of the Sugar River Shooting, now over seven years ago and fading from the national consciousness, replaced by other spectacular acts of violence in Oklahoma City and Littleton, Colorado. *The People's Talk Show* is heard only in DC, and while my agent would love for me to be syndicated, I'm not, and my show can't be heard in the Midwest. Wafer keeps pushing me, our bosses, and the engineers to make the audio available on computers, but that feels like a fad to me.

Wendy doesn't recognize me. "Do you live in the city?" she asks.

"No. I live in DC. I'm a radio talk show host. I'm on my way...to visit family."

Wendy is uninterested in my job. That's a first. When people find out what I do, they're immediately fascinated: it's not a common occupation, people assume I know celebrities or can get them free concert tickets. Her indifference is refreshing and, at the same time, mildly irritating, my ego bruised.

I suddenly feel the need to impress her.

"Wow, that's a long drive. Why didn't you fly?"

Because you can't take two grand worth of narcotics on an airplane. "I'm afraid of flying," I lie.

"Me too!" Wendy bubbles. "My family makes fun of me, but I will *not* get on an airplane. They tell me stuff like how it's safer to fly than drive and you've got a better chance of getting struck by lightning or drowning in a pool or attacked by a swarm of killer bees, but I don't care. I don't fly."

"So, tell me about *that*." I point at her wrist tattoo. "Why *forgiven*?" She rubs it gently, as embarrassed.

"It's just this thing that I need to remember. It helps me when I'm having a bad day."

I want forgiveness. I want the peace that comes from having an apology accepted. "Why that word, though? Of all the things to get a tattoo of, why that?" I'm persistent. Years of interviewing politicians who dodge questions have helped me perfect my technique. Plus, I'm pissed that my effort at forgiveness failed spectacularly on New Year's Eve, jealous that someone like Wendy found it so easily.

Wendy looks at me, both proud but bashful.

"It reminds me that I'm sort of a Christian now. I feel like I got a second chance."

"Why do you think you need a second chance? You seem like a nice person. The church people I've been around aren't handing out second chances to anyone, especially ones who could really use a break."

Wendy the Waitress, so talkative earlier, falls silent. She twists her ponytail in her fingers, twirling it around absentmindedly, looks at the pack of cigarettes, and gets up suddenly.

"Let me clear off this table," she says, and starts grabbing plates, stacking them on top of one another, squishing uneaten food under the weight of an ever-increasing tower of chipped porcelain.

"Hey, sorry about that. I didn't mean to get weird. I was just being nosy," I apologize.

"You didn't do anything! I just better clean off this table before Coach comes out here and sees us talking and the table all filled up with plates of food, and I need to wipe down some of the other tables before the morning crew comes in. I've got to wrap silverware and fill up the condiments too. You didn't do anything wrong. I've just been sitting long enough. I need to get my prep done and clean."

I protest. "You sat down for, like, ninety seconds. Put the dishes down. I'm not finished eating yet."

Wendy arches her eyebrows. "You're really gonna eat all this? It's cold and smushed on the plates."

"I paid for it. I'm hungry again. And if you sit with me while I eat, I promise you this—I'll help you wrap your silverware and fill the condiments before the morning crew gets here. I have experience at this type of work," I say, with a tone of ridiculous seriousness. "Years of training. Decades putting it into practice. I'm a sensei. A third degree blackbelt in silverware wrapping and condiment refills."

"I can't."

"No, you can. Five minutes. If Coach comes out here, I'll tell him I was having a panic attack and you were trying to see if you needed to call a doctor. It'll be fine. Sit." I point at the seat again. "Please."

Wendy is getting a little braver now. "I will under one condition."

"Deal," I agree before knowing the terms.

"Tell me what happened to your eye and your hand. You look like you got in a car accident."

I sigh. "Separate accidents. The eye is the result of me thinking I'd win a fight with a bartender who has more experience fighting and is way bigger than me. The hand is the result of me thinking that I could win a fight with a glass shower door that also had more experience fighting and was way bigger than me. In both cases, I was wrong. The bartender and my shower door were both formidable opponents."

I dramatically pick up my fork, scrape the cold eggs and hashbrowns together into a sticky pile of dried yolk and ketchup, and, with a flourish, shovel a massive bite into my mouth, using a piece of toast smeared with coagulated butter and clotted jelly as a trowel. Wendy's eyes widen. The combination of my story and this action must have left her with the understandable impression that I'm a crazy person.

She might be right.

"So, you got in a barfight and you punched some glass?" Wendy summarizes.

"Exactly," I say, my mouth still full of cold breakfast. I bite into a sausage patty and slurp coffee.

"Normal people don't act like that." I point my fork at her, nodding. I'm chewing for what seems like ten minutes before I can answer. "That is true." I take a big gulp of the orange juice. Somehow the food tastes better cold, scraped off the bottom of a plate, washed down with warm orange juice, than it did when it was fresh from the kitchen. I'm gorging myself, eating faster, elbows on the table, bandaged hand holding my hair back, my left hand clumsily scooping food into my face. Wendy watches, fascinated. I use another piece of toast to hoist the remaining eggs and another scoop of ketchup-slathered, soggy potatoes to my mouth. I'm intent on finishing what I ordered.

"You sure you don't want any of this?" I ask Wendy the Waitress through another mouthful of food.

"I'm definitely sure," she refuses. "I can't believe you're going to eat all of this. Cold."

I sip the coffee. It's icy bitterness. I chug the milk instead. In moments, the entire order of breakfast is gone. I polish off the orange juice. I drop the fork on a plate with a clatter and dab the corners of my mouth with my napkin like an aristocrat. Wendy finds this last bit of theater funny, and laughs.

I light another cigarette, get up, walk briskly to the nearby coffee pot, and refill my cup.

"Hey, you shouldn't do that!" Wendy exclaims.

"It's OK. I have restaurant experience. I got my certification in waitressing years ago. I'm not just a radio personality helping himself to the coffee. I'm part of the International Servers Guild." Wendy snorts. "It took years of working under the best waitresses, some of whom graduated shoulda-cum-louder." Wendy doesn't find the crude attempt at humor as much fun as the silliness. I don't know how to have a conversation with this person but for whatever reason I desperately want to impress her.

Suddenly, Wendy's eyes brighten. She points at the Christmas decorations strung up throughout the diner. Somehow I knew she was responsible for the Christmas shit. The cardboard cartoon cutouts and tacky tinsel and plastic garland are taped to the windows or dangling from thumbtacks poked haphazardly into walls stained yellow from cigarette smoke, humidity, and kitchen grease.

When I finish looking over the decorations again, I turn to see Wendy is absolutely beaming with pride.

"So, what do you think? Do you like my decorations? No one around here wanted to do anything for Christmas, so I asked, and they said it would be OK and then I realized I didn't have any decorations, so I went out and bought what I could find. They didn't have a lot to choose from by the time I got to the store, so I just got whatever they had. No one would help me but I put them up anyway and I think it looks really Christmas-y in here now! I guess I should take them down because it's January, but I don't want to yet. Maybe I'll just wait until Coach tells me to, or someone tells him to tell me. I really love it. We've gotten a lot of compliments from customers," she explains enthusiastically.

"I'm not really a Christmas person," I reply as I sit back down in the booth.

"What do you mean? Everyone loves Christmas!" Wendy is shocked. "Ho Ho Ho and holly jolly and Jesus Mary and Joseph and Frosty the Snowman and all the snow and mistletoe and good feelings and noel?"

"Jews and Muslims don't. And atheists." Why am I being difficult? Why can't I just humor this poor woman and lie and tell her that her decorations look festive and beautiful, just like every other lying bastard has when she's asked? Instead, I'm going to end up hurting her feelings, after a sarcastic half-assed attempt at deflection. I'm warring with myself, my mean streak, and my compassion.

"Are you a Jewish-Muslim-Atheist?" Wendy challenges me. She's appalled that anyone could be indifferent about Christmas, much less antagonistically dismissive.

"I'm more of a Halloween, New Year's Eve, St. Patrick's Day, Cinco de Mayo kind of guy. Unless your grandma has some brandy for the eggnog. Then I could like Christmas. Otherwise, it's really a kid thing and I don't..." I stop. Wendy looks up. "I guess since I don't have any kids... fuck Christmas."

("you don't want this baby at all, do you, Jeremy?" Michelle's tearful eyes, angry, disappointed, afraid)

"Don't say that about...about Christmas!" Wendy scolds.

"I'm sorry. I swear too much sometimes. I didn't mean it like that," I apologize, sincerely. What I really meant and cannot tell her was I'm completely disconnected from my own family and never had a meaningful Christmas as a kid, and I walked away from Michelle and her baby and sometimes wonder what Christmas morning would be like with them, presents and stockings and wrapping paper and hot chocolate and candy canes and fun arguments about a real or plastic tree and watching movies....

"You should be sorry. And Christmas *is* for everyone." Wendy puts her hands on her hips. "*Everyone* loves Christmas. You're a Grinch or a Scrooge. There's not a single good reason why anyone would not like presents and parties and lights and Christmas. It's fun! There's lots of food and surprises and you get to see your family. What kind of a person would rather celebrate Cinco de Mayo than Christmas?"

"A Jewish-Muslim-Atheist-Alcoholic who's justifiably proud of his Mexican heritage?"

"Jeremy Peoples doesn't sound like a name someone gets if they're born in Tijuana," Wendy says. I've genuinely offended her over Christmas, but I've also avoided insulting her terrible taste in decorations.

"My real name is Jeremias Personas. I go by Jeremy Peoples on the radio." I took Spanish for three years in high school. I've never used it for anything other than impressing people in bars. And now, apparently, failing to impress waitresses in diners on the South Side of Chicago on a Sunday morning.

"You think you're pretty clever."

It takes substantial effort, but I wink with my good eye.

"I guess you hate my decorations since you hate Christmas," Wendy has circled back. *Again.* Jesus.

I see my chance. "I don't like Christmas that much, but if I did, I'd put your decorations in a category all to themselves. I don't like decorations and trees and ribbons and lights and shit, but if I did, I would definitely say that these are the best diner decorations that I've ever seen, and likely ever will see."

Wendy has undoubtedly found my string of bullshit exhausting. She shrugs. "OK whatever."

I'm not as willing to let things go as she is.

"What did you mean when you said you were 'sort of a Christian'?" I have an insatiable compulsion to convince her to tell me about her secret tattoo story. "Is that why you like Christmas so much?" I gesture at the carboard K-Mart nativity scene.

"I don't know you at all," she says. "It's personal." Wendy's resistance to share is gnawing at me.

"You don't have to tell me, but I promise I'll sit and listen, and I won't make jokes, and if you feel like stopping, it's cool," I lie. "I've just never heard anyone say they were 'sort of a Christian' before. I mean, I grew up Lutheran. I'm sure I'm less of a Christian than you are. Why is it embarrassing for you to talk about it?" I'm pushing her too hard. I'm tweaked out and giving off an urgent, hard-edged energy.

I need to relax, my entire body is a live wire of tension and demands. She's not a guest on my radio show, or a caller. Wendy's the Waitress *believes* in forgiveness, and I need to know why.

I flop back, take a long draw on my cigarette, and blow out the smoke with a sigh. I ease my shoulders, all stress and knotted muscles, and unclench my jaw. I blink a few times to clear my anger.

"I'm not embarrassed," she corrects me. I like Wendy the more I talk with her.

"Spill it. Come on. Out with it. Why a 'forgiven' tattoo? What could you have done that you need to be forgiven for? You're probably the nicest person I've ever met in my life. Honest to God," I prod.

Wendy looks at my cigarettes again.

"I had an experience," she begins. "With God. I don't know what else to say it was."

Finally. I have to do better with Wendy than I did with the bartenders at Club Insomnia.

In the background, we both hear the "DING!" from the window counter. Wendy slides out of the booth.

I stand up too, throwing my hands up in the air in a dramatic display of frustration. "Are you going to tell me? After all we've been through together?!" I plead. "You can't just leave me hanging!"

"Coach," she blurts and her tone of voice says everything. She doesn't want to lose her job. Wendy is conscientious. She's not afraid of the conversation. I misjudged her. She has integrity.

"Saved by the bell," I can't resist saying as Wendy starts jogging toward the kitchen. I hope she's not in trouble. She's not the type of person I would ever seek out for friendship; I have no interest in her sexually. I'm an only child, but I feel like I'm talking to my sister. Wendy seems content. I'm certain she has dreams and aspirations, disappointments and discouragement, but it doesn't swirl around her like a fog of offense. I watched her talk to the customers, and how she talks to me. Wendy loves people.

She's happy, I guess.

I find it kind of obnoxious. It's got to be phony. Who's sincerely this content? How can a late-shift waitress feel good about her failed and stupid life?

A couple of minutes later, Wendy's back at the booth and I'm even more irritated. It's frustrating that she wouldn't answer my question about her God Experience, that she kept talking vaguely about forgiveness, evasive about the only thing I'm interested in learning about her. I don't care about the etymology of her name or her passionate defense of Christmas decorating or Coach or anything else she wants to overshare with me. I want to know why she feels forgiveness.

No. Not why. *How* she feels forgiven.

And if she calls herself a silly goose again, I'm going to scream.

She's not ready for what's about to happen. While she's been in the kitchen, I've loaded my verbal assault weapon with a clip full of words and vitriol, my frayed nerves and history the finger *and* the trigger. The cocaine and the stress and the exhaustion from the drive and anxiety about

Michelle's funeral and *just all of it* are coming up out of me and I'm too sloppy and selfish to stop it.

"Look," I say. That's a sure-fire Jeremy Peoples indicator that I'm about to finally say what I'm thinking. The word "look" has started many arguments over the years. "You're killing me with this tattoo. You talk to everyone about everything under the sun. You talk to me about everything except the tattoo. Why would you get a word tattooed on your wrist where the entire world can see it, and presumably ask about it, if you're never going to answer someone's question about it? It seems a bit fucking—I'm sorry—*freaking* bizarre if you ask me, which you're not going to, because you would rather this conversation didn't start, and you'd like it to end before you have to answer a simple question that makes you feel uncomfortable for reasons I can't begin to understand. If you didn't want to talk to people about being forgiven, why get the fucking tattoo at all? Or why not get it on your back or your ass or somewhere no one can see, but you can still peek at it when you need to be reminded of something good when you get out of the shower? If it's some religious thing, then why not learn enough about what you supposedly believe to be able to talk intelligently about it, debate it, hear an opposing idea that might open up your little worldview to something that could offer you more than just fleeting comfort while you drop off diner food to drunks at 4:00 a.m. on a Sunday morning and leave in a state of exhaustion to run to church and pray your prayer and give your little money and feel good about yourself again? I'm sitting here, a prime candidate for conversion, a poster child for proselytizing, your Billy Graham Crusade opportunity at Kay's South Side Diner and all you can do is say you're 'sort of a Christian' and bitch at me because I think Christmas is phony and I'd rather go drinking with friends on St. Patrick's Day than buy shit no one wants and give it to people I don't like? Jesus *Fucking* Christ."

I'm out of breath.

Wendy is frozen. Her expression hasn't changed, a grimace that appeared when I started ranting.

"Are you finished now?" is all she says. Her voice is shaking. I don't care. I'm angry. No, I'm hurt.

"Yeah, I'm fucking done." I bite down on each word, sarcastically. "Wendy."

"Please don't say His name like that again," she directs me. "Jesus. His name isn't a swear word."

I roll my eye. All I wanted was breakfast. Now I'm here with the Church Lady. Isn't that special?

"I mean it. You want to know about the tattoo? Then stop saying His name like that. I DON'T like it."

"Goddamn it." I can't help but try to provoke her one last time. Wendy turns on her heel to leave.

"Alright. OK. I'm sorry, I'm sorry. I'll stop. I promise I won't do it again. Honest Injun." I'll say whatever I have to say. I wonder if she's going to get Coach to come out front and drag me into the parking lot. Maybe he'll bash in my other eye so I can have a matching set. The escalation of my anger leaves me ashamed. I didn't intend to unleash on her, but it came out of me from a surprising place, a secret injury. It roared with the rage of betrayal and emotional impotence. It is looking for someone else to consume, insatiable and confusing. This shadow hate is a stealth explosion, with an antidote I've failed to find.

I'm sour. I'm bitter. I'm an active volcano.

But instead of running away crying or calling for help, Wendy stands her ground. "OK, Mr. Radio Man from Washington DC. I'll tell you about why I got my tattoo. Not because you're making me. Maybe you need to sit still and listen instead of talking at people and swearing. And try being nicer."

Wendy surprises me. "Hey," I start, "I'm sorry." She's not just nice. And genuine.

She has balls.

"You be quiet," she says firmly.

I obey.

"I was a foster child," she starts, slowly. "I was in group homes and foster homes a lot, especially when I was a teenager. Most of the people were good to me. Some weren't very nice, and one was terrible but the state found out fast and I got moved. It felt like I was always leaving, putting my clothes and toys and my diary in a garbage bag and sitting in a stranger's backseat. I don't remember my real mom or dad anymore, but I sort of remember remembering them. It really sucked. I mean, no one touched me or anything. Just lots of yelling and names. School was hard. I didn't get good grades, it was hard to concentrate on homework, and I was always new, and my clothes were never cool. But the last family I went to when I was sixteen was different."

"How so?" I murmur. She's so sincere. I can't stay angry at her for long. I'm not used to this. There are parts of her story that touch me with a sort of negative nostalgia, a wistful recollection of raging dysfunction. I willfully push back against those memories—it takes exceptional effort—and refocus.

"They had one other kid, a boy; he was younger than me. They made us both go to church. I hated it so much, but I liked them and didn't want them to get mad at me and make me go away when I was so close to graduating." Wendy is looking off to the side, remembering. It's so hard for the average person to recall their story. I can't relate, and I envy their dulled pain, the faded and erroneous details.

"After a few months we had to start going to Wednesday night stuff. I liked that a little better, because it was only for people my age and some of the girls were cool and there were cute boys and snacks. Sometimes there was music. I guess I went about three or four times, when it happened."

I'm really getting into this. "Your God Experience Thing?" Wendy is so corny, so awkward, so honest.

Wendy nods. "The teacher was talking about how God was a Father, and He let His Son Jesus go on a rescue mission to find lost kids. I don't know why I never heard anyone say it like that before, but I knew I was one of the missing kids that didn't have a mom or a dad, and I wanted a brother like Jesus to take me home. When I felt that, it was like I could hear a voice in my heart tell me that I could come home any time I wanted. I just needed to stop trying to run away."

Wendy is smiling again. Glowing.

I'm not sure what to say.

I went to church when I was a kid. People would pray, and they'd make me pray, they always needed money, they never seemed satisfied with anything I did, but still wanted more. Wendy doesn't feel like one of them. There's nothing in it for her. I had to drag the story out of her. That lends authenticity to what she's saying. It proves she believes it and doesn't care whether I do or not. It doesn't make it true, but she's not trying to convince me. She doesn't want anything, and that makes me curious.

"What did you say to the voice when it told you everything would be OK?"

"I don't remember. I said something, I'm sure. I didn't say anything to anyone for a week, but then I asked the teacher about it and she said that it was God telling me that Jesus wanted to help me, but I had to accept the help. God was a good dad and would forgive me for anything I had done. That part confused me, I guess. I didn't think I had really done anything wrong. I mean, I was a secret smoker, but so were other kids at church, so I didn't see how it was a thing God should care about it. Smoking was different in the 1980s. I said some ugly things sometimes, but I figured everybody says mean things once in a while. I understood needing to be rescued. But forgiven? Other people did things to me. Kids at school, my old foster family, they needed forgiveness, but I was good."

Wendy pauses, eyes closed, chest rising and falling quickly.

"That's it?" I'm incredulous.

"No—"

"Then what?" I keep interrupting.

"Can you stop interrupting? This part is kinda hard to explain. That night I went to the store on the way home. I was walking down one of the aisles and I see this little boy about five years old, all alone. I'm looking around and I don't see anyone else. And he has the biggest, bluest, widest eyes ever, but he doesn't seem scared. He just looks at me and then he sticks out his hands like he wants me to pick him up. I start to take the kid to the counter or find a manager or whatever, and his dad comes around the corner, sees him, chases him down, grabs him in a hug. He's saying stuff like, 'Hey, don't ever run off like that again. You scared me. I couldn't find you,' and that little boy said, 'I'm sorry, Daddy.' Right there in that grocery store, with that daddy and little boy, that's when I got it."

I jump in again. "Got what? You didn't do anything wrong. You said it yourself."

"I just knew the forgiveness I needed was for running away from Him all the time, when all He wanted to do was help, and it hurt Him. I hurt Him. And I was sorry after watching that dad. That's why I got the tattoo," Wendy finishes. "We want forgiveness for big things and little things. There's nothing too small for Him to not care about, and nothing too big He won't help with. I need to remember that feeling."

Clichés. After all of that, I get needlepoint-on-a-pillow Sunday school answers. I shake my head and sigh.

"Well, Wendy, that's a neat story. For you. It's got a real Neverland quality to it, that if you just believe really hard Peter Pan will come and take me to the land of fairies and pirates. I'm probably more of a Lost Cause than a Lost Boy, though. People like you get what you want. People like me get what other people think we need. You *are* sincere, though. Like Linus and the Great Pumpkin, Charlie Brown."

"But it's true," she says meekly. "It's what happened."

"I'm sure it's true for you. I won't argue that. I grew up around church people. You're all pretty certain that you've got the right answers. But people like me, we…we don't get fixed so easily. People like me don't get forgiven, because the stuff we've done—the stuff we're doing—it's either too big for people to forgive, or they don't think it's your fault so they won't let you take responsibility. And I can't forget what I've done. It stays with me. Forever. There's no church answer for what I'm dragging around." I speak with the certainty of a deeply insecure man who's trying to hide behind a wall of bravado and excuses. I will probably turn to science or philosophy if she decides to debate me. Maybe I'll use the Bible. I prepare myself for her Damascus Road and King David rebuttals. I've heard all the stories.

I've rejected them all.

Wendy shrugs. "You said you'd help with my prep. You volunteered. I didn't ask, but since you said you could roll silverware…I hate that job. I'll bring it over to the table, so Coach can't see what we're doing." For the second time this morning, she starts clearing off my table, stacking cleaner plates this time, making a racket with my cups and silverware on top of the porcelain tower.

I'm speechless. Wendy the Waitress is apparently fine to just live and let live. I've never met someone who believes in God enough to share their faith and is also unbothered that I have no interest in getting baptized and signing up for church softball. This is the first time I've encountered someone like her.

"Hey." She stops stacking the dishes again. "You're perfectly content to just let me go to hell, then?"

Wendy stares at me. There's softness in her eyes, not weakness. She seems less intimidated by me than she did earlier. Wendy has the confidence of someone who's unafraid because they have a bodyguard.

I fill the silence. I picked a fight. I'm not giving up that easy. If I can't get the answer I want, then maybe I can at least get her to show me that she really doesn't believe the way she does. I think I'll be less bothered by this disappointment if I can make her equally disappointed with her truth.

"I mean, that's what you believe, right? If I don't accept Jesus into my heart, then I go hell and get tortured with Hitler and Jeffrey Dahmer and child molesters? I remember the scary stories we were all taught in Confirmation. What if I get in a car accident when I leave here? Isn't it your fault that you didn't try a little harder to make me believe your story is The Truth, not just true?" I'm in full radio personality debate mode, trying to goad her into a confrontation, so I can make a point.

"It wouldn't be my fault. I'm not letting you go to hell. I just can't stop you from sending yourself."

My answer is ready. "Well, your loving Father and heroic Brother aren't stopping me either."

Wendy is patient, barely hiding her exasperation. "I'm not going to argue with you. You're looking for a fight and I don't like to debate. I'm not very good at it. I get my words and thoughts all mixed up. I know what I want to say and sometimes think of really good stuff after the argument is over when it's too late. Could we just not talk about it anymore? I did what you asked me to do and if you don't like the story about my tattoo and what I believe, I know I can't change your mind. I just know I'm forgiven."

She's so fucking honest.

And she's a teeny bit spunky.

"And there's really no more time because you have a lot of silverware to wrap. Night waitstaff have to do double what everyone else does since we're usually here alone. Two hundred rolls. You'll have to hurry, too. I don't know what time your family"—she looks at me, revealing she knows I've been lying—"expects you, so let's get the show on the road, Jeremy Peoples."

171

I want to feel triumphant. I want to believe that I've won the religious debate and forced her to capitulate because she can't answer my objections. I don't feel that way. She got the better of me somehow, and I can't make myself be mad about it again.

She's even making me do her prep.

I smirk. Wryly.

It takes me forty-five minutes to keep my word. I didn't consider my damaged hand when I shot my mouth off. My fingers aren't as nimble as they'd normally be unencumbered by an ace bandage and the shooting pain that jolts each time I torque or twist my wrist too quickly.

Coach never comes out from the back.

Wendy fills all the salt and pepper shakers and wipes down each table. She sweeps and mops.

Mercifully, only two or three people come in, and none of them seem particularly interested in why a customer is rolling silverware and chain-smoking. I saunter up to the register. Wendy sees me and says, "Give me one second!" with the exact same tone of voice she used when I walked through the door.

The clock, adorned with garland and tinsel, reads 5:03 a.m.

I'm suddenly in a hurry to get going again. Desperate, almost. Compelled by conviction to get away.

Wendy slips by me and rings up the ticket. I hand her a twenty. She counts my change out, giving me five ones instead of one five, and a small clutch of coins.

"Sorry I yelled at you earlier. I got a lot of shit in my life right now." I apologize, always with excuses.

"It's OK. I forgive you," she says without hesitation, but not off-handedly. Wendy seems to be offering me more than just absolution for my earlier rudeness. The way she's said it, so freely and yet with a certainty I can't explain, is momentous. As I choke down a sob, I get an idea.

172

It brings a warm joy, a thrill to momentarily replace the melancholy.

I'd started to shove the five-dollar bills into my wallet, but I stop, and instead take out my five remaining hundreds. It's the last of my cash. I don't care. I've spent a lot more on a lot worse in just the past twenty-four hours. "Here," is all I say, and hand her five hundred dollars. And then I give her the five ones. And then the change.

I give Wendy every last penny I have. "Merry Christmas." Tears are welling up in her eyes now; she makes no move to wipe them away, and they spill on to her cheeks.

It reminds me of Michelle Ramone.

I bolt through the door as she calls out a choked "Thank you!" behind me. I don't look back. I don't want her to see me cry and I don't want to see her smile. My life is too dead to have her breathe hope into it.

CHAPTER 18

On the morning of May 23, 1992, I was at Sugar River High School and I shouldn't have been. It was the Monday after prom and the official-unofficial, unsanctioned-sanctioned Senior Skip Day, an event that wasn't on any school calendar, but one that the teachers turned a blind eye to for years, letting graduating Seniors do whatever they wanted to do for one day before commencement.

A tradition.

The Class of 1992 was no exception. None of us knew exactly what we were going to do, but we convinced ourselves it was going to be awesome, and that's about as far as we got. We argued with each other, trying to reach a consensus. Part of the tradition of Senior Skip Day was that we all had to ditch together, and whatever we decided to do, our whole class had to go.

We were a small country school in a small country town. Sugar River, Wisconsin, population 1,640.

My hometown.

The Class of '92 had thirty-nine students.

I'd skipped any number of days throughout my four years as a Sugar River High School student, some for fun, some to hide secrets, some because I'd forgotten my homework, and occasionally I'd skip to work on the farm.

Senior Skip Day was a different kind of thrill. It was a rite of passage, and I was fucking it up.

I was at school. On Senior Skip Day.

My two best friends, Aaron and Derrick, were pissed. It was 7:39 a.m., sixteen minutes before the warning bell for first period. The weather was perfect, a sunny, cloudless day. We were supposed to be on our way to…whatever the hell we were going to do as a Senior Class. I was their ride, but I was also in love.

"Hey, Peepholes. Hurry the fuck up," *Aaron barked at me. We'd been better friends than we were at that moment. Aaron and I had both played sports, but our Senior Year I started something I should've done my entire high school career: writing about sports and student government for our school paper,* The Sugar River Sentinel. *I was far more creative than athletic, and felt more fulfilment seeing my words in print after a game than sitting on the bench during football and basketball season. He was shorter than me, and more muscular, a blonde-haired, blue-eyed Swiss with a mischievous streak that turned nasty when he got drunk. Aaron was headed to UW Madison after graduation, like me.*

"Dude, the whole point of a Skip Day is you are not supposed to be at school," *Derrick explained sarcastically. He and I had remained pretty close, partly because our class schedules had us together for five out of seven periods, and he'd also pulled back on sports to focus on his grades. Derrick was cocky, and at 6'6", towered over the rest of us. He had dark brown hair, a bowl cut, a patchy beard, and a gap in his front teeth that we said made him look like David Letterman. He would've normally driven himself, but his car had broken down and his brother wasn't going to be home to work on it until the following weekend. Derrick was probably going to be our class valedictorian. It was down to him and Veronica Miller. He'd already been accepted to Stanford. Derrick's parents could afford the tuition.*

I was looking for my girlfriend, Sarah Brennan.

I also needed to get that fucking Trigonometry textbook out of my car.

She wasn't at her locker.

I ran up a flight of stairs to check the library. No one. It was still too early for most of us to be in the building. We'd normally be out riding around having a cigarette, or a dip of chew, or stuck on the bus. The handful of students roaming the halls before school were underclassmen I didn't really know and never cared to meet. Freshmen and sophomores. I sprinted past without a word. A few teachers moved from classroom to classroom, making small talk with each other, carrying papers or coffee cups.

Was she not coming to school today? Because of what happened after Prom?

I scurried down the stairs, turned the corner, and scooted past Derrick and Aaron again, who both bitched and hooted at me about being pussy-whipped and fucking up their Skip Day plans.

"Why didn't you just wait in the car?" I snapped at them as I jogged to my locker.

"Someone had to drag you away from the snatch, Peepholes," Aaron scoffed. "You little bitch."

Locker 316 was disaster. My letterman jacket and a sweat-stained Chicago Cubs hat hung on a hook, the books and folders and papers and pens and gym clothes were all stacked up like the cross section of an adolescent core sample. The top shelf had five or six empty cans of Mountain Dew, one of which was a chewing tobacco spit cup, and a cheap camera that I used for the school paper and yearbook shit. There were candy bar wrappers in there too, and a cafeteria tray that we thought would be funny to steal.

A lump formed in my throat as I slotted the Trig book on top of the pile at the bottom of the locker.

That's when I saw her come around the corner.

Sarah was absolutely stunning: dark features, pouty lips, brown eyes, auburn hair that settled at her shoulders. She insisted we were the same height; I knew I was taller. We measured ourselves. I was right, but she continued telling everyone I had been wrong. Sarah had a thin waist, perfect skin—especially for a teenager—and a mole on her right cheek. It made her look like Cindy Crawford and she would blush when I pointed it out. She was more athletic than me, lettering in volleyball and basketball each of her first three years in high school. Sarah wore the Gin Blossoms T-shirt I bought her when we saw them together in Madison, and her favorite Guess blue jeans. She'd twist to admire how she looked in them in the mirror, and I liked to put my hand in her back pocket when there weren't any teachers around.

As always, one half of a "Best Friends Forever" heart pendant dangled from a thin gold chain around her neck. The other half stayed with Kelly Cantore, her neighbor from across the street. They'd grown up together, and the necklace wasn't just an idea. Sarah and Kelly had been best friends since age four. Things had gotten tense between the two of them over me, mainly because Kelly didn't like me, but Sarah balanced her time as best she could. It hadn't been easy, but she was thoughtful and prioritized relationships with uncommon emotional intelligence for a teenager.

It took me nearly a year to get the up the nerve to ask her out. It nearly ended just a few hours earlier.

Sarah saw me; she smiled. Was it sincere or forced? Sarah had the self-conscious smile of someone who once had crooked teeth and only recently got her braces off. She tended to look down and cover her mouth when she was truly happy, which is what she did then, as we made eye contact. She was perfect.

Dimples. I loved those dimples.

And she kept her promise.

I'd been holding my breath. I felt myself relax as I let the air out of my lungs with a suppressed sigh.

Maybe she really had forgiven me, and today, like I'd asked, we could pretend things were the same as they had always been between us. I knew tomorrow would be different, with so much still to face.

Sarah ran the rest of the way, covering the distance in a few seconds, and leaned in quickly to kiss me but stopped short and scrunched her nose. "Have you guys already been drinking?" she accused me.

"Yeah. I had a couple of shots of Doctor McGillicutty before we got here. Derrick raided his parents' liquor cabinet when I picked him up." I found it daring and funny. "But it's peppermint so if I see any teachers while I'm here they'll think it's mouthwash or something."

"No, they won't! Oh my God you need some gum! You shouldn't even be here! You're gonna get busted. One of the teachers will totally smell it on you. I hate you for drinking without me." Sarah pouted, sexy sadness and lip gloss. She grabbed my letterman jacket from my open locker, slid one arm in, dramatically slung it over her back and poked the other arm through. "You should stay here today. Don't go to Skip Day. It's already going to totally suck after summer. We'll never see each other. You'll be at U Dub. Without me." She handed me two pieces of gum from my own jacket pocket. "I'm totally kidding. Go skip. I don't even care. It's lame."

I held up the gum she'd given me, and then shoved it in my pants pocket. "Thanks, but I'm gonna put a dip in quick to hide the Doctor."

"Kiss me first," Sarah said, leaning up against the lockers, hiding herself from the view of my friends and any teachers. "I hate dipping so much. I want you to quit. I mean it. I hate it. I swear to God I'll never kiss you again if you don't stop." She flicked the plastic container in my pocket. THOCK!

I loved it when she picked on me. She thrived on the banter and I picked back. Sarah was smarter than me, but I was usually witty enough to keep up. "Why should I stay at school? You should come with me. What are they gonna do? The school year's almost over anyway. Come on. Come with me," I challenged.

"It's Senior Skip Day. Your class won't let me come. I'm a Junior. I'll get caught. My mom will freak."

"There's, like, less than two weeks left in the year. You'll get a detention or something. Do it."

Sarah looked down the hall at Aaron and Derrick. They jammed their fists into the bend of their elbow, extending their middle fingers at us. "LET'S GO!" Derrick bellowed. She shook her head at them and turned toward me, eyes semi-serious. "There's no way I want to spend the whole day with them. No offense, they're your friends and all, but it doesn't sound like fun to me. It's OK. Go be a Senior."

"I'll skip the Skip Day then, like we skipped the prom dinner. We'll go do something else. Fuck them. They can get a ride from someone else." I wanted to be with her all day today. Crippling insecurity had settled in. I wanted to lavish her with attention, cherish her, control the situation, try to steer her emotions toward my desired outcome. I didn't want her out of my sight. I was afraid what would happen if she had more time to consider what I'd done, what I had revealed. Would she change her mind?

Sarah looked me in the eye. "Go do the Skip Day. We can talk later. It's OK. I promise."

"OK. Aaron and Derrick are gonna kick my ass if I make them wait much longer. Call you tonight?"

"Maybe..." Sarah liked pretending she was always busy, barely making time for our calls and squeezing me into her hectic social life for a trip to our spot at the park where the river turns into marshland. "I'll see. I mean, like, I've got a lot going on right now. It's a really busy time for me. But I'll try."

Sarah snatched my Cubs hat out of my locker, pulled her hair back, and put it on, jauntily. Her hand shot out and snatched the Oakley sunglasses that were hanging from the front of my shirt and slid them on. The jacket, which was too big in the sleeves, along the hat and sunglasses, gave her the comical look she was going for. She stuck her tongue into her lower lip, mimicking a mouthful of Kodiak. "I'm Jeremy. I think I'm cool. My team always loses and I'm trying to get mouth cancer."

"That's our school you're talking about," I pretended to defend the honor of Sugar River High School.

"You know I'm talking about the Cubs," she refuted indignantly. Sarah liked the Brewers. We had plans to go see a game in Milwaukee over the summer, before I was supposed to leave for college. I told her I could be a fan of the Brewers, too: they were my American League Team. She said that was traitor talk.

"Duuude, come onnnn," Derrick and Aaron shouted at me from down the hall.

"Hey, for real, I have to go. What if McNally sees us here on Skip Day and, like, makes us stay?" Principal McNally was an older, stern man, who also coached Sarah's girls' basketball team.

Her face changed as she turned serious. "Did you mean what you told me, at prom?" That question was one that would take a moment to answer, in the right way, the only way, the perfect way for us.

"What did I say again?" It was my turn to play. She opened her mouth, feigning shock. "I'm spacing it out. I mean, I know it was important, but we drank so much, plus the weed, and it was like, all the way back on Saturday night and today is already Monday. Can you give me a clue? I'm sure if I get a hint, I'll remember everything. You know my memory, it's just not very good at times. I wanna remember."

"PEEPHOLES, YOU'RE WHIPPED!" Derrick bellowed. "HURRY UP!"

Sarah smiled, her head tilted down, hand over her mouth. She reached into my locker again, grabbed the Trig book that was sitting atop a pile of trash, clothes, and school supplies, flipped it over, and wordlessly pointed to her handiwork. As a joke, Sarah had wrapped the textbook in a brown paper bag book cover, like the kind we made in junior high. She'd written "Jeremy's Trig Book Handle With Care" on the front, and on the back, she'd inscribed, "I will love you forever, Jeremy!!" and signed her love note "from me." When I asked her who could have possibly designed such a wonderful book cover, and written such a meaningful note, she retorted, "There's only one me, and there better not be another me."

180

She gestured insistently at her doodle, face was brimming with anticipation.

I'd actually told her three times on Prom Night. I surprised her when I whispered it in her ear while we danced our only dance together. She made me repeat it. The third time was much later that same night.

"Will you say it again? Did you mean it? I mean really mean it, mean it?" she asked, quieter, more seriously, this time. Sarah took off the Oakley's, so I could see her eyes. They were hopeful. I realized this was a moment. Even as a teenager—who only seconds ago was joking, with my buddies yelling at me from down the hall, on Senior Skip Day—I could tell that I'd better not fuck this up.

I put one hand on the locker, just to the left of her face. I gently touched her cheek with my other hand, then moved my thumb and forefinger down to her chin and nudged her to look at me. Her brown eyes invited me to pause, her soft hair breezed against me. I carefully pinched her half of the "Best Friends Forever" necklace between my finger and thumb, fixed the twist in it, slipped it back, and promised her.

"I will love you forever, too, Sarah." I kissed her quickly, a young man's kiss, too eager, but with purpose. "And I'm so very, very sorry. For all of it. For everything I did."

She nodded instinctively, but then shook her head. "I know. But not today. We said tomorrow."

It was right then that I heard something. I was still leaning against the lockers, elbows locked, listening.

Sarah wiped her lip, her brown eyes glancing off into the periphery, without moving her head.

I couldn't tell what it was. A sound. I hadn't been paying attention to my surroundings. I'd been focused on Sarah. There was a commotion. The sound, it was sharp. A crack. Unexpected. I couldn't place it.

"What was that?" Sarah wondered.

I glanced around my locker door and down the hallway. Derrick and Aaron had stopped looking at me. They were staring toward the lobby, where a set of double doors opened into a secondary entrance. "Did you hear that?" I yelled. Both of them nodded. There it was again. And again. And again.

"What the fuck is that?" I wondered aloud. "Cherry bombs?"

Again.

Aaron or Derrick had left the landing, probably heading toward the cafeteria and the first-floor bathrooms across from the gymnasium entrance. The main hallway, with the school trophy case, was where most students entered the building before first period.

AgainAgainAgainAgain. Louder. No...closer.

"I gotta see this," I told Sarah excitedly. She grabbed my arm.

"No. Don't." Sarah was apprehensive. Her intuition, her instincts, warning her. Us.

"What? I don't want to miss a prank," I complained. "The school year's almost over. I can't get it in a yearbook, but I want pictures for the paper." I started to reach for my camera. Sarah let go of my arm. "What if someone is putting cherry bombs in the toilets?" I laughed. I wasn't so sure. I wanted to be right. "It's a Senior Skip Day practical joke. Someone from my class is going out in style."

AgainAgain.

It sounded like someone was yelling. A few people were yelling. The buses would have just unloaded a school full of teens about two minutes earlier. What if a class clown was dropping M-80s down the plumbing? AgainAgainAgain. Short pause. AgainAgainAgainAgainAgainAgainAgain. What the fuck?

Was that yelling or screaming? What kind of prank would everyone be screaming about? It didn't sound like fun excitement. I listened for laughter. Or an announcement over the loudspeaker. Just screams.

There was a swelling tide of noise building out of sight, down the hall, around the corner.

I knew what the noise was. It was the location that didn't make sense. There were a few more people in the hallway with us, teachers stuck their heads out of their classrooms, some of them ran toward the commotion. Students were buzzing, asking if anyone knew what was happening, laughing, guessing, deciding if they wanted to risk being tardy, only moments before the warning bell sounded, to run and join the crowd. But I'd been in the woods on Opening Morning of Deer Season since I was old enough to carry a gun. This sounded like that. Why would anyone shoot off a gun near the school?

My adrenaline surged, hands shaking. Mouth dry, heart racing.

"Oh my God, Jeremy." The color drained from Sarah's face. "That's a gun. Why is someone shooting?"

I assured her. Shook my head no. "No way. Nobody is shooting a gun at school, Sarah. It's a prank. It's fireworks." I turned to look at her. She was still wearing my letterman jacket and my Cubs hat, but she was no longer playful. Sarah had gotten a feel for the shock and panic and pandemonium. She sensed it and was intuitively afraid of it before I was.

I looked at the clock.

It was 7:53 a.m.

Everything inside of me screamed it was a gun, that we needed to go, that something historically horrific was happening and yet for some reason, I violated my instincts and reassured her, "It's not a gun."

CHAPTER 19

I made it to Wisconsin.

The final leg of the journey from Chicago is an exhausting blur; first toll roads, then desolate, harvested, and plowed cornfields. Silos and farmhouses in the distance. Highways, then back roads. Then here.

For over an hour I've been sitting on a picnic table—in the same pavilion, at the same park where Sarah and I went after the post-prom bonfire. Seconds ago, I tearfully came out of the memory of the worst day of my life with a surge of adrenaline and the need to vomit. I don't. I should. I'd probably feel better if I could wretch and enjoy the feeling of getting rid of some of the pain and sickness inside me.

I'm in Sugar River.

Water gurgles as it rushes by, the edge of the river a frozen crust. The current is hollow and amplified, flowing under a shelf of ice along the bank. Further out, it moves quick and cold, unimpeded. Distant. Unconcerned. The Sugar River is a tributary of the Pecatonica River, which itself is a tributary of the Rock River, and while the Sugar River has a shared history with the town that bears its name, it's actually the Pecatonica River that flows through town. Swiss, Germans, and Norwegians settled here in the 1850s and named the town after the wrong river. That's all I cared to learn about my hometown's founding.

Sugar River was wrong from the beginning.

I haven't been on the river in over eight years. A few of my friends loved to fish; it's a part of the culture in Wisconsin. You can get to any of the three main rivers in the area pretty easily, and spend the afternoon in a canoe, or trolling with a case of beer and a line in the water. I often wonder if—on Senior Skip Day 1992—we'd have ended up putting our teenage flotilla in the water at the boat ramp just a few miles down the road. Would Derrick, Aaron, and I have gotten drunk lounging on a raft or a pool float, spending the afternoon sneaking up on girls to untie their bikini tops? Maybe we would've tried to catch a small mouth bass or a walleye with someone else's fishing pole. I'm suddenly nostalgic for something I never much cared for, and only did back then because it was all there was to do.

I pick up a flat stone and throw it in The Pec, an arcing toss of nearly fifty yards. It splashes home.

The ground's unthawed, unusual for Wisconsin in January. There's a mix of mud and slush, polka dots of brown and white, smeared and smudging together. The trees are barren, aside from a few evergreens that bring a splash of green and a fresh scent to my nose. The area hasn't been kept up as well as when I'd lived here. The pavilion needs to be painted, or at least whitewashed. Garbage is piled up in the metal barrels used as trash cans, picked through by raccoons the night before. Tiny muddy rodent paw prints speckle the cement and the picnic tables. A stray cat streaks off into the underbrush.

A breeze momentarily swirls a handful of dry leaves into the air, then deposits them haphazardly.

I pick up the bag of weed I brought from the car. With my bandaged hand, I sprinkle a generous amount of pot into the creased rolling paper I'm cradling with the fingers of my left hand. I lightly lick the glue on the edge of the paper, and awkwardly twist a serviceable joint with fat and useless fingers. My Jack of Clubs lighter fires the joint and I draw in a deep cloud of welcoming intoxication. I cough, a wet and haggard hacking that rattles and wheezes painfully through my chest.

As soon as I'm able, I take another hit, hold it, exhale.

I feel cold and frail.

I wish that I could remember only the beautiful moments with Sarah, and discard the horror.

This is what I'm willing to settle for now.

I used to wish for her to be back with me, full of youth and life and promise. That I could undo all that I've done. That I could travel in time and save her. Save us, from me.

Now I'm satisfied, in my exhaustion and discouragement, to hope that my memories will start to fade like they do for everyone else. I'm so very, very sorry. For all of it. And it doesn't make any difference.

I take another hit from the joint and lift my gaze from the ground to the sky. It's so peaceful here. I didn't have the nerve to go into town—and drove nearly thirty minutes out of my way to avoid it—but I was drawn here by a haunted yearning to capture just a few minutes where Sarah and I spent so much of our short time dreaming together. It's the first time I've been back in this spot—our spot—since May 22, 1992, the Day Before, early in the morning, so early I still think of it as Prom Night even though it was Sunday morning by the time we arrived. I look down the slope, again to the icy banks of the river, where the specter of Sarah's life looms large. I can see her there, calling to me, waiting for me to come back ashore, so we could hold fast to new love. I'm still holding on, still holding on to her.

I miss her. I love her. I'd have told her every day for a lifetime. In a tragic twist of fate, that's what I did. I told her I loved her every day for the rest of her life.

.

All the memories of all the times we spent doing all the things we wanted to do spin through my mind with perfect clarity. Sarah, you won't be lost to history. I'm carrying your life forward, for both of us.

"Why couldn't I fucking stop him?" I cry. "Why did I just stand there and do nothing?"

(sneaking glances and then our eyes met in the hallway, a jolt of euphoria when she smiled, her hand over her mouth, relief when she finally accepted the invitation to go out for pizza with me after practice)

"Why was I such a fucking asshole to you, Mason?" I lament. It's a shout from my hell to the heavens. "Why couldn't I stop you?" The cat that had been lurking nearby skitters further into the woods through crunching leaves. I lob another stone at the river. This time it falls short, crashing through the thin ice before splooshing into the frigid water.

My joint is almost out.

I take another hit and hold it in.

(confused but committed, she chased after me in her prom dress, into the freezing river water)

Everything feels dead. I'm dead inside.

My future is dead. And now that Michelle is gone too, taking my show to New York City feels meaningless. The only hopes and dreams that I ever truly cared about are all lost to me, forever.

It's the end.

I'm on the verge of completing a meteoric rise to the highest levels of my chosen profession and I'd give it up instantly if I could touch her once more. Nothing feels real or vital. I've been chasing the storm, but after it's passed. I only see debris as I drive through, always minutes behind, unsure what I'd do if I actually got ahead of it. The passage of time and death, psychic trauma and guilt, is a force of nature, unconcerned with my demand that it be reversed at any personal cost. It can't be bribed or reasoned with, has no compassion, it makes no restitution.

It's 9:07 a.m. A dreary fog hangs in the Sunday air, undoubtedly because of the melting snow and ice.

Why did I really come home? I'm here to see Michelle laid to rest. I need to see it. She was my last true friend. I was comatose when Sarah's family held the memorial. Missing it shattered me. The lasting image I have of her is a violent one, so, to me, Sarah is never at peace. She's restless still. And I'm desperate to meet my son. There had been so many impossible decisions. Leaving my son behind. Missing his birth. Missing his birthdays. Missing his mother. I was a father and I was abusive in a new way, this neglect and abandonment and deception all born out of a false birthright. I've been given an unexpected opening into his life. I need to take it.

"I'm going to fuck this up, too," I predict.

I have to leave this place. I can't stay here.

I reach into my blazer pocket for my cell phone. I don't have it. I begin to run through—again, with perfect recall—every gas station, truck stop, and rest area that I'd used across six states, and then scrutinize the perfect mental image that I have of Kay's South Side Diner. Nothing. I go back even further and see it sitting on the bar in my condo. It is a victim of priorities; in my manic dash to escape the Floyd Chicks and DC and run headlong into the unknown, I'd simply neglected to take it.

I hate cell phones. I've never gotten used to people being able to call me whenever it's convenient for them. I miss the days of being unavailable, affirmed by how unbothered I've been without my phone until now. But I need to call Stacy and see if he's still at the same address he evicted me from at gunpoint nearly four years ago. I'm dreading the last few miles of this journey, a reunion, a funeral. Did I come home to get answers about Michelle? I need to know, but I'm afraid to ask.

Nothing I'm going to learn will change anything.

There's a weight sitting on my chest. My eye is killing me. My hand has a dull, incessant ache.

I flick the smoldering roach into the mud.

"Why didn't I listen to her intuition? Why did I try to convince her that she wasn't hearing a gun when I *fucking knew* it was gunfire?" I ask the Universe. The same questions I've asked thousands of times.

The Universe doesn't answer. It never has the answers.

A bright red cardinal lights on the skeletal branch of a tree not ten feet from where I sit. It's possible that I'm perfectly stoned, but the bird seems to sit and stare at me. He cocks and jerks his head from side to side but never looks away. He's a fluffy splotch of radiant red contrasted against barren trees, dead grass, mud, decay, coldness, and a forgetful river that pays no respect to friends who no longer visit. I don't budge, holding my breath, afraid he'll hear me and escape. He hops and twitches and nearly takes flight, but settles in again, shuffling his wings and puffing his chest feathers, picking at himself with his beak and chirping. The black feathers on his face are a mask.

Unprompted tears well up in my eyes.

I've always cried easily, but the past few days I've reverted to how I was in the months after the shooting. Dr. Darby has reminded me that I'd been numbing my emotions instead of processing them, but now I'm healing and "building a foundation for positive growth." I've lost the people in my life that mean the most to me, either through death or disaffection, and now I'm in the orbit of people who are using me and using me up. I feel like that fucking bird. Alone. My agent, my ratings, and my contract say otherwise, but I don't see it in myself, surrounded by dirty, cold lifelessness.

"What the fuck are you doing here, bird?!" I finally shout at him. "Fucking go."

He flies. I instantly regret it and want him back.

I wipe my eyes and pinch the bridge of my nose with my bandaged hand.

"Why didn't I see what was happening? Mason, you motherfucker! Why didn't I just do what I said I was going to do? Before you came upstairs, before you came down the hallway, and saw us, you'd have just seen me, and you could have killed me, and you wouldn't have killed her! Why did I have to push you so fucking hard? Why did I have to keep pushing and pushing and pushing? Why'd you say all of that shit to me on the radio? What does it mean? I don't understand any of this."

I'm sobbing. Raging. Unforgiven.

I feel Sarah's presence here, so close to me that I turn around to look for her as cold air again breezes through the park. I remember her dimples; she's wearing my letter jacket and my Cubs hat.

This place is sacred.

Echoes of gunfire and sex and mocking violence and laughter and our promises of love forever mingle together in my mind's eye like a witch's curse. They're not the normal scenes that overwhelm me. These are regrets. Emotions without images. Moments and ghosts. Unjustifiable hatred and the actions they provoked. Unrequited love—longingly left behind by death—warps into a sustaining grief, roaming for its rightful place in open arms now folded in a casket. It's impossible to let go of something I promised to hold on to forever. Sarah hasn't let go. She *never* will. I'm now clutching joy and sorrow equally. Only minutes earlier, I was wishing these horrors and remnants would fade into a white haze of amnesia, but I know I don't want to abandon them. In those final, defining moments, Sarah and I came to the end of our past. She is unchanged and idealized, timeless and everywhere, haunting and perfect.

I am none of these things.

I am nothing.

Sarah's not here. She's not coming back. My only option is to go to her.

Every blink is another memory of our short time together, flashes in the fleeting darkness.

I screw my eyes shut, hoping to sustain a phantom image. It dissolves into blood.

I'm lost. Sarah. Her name sweeps me under.

I'm discarding the will to keep going. My hope is extinguished. I'm finished. I'm at the end. Again.

Waves of anguish crash over me. My body is wracked with heartbreak. I'm pierced with a thousand self-inflicted sorrows. I'm in a pit, a prison, tormented by a captor who looks just like me. My breath comes in shudders. The world washes out almost completely. Sounds, smells, sights, all muted and blunted. I'm not afraid to die. I'm afraid I might stay alive. I'm involuntarily rubbing hesitation wounds and pressing my thumbs into the deepest scar on my wrist. Worn out—worn down—the darkness is calling me home.

I need a reason to keep going.

I remember Michelle's letter.

I pull it out of my back pocket, fumbling with it and dropping it onto the damp cement. It makes a small tent, landing face up, my name in smudged purple-cursive, a prophecy written by one of the fellow damned. Somehow the letter is a talisman, exuding power over me, a type of written reminder that I'm trapped inside a spell. Could I break its hold on me if I just read it like an incantation?

I still can't open it. I can't face the pain and disappointment of what it might say. I need to read it. Avoidance is my default response in situations when fear of an uncertain outcome overwhelms me.

"Fuck it," I say. "Fuck you," I declare, to myself, to Mason Reynolds, to everyone. "Fuck. All of you."

I snatch the letter off the ground and cram it back into my pocket. When the time is right, I'll know when I need to read it. I'll know when I'll be ready to confront it. Not here. Not while I'm among the ruins of lost love, and the shadows, unprepared and vulnerable. Not when I'm finished and weak. I'll crumble.

I'll read it when I see Michelle safely laid to rest. When I know she's at peace.

I take one last look around. I'm never coming back here again.

Shivers travel up and down my body from the damp air. With muddy shoes and a macabre resignation, I climb back into my car, and ten minutes later I cross into the Town of Sugar River, Wisconsin.

Small towns don't die anymore. They pause and get angry at being left behind by the passage of time. They change, more decay than evolution. It's like an old family photo in a childless home: the dead-end genealogy of the desperate, subsisting on bitterness and dwelling in the glory of yesterday's tired achievements and faded optimism. Houses need paint; most of the stores have gone out of business but the buildings remain, unoccupied. The holiday weekend, and church, make for quiet roads this early on a Sunday. Main Street is now just the three farmer bars that have been there since my childhood. I cut down an alley to avoid having to look at Sugar River High School. I drive across the old bridge, rusty wrought iron rivets and concrete in need of repair, atop a dam built during the Great Depression.

I was taken from Sugar River in an ambulance the morning of the shooting. I haven't been back since.

There was a graduation "ceremony" for the Senior Class months after the shooting that I chose not to attend. There was a five-year class reunion; I have no idea how many of the survivors attended. I should've gone. Maybe, somehow, someone could've helped me find what I'm looking for, but I doubt it. No one ever talked about what I did to Mason at the bonfire. Not even under oath during Mason's trial and appeal. Our silence was a town secret. We didn't conspire. We all just kept our mouths shut.

I heard that my parents divorced nearly three years ago, the family farm no longer in our family. I don't talk to either of them. The last I heard my mother is somewhere in Utah. I don't know where my dad is, or if he's still alive. I half expect to see him ambling down the street just now. I don't. Thank God.

I don't know what I'd do if he saw me.

I pull into the parking lot of this dying town's last gas station to call Stacy. Bolted to the wall near the entrance is the payphone I used to make prank calls on with Derrick and Aaron; we had nothing better to do than harass people and waste hours on idiotic and vulgar fun. When we ran out of quarters, we'd pelt school board members' homes with rotten eggs, and toilet-paper the same trees, over and over.

I can't make a phone call. I have no cash. I gave everything I had to Wendy the Waitress.

I fish around under my seat, in the glove compartment, in the console, under the floor mats. I can't even find enough change in my car to make a phone call.

I'm going to have to go inside. "RJ's Kwik Stop Gas N Go." Even the name is the same as it was in 1992.

When I walk through the door, I see something that momentarily makes me smile, catching the attention of the teenager working behind the counter. He's too young to smoke or drink legally.

"What's funny?" he asks.

I point at the ATM machine.

Only, no one calls them ATMs in Wisconsin.

Thanks to someone's attempt at clever marketing, they created a memorable acronym out of the phrase "Take Your Money Everywhere." When you need cash, you go to the "TYME Machine." I remember the look on the face of the first store clerk I spoke to in Washington DC, when I asked where I could find the "Time Machine." Deadpan, he replied, "My DeLorean is in the shop." I didn't immediately get the joke.

I've wished nearly every day for a real time machine.

The kid has no idea why I'm smiling and pointing at the TYME Machine, but he apparently doesn't care enough to ask, and goes back to watching a bass fishing show on the tiny TV mounted on the wall.

"Do you have a *Capitol Times* here?" I ask Convenience Store Kid.

He points at the newspaper stand that is literally right next to me, stocked full of Sunday editions.

I pick one up, opening and closing it like an accordion until I reach the obituaries. I look for her name.

No mention of Michelle Ramone. Maybe it's only in the *Stoughton Courier Hub*, their local paper.

I get a hundred dollars in twenties, then buy a bag of Skittles, a can of Mountain Dew, two packs of Marlboro Lights, ask for quarters with my change, and breeze out to the payphone. I wonder if I'll run into someone I know, or someone who knows me, but there are only unfamiliar faces grabbing snacks and filling up their farm trucks. It's a small town. It's a holiday weekend. There aren't many people out and about.

I don't want to make this phone call. My eye is pounding. My head is killing me. I should take…more of…what I've got. I'm still stoned, but the joint only made the throbbing in my head worse.

The past—playing like a split screen with the present—has taken it all out of me.

Guilt sits in my throat as I try to dial Stacy's number. But I'm also afraid. Stacy wanted to kill me once.

Michelle was the only good thing to happen to me after this goddamn place tried to send me to hell for my sins. It isn't my fault that her goodness didn't belong to me.

I deserve to be hated, but I don't hate Stacy for it. He was the first man to show me any true kindness and didn't want anything from me in return except friendship and loyalty. I didn't esteem it the way I should have. Stacy hadn't just filled a void in my life. He'd reached out to pick me up out of the gutter—literally—and brought me into his life, opened up his home, when I had nothing and nowhere left to go.

Almost like a father.

And I fucked him over.

CHAPTER 20

I didn't expect Michelle to come home when she did. I also didn't expect her to be alone.

It was the night before Thanksgiving, and she asked me to help her carry in some groceries.

"You don't pay rent. Make yourself useful," was how she put it, exactly.

I slipped on my flipflops and lugged in brown paper bag after brown paper bag of food for the small number of people who were going to be stopping by our (their) house trailer the next day. I'd been drinking since noon, a regular occurrence for me over the past six months. It was 7:14 p.m. on November 22, 1995. I watched a documentary on the Kennedy assassination earlier in the day.

"Where's Stacy?" I asked, surprised he wasn't with her. Stacy was supposed to bring home weed—bricks of it—for me to break down into half-ounce bags and unload over the holiday weekend. After he wrapped up at the tavern, I expected him to lure one of our friends over for a night of card games.

"He's working a double. They're staying open now until 2:00 a.m. because they expect a big night since no one has to get up early tomorrow." Michelle looked right at me, clearly irritated. "Most people don't have to get up early. But women who work full-time jobs and are also expected to cook

a Thanksgiving dinner tomorrow have to set an alarm." She pulled her hair back and started stacking cans and shoving things around on the counter, filling the sink with warm water. "So yeah. He's working late. Again."

"Isn't it too early to thaw the bird?" It wasn't meant to sound like a challenge, but it came out that way.

"Hey, Mr. Know It All, you want to make the food for tomorrow, or do you want to shut up and let me?"

I chose neither option. I changed the subject. "Who all's coming over tomorrow?"

"What is this, Twenty Questions? And how much have you had to drink today?" Before I could answer, she opened the fridge and saw the case of Ice House—full when she'd left the house that morning—was missing thirteen of the original twenty-four bottles. "Jesus, Jeremy. How are you not hammered right now? I have never seen anyone drink like you drink every day. Your tolerance is freakishly high."

There were times when cramming three people into a two-bedroom, two-bathroom doublewide meant everyone was in the business of everyone else, and sometimes our bad habits got on each other's nerves. Michelle sporadically commented on my inebriation with sarcastic judgment. She was also frustrated with Stacy's work schedule. I guessed she was conflating annoyances and beating me up for both of us.

"I'm German-Irish. I come by my alcoholism honestly. Genetically. Holding my liquor is the only thing I do well. I could also hold your liquor if you want. And any of your friends and family, if it helps."

"Alcohol isn't a good way to solve any problems," Michelle said.

"But it's a fun way to create some new ones," I laughed, delighted by my own spontaneous wit.

Michelle tried to stop herself from smiling and couldn't, so she turned back to the sink, tested the temperature, and hoisted the frozen turkey into the water. Michelle took care of herself. Ate well. As a nurse, she was on her feet at least ten hours a day. Her freckles were wonderful. Michelle was beautiful.

We had a natural, conversational chemistry. I was drawn to her, but kept my distance out of respect for Stacy. Our business partnership was profitable enough for him to look the other way when it came to other self-destructive tendencies, but he'd never forgive me if I made a move on his wife. Stacy was rational when his life was ordered in the way he expected it to be. He was wildly unpredictable when things did not go according to his plan. The last three months, Michelle and I found ourselves alone more often. At first, she was just my friend's wife, then my roommate, then we became friends.

I felt it happening. I tried to think of Michelle as my sister to change my emotions. I couldn't do it.

After I'd been discharged from the hospital on Monday, September 21, 1992, until Stacy found me in a tavern parking lot, I had refused to stay with my parents and lived from day to day for 621 days. Couches. My car. Parks. I'd hold down a job for a month and crash with a co-worker.

Stacy and Michelle Ramone had become a surrogate family.

I had no other place to go, I had worn out my welcome everywhere else, but against my will, I lusted for her.

"Why don't you take a picture, it'll last longer." She startled me. I was staring at her ass.

"Not for me it wouldn't," I quipped in return, reminding her of my picture-perfect memory.

I lit a cigarette and sat down at the table positioned against the wall in the tiny kitchen—between the short hallway that led to a bathroom, a backdoor, and my bedroom—and the living room. Scuffed, lime-green linoleum in the kitchen ended where the threadbare brown carpeting in the living room began. The front door opened up to a rickety wooden porch; to the left of the door was another hallway that led to Stacy and Michelle's bedroom, our second bathroom, and an alcove with a stackable washer-dryer.

I cracked open the window next to the table and watched the cold November air suck the smoke outside. "So," I tried again, "who all is coming over tomorrow? Do I need to leave?"

Michelle walked over to the cabinet stereo and started browsing the cassette tapes that filled two black plastic racks screwed into the paneling. Stacy and Michelle were both about five years older than me. While I spent my childhood listening to the same music they did, I came of age when Nirvana, Smashing Pumpkins, Pearl Jam, Stone Temple Pilots, Alice in Chains, and Soundgarden were on the cover of magazines and getting airplay on all the rock radio stations and MTV. Stacy and Michelle, on the other hand, held fast to the '80s, forever fans of Mötley Crüe Dokken, Night Ranger, Bon Jovi, White Snake, Warrant, and Cinderella. Our combined tape collection was massive; we'd not switched to CDs yet.

Michelle put in U2, "Achtung Baby." I was surprised, and delighted, but didn't say anything.

"Why would you have to leave?" she asked. "What difference does it make who comes over?"

"I don't want to be here if your family is coming over. I don't want to be a sympathy guest on Thanksgiving. I'd rather go get smoked up somewhere than sit around with your family and have them ask me how long I've known you guys and was I that Jeremy Peoples that they read about in Time Magazine. I don't know them and they don't know me, and I can eat turkey leftovers on Friday. I don't care about the Lions or the Cowboys, so missing the game isn't a big deal to me." Why was I so jittery?

"I have so many thoughts," she said absent-mindedly. "My family is coming over, yes. It won't be as weird as you make it sound, but you don't have to eat if you don't want to. I think the others are coming over later anyway, after my mom and dad leave, so just come back then. You're overthinking it."

Michelle then did something she shouldn't have. She opened a beer and sat down with me at the table. "Cheers," she said, clinking the top of her bottle to my empty one. I tossed mine in the trash, stumbled two steps to the fridge, snatched another Ice House and cracked open my fourteenth of the day.

Michelle didn't drink much. She was usually the sober one in our crowd of rowdies.

We sat there for a few minutes, neither one of us talking. It didn't feel awkward. I zoned out and smoked, staring out the window and wondering where I was going to get weed now that Stacy wasn't coming home for another eight hours. When Michelle spoke again, she startled me. "Earth to Jeremy!"

I blinked away my blank stare.

"You didn't hear a word I just said."

"You," I intoned, slurring, "are one hundred percent correct. I did not." I tipped my beer bottle at her and smiled.

"I was asking if I could have one of those." Michelle pointed at my cigarettes.

She didn't smoke regularly, but she had been drinking. Michelle had the willpower to buy a pack of cigarettes and smoke four or five and then give the rest away. I sort of hated it, but I admired it too.

I shook out one of my Basic Light 100s and slid it across the table. Michelle put the cigarette in her mouth and asked, "What's a girl gotta do to get a light around these parts?" like she was in a black and white film. I flicked open my Jack of Clubs Zippo and playfully tried a Humphrey Bogart impression.

"Here's lookin' at you, kid," I said, using the only line I knew from a movie that old.

Michelle leaned into the flame. She wore a button-up shirt, and the third one from the top had come undone, allowing me a peek at lace and previously unseen freckles. I glanced, more tactfully than when I got caught gawking a few minutes earlier. I've always been better in the middle of a conversation and I'm brilliant at ending one, but I almost always struggled to find an entry point with someone.

I wanted to tell her that I had feelings for her in places formerly dead and dormant.

I wanted to ask her if she knew I was broken and helpless, that I wanted to be touched again.

I wanted to see if she could bring me back to life, giving me more of her than I have seen so far.

I wanted to, but I couldn't.

"You don't have to talk about this if you don't want to," Michelle started. "But I feel like we've known each other long enough now that I can ask. I can't believe we've never talked about..."

Sooner or later, they all ask. "The shooting at my school." I'm sort of happy she respected my boundaries enough to keep from interrogating me about it until tonight. I'm also sort of pissed that she still felt the need to get into it with me, when it seemed obvious I don't want to talk about it. Ever.

She nodded. "I read about it when it happened. Everyone watched the news. I remember seeing you on TV. I can't even imagine what it was like to go through all of that. You never talk about it with me. You've been here for over a year. Stacy told me you bring it up sometimes when you've been drinking, but he hasn't really told me what you say. I'm not really sure what I expect from you right now. I'm worried about you, a little. A lot, I guess. Like I said, if you don't want to talk about it, I get it."

"There's not much to say that I didn't say on the stand. Mason Reynolds killed my girlfriend Sarah and six of my classmates. He shot twelve more, including me. My friend Aaron got paralyzed and my other friend Derrick died. I got shot twice at close range. Mason just...ran out of ammunition and then sat down and waited for the cops to come. I nearly bled out but didn't and woke up days later in the hospital."

I recited the version of events that I have prepared for when nosy people pry.

"Did you get any therapy for what happened to you"? Michelle was clearly unsatisfied with my answer.

"What, like, physical therapy? Yeah, sure, I was in rehab for a long time. There's shrapnel from the locker peppered near my heart and lungs, and a bunch of my stomach had to be surgically rebuilt. Plastic surgery too. I was on kick ass painkillers for months. Lots of therapy." I was being intentionally obtuse. I knew she was asking about my mental health, but she waited patiently for me to finish.

"You never had a psychiatrist or a psychologist or whatever? Like, a counselor on something?"

"A few." I shrugged.

"And...?" She pushed.

"And...nothing really. I stopped going. It was all bullshit."

Michelle took a moment to consider my answer. "You brought up your girlfriend first, before any of your friends or even yourself. I've never hear you talk about her." Her eyes, and her voice, were soft.

"What the fuck am I supposed to say about her?" Defensive. Protective of her memory. It was mine.

"It's OK, Jeremy. We don't have to talk about it anymore. I'm your friend, but it weirds me out that you never talk about all this with anyone. I'm worried that you keep it all inside and don't let it out. It's a lot of darkness and trauma to carry around. I've seen what it does to people at the hospital. You don't have to tell me, but maybe just talking to someone else about stuff is a good idea. You're just...you're just drinking a lot more and really dipping into the product and I don't know that you realize or care."

"I'm not worried about anything. I'm good." It was an answer designed to be frustrating.

Michelle finished her beer and dropped the cigarette down the bottleneck to a hissing death.

I was surprised to see her immediately get another beer. Something else was on her mind.

"I don't want to talk about it. I want to forget it ever happened, but I can't because I remember everything perfectly. When I think about it, I feel the pain of the bullets—"

(through my body tearing through my chest and ripping through my back and the searing fire and comprehension take a second, no three seconds, to catch up with reality Oh My Fucking God)

"—and the adrenaline and the image of…everyone…dying…never fucking fades." I'm out of breath.

(straining to lift my head and I see blood soaked blue jeans and I know who it is and I can't bring myself to look but I have to see her face, to know, and I see her eyes I'll see them until the end of my life)

"It's like it happened twenty minutes ago. I think about it thirty times a day. I can't function if I talk about it. I want to talk less about it. I don't want people to ask me about it. I want to be normal, and that's part of why I like it here. Stacy doesn't ask me. You didn't ask me. Imagine your worst day, the worst thing you ever did, that ever happened to you, a horror show, and then imagine you have to look at it and you can't turn away and you see it when your eyes are closed and when they're open and you dream about it and you can't ever un-remember so you just keep reliving it, re-feeling it constantly. That's what it's like. There's two movies always playing. Right now and that worst day. Side by side. Sometimes the past takes over and I lose sight of the present. But I never completely lose sight of that worst day. Ever."

"I'm so sorry," Michelle apologized, and I believed she meant it.

"No, it's cool," I lied. I was pissed that she brought it up, but strangely gratified, too. I felt anger and relief and a vulnerability with her that I hadn't felt with another person since Sarah.

Could I tell her about the feelings I had? Could I tell her about the guilt, the responsibility I bore for the shooting? For Sarah's death? Would she listen and understand that I had lost the love of my life and couldn't figure out how to recover? Could she possibly have the right words for me, in spite of the mounting self-hatred and shame boiling to the surface, corrupting all that it touched? Or would Michelle just nod and not understand and regret ever bringing it up in the first place? Did she really want to know, or would the intensity of the emotions and the finality of my outlook intimidate her into retreat and silence? Would she see me for what I was and reject me? Would it change our friendship forever, making it awkward whenever we were together, where it had mostly been fun and easy? I didn't want to take the risk. I was conflicted. It would feel good to tell someone about how much I love Sarah. I needed to heal and see if there could be someone else. Is this how traitors feel?

I wanted to tell her all of it.

"I feel like I've been doing a lot better lately," I heard myself say. "Staying here has been good."

"It's been nice having you here," Michelle agreed. Then she added, "Most of the time, anyway." She was extending an olive branch of gentle teasing. She continued with her own vulnerability. "It was quiet here before you moved in. All the time. I mostly like it, but sometimes it's too much. Stacy is gone, well, you know. He's at the restaurant all the time." She looked at everything but me. "I feel like people are constantly watching me at work. I'm exhausted. I get home and watch TV. We don't go out anymore."

Michelle was a nurse at St. Sebastian's Hospital, and had gained access to the pharmacy. She supplemented our street drug sales with prescription drugs. The constant fear of getting caught, along with the normal stress with being a nurse in a busy hospital—and her disconnection from Stacy—had taken its toll on her. I'd never considered her burden before. She'd become a drug mule.

I couldn't imagine that this life was her childhood dream come true.

She sipped her beer; a dribble squirted from her lips and trickled down her chin.

"That's enough for you, woman. You are officially over the legal limit. Intoxicated turkey preparation in the State of Wisconsin holds a maximum penalty of thirty months in Taycheeda. I'm cutting you off." My arm was resting on a dish towel. I tossed it to her, and she wiped her mouth with it, laughing. "That's what you get for saying that it's nice having me here 'most' of the time." I was really slurring my words. "Do you know if Stacy has any weed stashed here? He was going to bring back our supply to baggy-up for tomorrow, but since he's not going to be here until, like, Christmas, I don't want to wait and I don't feel like going anywhere and I've called six people and no one's holding anything right now."

Michelle got up and stretched to open the cupboard door above the fridge. She had to get up on her tippy toes; I sneaked a glimpse of her toned midriff as her shirt pulled up while she reached. Her fingertips got hold of a small blue tin, tucked away, nearly out of sight. Michelle pried off the lid.

Inside the square tin was about an eighth ounce of weed and a one-hitter.

"What the hell, Shell?! You been holding out on me. You smoke weed? When did this start?"

"I'm good at keeping secrets," she informed me.

"Are you now? Can you keep all the secrets, or just some of the secrets?" I reached for her Magic Blue Tin and she snatched it out of my drunken grasp. I wasn't in the mood to play for it. Exasperated, I threw my hands up in disgust. "Dude. Really? I've been waiting all day to get high. Come on."

"What's the magic word, Jer?" Michelle was buzzed and silly from one-and-a-half beers.

"Wait. What's this 'Jer' bullshit?" I wasn't as annoyed with her as I was acting. "I am not a Jer."

"So you can call me 'Shell' and think that's cool, but I call you 'Jer' and you get weird about nicknames all of a sudden? What if I don't feel like being a Shell? What if I like Michelle exclusively? Or I want to be Shelly?"

She emphasized the "EE" in Shelly. "Shell-EE. Or maybe...I want to be Mich." It came out "Mish" when she said it and it was so absurd that we both started laughing.

"Mish, huh? OK. Cool. I will be Jer but from now on you are Mish. I'm making t-shirts."

I'd never seen Michelle laugh that hard.

"To Jer and Mish." She toasted, we touched bottles again, and she finished her second beer.

"Fucking cheers," I saluted. Michelle nodded. "Now would you please, for the love of God, give me that fucking weed before I lose my shit at you?" That sent her off into another round of laughter, so much so that she set her head down on the table and handed me her stash without even looking. "Dude, are you drunk on two beers?" Her laughter made me giggle.

"Uh huh," was all she could muster, snorting and laughing. I shook my head and laughed along with her.

I packed the one-hitter, cached it, packed it again, cached it, packed it a third time, and handed it to Michelle. She held up her hand. "I haven't been piss-tested in a while. I'm overdue. I can't."

"More for me," I said and finished the packed one-hitter, setting it down empty in the ashtray. Michelle got up, opened the fridge, and grabbed a third beer. Nothing about tonight seemed in character for her.

"I feel like I can tell you something because you will understand." Michelle was suddenly serious. I didn't say anything. "Because you're always talking but never about what you're really thinking about."

I normally struggled to make eye contact with people, but right then I was locked in with her.

"I feel alone all the time." She just said it and then didn't say anything else. She looked off into space.

I waited.

She drank her beer. "I'm lonely and I feel like I'm under pressure twenty-four/seven doing what we're doing."

I barely nodded and said nothing.

"I feel like you get it. You understand being lonely even when there's a lot of people around, don't you? You know how it is to not have what you want in your life, don't you, Jer? Because of Sugar River."

"Loneliness is the demon that exhausts you with noise from people you don't want to be around and silence from the people you can't be without." I explained it in the only way I knew how, at that time.

Michelle's eyes widened. "Holy shit, Jeremy. Where did you read that? That's exactly what I mean."

"I didn't read it. It's how I feel. I'm exhausted by noise, and silence. I hate my life. I hate everything about everything." I could feel the dam breaking. I'd been holding back my thoughts and feelings for too long.

"I knew you feel it, too. I try to talk to Stacy, but his head is too much in the money. I don't think he understands. He doesn't listen. I don't care about the money as much as he does. I would be OK if I just stopped and he stopped, or we just worked the jobs instead of using them for the other shit. It's like the thing we're doing to get our money together so we can have the stuff we want and do the stuff we want is driving us apart and he doesn't get it," Michelle vented. "It doesn't feel like we'll ever get out. Even if we buy the tavern like we said. I think Stacy will keep running drugs, even when he's the owner."

Side One of "Achtung Baby" ended abruptly.

I jumped up and flipped the tape over, hit fast forward for two seconds, and started it perfectly on "The Fly." I felt my head spinning. I was stoned and drunk, past the point of no return but not totally wasted.

"You should be a DJ," Shell said. "You run the stereo like one. Always perfect on the starts, and you make the best mix tapes. Honest to God, you should be on the radio or something. You'd be so good at it."

"*Never thought about it. I just like music and I don't want it to stop once it gets started. And I love this album,*" I recalled. "*I played it a lot during my senior year. I wanted 'One' as the Prom Court song, but they picked 'Love is on The Way' by Saigon Kick. Fuck me. Terrible fucking song. My class sucked.*"

The thought of prom, and my casual discussion of our class debates over prom music brought another wave of perfect, horrifying memories cascading in on me. I saw dead faces and crippled bodies mixed together with our emphatic arguments over song selection, and how important it seemed at the time. It was a nothing moment that we'd made into an ordeal. "*My best day. Then, my worst day.*"

"*The things we want we won't get, because we're chasing things we're not supposed to have,*" *Michelle sighed.* "*I really am sorry for what you've been through. I'm sorry for all you lost. It's so terrible.*"

"*I lost everything.*" *We sat in silence again. I watched the kitchen clock, fighting the urge to be honest. The beer, the weed, the compassion, I couldn't stop myself from talking. Opening my heart. Letting it out. Exposing my vulnerabilities despite everything inside me screaming at myself to stay protected, quiet, hidden. It was too late. I wanted to let her into my world. So I did.* "*I love her, Shell. I love her so much, and she's gone. She is the best thing that ever happened to me. That will ever happen to me. I can't believe she's gone. It's like she's not really gone but was never really alive. It's my fault…*"

Michelle tried to interrupt me. "*None of what happened in Sugar River is your fault, Jeremy.*"

"*Don't. Do. That. You weren't there. You didn't see what happened. You don't know what I did. You don't know that Sarah wanted to run, but I wanted to see what was happening, and if I'd listened to her or let her run she'd still be alive and I'd be dead. I don't want you to tell me it's not my fault. It IS my fault. It's ALL my fault. I caused it, and I stopped her. Why did I do that?! And I didn't save her. I didn't do anything. I just stood there and let him shoot her. I love her and she's dead and I can't fix it and bring her back. I'm just as responsible as Mason. I need someone to tell me what I can do to make it right again because it's all wrong. I'm sorry, I'm so sorry, Sarah, I'm so sorry please, please forgive me..."*

I didn't want to cry but was about to.

"You're not alone in all of this, Jeremy. You don't have to do this by yourself. We care about you. I care about you," Michelle comforted. "You can't keep carrying this around. You have to get help."

"I need to keep it. It's all I have left of her. I love her. I will love her. Forever. She loves me. I'm all alone, too. I understand how you feel. I get it. I hate it. I live in this ghost story! I'm always alone, and I'll always be alone, and I don't want to be alone, but I need to stay alone because of what I did."

Michelle had tears in her eyes. I couldn't let myself cry with her. Getting it out in the open felt good. But it also felt like a betrayal of Sarah's memory. I had fallen for Michelle. It's why I trusted her. How could I love Sarah forever if something happened between Michelle and me? I was being unfaithful.

Spiritual infidelity.

"Looks like we're alone, together," was all she said, but she looked at me when she said it.

It was then that my favorite song on the album started. Haunting music and lyrics of desire and despair. Lyrics that were predicting the future for us, though we couldn't know it then, drunk and oblivious.

"Love Is Blindness."

Michelle peeled the label off of her nearly-empty beer bottle, averting her eyes. What was she thinking? Was she weighing the consequences of the different paths the night could take? My autobiographical memory gifted me nearly every detail of her life, what she'd revealed and secrets she failed to hide. I saw her clearly for who she appeared to be, and I finally understood what she wanted to be. But...was I mistaking the signs? And...did I want to do this? Could I? Should we do this?

"Have you...thought about us? Like this? More than...what we are now?" Michelle wondered.

The song ended, hissing background noise for a few seconds, then a click and silence filled the trailer.

I wanted her.

"Jer." Michelle smiled, pulling me out of my trance. Our gazes met. It was then I realized that her Irish green eyes were the same color as mine, bleary with alcohol. She'd let her strawberry-blonde hair fall to her shoulders. "It's OK if you can't." She got up from the table, downing the last of her beer. "I need sleep. I have to get up early and cook a turkey. Come on. You should call it a night, too."

"It's, like, 8:30, Shell. You're going to bed at eight fucking thirty?" My head was spinning.

"I worked ten hours. I need a shower. I think I'm a little drunk," she giggled. "Yes." She pointed. "Bed."

"Stay. Stay up. Get high with me." I was paralyzed, but I couldn't let her slip away.

"I told you I can't," Michelle reminded me. She also didn't leave.

I knew I had to say something.

I said the most ridiculous thing.

"I don't want to go to bed alone. Not tonight." I stood up from the table and wobbled in place.

She didn't move. I held my breath. I hadn't been with anyone since Sarah. My heart pounded in my chest and I was blushing. I felt myself stirring. Nervous. My mouth was dry. What would she say?

"It can only be tonight. He can never know about it. It can never be more than tonight."

I dismissed the thoughts of betraying his trust, stabbing him in the back, disloyal ugliness overtaken by loneliness and lust and selfishness. I'd made my decision. I believed she had as well, maybe weeks ago.

"All we ever have is right now, and a lifetime of yesterdays. Tomorrow's just a lie." I felt poetic in my drunkenness.

Indecision hit suddenly. Michelle protested. Weakly. "Jeremy, I don't know." Her face revealed her conflict: sad yet wanting eyes, lips pursed, brow furrowed. She was a good but desperate person. If Michelle hadn't been drinking, she might've decided differently, unable to hurt her husband, even unknowingly. Michelle might have found a resolve to remain in her unhappiness, conscience clean.

"I don't either," was all I could think to say. I didn't know. It felt like a perfect mistake. "Just tonight."

I took one tentative step closer.

"Jeremy, we shouldn't do this. I'm sorry. I shouldn't have let you think..."

It was on the verge of rejection that I saw Sarah again, almost as an overlay of scenes, yesterday and now, Michelle and Sarah, together across time. "I will love you, forever" I had promised her. She'd entered forever; it hadn't even begun for me. How could I love her forever if this happens?

Her smile flashed in my mind's eye, dimples, hand over her mouth, face turned down.

What we had shared would no longer be unique if this happened. I held on, but my grip weakened.

Then blood-soaked hair, her mouth choking out incomprehensible, soundless last words.

Her idealized specter both urging me toward freedom and bewitching me to stay beholden, and alone.

I just wanted the fucking pain to go away.

I reached out for Michelle and I kissed her.

Her words turned into an "mmmhmmmm" as the kiss deepened. She didn't pull away. She let go.

I embraced her, she wrapped her arms around me, clenching me with her tensed fingertips, running them across my shoulder blades and down to my lower back. My mouth moved to her neck as she closed her eyes, I gently touched my lips to each eyelid, then kissed her again.

I suddenly knew we were on the verge of a terrible goodness. I only made thoughtless decisions after Sugar River. I was contemplative only when it came to the past, what I had wanted and what I had lost. I only did what I wanted to do in the moment, without care or consideration of the consequences. I wanted the hopelessness replaced, the emptiness filled. I voided the risk, ignored the threat of a fallout. Tonight held the promise of a momentary reprieve, and a fellow traveler to get lost with in a fantasy.

Not just numbing the pain. With Michelle, could I bury it?

I finally stopped thinking.

We were in my room in seconds.

I closed the door, locked it. We fell on my bed, looking into each other's eyes. Our hands searched for the places they wanted to be, touching, pulling, unzipping, slipping, carefully, patiently, and lovingly down to skin on skin. It was moving, slow and open, like we'd been waiting years for our moment and had finally and secretly discovered it. My necklaces dangled, a crucifix and a St. Jude's medal, falling softly to her throat, sliding gently across her breasts. We instinctively knew what the other wanted, needed, and yearned for. It didn't have the clingy clamor of a drunken mistake. We were old soul lovers, together at last. Our bodies and souls were one, the formerly separate story of our lives converging in chemistry, just in time, loneliness and emptiness, gone. We chose to become a rumor.

"This could be bad," she gasped, but didn't stop me.

"I know," I agreed, and we kept not stopping for hours.

CHAPTER 21

"Jesus Christ," I say to myself. "What am I doing?"

I'm still at the payphone in Sugar River, holding the handset that is now honking an off-hook tone at me. Will I be able to talk if Stacy answers? He hates me, justifiably. Stacy's gun in my face is the lasting memory I had of him until New Year's Eve.

Although I'm home at his invitation, I'm unsure if the secret about my son remains hidden.

Why did he really want me to come back?

I shake my head, hang up, then pick up the handset again, drop two quarters into the slot, and reluctantly dial Stacy Ramone's telephone number from memory.

It rings once. Stacy answers immediately. "Who's this?"

(the door is open, adrenaline screaming through my body, disrupting my ability to think clearly, to lie effectively, Stacy pressing his gun to my forehead, rage and betrayal on his face, Michelle calmly says—)

"Hey, dude. It's Jeremy. I'm uh, I'm at a payphone. I'm in Wisconsin."

"I didn't think you were coming." His voice is flat, emotionless, the same as it was on the radio.

Only moments after the flashback to my first night with Michelle, Stacy's voice triggers memories and emotions that rip into sight as I stammer and struggle to find the words to say, something I rarely do.

"I drove." I don't know how to talk to him. It was easier on the radio, with my focus on the show, the audience, Wafer, and Sammie, the rest of the visitors gawking at the unfolding melodrama.

Now that it's just the two of us, I've lost all confidence.

"You drove? That's a long ass drive, hoss. I figured you'd fly. Even on short notice. Don't rich radio DJs in big cities have all kinds of contacts with influential people and shit? Especially ones in DC?" There's a subtle provocation in how he's talking about me, and not to me. It's not hostile, but there's an edge.

I'm stoned. The Floyd Chicks did not let me down. The weed is killer.

"Yeah. I mean no. I didn't fly. It's not really that bad. Holidays. No traffic. I just couldn't get out of DC until last night. Work shit," Nervous half-truths. "I'm in Sugar River right now. I haven't gotten all the way up your way yet. I have some shit to do before I get to Stoughton. You in the same trailer?"

"Yeah. Same place. I know you know it." It sounds like he's taking a drag off a cigarette. "Coming over this morning? We can just chill out here. I don't have anywhere to go today. Nothing open anyway."

"I'm forty-five minutes away. I didn't make any hotel reservations. I gotta sort that out first."

"You don't need a hotel. Stay here, hoss. You can stay in your old room."

There's no way in hell I'm staying in that trailer. I scratch at my beard growth, touch my tender eye, scrutinize my blood-speckled bandage, and instinctively reach for my cigarettes, stalling.

"What about," I hesitate just slightly, "Stevie? Isn't he in that room now? No man, thanks, it's okay, I'm getting a hotel."

Stacy doesn't say anything for a moment, and then agrees. "OK. Thanks for coming, man."

I hear music in the background. Are there people there? Stacy told me he needed me to come back because he didn't have anyone. Maybe it's the TV. Who would be there? Michelle's family?

"Yeah. It's…it's OK. I mean, I guess it's not OK. It's all just so fucking unexpected. I haven't talked to you in almost four years. And the news. About Michelle. It's just. I can't understand it. What happened? Was she sick? Was it an accident? I'm totally in the dark here, bro," I blurt out. I hadn't planned on asking Stacy any questions about Michelle until we met in person, but sadness and curiosity are driving me. And I'm high. "I looked for her obituary, but I didn't see it. How is Stevie? I mean, he just lost his mom…"

Long pause. Long enough that I think we got disconnected. "You still there?"

"Yeah. I don't wanna talk about this right now, hoss. Go do what you said you need to do before you come over and I'll tell you everything. There's a lot. It'd be better if we just sat and talked." I knew this would be painfully uncomfortable. My defenses are up and Stacy seems evasive.

"I understand," I lie. "I'm gonna let you go. I'll be by later. We can talk then. It's cool."

Instead of hanging up, Stacy asks, "What are you doing in Sugar River?"

It's been nearly twenty-four hours since I've slept. I'm stoned. Paranoid. I don't want to answer him, but I do.

"I don't know, dude. I'm just here. I'm not sure what I'm trying to do. I don't know," is all I can say.

"You don't know what you need to do while you're here? Huh. You don't have to say. It's cool, hoss." Another weird, calculated pause. "Thanks again for coming. It really means a lot that you're here."

"No problem. I'll see you in a few hours," I promise, and quickly hang up—even before I hear Stacy say goodbye—so he doesn't have time to ask me any other questions. Relieved, I exhale and light a cigarette. Suddenly feeling exposed, I take a few strides back to my car and pretend to hide behind the tinted windows. I turn the car on, then the radio. It's the Classic Rock station my dad used to listen to. The Moody Blues, "Nights in White Satin" is playing. I turn it up loud enough to drown out my thoughts.

It doesn't work.

I'm never going to come back here again. If I'm going to do this, it has to be today. If I'm going to do this next final thing, it has to be now. Get it all out of the way at once. Confront the places in the present that assault me from the past. I'm alone in this pursuit to find what I need. Can I kill the past by seeing it as it is now? New memories of an old place, powerless and empty, instead of filled with revenge and dead bodies? I can't hide from my past. Leaving hasn't helped. It follows me through incessant recollections. My new life hasn't supplanted the old one. Can I find closure? Answers? Something I never saw in the days and years since Sarah's death in my mind's eye that can help me find peace, somehow?

I'll do anything.

Anything.

I pick apart a small, aluminum foil packet of pure China White Heroin with my fingernails and spill it out onto the Alice in Chains "Dirt" CD case. Using my driver's license to make two short lines, I roll a dollar bill and snort both lines without hesitating. I lick clean what's left in the packet. Heroin drains down the back of my throat like an acid wash, the unmistakable taste of emotional anesthesia.

My heart rate dips.

My eyes droop, my head nods, the familiar blood rush in my ears.

"OK," I sigh. "OK." I let go, slumping into the descent. *Let the fucking China do what it does.*

Everything slows down.

Even the onslaught of distant replays. The memories never go away completely, but my mind relaxes inside a cloud of opioids and the pain isn't as sharp. It's almost as though I'm watching someone else's dismay, upsetting but impersonal. Sarah and Stevie and Michelle and Stacy and Mason and my dad appear like characters in a movie I saw years ago.

Their faces are just as vivid, however. I reach out my hand to try and touch the images in my mind.

I am in the present, right? I'm shaking. Cold. The damp January air has settled into my bones. I turn the heater up. My mouth is dry. I sip the Mountain Dew. I'm clenching my jaw, grinding my molars. My jaw pops when I open and stretch it. People have to be watching me. I look around. No one is paying attention to me. Actually, I don't see anyone, anywhere, anymore. I look around again anyway.

I'll smoke a cigarette. That'll help. I'm still smoking the one I lit after I finished the phone call with Stacy. I take a drag and let my hand drop to my thigh. Ashes plume and sparks dot holes in the upholstery. I'll be pissed later but right now I'm only vaguely aware and it seems distantly important.

I'm in no condition to drive. I try to start my car. It's already running and the starter grinds.

"What the fuck?" I mutter, and pull my hand back. My eyes are barely open. I shift into DRIVE, pull slowly out of the gas station parking lot, on to Main Street, and turn toward Sugar River High School.

CHAPTER 22

It's a haunted house.

Sugar River High School looms at the top of Main Street Hill like a red brick tombstone.

I wish they had torn it down. Why hadn't they? It has stood near the center of town in silent testimony for over seven years. The School Board and City Council had voted to condemn the building after the Wisconsin State Police, FBI, Dane County Sheriff's Office, and the Sugar River Police Department had collected all the evidence and decided it was no longer a crime scene. Two months after the shooting, parents, students, and teachers took home anything forensics left behind. I assume the contents of my locker are somewhere with the diploma I've never seen. There'd been a memorial service and prayer vigil that summer, but I was in rehab, despairingly in pain. That fall, Sugar River students went to a neighboring school district to allow for a new, consolidated high school and junior high to be built. The Class of 1994 was the first group of seniors to graduate in the town of Sugar River after the shooting.

Why didn't they tear this place down?

The fact that the school still stands condemns me.

I no longer speak to the witnesses or survivors. After the trial and appeal, we went our separate ways and I quickly lost track of them. I reached out to Aaron once, with the hope he would understand my regret and share the desire to take responsibility. Partially paralyzed, he hadn't recovered from his physical injuries as fully as I had from mine, and he was opposed to revealing what we'd done to Mason at the bonfire. Instead, he started a charity to help people recover from brain and spinal cord injuries. The last time we spoke, we again argued over telling the full truth. I was drunk, in a dark mood, and he asserted unequivocally that he would no longer look back, only forward.

I can't do the same.

"I can't believe it's still here," I choke out a whisper, my words coming slowly, slurred and pained. "I can't believe that I'm here. What am I doing here?" I'm talking to an imaginary audience.

So many lost and ruined lives.

The enormity of what happened in this spot has warped the size of my high school into something gigantic in my memories. I circle around the block twice, at ten mph, looking at the school from all angles, unwilling to stop. I'm leaning over the steering wheel, drugged and gawking like a tourist.

Sugar River High School was built in 1920, a two-story brick box that had been the pride of the community. Now, rows of windows running parallel to each other on both floors are smashed and broken. The two primary entrances and three side exits are boarded up. The main entrance had led to a trophy case, a set of six doors that opened to the gymnasium, and a staircase that zigzagged up to the principal and guidance counselor's office and several more classrooms. The other entrance, which we all called "The Secondary Main," was on the opposite side of the building facing the street. It was a set of double doors with a small landing that split in three directions: up the main stairs to the second floor, down to the basement and the boys' and girls' locker rooms, or straight through to the Senior

Hallway. A student parking lot that accommodated forty or fifty cars is out back, with another set of double doors that opens into the other side of the gym through a stage we'd used for school plays, choir and band concerts, and graduation. Each end of the building had another, single door exit: one was accessible from an alley, the other from a small patch of grass between the school and a side street. I look for the beautiful pin oak tree that stood guard over the property—it was easily a hundred and fifty years old—but it's missing. Someone must have cut it down, or maybe a storm toppled it.

It's gone, without so much as a stump for a memorial to a majestic, patient, and silent observer.

Sarah and I sat under that tree for hours, studying and dreaming about our future together.

I'm shaking uncontrollably. I feel old. The school is so different than I remember. Neglected. And yet, everywhere I look, memories explode into life, out of the past like ghosts in a landscape.

The trimmed strip of grass that once circled the property is nothing more than a ring of overgrown weeds and trash. Vandals spray-painted the building in various places. The blacktop parking lot surface has gone unused for so long that volunteer trees have sprouted up through the cracks in various places.

I drive down the alley. I've lost my nerve. I know I can't go inside.

Yet I still make the turn into the student parking lot. The "Sugar River Raiders" logo is faded and barely distinguishable on the wall of the shop garage. The Class of 1990 had painted it so visiting teams would see it when their buses pulled up to our home games. It wasn't all that intimidating but it was high quality work for a bunch of high school kids, and we thought it was pretty badass at the time.

It's been two thousand seven hundred and eighty days since I've set foot in this building.

I was unconscious when they took Sarah away. What if she's still in there, hemorrhaging on the floor next to Locker 316, wearing my letterman jacket, her favorite Guess jeans, and one half of a Best Friends Forever pendant? Eyes open, fixed and dead. I know she's not, but it *feels* like she could still be there, waiting for me to finally save her, or carefully return her to her final resting place.

"I cannot fucking go in here," I remind myself. "Under no circumstances should I do this." Bottles and cigarette butts and other trash are strewn about, wet and stuck to the pavement. The normal snow and ice have mostly melted away, leaving only grey splotches of slushy filth.

I put my car in park, turn off the engine, and, aside from the pings of a cooling motor, it's quiet. No one has been here in months. Years. Even vandals have grown bored; the graffiti has faded away with time.

Sugar River High School is alive with death, waiting for me to return. I'm its final victim, escaping temporarily, and now lured back with the false promise of closure and absolution. It's as though it's balancing a ledger, correcting the cosmic carelessness that inexplicably allowed me to survive.

The building is going to try and kill me again the moment I set foot inside. I can feel it. I know it.

The dark holes of jagged glass scream soundless accusations at me.

Staggered from the effects of high dollar heroin and dread, walking in slow motion, pushing into psychic resistance and spiritual turmoil—against my better judgment—I trudge toward Sugar River High School.

Each step is an effort.

I have to go inside.

I need to. I don't want to. I have to see.

I don't want to see. But...

Sarah could still be here. Maybe this time I can trade my life for hers, stay behind and let her run.

("Oh my God, Jeremy. That's a gun. Why is someone shooting a gun in here?")

Mason might be here too. He's not really in prison. He's waiting for me. CLICK. CLICK. CLICK. Rifle empty, damage done, yet unendingly he pulls the trigger, an echo throughout time. CLICK. CLICK. CLICK. CLICK.

("Look what you made me do!")

"He's not in there!" I yell at the building, gunshots ringing in my ears from the most powerfully resilient memories of that day. There's a slight breeze against my face as I shriek. "I am NOT coming in there!"

The boarded-up doors no longer look like a fortification. The plywood barricade is a ruse, rusty screws that once anchored it to the brickwork have pulled free of the mortar. It creaks ever-so-slightly, showing me clearly that there is an opening that I could easily squeeze through.

It's a trap.

"FUCK. YOU. MOTHERFUCKER." I point at the door.

My mouth is my weapon. It is a trusty defender but seems useless now, all bluster and bravado. Sugar River High School sees through it, sees past the angry façade and directly into my hidden craven heart.

An icy shudder courses up my spine, jerking my head and neck. I have to shake my arms. I light a cigarette, and take a deep inhale. I'm wracked with another wet, hacking cough. I choke, struggling to catch my breath, a pathetic, wheezing failure that only leads to more coughing spasms. I bend over at the waist, put my fist to my mouth, and force myself to choke out some spit and phlegm and the drainage-remains of the heroin I snorted minutes earlier.

I'm weakly aware of the irony:

The building doesn't need to kill me; I'm doing it myself—albeit inefficiently—without any help.

I flick the cigarette into a slush pile, grab hold of the plywood over the doorway, wrench open a gap, and clamor through without incident. Aside from a dim shaft of light coming from outside, I'm in darkness.

"Here I am. I'm fucking here!" My voice carries, echoes, and reverberates perversely. I'm in the gym.

My eyes adjust. I see the outlines of bleachers, pushed tight against each wall. The basketball hoops are retracted into the ceiling and remnants of the Class of 1992 Prom decorations still visibly adorn the stage, tables and folding chairs and an empty punch bowl. Time ended here at 7:54 a.m. on May 23, 1992. Everything remains in place, both joyous and tragic, youthful and dead, fleeting and eternal.

I'm less than ten feet from where the first shots were fired.

Vacant buildings usually smell like decay, but it's something worse. Rotten. The dampness clings to my nostrils and inside my mouth. Death this old and offensive has a cold, sickening odor. Unmistakable.

I push on the door handle, exiting the gym into a hallway, and nearly fall down. All the windows are broken, letting more light stream through. A film of dirt has crusted over everything. Dried leaves have drifted in. The cafeteria is directly across from the gymnasium doors.

I look in.

There's blood everywhere, dried in crusty pools, blackish-red, splattered and smeared in various places.

I'm petrified. I know this is where Derrick was killed. I saw crime scene photos in court. He was shot through the throat and died alone as everyone ran in terror. Derrick wasn't even supposed to be here.

It was my fault. I murdered him.

I feel the wetness of tears on my face.

There's no way I could have known, but the truth is meaningless.

Everyone was killed because of what I did. Because of me.

I can't tell if what I'm seeing is real or I'm still out in my car, passed out on heroin, having a nightmare about what Sugar River High School must still look like inside.

I look down the hallway on my right, toward the trophy case. All that remains is a metal frame and shattered glass. I turn in the other direction, toward The Secondary Main entrance. There's a paper banner, hand drawn with markers, still hanging over the archway, torn almost completely in half.

It reads "Welcome Class of 92 Senior Prom! Love Is On The Way!" There's blood spatter on it.

Bullet holes in the walls and ceiling.

This is a mayhem museum. The oppression I felt outside is ten times greater now that I'm inside.

I swear I hear voices, screams, gunfire, sirens, even water falling from the ceiling. My clothes feel wet. I taste the acrid memory of blood and gunpowder. The looming shadow of Mason, replaying his merciless march forever, stops only when he runs out of bullets, and then restarts again, always with the same deadly result. It's a ghastly loop. This moment is locked in time, repeating over and over. And over.

I'm compelled to keep going.

I need to see the empty hallway, confirm that Sarah's body is gone.

I need to see the empty hallway, confirm that Mason isn't still shooting, pointing, blaming.

I need to see the empty hallway, confirm that I'm not still here, a corpse propped up against the lockers.

There are only six steps from the landing to the entrance to the Senior Hallway. My legs are heavy. Sweat pours down my face. I take my sunglasses off and wipe my forehead with the sleeve of my blazer.

I'm walking in Mason's footsteps like a macabre reenactment.

("Last four, motherfucker!!" Mason is screaming, wicked wild eyes, putting the rifle to his shoulder)

The hallway is a mineshaft, horrifically elongated, a terrifying amusement park funhouse. I'm stunned that there aren't any bodies. I strain my eyes, blink, make sure that I'm not overlooking the evidence. Mason isn't here. Sarah isn't here. I'm here, but not lying in a crumpled heap next to Locker 316.

I'm here now, two thousand seven hundred and eighty days older, still trapped and dying.

Hot tears are falling. There are tape outlines on the ground noting where young lives ended.

My heart is pouring out in the only way that the inexpressible can be expressed.

This is a waking nightmare. My cries echo back at me.

I'm steps away from where Sarah's life was taken. I try to yell again, but the words are trapped inside me, a silent, a one-man funeral procession, a single pallbearer, carrying the perfect memory of what happened to an undug gravesite. This was a terrible idea. It's even worse than inviting Mason Reynolds on my radio show; at least then I had the protection of distance and theatricality. But here, I've wandered back into the shooting gallery alone, unprepared for this onslaught of remembrance. I thought I could do it. I'm punishing myself by being here, with no one to hear my confession or acknowledge my regret. My visit only bears witness to the idea that the guilty return to the scene of their crimes.

I'm standing in front of Locker 316.

There are two perfectly round holes punched through the metal. Blood is still visible, spattered and smeared on the lockers next to mine. None of my stuff remains inside. Someone cleared everything out.

"That's my blood." I'm in awe. "That. Is. My. Blood." Seven years, seven months, and nine days ago, it exploded from my body in a spray, and drained out of me onto the tile floor. I'm in the exact spot where Sarah lost her life and I lost everything else. I reverently touch my blood, my resurrection.

(*"Your fucking boyfriend, you stupid bitch..."*)

I take a step closer to where Sarah fell. My knees wobble. My head pounds with tension. I hold back vomit, but I have to bend over to do it. I stumble forward, trying to stop myself, but can't catch my breath. Am I having a heart attack? They never cleaned up the crime scene? I can't be awake. Right?

"End it already! It's overdue. I'm ready. I've been ready! I miss her. Take me! Kill ME!"

I collapse to the floor and contort my body to fit inside the tape outline of Sarah's body. It's the only thing I have left. It's the last tangible trace that she was ever here.

It's the only way I can ever be inside her again.

As I lay in her place I beg and plead for the past to be rewritten.

That's when I see it, on the floor, a few feet from my face.

A thin gold chain, a heart pendant, made to look broken, half of the words "Best Friends Forever" etched so I can still tell what it says, even without Kelly's half. I reach for it, extending my arm, straining my fingers, desperate to reclaim this relic of lost love. Can I touch it, pick it up, secure it? Is it real?

"End it! It's overdue. I'm ready. I've been ready! I miss her."

The hallway dissolves into a pinprick of light. Then nothing. Blackness. A silent empty. I try to imagine that I'm dying her death, in the same spot, in the same manner, in her place. I want to rest.

Is this a dream? Am I waking up? Am I'm passing out? Is this real? Does it matter? I let go.

CHAPTER 23

I was discarded in a barren field, surrounded by charred trees and grey ash. Gagging.

Everything else had burned down to the ground. Desolation.

Stripped naked, I was smothered in a grimy filth, a burning irritant in sensitive, sweaty crevices.

Heat came from above and below, a scorching furnace that cooked life from my flesh.

The sky was streaking smoke, blurred and silver at the horizon, rushing upward and away from me. Bleach and ammonia stung my eyes. Vultures circled. Hundreds of them. A roar of shrieks.

I was petrified.

And I couldn't breathe.

Someone had wrapped my face—my entire head—in plastic and stuffed my mouth with a gasoline-soaked rag. I sucked in bitter smoke, desperate to fill my lungs, no matter how polluted and poisoned it was. The plastic fogged with droplets of smothered respiration. I strained and gasped. I felt the blood vessels in my eyes burst. Voices, an unseen crowd, considered my state and judging me as I suffered.

I screamed soundlessly. Panic erupted as I suffocated. My lungs broiled inside my chest, my throat cracked open. I tried to reach for my face, desperate to claw the plastic away, but couldn't move.

Dozens of waxy yellow tapeworms and black leeches had chewed into the veins in my forearms. They gnawed, draining my body and regurgitating venom into my bloodstream, heaving and sucking and bulging as they sated themselves. Several of the tapeworms slithered across my bare chest and under the plastic, burrowing into each nostril and into my sinuses. I tasted their meaty invasion in the back of my throat. Leeches fed at my festering groin. Their razorblade teeth burned like an infected animal bite, a constant ache that stabbed with sharp agony when I tried to shake them off.

The vultures grew bolder, still circling, but closer now than they were when I first noticed them.

I swiveled my neck to see that I was flopped across a massive dirt mound, discarded like trash, horrified to see hundreds of thousands of fire ants swarming from the earth, red and angry, biting and stinging.

Two diseased bullet wounds appeared. One in my chest, the other in my stomach, each a gangrenous bloody-black scab. Biting flies swarmed above me, a diseased cloud of parasites, feasting. They were the size of handgun bullets, plunking against the plastic over my eyes, smelling the blood that ran freely down my cheeks, into my ears, pooling under the back of my head. Some of them laid hard red eggs in my infected flesh. Fistfuls of mealy maggots uncoiled and began eating into my body. They squealed their delight incessantly, a thousand high-pitched, wordless, childlike voices in my torso.

In all directions, far off in the distance, was a ring of fire that cast a blinding orange hue against the gun-smoke gray-blue sky. I heard it, a hot roar, a raging inferno, a thousand miles away, hundreds of feet high. It was consuming everything in its path, moving toward me on all sides. I saw no one, no saviors.

A hot wind scattered the biting flies.

The vultures had waited long enough. They were descending.

As they drew nearer, I could tell they weren't birds.

They were demonic shadows with human eyes and gnashing mouths filled with raging accusations. Grotesque leathery wings kicked up clouds of ash. They had tiny hands and twitchy fingers with ragged fingernails, torn and bloody as though they'd scraped their way out of a grave. Each demon had hundreds of names tattooed on its torso, but mine was the only one branded on all of them.

JEREMY PEOPLES.

The swarm buried me, scratching me with their baby hands and broken talons, breathing their hot breath on me, a stench like dead animals and fermented manure, ammonia and carrion. I thrashed against them but there was no escape. Hundreds of them clawed and screeched the ugliest half-truths they could muster. They crushed me into a crater of condemnation. Their bloodshot eyes took turns staring into mine, as they roiled and battled for position, a pile of leathery wings and moist breath on my skin. Pinpricks and blisters rose where they touched me, spreading like a fiery rash across my entire body.

SOMEBODY. ANYBODY. SAVE ME FROM THIS. LIVING. NIGHTMARE.

My heart throbbed in my chest.

My brain memorized every violation.

For a moment they fell silent, a pause for the briefest taste of hope, and then one by one, dozens, hundreds, thousands, all of them, began repeating something hauntingly familiar and terrible.

"LOOK WHAT YOU MADE ME DO!"

It was a cacophony of blame, Mason Reynolds' words, his voice even, pouring from the snapping mouths of my tormentors. "LOOK WHAT YOU MADE ME DO!!" They were chanting, a rising stadium roar, impossible to distinguish one demented voice from another, until they again fell silent. I found myself unavoidably looking into the bloodshot eyes of the beast nearest to me, who hissed "LOOK WHAT YOU MADE ME DO!" and lunged at my throat, biting and gnashing, spit flecking across my face.

"JESUS CHRIST!" I finally found the strength to scream through the weight of the horde and the draining weakness of the worms and the stinging flies and the scabrous rash and infected debilitating wounds.

Bright light. White. Quiet.

I slowly opened my eyes.

Pain. My whole body was broken. It took my breath away.

There was a searing discomfort in my stomach. My chest felt like it was crushed in a vice.

Tubes in my arms. One in my nose. Lips dry and cracked. My tongue was stuck to the roof of my mouth.

I tried to ask for help. Nothing. I tried to turn my head. I couldn't. I was in a bed. Where was I?

Can't move.

I patted my legs with my fingers. My feet were tingly and heavy, like they'd fallen asleep.

Something was beeping. Faster.

Everything was fuzzy. Blurry. I couldn't focus my eyes for more than a few seconds at a time.

I had no idea what day it was, what time it was, where I was, how I'd gotten here, what had happened. Why can't I remember? I can always remember. I should be able to remember. I need to remember.

"Jeremy," a kind voice said, speaking deliberately, pausing patiently between sentences. "Can you hear me? You were on life support. We intubated you. Do you understand? It's OK to nod if you can't talk yet."

I understood. It registered with me what I should do. It took ten seconds. I nodded slightly and immediately felt a wave of exhaustion roll over me. Who was I talking to? Where are they?

"Good, good. Excellent. Can you feel your fingers and toes? Nod if you can."

I did. There was a conversation. I realized there was more than one person standing near me.

The white light in the room made it impossible for me to see faces, only shapes. My eyes burned.

"Jeremy, do you know where you are?" the voice asked. It was a woman's voice.

"Uh-uh," I tried to say, but it was more of an exhale than an admission of confusion.

"OK. That's OK. You're at St. Sebastian's Hospital in Madison. I'm your doctor, Doctor Benedict. You've been here for several days now, Jeremy. There's a lot of people who've been worried about you. Do you have any recollection of the last week...of why you're in the hospital?" Her voice had a soft confidence that coaxed me into trying harder to remember.

Why was I in the hospital?

Did she say for the past week?

What had happened to me?

Did I fall? Did I get hurt on the farm? Was there a car accident?

I could not recall why I was here. I slowly shook my head as anxiety rose in my chest. I winced.

"That's fine, it's fine. Relax. You've been in a coma, and then sedated. It's looked like you've been coming around for the past four or five hours. Your family is here to see you. Do you want to see your mom and dad, Jeremy? We called them when you started to wake up. They're just outside in the hallway."

I shook my head. "No," I whispered.

"No?" Dr. Benedict asked, confused. "Are you sure that's what you mean? Mom and dad, Jeremy?"

"No," I said again, pushing against my burning throat, fat tongue, and chapped lips. "Sarah." Silence. "Is Sarah here?" It was almost impossible to speak, I was so weak. It took everything out of me. "Can she come in?" The room was too bright. I couldn't see Dr. Benedict, just her outline, a white coat, featureless face, her voice coming from somewhere above me, calm and careful, insistent and mindful.

"Jeremy, I need you to try and remember why you're here," Dr. Benedict persisted.

My body reacted before I understood why I felt the way I did. Sudden, spiraling despondency. Terror. What had I done? Why isn't Sarah here to see me? Is she OK? Why can't I remember anything?

"I...can't...think," I croaked. I pushed myself to search out the answer from within. "What...did...I...do?"

"Jeremy—" the voice began, but I lifted the fingers on my right hand off the sheets and she stopped.

My memory wasn't going to protect me. It had every detail. It was just waiting.

And then it started to come.

Teal and black.

Prom. Lights and streamers and Sarah's breath in my ear.

Nothing Else Matters.

I will love you forever.

I closed my eyes again and relaxed. Sarah and I had gone to prom. The night had been amazing.

A bonfire.

What was I doing? Sarah was yelling at me, crying, people were staring. Humiliation. Anger.

Who was there? Derrick. Aaron. Sarah. Others. My math book. Why did that matter?

Skip Day. Driving. Derrick and Aaron in my car. They were pissed. I pulled up in front of the school and went in. I needed to go to school on Skip Day to see Sarah. Something happened between us.

Mason.

Mason Reynolds.

Oh my God. OH. MY. GOD.

He had a gun. He shot me. Twice. Did I die?

Mason Reynolds shot me. At school. I heard his voice. "LOOK WHAT YOU MADE ME DO!!"

I had almost set him on fire. I had stripped him naked. I burned his clothes. I left him alone in a field in the middle of nowhere. I beat him up. I laughed in his face and ridiculed him in front of everyone. Events unfolded out of order, but I knew they were true and not a dream, not my imagination.

"Sarah," *I said, my voice stronger.*

"Jeremy," *Dr. Benedict said firmly,* "I think you should let your mom and dad come in now." *I blinked, my eyes full of tears, and as they adjusted to the fluorescent lights in my room, I got a sense of my surroundings. I was hooked up to several machines, IV bags inserted into my veins. Dr. Benedict consulted with a nurse, who appeared bedside with a plastic cup and spoon to put ice chips to my lips.*

It soothed my throat and loosened my tongue. "I want Sarah. Not my dad," *I whispered hoarsely, but Dr. Benedict had already ushered my mother and father into the room.*

I slammed my eyes shut and flailed at the nurse's hand, sending the cupful of ice chips clattering to the floor. "Boy," *my dad said.* "You need to settle down and listen to your doctor. Look at me."

I refused. "What happened? Dr. Benedict, did someone shoot me?"

There was a long pause, long enough that I almost opened my eyes to see if I was alone. "Yes, Jeremy. You were shot two times. Once in your stomach and once in your chest. It's a medical miracle you're still with us."

There was discussion between my parents and Dr. Benedict, and then my dad spoke again.

"Just tell him everything. Jesus Christ, he's eighteen. He's a man. He can take it."

Someone sighed. Dr. Benedict continued. "Mason Reynolds shot you and several other students and teachers, Jeremy. The first shot hit you in the stomach and somehow missed your kidney and spine. The second bullet went through your chest, collapsed your lung and broke several ribs but fortunately missed your heart. You've had two separate surgeries, but I'm fairly confident you'll make a full recovery. It's going to be a long road back, lots of physical therapy, and at least one more surgery, but you are a very, very lucky young man. If either shot had been a few centimeters in any direction, you might not be here."

I kept my eyes closed. "Where...is...Sarah? Why won't anyone tell me...is she's OK?"

I heard my dad again. "He needs to know."

Then my mom. "He just woke up. It's too soon."

Dr. Benedict. "I agree with Mrs. Peoples, respectfully, sir, this is still a very delicate time for his recovery."

My dad again. "Oh for Christ's sake. Jeremy. Jeremy, open your eyes and look at me. I mean it. You can do it. Open your eyes. You need to hear this from your family, and not from some doctor or on the news."

I looked into the face of my father, Stanley Peoples.

He was a few inches taller than me, and we shared the same hair color. He needed a haircut, with sweaty flips of black hair sticking out of each side of his mesh John Deere ballcap. My dad's beer gut pressed tight against a stained but clean, white t-shirt, and hung over the belt of his Wrangler jeans. His eyes were dark and unforgiving. He didn't look concerned. Or relieved. Dad looked as he always looked.

Angry.

He was cleanshaven, of the belief that every day started with a shit, shower, and shave. The only one of four brothers raised in a military family that wasn't a veteran, he had still retained all of my grandfather's severity and routines. My dad's fingernails were dirty, engine grease embedded under them, knuckles scarred and forearms veiny. His flannel shirtsleeves were rolled up. Flecks of chewing tobacco speckled his crooked teeth. Dad wiped his nose with the back of his hand.

"Sarah's dead. The Reynolds boy killed her before he got to you."

The will to live left my body. A flood of images assaulted my senses.

Blood-soaked hair.

Open eyes, black, dead, staring.

A pleading voice, begging me to listen.

Water pouring from the ceiling. Sparks. The clock reading 7:53 a.m.

Her blue jeans—soaked and stained—had two tiny rips in the seat, at each back pocket.

Sarah was flopped forward on her stomach, head turned to the left, right cheek on the floor.

Her mouth was moving silently. Opening and closing. The words were lost to the afterlife.

She was dead. Sarah was dead.

CLICK. CLICK. CLICK. CLICK. CLICK.

Mason sat on the floor next to me with an empty rifle to watch me die, too.

Why hadn't anyone saved her?

Why was I alive and not Sarah?

Rage and anguish roiled inside of me until it couldn't be contained and it poured out of me, and my dad and the nurse were suddenly both holding my arms down to keep me from getting out of bed.

"Why? WHY?!" I sobbed and begged and slobbered. "I want to see her! I need to see her!!"

"This is why I thought it best to wait," Dr. Benedict admonished my dad. I knew he didn't give a damn.

"You can't see her, boy. She's gone. You need to stop fighting or you'll pull out all your stitches and the IV. I mean it. Stop fighting. Can someone give him some kind of drugs or something?" my dad shouted.

"Stanley, he just woke up!" my mom cried out.

"Why can't I see her? I want to see her face! I want to see her body! She's not dead, she's not, she's got to be OK, she can't be dead I love her and we were going to live in Madison together she can't be she can't be I want to see her I don't care what she looks like bring her in here!!" I ran out of strength.

Two more nurses burst into the room.

I'd pulled out my IV and knocked it over in the commotion. Shoes squeaked on the wet floor. There was an announcement over the PA. Dr. Benedict kept repeating, "Sir. Sir, please. Sir."

"You can't see her, Jeremy." My dad elevated his voice over everyone else's in the room.

Tears streamed down my face. Why was this happening? How could this be true?

"He needs to know. Get it over with all at once, then he can get on with getting right again. He's a man, he can take it. It can't get dragged out and on and on." Stanley Peoples, my father, pointed at me without a shred of empathy and barked, "Her funeral was two days ago. You can't see her. She's gone, boy. Dead. Nothing you do right now can change anything about how things are."

I had missed her funeral, too?

She died in the hallway, without me.

She was buried alone, without me?

She's in the ground, she's worm food, alone, without me?

Lying in bed, devastated, I began to believe that there was nothing terrible left to be done to me. I had nothing to lose. Everything important to me was gone. No one could hurt me any worse than I'd already been hurt. My last chance to see Sarah was stolen from me, and even now my dad intimidated me into being quiet, to accept it instantly, to behave, to obey, to listen to him or else. To do it his way. I hated it. I didn't want to lie quietly and suffer.

Sarah said she would help me, and now she couldn't.

I wanted all the pain to stop.

Everything had been taken away from me. Everything. And I wanted to take something back.

I wanted revenge for my fear and despair. I wanted to torment someone else with that feeling.

I lashed out at my dad. He deserved it. "I'll tell everyone," I whispered. "I'll tell them what you did."

He stepped back from the bed, startled. "I don't, I don't know...what are you talking about?"

One of the nurses looked at me, then at my dad, and Dr. Benedict asked, "What does he mean?"

"Dad," I said, suddenly calm. He seemed to shrink in stature and importance. "Take Mom and go. Don't ever come back." It took all of my remaining strength and courage to confront him.

Dr. Benedict was close enough to hear me and tried to intervene. "It's OK, Jeremy, you don't have to—"

I ignored her. "Leave," I told my dad. "Go." I couldn't see my mother. Had she left the room?

No one moved. I shifted my eyes from Dr. Benedict to the nurses and back to my dad. Everyone stared at me. Dr. Benedict was perplexed and seemed to be considering what to do. The nurses had frozen in place. My dad was pale. I wanted to infect him with my fear, punish him with my wrath, I wanted him to feel defenseless to stop it. I was strangely empowered by the loss of everything else. He was disarmed.

"I hate you," I told my dad. "Don't come back here again! Leave me alone and don't ever EVER come back again. I swear to God I don't ever want to see you again. Stay away from me!"

My dad. Smaller still. A small man. Vanishing forever. Still oblivious to his public defeat.

"You can't make us go," he tried. "Boy, I know you been through a lot, but I'm still your father! You don't use that kind of language with me, I don't care what all is going on, you need to respect me—"

"I want him to leave," I told Dr. Benedict. "Make him leave. Make them go. Don't let them see me."

"Jeremy," Dr. Benedict said firmly. "Please. I want to help you. Tell us what? Try to breathe."

"You shouldn't have let them bury her without me!" I was crying. "You should have waited. You can't tell me how to feel you can't tell me how to act you can't tell me to be calm and not be upset! You can't make me do what you want me to do anymore there's nothing left I don't care about anything else anymore you're my dad you should've looked out for me you should've let me see her!"

Dr. Benedict grew stern, but not with me. She looked at my father and took my side. "Mr. Peoples, you and Mrs. Peoples really need to leave, please, we may need to sedate him again—"

Dad interrupted her. "We're leaving." His voice was shaking. He looked afraid. I felt victorious.

I laughed, weakly. "That's right. GO!"

But the despair returned almost instantly.

"Don't come back. I can take care of myself. Just leave me alone. Dr. Benedict, please don't let them come back in here please just make them stay away please can someone take me to Sarah's funeral so I can see her one more

time she said she forgave me so this can't be what happened I was going to fix everything but I'm not a fucking pussy I got shot twice and I lived and I don't want my dad around me anymore please just keep them away from me and take me to her just take me to her please..."

CHAPTER 24

"Hey, Wafer, it's Jeremy. I'm not going to be back for the show tomorrow. I'm in Madison..."

I'm in my room at the Mansion Hill Inn, a few blocks from the State Capitol. It had been nearly impossible to pull myself out of the emotional darkness after my visit to Sugar River High School and the gripping memories that flooded back over me while I laid in the dirt and dried blood. I recall the drive to Madison—vaguely—and I'm amazed that I didn't wreck my car or get pulled over and arrested, and somehow checked into this hotel while high and emotionally devastated.

It's Wafer's machine and I'm leaving a message, thankful that I won't have to talk to him.

Suddenly, there's clatter and feedback and I instinctively pull the phone away from my ear. Wafer is apparently wrestling with his phone cord and pressing buttons, trying to turn his answering machine off and pick up the phone to talk to me. I feel my exhaustion shift to an edgy irritation.

It's 7:13 p.m.

Wait. No. It's 8:13 in DC.

Sunday, January 2, 2000, never ends.

"Hey. Jeremy. Dude. Hang on. Don't hang up." Wafer stopped the tape, which stops the feedback, and is clearing his throat. His voice sounds tired, like I just woke him up. It's not entirely out of the ordinary, considering he's been on a night schedule producing my show for the past several months.

"Did I wake you up? I can call back tomorrow or whatever." I want to ask him if Sammie is there, but I choose to respect his privacy. For now. Wafer's inability to get his phone untangled pisses me off. I just wanted to leave a fucking message, and I'm already feeling anxious and disoriented.

"No, it's cool. It's cool. What's up, man? Did you say Madison? Like, Wisconsin? When are you coming back? I left a message on your machine. Your cellphone just rings. Is everything OK?"

Everything is *not* OK. I wonder if I should tell him anything. Or everything. Or nothing.

"I left my phone in my apartment. I'm at a hotel."

"Dude, you forgot your phone? That sucks. You good? You fly out there? You flying home tonight?"

"I'm good. Look. A lot of shit has happened since the show on Friday. I drove here. Met some new demons and spent time with some old enemies. I think I passed out in my old high school, but I'm not sure if what happened before that was a dream or real. I think it was real because I'm dirty. The cardinal at the park was definitely trying to tell me something, but I don't know what. And I met Wendy from *Peter Pan*. She's the biggest fan of Christmas I've ever met, so I gave her all my money. So, yeah, I went home but I still haven't opened the letter and for whatever reason her obituary isn't in the paper. I'm not gonna see my folks, but I am going to see my son. And then the funeral. But Syd told me not to come back." Everything I tell Wafer seems vital in order for him to understand what I'm going to tell him next, but it's coming out jumbled and confused.

I start to say something else, and Wafer finally interrupts me. "Your son? Jeremy, I don't understand what you're talking about. Who's Syd? You're not making any sense."

"I don't think I'm coming back to DC. I think I'm gonna quit the radio show." Saying it feels right.

There's a pause. "What the fuck are you talking about, man? You're quitting? Now?" Wafer is understandably upset, almost groveling. "Jeremy. We're on the verge of something big here, man."

"I know. I'm just...I'm all fucked up. It feels wrong. Like, this isn't what I want to do anymore. I don't think I ever wanted to do this and I can't come back to DC. I can't keep from doing shit I shouldn't do."

Wafer stumbles over his words, trying to keep up. "What do you mean, you *can't* come back to DC? What happened? I thought you were just leaving for that funeral. You're just...leaving? Why?"

I don't like getting pushed into explaining myself. I'm abruptly uneasy. "The show with Mason wasn't about getting publicity and ratings. I needed something from that show that I didn't get."

"What?" Wafer asks.

"I needed Mason to let me take the blame for the Sugar River Shooting so I can get off this cycle, this downward spiral. But he didn't. And then he got in my head with all that shit he was saying. And now I need to get away from some people I'm tangled up with. If I'm there, I won't stop. They know it. I can't stay away and I need to get straightened out, but I can't do it there. I need distance or I'll just keep going back again and again and I think they're going to fuck my whole life up and I'll let them."

"Sammie and I talked about it, dude." Wafer cares about the show, but I believe he cares about me, too. "Why don't you go into rehab or, like, intensive therapy for a while? Get sober or clean or whatever, take some time off, and then come back fresh and we can build on what happened on New Year's Eve?"

I sit up.

"You're not hearing me. I'm not coming back. For a while. Or Ever. My life is a fucking mess and I can't keep it up, I'm not even thinking about all the shit I need to be thinking about to take the show to New York. I can't. The details. It's all too big for me right now—"

Wafer cuts me off, arguing gently. Reassuring. "You've been through the ringer, bro. That Mason interview was brutal to listen to. I don't think anyone can understand what it was like to admit to all of that. And the call from that dude and his wife dying. But just take some time, get your shit together, get clean, get help, come back, slow it all down, and we'll take it to New York, or go for syndication, when you think you can handle it. Let me do more. Let your agent do more. You don't have to do all of it. We want to help you, man. You're not responsible for that shooting. You're not."

I'm suddenly filled with rage.

"Look. You want to fucking help me? You want to use me to make your name in the industry? If you wanted to help me, you'd stop pushing me to do this when I don't want to." I hate being told what to do. It's like I'm in a corner, being punished for my preferences and ordered around, people forcing me to violate my internal boundaries so they feel better about themselves and get what they want.

Right then I decide, no matter what happens while I'm in Wisconsin, I absolutely will never go back to DC ever again. Fuck my job, my condo, the Floyd Chicks, all of it. I'd been indecisive before, giving myself an out, qualifying what I told Wafer, couching my revelation with "maybe" and "for a while" and "right now." Stubborn resolve stiffens in my jaw and neck. I'm leaving because I want to leave, not because Syd told me to. It's my life to fix on my terms. And no one can convince me to come back.

"I'm not the enemy, bro. I'm just trying to figure out what the fuck is going on, and it's my career, too. It's my job on the line, too. You go, I'm probably out. Or I'm on with some new asshole that I don't even like. And Sammie, too. We like working with you, bro. I'm just saying it doesn't have to be all or nothing. You can get help. We can keep doing the show. We can go to New York when you're better."

I stand up.

Seething anger is a coiled snake, striking now with speed and ferocity, fangs and venom.

"Goddamn it, you fucking selfish asshole! I DON'T WANT TO GO TO FUCKING NEW YORK, WAFER! You work *for* me! You aren't shit *without* me. If we go to New York, it's *because* of me. If we don't go to New York, that's *my* decision. Nobody gives a fuck about you. You're nothing. It's over because I say it's over. I can blow this whole thing up whenever I want to because *I am the goddamn show*."

I'm pacing the room, twisting the phone cord into a tangle of knots as I lash it back and forth from out in front of my feet. Wafer is quiet. I'm out of breath, furious, gripping the receiver with white knuckles and panting. I want to fight. I provoke him further. "Nothing to say? Does the fucking truth hurt? I call to tell you I'm cratering and all you want to talk about is *your* career?"

Wafer doesn't fight back. He apologizes. "I'm sorry, Jeremy. You need to do whatever you need to do to get better, to get right. The show doesn't mean anything if you're not healthy, or worse." Wafer's empathy, kindness, and understanding fills me with shame. Self-hatred. He's a better person than me.

I still can't wind down the rage. "And you're just gonna back down like that? You fucking pussy." Those words aren't my words, but it's my voice, from my heart, filled with my anger, and my inability to let someone be my friend. Wafer is a decent person and acts accordingly. My awareness of the stark differences between us, and the disconnect between my intentions and my words and deeds, stops me.

Wafer finally speaks. "OK, man. Whatever." He's indignant, but doesn't sound nearly as bitter and offended as he has a right to be.

I want him to fight back. So I can hit him again and again. And again. FIGHT. BACK.

I want him to tell me to stop. Beg me to stop. Beg for forgiveness so the punishment stops.

Even though he hasn't done anything wrong. FIGHT. BACK.

Just hit back so I have the fucking justification I need to let my hatred and humiliation punish you.

FIGHT. BACK.

You fucking liar. You don't *care* about me. You need me, but you don't even like me.

You can't control what I do anymore. You can't hurt me. You can't make me hurt myself. I can stop it.

I can stop it?

Jesus Christ. I'm not just being an asshole. I'm treating Wafer like I treated Mason. Mason wasn't the monster. *I'm* the monster. I should stop. There's no one here to stop me this time. Sarah's gone. There's no one to save me from myself. Michelle's gone. It takes me a second to process that realization. History is repeating itself; I'm in a circular loop of action and reaction, lashing out with viciously unwarranted, irrational responses, even while I'm desperate for absolution for past sins. I haven't learned any real lessons that lead to change or true remorse.

"Wafer, I'm…I'm sorry. I have got too much shit hitting all at the same time." I can't apologize without making excuses. I want to justify the unjustifiable. An unequivocal apology sticks in my throat.

He doesn't respond.

"Did you get cut off? Are you still there?"

"Yeah. I'm here. I'm deciding whether or not I want to accept your bullshit apology."

Wafer's blunt answer puts me further on the defensive. I'm still disgracefully seething, but I'm also wary of myself, fully self-aware and indecisive about my tone of voice and what I should or shouldn't say.

"I deserve that." Rarely cautious with my words, I'm now self-conscious. "I mean it though. I'm sorry."

I wonder if I'd only apologized to Mason Reynolds, and helped him, would Sarah still be alive? Would I be on a path to healing from other things, instead of tortured by memory and the consequences of my sins, and my pride, and my hardness of heart?

"You've got a real problem with basic human decency. Like, you're two totally different people. Sometimes you're cool, but most of the time you're a fucking dick. And you can get away with that shit because you're legitimately talented. But I don't want to put up with it anymore. Honest to God, I believe you when you say you're all fucked up, but how much of that is your own fault? And none of what you're going through gives you the right to be a dick to people all the goddamn time."

I grit my teeth to keep my mouth shut. Wafer's right, but everything in me wants to counterpunch. The fact that what he's saying is cuttingly accurate is precisely what's making me defensive.

Because it's the truth.

Possibly feeling as though he has nothing to lose and emboldened by the eight hundred and fifty miles between us, Wafer continues to stand up for himself. "If you want to blow up your career and your life, no one can stop you. Hell, Jeremy, no one can ever talk you out of anything once you make up your mind. But you could at least pretend like you give a shit about how this fucks me and Sammie up. We thought we were on our way, man. Like, a team. Yeah, dysfunctional, but still. A team. We built this thing, man. Your ratings are killer and that's all of us. A major market deal or syndication? That us, too. Not just you."

Somewhere along the way, my self-preservation had warped into selfishness. I was so concerned with making things right in my past I'd continued to make things wrong in my present.

"Yeah man, I know," is the best I can do. I want to apologize again, but I don't. I want to tell Wafer that he's right, but I don't. "You've done a great job. You and Sammie both. You'll be alright. The radio station will keep you. Both of you. They know what you know. You're valuable."

Wafer softens. "Come on, man. Don't quit. We're so close. *We can still do this.*"

This time, his desperate attempt at convincing me doesn't make me angry. It stings. Tears start to come again. My emotions are so close to the surface; there's too much unresolved instability and confusion.

I don't want to say it again, but I do it anyway.

"None of it matters to me after New Year's, Wafer. I don't think it ever really mattered to me for the right reasons. I can see the success I could have, and it does nothing for me. I don't know what I want, but it isn't this anymore. I wasn't doing it for me, I was doing it for the people who talk to me in the night, in my mind, from my past, from everywhere and nowhere." There it is. "I'm sorry. I really am."

There's a long sigh across the phone line. Perhaps it's resignation, if not understanding. Wafer likely sees the futility of his persistence. He sounds disappointed, but relents. "It's OK, man."

I'm exhausted again. The effects of the heroin haven't worn off yet, but still my mind is racing. I either need to go to sleep—just a nap, maybe, before I go to Stacy's—or I need an upper. Wafer's still talking. "...I meant what I said. Get better. What do you want me to tell everyone?"

I need to get off the phone. I feel exactly like I do after a therapy session with Dr. Darby. Totally spent. The bed is inviting. I sit back down, lay back down. Rage has left my body. I'm deflated. One last thing.

Tears are draining from my eyes, one after another, streaking down my temples and dripping on the blanket. I screw my eyes shut to stem the sorrows. My nose is running. I clear my throat. "Just tell the Suits I'm not doing the show tomorrow. Fuck it, I don't care what you tell them. Lie, tell them about this call, whatever you want. It doesn't matter. Tell them I'm not sure if I'll ever be back, like Syd told me. So, thanks. Don't look for me. I don't know where I'll be. I'm really fucking sorry, Wafer."

"Who's Syd? Wait, Jeremy—"

Wafer is still protesting as I hang up.

CHAPTER 25

Michelle's and my only night together lasted until January 28, 1996, Super Bowl Sunday, when our recklessness caught up with us. It wasn't that we were together often. We would, with varying degrees of success, try to resist temptation. Sometimes, in sober-minded moments, we'd agree that it had to be the last time, for our own good, for the good of the business, for the greater good, because we were afraid Stacy would find out, or felt guilty that he hadn't; whatever our reasons, it just had to stop. Then, within a day or two, we'd relapse and fall into another careless, passionate moment. People get hooked on risky behavior; we were addicts. The adrenaline of speculating if anyone might suspect what was happening between us, the thrill of sex in less-than-discrete locations, and the distraction from our mutual loneliness spun an inescapable entanglement. We had become so connected I couldn't imagine what I'd do without her in my life, but I couldn't see our future together, either.

We were snarled together, a mess. It was completely self-destructive. And wonderful.

We had all the behaviors of a couple at the start of a passionate partnership. The symptoms of our relationship could even be mistaken for love. I made her laugh. Our chemistry was undeniable, but the circumstances were toxic to any hopes of anything real and healthy. Michelle and I were sleeping with each other behind Stacy's back, selling drugs in a small town, while all three of us lived together.

Every day we didn't end the affair was a day closer to an evitable, predictable disaster.

But it was also the first time I'd felt alive in years and I held on tight. The memory of Sarah still cast a long shadow, but it wasn't as dark and all-consuming. I had hope again. And moments of happiness.

Michelle was much less content. She'd escaped loneliness, found release, and seemed more vibrant, but had weighted herself down with guilt. She shared how she was violating her conscience, living out a physical and emotional fantasy—sometimes she called it a lie—that satisfied only one small portion of a greater, holistic need. She struggled with the shame of what she was secretly doing to her husband. Michelle told me she wouldn't leave Stacy, she just wanted him to change some things, but as time went on her feelings for me had deepened. Her introspection turned into self-loathing. We fought. I'd brood, she'd analyze and worry, I'd try to talk, she'd withdraw, and then we'd switch roles and start over.

Disgusted with herself, Michelle always returned to me.

I was constantly afraid of getting caught, but was so thoroughly enamored with Michelle that I barely felt the same deep guilt that she did. I was well acquainted with the demon of self-hatred and would try with sporadic success to coax Michelle out into the open when she'd descend into silence. At the same time, the intensity and happiness I experienced when we were together had a side effect: when I made Michelle happy, I felt less shame over Sarah's death. I was finally healing. The present was so positive, giving me something to look forward to each time I thought of Michelle, that the past—when it presented itself uninvited, as it always had—was becoming manageable. The horrors and regret would always be there, the love I promised to Sarah was still hers and hers alone. I had decided that as long as I never said those words to Michelle, I wasn't betraying Sarah's memory. I was on the verge of falling in love again, even if I would never allow myself to use those words. Almost in love was beautiful, exactly what I needed, right where I wanted to be with her. We were nearly together. It was perfect. For me.

I also had no misconceptions that things wouldn't end in tragedy, but I wanted to be with her and was willingly satisfied with whatever small, secret portions that time and opportunity afforded us. She was beautiful, daring, and brilliant, showing me that even if I wasn't healthy yet, I could catch tiny glimpses of how it would be when I finally was. I poured myself into her. I thought about her constantly.

Michelle made me feel a little better about myself. It was one of the things I adored about her the most.

I wanted to believe I brought out the best in her, but I also believed I was a temporary convenience.

Ironically, the end came on a day when we hadn't even slept together. I'd sold weed all day, getting high with our regular customers as they dropped by, and was staring into space listening to the Smashing Pumpkins double album "Mellon Collie and the Infinite Sadness" when Michelle got home. I barely flinched when she flung the door to the trailer open, still in her hospital scrubs, strode over to the stereo and punched the power button, cutting the song off. I started to object, but I was too stoned and she had a smile on her face. Work at the hospital hadn't been terrible.

"We gonna watch the Super Bowl?" Michelle asked playfully.

"Yeah. Even if the game sucks the commercials are funny. And I put a thousand dollars on the game so I have to watch. I didn't really care about the teams but now I do," I laughed. Michelle shook her head. She knew I didn't have a thousand dollars to put on the game. "I'm broke, so the football gods must smile on me, man."

"I'm not going to say anything, Jeremy. Not a single word about how that's really stupid and you shouldn't do it and I won't even ask how you found someone to take a bet when it's not like we live in Vegas or Atlantic City. But I won't get into any of that with you. I hope you win, for your sake."

I pointed my stubby cigarette at her. I was on my back, head propped up on a throw pillow, ashtray on my stomach, a room temperature can of Mountain Dew balanced on the edge of the end table. My red-rimmed eyes were barely open, my mouth dry and sticky as I replied sarcastically, "Yep. Thanks for keeping all of that to yourself and not bringing it up."

Was she going to get mad? No. She laughed.

"I talked to Stacy about an hour ago." It was understandably awkward when she mentioned his name, but not as weird as it should've been. "He's going to stay at the restaurant until after the game. The bar is slammed, and he thinks we can pull down another fifteen thousand dollars tonight. This is like a bonus Saturday night. I told him to stay and work. We need the money." She shrugged, her smile thin and tight. "Well, you do. Especially if your bet doesn't come through. In fact, now that I'm thinking about it, I can't remember a time you've ever won any money betting on anything."

"Is this you still talking about something you said we're not talking about?" I picked at her, but if Michelle was happy she'd leave something alone even though she wanted to fight about it. When she didn't take the bait, I changed the subject. "No one coming over, Stacy working, that sounds good."

Michelle was emphatic. "No. Nothing is happening today. We need to keep being careful."

I protested. "You don't even know what I was going to say!" I took a quick drag off my cigarette, poked it into the ashtray, rolled over on to my side, and put it on the floor. Michelle was smarter than me, a quicker wit, and usually got the better of me when we bantered. Especially when she was sober and I'd spent hours of the day getting stoned and was now silly, dulled and oblivious.

"What? What could you possibly plan to say that doesn't have anything to do with this?"

"I was going to say," I paused dramatically, "why don't we order a pizza and a two-liter? For the game?"

251

Michelle looked at me, hands on her hips, strawberry-blonde hair tousled, and said, "You lie. You. Lie." She could barely hide her smile behind a pretend scowl and twinkling eyes.

"I'm offended." She was in a better mood than I'd originally thought, just not in the type of mood I'd been hoping for. "I've had a deep, abiding desire...for...a piece...of pizza. All day. It's all I can think about. This passionate yearning for the companionship that comes from a two-liter bottle of Pepsi along with that pizza would only make for the perfect ending to a perfect day."

"You're such a smartass, Jer." Michelle giggled and relaxed, realizing that I wasn't going to sulk. I'd decided to be content hanging out and watching the Super Bowl. "I need to take a shower. I stink. Do I have time before the game?"

"You don't stink. I mean, you do, but it's a good stink. Like how sometimes a skunk smells bad, but it's so bad it's kinda good? That's you. You're not gross. You're like, a good stinky." I felt playful that night, too.

"Good stink? What the hell are you talking about, Jer? There's either good smells or bad smells, but not good, bad smells. Body odor and latex isn't a good perfume. Are you high?" Michelle giggled again.

"I am high," I admitted the obvious, "I'm totally fucking baked, but you know I'm right. Sometimes you just sniff your own arm pits because it's a good gross. Don't you ever do that? The B.O. is perfectly ripe, so you know you stink, but you can't stop from sticking your nose in there and smelling it?"

She wrinkled her nose and pretended to put a close pin on it. "Uh, no. You're being a weirdo today. So, like I said, I'm going to get unstinkified, much to your personal chagrin, you armpit sniffer, and then we'll watch the game. Don't go huffing garbage while I'm doing super disgusting stuff like using shampoo to wash my hair and soap to clean sweat and blood off me. OK? Can I trust you?"

I shrugged. She laughed again and padded down the hallway and out of sight.

Michelle had worked a double shift at St. Sebastian's Hospital the day before, and then stayed up most of the night sorting pills with me. She only slept a few hours and went back to the hospital for a Sunday shift when there were even fewer eyes than usual so she could score again. She had to be exhausted.

By the time we started watching the game, my insomnia was approaching sixty hours. Michelle sat cross-legged on the couch in a Queensrÿche "Operation: Mindcrime" T-shirt and a pair of cutoff blue jean shorts, despite the Wisconsin winter weather. The heater was cranked up, the fan ran constantly. I was in track pants and a t-shirt. We were lounging around the trailer, eating taco pizza. Comfortable. Relaxed.

The lack of sleep caught up to both of us at the same time.

There was 3:45 left in the third quarter, with Dallas leading Pittsburgh 20-7, when I scooted down to Michelle's end of the couch, stomach full of cheap pizza. I stretched out my legs, kicking them over the arm of the couch, flopped over on my side, and laid my head in her lap. Michelle didn't object, her eyes bloodshot and droopy. She stroked my unkempt hair, her other hand on my upper arm, and I reached up and clasped my hand over hers. I squeezed. Michelle squeezed. Neither of us wanted to let go.

I put my other hand between her legs, just above her knees. I was slipping off to sleep, finally, with Michelle rubbing my head and holding my hand, a blanket balled up around my feet. She kissed my cheek. I twisted my head so I could look up at her. She bent her face toward me again, this time kissing me softly on the lips.

"Jer," she said. Her expression was a mystery to me.

"What?" I asked.

She was quiet, and then said, "Never mind."

"Just say it," I pressed.

"No. Never mind. Watch and see if you win your bet."

For the first time—possibly for the first time in my life—everything seemed normal for me. This was how I thought life could be. It felt good, and safe, even if it was wrong.

I fell asleep for what couldn't have been more than a few minutes. I was dreaming.

It was one of the recurring dreams I still have about three times a week.

I'm trapped in Sugar River High School, but nothing terrible is happening. It's the first day of class, I'm lost, and the entire school is a mysterious labyrinth. Nothing leads me to where it should. I'm running desperately from one room to the next, down serpentine hallways, forgetting my locker combination, interrupting classes, barging through libraries, unsuccessfully trying to find the room I'm supposed to be in. I finally find the right class, but it's the wrong time to be in that class. Teachers yell. Students laugh. Time slips away. Somehow the entire school year is unfolding and I'm not turning in assignments and I'm sure I'm failing every class because I can't ever get my schedule right. Day after day, a time lapse, it's the same. Lockers whiz by, teen faces are a familiar blur, voices tell me to "try this door, takes those stairs, you're already tardy, stop running, you dropped your books, what teacher did you say you were looking for?" as I grow increasingly desperate, realizing I'm going to miss the entire school year if I don't figure out how to navigate this carnival funhouse version of Sugar River High School.

In my dream, I never find out where I'm supposed to be, and I never find out what the consequences are.

I woke up when the front door slammed shut. "What the fuck?!" *Stacy erupted, then froze and stared.*

Michelle and I both immediately scrambled off the couch, guilty with the secrets of the past nine weeks. Stacy had seen my hand between Michelle's knees. Stacy had seen her hand resting in my hair, my head in her lap. We'd both been asleep, holding hands. The time for hiding and pretending was over.

"Hey, bro," *I tried to stay calm.* "This isn't what you think it is. It's not what it looks like. It's not."

"Hey Jeremy, why don't you SHUT the FUCK up?" Stacy was bigger, taller, and stronger than me. He stood about 6'3" and weighed a solid two hundred and twenty-five lbs. He had a swath of wavy, dark brown hair that could only be brushed when it was wet. His piercing, crystal blue eyes were set back into angular features, pronounced cheekbones, a strong jawline, and ears that were slightly too big for his head. He didn't work out, but he'd mostly retained the physique he earned in the Marine Corps. Stacy wore horn-rimmed glasses and tight jeans, a remnant of the 1980s that he refused to abandon. His intense demeanor put people on edge, yet he could also unwind, laugh, and party without much prompting. Until today, he had been almost paternal with me, and assumed I was a badass because I'd survived the Sugar River Shooting.

He was wrong. I wasn't a badass.

But that may have been what held him at bay when he barged through the door. I was shocked that he hadn't already thrown me to the ground and stomped my face in. I tensed for it. Stacy was cemented in place, fists balled, eyes bulging, veins in his neck and forehead pulsing. He had turned bright red, punchy snorts of breath exhaling from his nostrils.

Stacy tossed a stack of cash into the chair next to the door, easily more than ten thousand dollars.

He turned to Michelle and his expression changed. Rage turned to devastation.

Michelle remained calm, standing silent with a look of compassion and sadness on her face. She never panicked, never once turned toward me, her gaze always on Stacy, striving to make eye contact.

Stacy turned and stalked down the hallway toward their bedroom. I heard him kick open the door.

I mouthed, "What the fuck is he doing?"

She whispered back, "I don't know. You need to get out of here. Run."

It was too late.

When Stacy returned to the living room, he had a revolver.

"Stacy, no. Don't do this. You'll destroy your life. Our lives." Michelle was wise, choosing the perfect words, ensuring he knew she loved him and cared about their marriage without defending or justifying.

The sight of the gun calmed me down immediately.

Stacy took three steps toward me and pointed his pistol at my forehead.

"If it's not what it looks like, then tell me what it is," he said. "Because what it looks like, to me, is you are comfortable enough with my wife to lay down in her lap when I'm not home." He glanced at Michelle, who remained tactically silent. I made the only decision I felt I could make in the moment.

I was honest. "I'm sorry, Stacy," I apologized. "I can't. I don't need to. You know."

Stacy pulled the hammer back on his .357 magnum and took a fourth step toward me. The barrel of the gun was an inch from my face. Relief came from deep within me.

Finally.

"Stacy," Michelle pleaded. "Please. Don't. This wasn't just him." The likelihood of de-escalation was possible with calculated honesty. Stacy glared. There were no tears, but tortured betrayal and chaotic, conflicted emotions were a lit fuse of instability.

"How could you do this to me?" Stacy asked. His hand never shook, arm extended, gun steady.

"I don't have a good answer. I made a mistake. I shouldn't have. I should've tried harder to fix things between us. They were my problems, not yours. I should've stopped myself when I knew where things were going with Jeremy in the house. I should've made him move out. I should've told you why. You and I should've went away. We still can. Figure this out. I can figure this out. We can make this work together, I want to fix this, but we can't if you shoot him. You can't come back from that, honey."

"Do you love him?"

Michelle shook her head no. I suspected the truth was more complicated, which is why she never spoke.

Stacy switched the gun from one hand to the other, resting his arm. His left hand didn't shake either.

"When did it start?

Michelle answered honestly before I could speak. "The night before Thanksgiving."

Stacy's face burned red again. He flinched. Blinked.

"How many fucking times between then and now?" He demanded.

"A few. I don't know exactly. Not many." Her first lie, but she sounded sincere.

He looked at me with accusing eyes. "You motherfucker. I brought you into my home, and you fucked me. I treated you like a fucking brother." My eyes never left his trigger finger, curled and twitching. "You're always running your smart-ass mouth," he continued. "Nothing to say to me now? Is that how it's gonna be? You don't have anything to say except you're sorry? You think you're some big fucking man, taking my money, staying at my house, sleeping with my wife!?"

There was no way out of it. Right then I knew that Stacy was going to shoot me in the face.

Every bit of survivor's guilt, born inside Sugar River High School, melted away. My heart rate slowed. I nearly smiled. The heat in my flushed face subsided. I wasn't afraid to die. I was ready. As the seconds slipped by, I wondered if I had wanted to get caught by someone with more balls than me, who would do what I'd wanted to do but couldn't. Had my subconscious sabotaged me, allowed me to fall asleep despite my insomnia, to let Stacy encounter us, to end it for me, finally?

Stacy drew closer, squinting behind his glasses, noticing something on my face.

I closed my eyes.

257

"Is that lipstick? On your face?" Stacy sneered. I still felt the tenderness of Michelle's lips.

It must be. I couldn't see. I nodded. My eyes were still closed.

The cold steel of the gun barrel pressed against the spot where Michelle had kissed me.

It was liberating. I knew it was time.

"I fucking trusted you!" he yelled.

"I know. I know. I know," I just kept repeating myself. I didn't know what to say. "It's OK if you do it."

He was confused. "It's OK if I do what? I'll do whatever the fuck I want."

"Stacy, please, no, please don't, please! He's not worth it," Michelle cried out.

I opened my eyes again and looked directly at him. Stacy was a man who'd set his course. He was going to kill me; I could see the conviction in his searing blue eyes. The artery in his neck pulsed, his heart thumping through his shirt. Stacy's mouth was twisted into a demented grimace, baring his teeth and clenching his jaw, squinting his eyes as though he was steeling himself for the recoil and spatter. The trailer seemed to shrink in the flickering shadows given off by the TV, the room closing in around us.

I eagerly expected the end at any second.

But it didn't come. Michelle spoke again.

"Can we just sit down and think about this? This doesn't have to go this way. It can go different."

I didn't want it to.

"Stacy." Michelle was firm in her tone. "Don't do this. You're giving him what he wants."

I flicked a look at her.

"Look at him. He wants you to shoot him. We may get away with it, but he is the only one who gets exactly what he wants if you pull the trigger. The

only way you can really hurt him is to let him live with himself." Michelle used my Sarah, Sugar River, my guilt, and the aftermath, and turned it against me. She'd found the right combination of ideas to give Stacy pause. Michelle was calculatingly strategic under duress. Perfectly calm.

Stacy hesitated. He looked confused.

"He wants to die," she revealed. Michelle was saving me.

I was furious.

"What are you talking about?" Stacy snapped at Michelle.

"He's in love with his dead girlfriend and thinks if he dies, they'll be together." Michelle was coldly laying out everything I had told her, my most intimate secrets and sadness, and was using it to keep me alive. If I acknowledged that she was telling the truth, he might let me live, to prolong my suffering. "He blames himself for the shooting at his school. He thinks it's his fault. Letting him live is torture."

It was right then that I knew Stacy wasn't going to shoot me after all. My death wish was the beast that could keep the peace. When people want to die, they're harder to kill. The murderer's power is usurped, they lose the control they demand, their satisfaction denied and their revenge tainted.

Stacy let his arm drop to his side, holding the revolver loosely.

Michelle was brilliant. It was infuriating.

I was torn about what I should do next. I envisioned screaming at Michelle, calling her a fucking bitch and lunging for her, causing Stacy to defend her and shoot me. I envisioned getting on my knees and begging for my life, hoping that Stacy would think I wanted to live despite what Michelle had said. I pictured confronting Stacy, attacking him, screaming accusations and trying to gain the upper hand just long enough for his military instincts to exert themselves. I thought of blurting out graphic descriptions of my time with his wife, wondering what I could say that would get him to fire that gun.

But I said nothing. I did nothing.

Stacy sat down on the couch, still holding the revolver. He put his head in his hands. I considered running for the door but couldn't move. Michelle looked at me, looked back at Stacy to make certain his head was still down, and mouthed "I'm so sorry" to me. I blushed with anger and frustration. Her eyes were filled with a tragic sadness, knowing she'd saved me against my will. She'd inflicted deep wounds doing the right thing; what she had said was true. Allowing me to live was a far greater punishment.

Michelle shoulders untensed, slightly. She exhaled, quietly. Her face relaxed, barely noticeable.

Stacy said nothing for seven minutes. I watched the clock. When Stacy shifted or looked at me or Michelle, a thrilling burst of stress hormones coursed through my body. He smacked himself on the side of the head with the butt of the pistol, two, three, four, five times. Michelle never took her eyes off of him, so that every time he looked at her she was making eye contact with him.

Stacy spoke, finally, to Michelle. "I came home early to surprise you. I thought we could go to a late dinner. I've been gone so much, we fucking killed it at the bar tonight, and I wanted to surprise you. Get a bottle of wine and a steak and you could get whatever you wanted, and we could just..." His voice trailed off. "Why'd you have to fuck everything up, Michelle? Why?"

It was then I thought Stacy had decided to kill Michelle.

"You won't like the answer, but I'll tell you," she said.

Michelle had remained impossibly calm. I knew it was due to her years of nursing experience; she had to be cool in high-stress environments, and life-or-death situations. She was remarkable under pressure.

"Jeremy was here, and you weren't, and I was lonely and stupid and made bad choices. I fucked up."

Stacy's face contorted as he recognized the truth. Michelle had found the exact right thing to say in the exact right way, and he came to conclusions that she wanted him to believe were his own.

It was a masterclass in crisis management. Or manipulation.

Stacy pointed at me. "I want you fucking gone," he snapped. "Tonight. No." He shook his head. "Now. Get the fuck out of here, or I swear to fucking God I'll kill you, man. If I see you again, if I hear about you again, if I run into you at the goddamn mall or a restaurant or on the fucking street, you're dead. None of my connections are open to you. You're dead to them, too. This money from tonight? Mine. You're buying yourself ten minutes of life with your share. Get whatever shit you can get…In fact, fuck that."

Stacy sprang from the couch. He pointed the gun at me again. "Stay right there."

He thundered down the hall to my bedroom and smashed open the door, springing the hinges. He flung open the back door of the trailer and began hurling everything I owned out into the snow-covered backyard. Clothes, music, all of it. Stacy manhandled the mattress and box spring out the door. Then my dresser. It flopped off the wooden stairs and splintered when it hit the ground. Blankets, sheets, mementos, all of it, strewn and piled up like a disorganized winter yard sale. I watched from down the hall as he maniacally dragged my few possessions out of his life. It all took less than five minutes and Stacy never set the gun down. Michelle stared at the floor the entire time, rubbing her arms as the chill from the open door gave her goose-bumps. She never looked at me; I could tell tears welled up in her eyes because she dabbed them away with the bottom of her t-shirt.

When he returned, Stacy's eyes were still wild, but the adrenaline-fueled eviction left him winded and sweaty. He again pointed the revolver at me. "Get the fuck out."

I thought Stacy still might shoot me in the back as I left. I didn't want to leave Michelle, but she'd proven she could take care of herself—and me—far better than I could.

I didn't know what to call what Michelle and I had exactly, but she was my best friend and I had lost her. I had spent hours a day with her, talking and making love and growing as close as any two people could.

I was heartbroken. The hatred I felt as Michelle told Stacy my secrets dissipated. I couldn't be angry with her. I wanted to tell her goodbye. Even stranger, I wanted to thank her.

Michelle made me care again.

I had been desperate to feel alive, willing to do anything, with a callous disregard for consequence. Remorse came on suddenly, as my next thoughts turned to what I had done to Stacy—what I'd done to our friendship—someone who had consistently helped me and looked out for me.

I was a fucking traitor.

I glanced at Michelle one last time; her strawberry-blonde hair was disheveled. She'd lit a cigarette. I'd never felt more distant from her than I did right then, only six feet away. Certain I'd never see her again, I trudged down the hall, through the open back door, and walked barefoot out into the snow.

CHAPTER 26

It's 3:16 a.m., because the alarm clock in this strange room tells me it is.

I'm not at home. This is a hotel. In Madison. I'm at The Mansion Hill Inn.

What day is it?

Is it Monday? Yeah, Monday. I must have fallen asleep after talking to Wafer. Why am I awake?

Wait. This isn't what I was wearing on Sunday? What the fuck did I do yesterday?

I sit up. I'm fully dressed under the blankets. My room is in a normal state of hotel disarray: open suitcase, clothes strewn, empty bottles on top of the minibar, the bathroom light is on but the door is closed. I look back into the darkness of my normally perfect memory, straining to recall any clues about what happened. Did I go anywhere? Why did I change clothes? How long have I been passed out?

I call the front desk. A woman answers. She tells me it's Tuesday. I quickly do the math from when I spoke to Wafer, until now. I passed out for almost twenty-nine hours. I lost an entire day?

It's fucking *Tuesday*?

Suddenly paranoid, I scramble out of bed and reach for the brown leather shaving bag in my suitcase and sort through how much of my drug stash remains. Everything that was there on Sunday night is still there now. I must have blacked out. I sniff myself. I've taken a shower. I don't remember that.

My intuition tells me I've been out of the room, but was I? It feels like something happened, aside from dropping into a catatonic state, taking a shower, cleaning out the minibar, and changing clothes. Hell, I'm even wearing socks and shoes, and my wallet is in my back pocket. I turn to the bathroom. Is someone in there, with the light on and the door closed? Did I pick up a woman? I have no recollection if I did.

I creep across the room and find the door unlocked. The bathroom is empty.

That's when I notice my hand. It's freshly bandaged. Where did I get a new dressing? The cuts twinge when I roll my wrist and try to stretch my fingers. I gingerly pat my eye with two fingers. It feels less swollen, and I think I can see out of it better. It's tender, but the stabbing pain is gone, replaced with a dull ache. I'm healing. My body must have just shut down on me.

I call the front desk again.

An older gentleman answers this time. "Front desk. Scheduling a wake-up call, Mr. Peoples? As I mentioned last night, room service ends promptly at 2 a.m. My apologies. How else might I assist you?"

"We spoke last night?" I probe.

"Yes, sir. You called to ask about food delivery, and nearby establishments that serve adult beverages, gentlemen's clubs, and a restock of your minibar. You also requested that someone check on the status of your vehicle, which I reminded you was valeted at our suggestion when you checked in on Sunday evening. We delivered a full complement of beverages soon after. I believe that's the full report."

I have no memory of this conversation.

"Did you see me leave yesterday? Did anyone come to my room?"

"Well, sir, I'm only the night desk manager, so I can only share with you the details of what has transpired since my arrival at approximately 8:00 p.m. last night. I can inform you that if you left, or someone visited you, it happened without my knowledge. Aside from the minibar restock at your specific and insistent request, you have a 'Do Not Disturb' notice on your door, and therefore we did not fully service your room at any point yesterday, according to the notes left behind by our cleaning crew. Are you in need of fresh towels, sir? Or another delivery to replenish your minibar?"

"I don't know. Maybe."

I must have blacked out, finished the minibar, and about six hours ago called the front desk, got ready to leave, drank some more, and then passed out again. I don't think I left the room. I hope I didn't. Jesus.

Why does this keep happening? I remember everything or I remember nothing. Forgetting is frightening. How do normal people do this with regularity?

"Will there be anything else, sir?" the Night Desk Manager politely presses.

"Yes. When the morning people arrive, can you have them call my room? Especially if they are the same people that were working yesterday. I need to talk to someone about Monday. Thank you."

"Absolutely, sir. I have one final question, if I may. When you checked in, you did so without specifying a check-out date. You'd left it open-ended, and while we requested that you provide a check-out date, you emphatically refused. It is not our general policy to…lease a room as though it were an apartment, especially an executive suite. You've left your credit card with us, and there are no concerns about the payment, but we will need an approximate check-out date as soon as you have solidified your ultimate travel plans. Just a reminder, sir, of that conversation we had on Sunday."

"When I know, you'll know. Thanks for the reminder," I say, and drop the phone on the hook with a clatter. My head is clear, but I'm hungover and almost claustrophobic. It's the middle of the night.

Then it hits me.

I told Stacy—when I was in Sugar River on Sunday morning—that I'd see him in a few hours. It's now almost two full days later. Is today Michelle's funeral? What if it was yesterday? What have I done? The thought of missing another funeral fills me with a painful wave of familiar remorse. I couldn't have. I may not remember leaving the room, but I *know* I'd remember being at the funeral. I can't allow myself to believe that meeting my son and laying Michelle to rest could be blotted from my memory forever.

I have to call Stacy.

No, I need to get to his place. I need to go now. I'm sure he's awake. If he's not, he'll get up. Stacy had been there to literally pick me up out of the gutter. And I owe him. I owe him for what I've done to him.

I once told Stacy, before Michelle and I slept together, that if he ever needed someone and only had one phone call, no matter where I was, I'd be there for him. I'd drop everything and help him.

For years, I'd set that commitment aside, nullified by my own treachery and banishment at gunpoint.

Now that Michelle is gone, I reconsider my word once more.

Stacy was—no, is—my family. I owe him. I need to make things right. I feel bound by an oath that precludes logic, common sense, and self-preservation. Without fully considering the consequences, I have to go because I promised I would. This is a loyalty test that transcends reason, linking us. I don't know what else to do. I can't undo the past. I can't stop myself from feeling deeply for Michelle, and her death can't be undone, but maybe I can fix things between Stacy and me.

And maybe…I'll meet my son for the first time.

This is the clearest-headed I have been in weeks, maybe months. I've slept. I'm rejuvenated. It was a taste of freedom, telling Wafer I was abandoning the show. It was liberating to walk away. Empowering. It also feels like I am doing the right thing for me, finally, even if I'm going about it the wrong way.

I'm trying to put things in order, finally, and all at once.

I snatch my leather shaving bag, find my room key, and I'm out the door, jogging down the hall to the elevator, mashing the down button repeatedly.

Too slow. I'm taking the stairs. I have to get out of here, I need to get to Stacy's house.

I get to the lobby and try to claim my car from the valet without my ticket.

He won't let me. I argue, I swear at him, he gives me the "enough is enough" look and I relent.

I have to run back upstairs, dig the crumpled ticket out of the pants I was wearing yesterday, run back downstairs, and flick it at him. It sails through the air, landing like a glider on his podium. "See?" I say.

He slowly pulls my keys out of a lock box hanging on the wall, and saunters through the sliding door toward the garage. I follow him outside into the brisk January air, patting my blazer for my cigarettes.

The Capitol Dome glows in the night sky, only blocks away. There's almost no traffic. Madison is quiet.

I spring open the lid to my Zippo, and stop to look at it more closely. The Jack of Clubs engraved on the silver case that protects the guts, the lighter-fluid-soaked cotton, the flint and circular striker. On the back, the initials. My initials. "JP." A date. "3/16." My birthday. I look straight up, a lump in my throat.

The clear night sky is drawing me into a wistful remembrance, an unanticipated crossroads in my life.

CHAPTER 27

I tilted my head to one side, spit out a wad of blood and phlegm and looked up. Only this time, I wasn't starting into the cloudless summer night sky. It was the bartender who just watched me get my ass beat.

"What?" was all I could think to say.

He didn't answer immediately, so I tried to get up. "OK. OK, I'm going, man. Don't call the cops on me. Just need to find my keys. Give me, like, five seconds, man, and I'm out of here. Swear to God."

Silently, he extended me his hand.

Warily, I accepted his offer and he hoisted me effortlessly to my feet.

"That guy broke your face when he hit you with the pool stick," he finally said, impressed, laughing.

I laughed with him and spat another mouthful of snotty blood. "You think? He fucked me up good."

"Your nose is broken for sure. They kicked your ass." This guy was solidly built. Crazy hair. Penetratingly clear blue eyes behind thick glasses. He was waiting for me to get my shit together.

I reached up to pinch the bridge of my nose, and that's when I noticed my left pinky and ring finger were distended in a disturbingly unnatural direction. My hand didn't hurt until I noticed my dislocated fingers; upon recognition the pain was excruciating. I was a fucking mess.

"I'm not gonna call the cops," he assured me. "I know who you are. Figured it out when you came in."

Every time someone recognized me, they'd call me "That Sugar River Shooting Survivor" like I was the only one who lived. I had a love-hate relationship with it. Treated as a local celebrity. I sometimes got free food or drinks, but those perks had stopped as time went on. Most people shamelessly lacked self-awareness, asking for autographs with no consideration for the trauma I'd endured.

"You're Jeremy Peoples."

I warily nodded my acknowledgment. "Busted." He didn't mention the shooting, but where else could he possibly know me from? Eyes watering, I held up my hands in mock surrender. "You got me. Now what?"

"I'm Stacy Ramone. Come on, hoss. Come back inside. Let the house buy you one."

I felt compelled to be honest. "I'm not twenty-one. No one ever cards me."

"I don't give a shit about that. Just keep your fucking mouth shut. I got this," he promised.

I took one final look at my newfound treasure, the Jack of Clubs Zippo, and tucked it into my pocket. Stacy put his hand on my chest and brushed the glass and gravel off my back and out of my hair. "And I've got something for you that will help with your broken face. Something strong."

Stacy Ramone led the way back into The Brew Haus. "Are the fucking shitkickers gone?" I asked.

He nodded. "You're not the only one worried about cops. They're not coming back tonight, hoss. You can relax. I got your six." I didn't understand that term or what it meant, but it sounded good in the context of our conversation so I agreed.

"Cool."

The Brew Haus was a typical rundown Southern Wisconsin establishment with a German motif. Low light, hardwood floors, pine wainscoting about halfway up the wall, a smoke-stained green and yellow paint job running the rest of the way up to the ceiling. Photos of Wisconsin sports history were thoughtlessly displayed: 1963 Badgers, The 1982 Brewers, decades' worth of Green Bay Packer seasons. They sold burgers, fried cheese curds, brats, and pitchers of Old Milwaukee served by waitresses in jeans and Brew Haus t-shirts in a large dining room made up mainly of wooden high back booths.

I don't know why I decided to stop here for a drink. I just pulled in. I wasn't hungry. I don't know why I had stayed. I didn't like cover bands, although "High Voltage" did a decent job with "Dirty Deeds (Done Dirt Cheap)." I didn't know anyone who drank here and didn't want to know anyone. The bar had looked quieter from the street, but that was three hours earlier, and the atmosphere had changed while I drank.

The second floor of The Brew Haus was apparently known as "The Attic." It was just a C-shaped bar, a couple of pool tables, dartboards, and a cigarette vending machine on one end of the room, and a small stage and dance floor on the other end. There were two staircases to The Attic: the one I'd taken from the dining area, well-lit and inviting; the other was a seedier, back entrance from the parking lot.

It was that back staircase Stacy and I navigated, returning to where less than ten minutes ago I'd gotten thrashed by two maintenance workers who were still in uniform. "Randall" and "Donald" (their names had been embroidered in dark blue thread on their light blue, short-sleeved uniform shirts) were gone.

Stacy poured me a shot of Absolut Vodka. I knocked it back, winced, and indicated I wanted another.

Instead, he reached into this pocket, pulled out two white pills with a line across the middle, and two smaller blue pills. He handed them to me, poured a tap beer—probably Old Milwaukee—into a glass mug and slid it across the bar.

"Take these," he ordered. I looked around. No one paid any attention to us. The music was loud, the dance floor was packed. I popped all four pills into my mouth and washed them down with sudsy beer.

"What were they?" I asked.

"Valium and Vicodin." Stacy held up both hands in the "peace symbol" gesture, but in this case, it indicated the Triple V of pain relief. "Have a Vodka and Orange Juice, and in ten minutes you're not gonna care about your nose, your fingers, or who killed Kennedy. Lemme know if you need anything else. Sorry about Randy and Donnie. I don't know what started it, but when you call people shitkickers and get in their face around here, they won't walk away."

The Attic at The Brew Haus was raucous.

Stacy rolled back to my end of the bar. I'd zoned out. How long had he been gone? Five minutes? Twenty? I felt great, like I was floating. Lightheaded, grinning, numb. The barstool barely held me up as I turned to booze, slouching and sipping. I smiled at my new friend with dull glassy eyes.

"Hey, I've got an idea, hoss. You can tell me no, it's all good. But my wife is a nurse. If you can hang here until we close at 2:30 a.m., I can take you by my place and have her take a look at you. Maybe get your nose set and your fingers taped up. You don't seem like you're in too big a hurry to go to a doctor, so I thought I'd throw it out there. Think about it. Either way, up to you," he offered, and went back to work.

People were always nice to me when they realized who I was. I hated it. My disgust that people were drawn to a tragedy that had taken everything from me, combined with the guilt I carried as the one responsible for that tragedy, formed a palpable disdain. I loathed them as much as I loathed myself.

I took another sip of my Screwdriver. I probably should do something about my fingers and nose. I looked at my left hand and wiggled my disjointed fingers, bemused. Nothing hurt anywhere in my body. Not my nose. Not my fingers. Not the nerve pain that still screamed at me from surgical scars and bullet wounds. I was soaring above the temporal plain, barely lucid, on the verge of melting into a puddle on the floor, but I was pain-free. I didn't need a nurse. I needed more vodka and Vicodin and Valium.

The music sounded far off in the distance, replaced with a droning "WAH-WAH-WAH-WAH" in my ears. I'd completely forgotten about my broken face when Stacy came back again. I started to tell him that I didn't want to go to his place, I was all good, but he had something he wanted to say and jumped in.

"Here's the thing. I get where you're at. I'm a Marine. I was in Beirut in 1983 when those fuckers blew the barracks. I was eighteen. Two hundred forty-one of us dead. Could've easily been me. But I'm still here. Like you. That crazy kid killed how many of you? Thirty?"

I don't correct him. How many died? Sarah, me, Derrick...other people. It was so long ago. Had I really forgotten? Forgetting was a new feeling. Wonderful. Stacy understood. And was helping me forget.

"And then he tried to kill you. I know you got shot two or three times. I remember seeing it on the news. They even had footage of you on life support in the hospital that they'd show when they'd do a story about the trial or whatever. But that kid couldn't kill you either. You're badass. Hard-core."

Stacy leaned in closer, almost whispering now.

"There's shit I won't tell anyone about what it's like. It's none of their fucking business. But I can tell by looking at you that I don't need to tell you shit about how it is, and you won't ask. And neither will I. We've seen the same shit. You and me, hoss, we're the same. This place, these people, they won't ever know what it's all about. You do. I know you know. I got your back—"

"My six!" I drunkenly interrupted, slurring.

"That's right, hoss. I got your six. You've seen things that no one else will ever see. I've seen them, too. So, before you say you don't need any help, you don't need to get patched up, just set that shit aside."

The combination of the drugs and listening to someone relating to what I've been through was hypnotic. Someone who helped me. Someone who didn't seem to want anything from me. Someone who had helped the pain subside and bring on the fog of fading memory. Someone who looked out for me.

Stacy Ramone was the first man who'd treated me with kindness and apparent selflessness. I had no brothers. My grandfather died before I knew him well enough to form a memory. Teachers had tried, but it was a transactional arrangement, never able to close the arms-length gap I'd put between us. Family friends mostly ignored me unless they wanted a demonstration of my freakish memory. Stacy had invited me to come to his home before he ever knew me.

"Yeah. OK. Sounds good." I nodded in an exaggerated fashion. "Fuck it, why not."

Stacy gently tapped his fist on the bar. "Fuckin' A. We're out of here in less than a half hour."

I never finished my drink. I descended into a fugue state. Thirty minutes vanished. I was startled when Stacy said my name loud enough to get my eyes to fix on him. The band was done, the crowd leaving.

"You ready? I opened. They're closing." Restaurant talk. He jerked his thumb at his co-workers.

I stood up and followed Stacy like an obedient toddler, floating across the floor, vaguely aware that I could fall at any moment, legs barely functioning, blurred double-vision, distorted perceptions. No sense of personal space. I bumped into everyone, staggered, and apologized. The stairs were an adventure.

Magically, we were in a car. Stacy told me it was his, a 1972 Pontiac LeMans.

Stacy talked to me the entire trip, but I retained nothing. I stared out the window at telephone poles, the white line along the shoulder of the road, and winking stars that seemed brighter and closer than usual.

Suddenly, we pulled up to a house trailer in a small town outside of Madison. How long were we driving? It seemed like only seconds. What town was this? It was reminiscent of Sugar River, a rural farming community. Poor, but not desperately so. Small, but not disappearing completely from the map just yet.

"This is Bump Fuck Egypt," I said.

Stacy started laughing. "You're in Stoughton, hoss. It's a suburb of Bump Fuck Egypt."

"Why are we way out in the sticks, dude?" I was confused; the "Triple V" of Vodka, Vicodin and Valium and a mild concussion had scrambled my thoughts. Not having total recall was newly unsettling.

"This is my house. I'm going to have Michelle—my wife, remember?—take a look at your face and fingers. I forgot to call first, so she might bitch a little about you being here but trust me, it's all good, she's cool. I'm serious. I can't wait for you to meet her. You're gonna love her, man."

Stacy leapt over all three stairs in one leap, thudded to the top of the deck, and shoved his keys into the lock before I'd closed the door to the LeMans. Even in my condition I recognized how intense Stacy was. He did everything at full speed and gave off waves of kinetic energy. His clear blue eyes were restless.

"Watch out for the middle step, that second one. Just step over it if you can. Hey, hang out here on the porch for a second. I need to make sure that Michelle is still awake. Two seconds." Stacy's words rattled out of him like an auctioneer, enthusiastic and demanding. He charged through the screen door and then their main entrance, slamming both behind him. I wobbled outside at the foot of the stairs, uncertain about which step I was supposed to avoid, and how serious it might be if I guessed wrong.

Stacy came back out, consoling and apologizing through the door as he beckoned at me to make the trek up the mountainous steps to the porch and come inside. One foot on step one, then the other. Skip step two. One foot on step three, then the other. One foot on the top step, then the other. I had to watch my feet to ensure that I didn't topple to my death, a staggering thirty inches to the ground.

"Dude, did you get a concussion? Why are you walking so slow?" Stacy mocked my movements, extending his arms out in front of him and stomping like Boris Karloff's Frankenstein.

"I'm not sure. It all feels so important," I said solemnly, my response not matching his question.

Seconds later, finally inside, I came face to face with a perturbed strawberry-blonde in nursing scrubs, scowling, hands on her hips, with tiny diamonds in her ears, freckles, and furious, emerald-green eyes.

"Irish eyes are smiling," I whispered without even thinking. "Ah, yer a bonnie lass for providin' me such wonderful medicinal aid in the wee hours of the mornin'." My Irish accent was more of a slurred and absurd Lucky Charms commercial. Stacy threw back his head and laughed.

His wife did not.

Stacy was wearing a heavy, black leather jacket, chains jingling, even though the night air was muggy with June humidity. The flaps and zippers reminded of something Axl Rose wore in one of the "Appetite for Destruction" videos that Guns N' Roses did. Or a cover photo for Kerrang! Or Spin magazine, maybe? Stacy had bunched the sleeves up at his forearms. The coat— scuffed and memorable—had character.

Stacy gestured like a master of ceremonies. "Michelle," he announced, "this is Jeremy Peoples." Michelle's eyes widened a touch, barely noticeable. I expected her to start preening and cackling about how she'd seen me on TV or try to impress me with how much she knew about The Sugar River Shooting and ask a bunch of gross and personal questions. Instead, Michelle rubbed her eyebrow with her right hand and gave me a disapproving once-over. My head dropped, averting my eyes from her glare. When I looked up again, sheepishly, she was still frowning at me.

"This is the only time you can expect me to clean up one of your messes," she informed me.

Stacy shrugged. "He's all fucked up. What was I supposed to do?"

"Tell him to stop drinking and fighting and go to the emergency room. He's not a stray dog. It's 3:16 a.m. I worked a double shift today. Didn't plan on opening a free clinic for Brew Haus bar fight victims."

I started to apologize, but she interrupted me. "You be quiet." Michelle looked at my nose, and then my dislocated fingers caught her attention. "That's no good. Let's get these fixed up first. Yikes."

Stacy sat down at the kitchen table. I followed him and flopped down in the chair to his right. Michelle had quickly ducked into the bathroom and come back with a first aid kit and a washcloth. I groped for my cigarettes. Michelle scrounged around in the freezer and took out three popsicles: two greens and a red.

"Pick a flavor," she demanded.

"I'm good. I don't want any ice cream," I refused. "Thank you though. Sorry."

Michelle had a patronizing smile and Stacy raised his eyebrows.

"I'm sorry, I didn't offer this to you. I told you to pick a flavor. And this isn't ice cream. It's a popsicle."

"Why do you have popsicles? Do you have kids or something?" Why didn't they offer me a drink? Or a sandwich? Or more Vicodin? "I don't really like popsicles," I slurred. "Maybe if I was nine years old and we were at the Fourth of July or a family reunion. Sweet shit sounds gross right now. How about chips?"

"Red. Or green," Michelle repeated.

"You better take one," Stacy laughed. "She will fuck you up, and you need people to stop fucking you up tonight. Take the popsicle, hoss." It was Michelle's turn to raise her eyebrows.

"Green," I pouted, tore the wax paper wrapper with my teeth, and bit off a chunk, chewing as it melted.

"Who bites a popsicle?" Michelle exclaimed. I took another emphatic bite. My tooth chomped on the wooden stick. Michelle shook her head. "Some things should be savored. Popsicles shouldn't be eaten. They should drip on your hand a little bit. If they don't, you didn't enjoy them as much as you should."

"She's making you pay for me bringing you here tonight without calling first," Stacy said.

"No, I'm not. I'm giving him a treat before the treatment. So he'll be a good boy."

Michelle also chose green and left red for Stacy.

"We're both greens," I giggled. It seemed funny to me. Stacy and Michelle exchanged glances.

"What happened to you, Jeremy Peoples? Whose Cheerios did you pee in tonight?" Michelle asked.

"Some shitkickers," I complained. "I didn't think it was as big a deal as it was. I get tired of people asking me to do shit I don't want to do, so I told them to get lost or I'd kick both of their asses and they laughed and I called them shitkickers and the one guy said something that pissed me off so I shoved him but the other guy jacked me. One of them rocked me with a pool cue, I think. That's what it felt like. They took me outside and left me there. One shitkicker kicked me in the chest before he left. That's the story."

I took a breath.

"Fucking shitkickers," I said again.

Stacy and Michelle both laughed.

"I've never heard the word shitkickers used that many times in such a short amount of time," she said, between giggles. "I'm pretty sure I've never heard anyone use that word in conversation, ever."

Stacy took off his glasses. "What did they ask you to do what you didn't want to do?"

I normally would have withdrawn behind a wall of silence or deflection, but I was intoxicated and felt at ease in their home. I set my popsicle stick on the wrapper and again patted myself for my cigarettes. Stacy tapped a Camel out of his cellophane-wrapped soft pack and flicked it across the table at me.

"They wanted my autograph. Like I'm a musician or an actor or something. I said no, and they wouldn't let it go. Wanted me to sign a bar napkin. If anyone had a camera, I'm sure they would've wanted a picture. Don't you think that's a weird thing to want? I'm famous because someone tried to kill me, after killing my friends, not for like, winning a fucking Grammy." My hands had started shaking.

Michelle remained silent as her sad eyes spoke volumes of compassion.

Stacy took my side. "Shitkickers," he said, and all three of us fell into hysterics.

By the time I smoked my cigarette, Stacy and Michelle had finished their popsicles. Michelle licked a dribble of lime green that dotted her hand. She took my wooden stick along with the other two and rinsed them in the sink. When she came back to the table, she looked me in the eye and promised, "I'm going to tell you right now, this is going to hurt you a lot more than it's going to hurt me."

I didn't have time to consider it further. Michelle grabbed my hand and firmly relocated my two fingers. There was a distinctive pop, a blast of pain, and then instant relief. I held my tongue. Stacy cringed.

"God. Damn!" he yelled. "Snap, crackle, pop! Way to take that shit, hoss. Fucking badass!" He slapped the table emphatically, rattling the ashtray and glasses. "That shit sounded like Rice Krispies. Hoorah!"

I wondered if all Marines were like this. What were they called? Jarheads? Stacy was a little nuts.

"Not done!" Michelle barked. I had tried to jerk free, but she held tight, turned my hand over, and used three popsicle sticks and some gauze to fashion a makeshift splint, stabilizing my traumatized fingers. "This isn't going to be perfect," she continued. "Be careful not to bump it and don't get it wet in the shower and don't take this off for a few days. By then, most of the swelling in the joints will be gone, but everything is all loosened up in there from popping them out. You need to give it time to heal. OK?"

"Popsicles." I was awestruck. "Huh." Expertise and ingenuity. Two greens and a red.

"Let me get a look at that nose now." Michelle took the washcloth and gingerly touched the bridge of my nose. I leaned back in my chair—a reflex—but she shot me another severe look. I braced myself, and seconds later a sickening wet crack announced Michelle's success in realigning broken cartilage.

"Fuckin' A," Stacy said. "Gristle. Hard-core." He struck the table again, but with less gusto.

I moaned, surprised that my nose wasn't bleeding. Michelle got up while my eyes watered, opened the freezer again, and picked out a bag of frozen peas. She punched it with her fist, and then handed it to me. "Hold this on your face, right across the bridge of your nose. No, no…wrap it up in the washcloth and then press it right there…yeah, where it was busted. Put a little pressure on it. More. Yep, like that. Just keep it on there until I tell you to take it off. That break was clean. It'll heal straight. You'll live."

We sat in silence for a few seconds, before Stacy spoke again. "What kind of music you like?"

I opened my eyes. Stacy was no longer seated next to me. He was a few paces into the living room, in front of their stereo, scanning wall-mounted racks of cassette tapes. "Um, Grunge, alternative mostly, '60s, '70s, really almost anything but Country. Well, not true. Johnny Cash, Waylon, Willie, that's OK. I listen to a lot of Top 40 radio, too. Some rap. Tupac. The Fugees. Dr. Dre and Snoop Dogg. I like a lot, I guess."

Disappointment shot across Stacy's face. "Grunge? C'mon, hoss. You're kidding me, right?"

Michelle looked at me and rolled her eyes. "Here we go. You don't know what you started, Jeremy."

Stacy was animated. "Nirvana? That's shit music. You think you got credibility because your album sounds like you recorded it in a garage? No fucking way. I could make that music tomorrow."

I leaned forward in the chair, twisted, and peered across the room at the tape collection on the wall. White Snake. Ratt. Dokken. Night Ranger. Queensrÿche. Cinderella. Yngwie Malmsteen. The Scorpions. Quiet Riot. Twisted Sister. Bon Jovi. It went on and on, a massive collection of '80s Rock. This was the House of Hair. Guitar Gods and eyeliner. Spandex. Hairspray. Makeup.

"Hey, put the peas back on your face," Michelle reminded me. She used her nurse voice. I obeyed.

"I'm not into Duran Duran and Billy Idol and Tears for Fears. I need Pearl Jam and Alice in Chains and Stone Temple Pilots. Music that wasn't invented in a Los Angeles corporate record company office. I want authentic. A garage is better than some company selling image to me. Live, Skinny Puppy, Fugazi are better bands because they're making something that's ours. That '80s shit is sell-out rock, bro."

Stacy was irritated. "I'd take Motley Crue over Soundgarden."

"And I'd take Smashing Pumpkins over Warrant," I countered. "We can do this all night."

"You really think the flannels and the fame-hating and the heroin abuse isn't just a different image the record labels are selling you on? LA or Seattle. Cocaine or heroin. Leathers or flannels. It's all corporate-approved rebellion. Punk rock was hating The Man when Eddie Vedder was in diapers. Gen X didn't invent it." Stacy was holding two or three tapes in each hand, his face serious.

"The Seattle Scene was real. Some bands sold out. People are making money. But that's not the same. You're just pissed because there's no Hair Metal on the radio. People are singing about shit other than cherry pie and once bitten twice shy and whatever the fuck." I was honor-bound to defend my music.

Stacy roared with derisive laughter. Outraged. "Lyrics? Nobody can understand what the fuck any of these bands are saying and when you read the words in the liner notes they're total bullshit, hoss!!"

Michelle stood up and laughed. "OK boys. Enough is enough. Why don't we compromise with the '70s?" She shrugged. "Stacy's not used to someone not immediately bowing down and telling him his taste in music is perfect." It was the first time I'd met someone who seemed to take their music as a personal reflection of their self-worth.

"Your house, your rules, your music. I didn't start this," I pointed at Stacy. "Sebastian Bach did."

Stacy put in a well-worn copy of Alice Cooper's "Welcome to my Nightmare." He came back to the kitchen table and sat down. "Kurt Cobain kills himself and the whole country bows down like the guy was John Lennon. Total bullshit. His lyrics don't even make sense. You can't understand what he's saying. We went from Steve Perry to guys who can't sing because one band—hell, one song!—went huge on MTV. Now everyone's doing it. You don't think Grunge is as much a sellout as anything else now?"

Michelle waved her hands and sat back down. "Enough. This isn't getting settled tonight. Coke versus Pepsi, McDonald's versus Burger King, and Democrat versus Republican. It's a matter of taste. Some people have it—" she gestured at Stacy "—and some people like Grunge."

Stacy nearly fell off his chair laughing. I pretended to bow in Michelle's direction.

I guessed Michelle was about three or four years older than me, and Stacy two or three years older than her. Michelle came across as shrewd, intelligent, and mindful; Stacy seemed edgy, brawny, and reckless.

I liked them. Michelle was cool. Stacy had my back.

Neither of them wanted anything from me.

"Can we talk about something else?" I asked, and we all laughed again. "Movies? Politics? Religion?"

"Let's get high," Stacy announced, and pulled a bag of weed out of his front pocket.

"With that," Michelle pushed her chair back from the table, "I'm going to bed. Jeremy Peoples, it was nice to meet you. Remember: keep the splint out of the shower for a week, and ice your nose again tomorrow for a few hours. That will keep you out of the hospital." She smiled at me, wanly. "Oh, and try to stay away from shitkickers and alternative music. They're hazardous to your health."

I tipped an imaginary cap.

Michelle tottered across the living room without glancing back. I appreciated that she hadn't asked me about Sugar River, even when she recognized me, and I could tell she wanted to. I felt the urge to joke.

"Good night," I called after her. "Thanks for the nose job and fingering me."

Stacy didn't laugh, but I saw Michelle's shoulders shrug up and down, her hand going to her face. A hidden laugh. She disappeared down the hall, silently flicking the light off as she went off to bed.

Stacy packed his wooden dugout, smeared some hash across the top with a pocket knife, and slid it across the table. I didn't hesitate. We passed it back and forth, rekindling the music discussion, but instead focusing on the bands and artists we agreed were underrated and underappreciated from different eras, each trying to outdo the other with obscure references.

It was fun.

There were no interruptions from my memory. Sarah never demanded to be remembered.

I was stoned, drugged out, happier than I'd been at any time since May 23, 1992.

The sky had grown faintly brighter. It was after 6:00 a.m. I'd been there for over three hours.

I was suddenly worried. "Hey, man. I need a ride back to the city. My car is still at the Brew Haus."

"Chill out, hoss. Sleep on the couch. I work today, too. I'll take you back with me. You don't have a job to get to or anything do you?" Stacy was unconcerned. He again decided and again I obeyed.

"I did. I'm quitting," I informed him. "Today. Today is my last day. Well, yesterday was. Fuck them."

"Wait, like your two weeks' notice or some shit?"

"Nope. I just decided right now. Fuck that place. I quit. They'll figure it out when I never come back."

Stacy roared with laughter. "OK, hoss. You living anywhere?"

"Yeah. I live with one of the guys I work with. We don't really get along, but we have work in common. Well, we had work in common." I started giggling. "I'm probably evicted now since I won't have any money and he doesn't like me. Fuck him, too, I guess." I was laughing so hard my nose was hurting again.

It felt great to walk away from something with impunity. I flicked open my new Jack of Clubs Zippo and lit my last cigarette. Stacy set the baggy of weed in front of me and squinted at me with bloodshot eyes.

"Smoke another one?" he suggested.

"Fuck it. Yes. From now on, I always say yes," I decided.

CHAPTER 28

"No. No way," I say to myself. "I can't do it." But I know I'm going to. I have no idea what happened, but I didn't drive across the country to sit in my car a block away from answers only to leave without them.

But it was fucking tempting.

It feels like everything between Stacy, Michelle, and I erupted minutes ago, instead of years in the past.

(crystal blue eyes raging, icy gun metal against my forehead)

I'm sitting at a four-way intersection not moving, headlights off, one block from Stacy and Michelle's trailer. I keep calling it "Stacy and Michelle's." She's not in there, and never will be again.

But there's a motherless boy inside. And an avalanche of baggage. And a friend. And I gave my word.

One left turn away. It's the fourth place on the left after the intersection and I cannot bring myself to finish the final few feet of my journey. There's no one behind me. It's too early. I'm watching the trailer.

Three or four cars are in his driveway, including a 1972 Lemans.

No lights, not even a TV flickering in the window. The blinds are drawn.

It's 4:22 a.m. and the need for resolution gnaws at me, but there's something else building inside of me.

For years, I've tried to bury any paternal feelings of responsibility for my son, made easier by the fact that I've never seen his face, and have no recollection of him as a part of my life. Stevie was Stacy's son, a lie I repeat to myself when I think of Michelle's decision and my consent. The truth could never be fully expelled from my thoughts, but the lie gives room for my justification.

I ignored him.

Deep inside, something awakened when Stacy called me on New Year's Eve. I have a growing conviction that I *need* to see Stevie. I'd convinced myself that because of what I'd done and what I'd gone through, I was unfit to be a parent. Leaving was protection. The truth is revealing a larger reality. Everything I imagined would happen if I had stayed ended up happening because of my absence.

The past is weaving a devious conspiracy with the present. Repeating itself. I'm right back where I started. Despite my constant avoidance and myriad of escape attempts, here I am.

Maybe, in the same way I have a burgeoning and renewed loyalty to Stacy, I now have an awakening sense of responsibility for Stevie because… Michelle's gone. Am I trying to fill the void left behind by Michelle? How could that even be possible? My thoughts are incomplete and erratic.

"He's a-fucking-sleep," I decide. "Why didn't I call first?" I had thoughtlessly stormed out of my hotel room with the Stacy of 1994 in my mind, the bartender/cook who worked the night shift, the guy I sat up and smoked weed with until sunrise, the person I never saw asleep before dawn or awake before noon. It never occurred to me that he wouldn't be awake in the middle of the night. He always was.

"But there's no lights on. It's almost 4:30 in the morning. Of course he's asleep. He can't stay up all night like he used to, right? Not with a kid in the house who doesn't have a mom. He couldn't have worked last night.

Not with all he's got going on right now. Right?" I'm talking myself out of going inside. I need to talk myself into it. "Stacy's always been a night person. He's awake. Just go inside."

I need to find out what's going on. I swear to God I better not have slept through Michelle's funeral like I did Sarah's. Even though I haven't seen or spoken to her in years, Michelle is—*was*—my best friend.

(nurses restrain me as I pound my fists on the bed and pull IV needles from my arms and I scream and curse my parents and Sarah is in the ground cold alone rotting dead without me)

I blink away an image so vivid, the memory of Velcro restraints raises the hair on my arms.

"What am I supposed to do, just knock on the door like a fucking idiot? Just keep pounding until he answers the door? What if I wake up Stevie? Why the FUCK did I leave my goddamn cell phone at my apartment?!" I jab the heel of my hand into the steering wheel. "Just leave, call him later, tell him what happened. Go to a restaurant, wait a few hours, call him then. People stay up late or get up early in Stoughton, don't they? People eat. People need coffee. Shit must be open somewhere."

When I put the car in DRIVE, I don't turn around. Instead, I start creeping up the street, absurdly slow. "Jeremy, what are you doing, bro? You had a plan. It was a good plan. This new plan is a bad plan."

Finally, I join the mini caravan that is crowding Stacy's driveaway.

Deep breath. Grab the brown leather shaving kit, my portable pharmacy.

I wish I had a gun. Why don't I carry a gun? Or a knife? Or a baseball bat or something?

"Dude, you're losing your mind. He called a radio show and went on the air live. Everyone would know right where to look if you disappear. He knows that. It would guarantee premeditation. It would guarantee he'd be caught in days. Hell, hours. What is he, sitting around with a bunch of guys, waiting for me to randomly show up almost forty hours late? This doesn't make any sense. I mean, he is an ex-Marine. He's done some crazy shit. What's forty hours of waiting compared to storming Iwo Jima?"

My imagination is running away with me.

I get out the car. Puffs of steam float from my mouth into the starlit night. There's a full moon. I ascend the rickety stairs, remembering to skip the middle step, remembering my first time here.

I knock on the door. Softly. No answer. I gently tap again, twice. I can't hear anything. I cup my ear to the door. Nothing. I reach for the door handle, breathe out, and whisper, *"What am I dooooooing?"*

The handle turns. The door opens with barely a nudge.

The living room is completely dark, but my eyes adjust and I can tell that there are people here: someone is laying on the couch snoring, another is slumped in a chair, and a third is sprawled out on the floor. Everyone's asleep. No one stirs as cold air fills the room. I carefully close the door, pushing it tightly into the jam while twisting the handle, letting it click almost silently into place.

A lit cigarette glows, seemingly suspended in midair, from across the room.

Stacy is sitting at his kitchen table. He watched me come in, he must have heard me tapping but never came to the door, and is looking at me from across the room, saying nothing. I immediately regret my decision to come in unannounced. A soft glow from the street light has backlit me like I'm on stage.

"It's come full circle," Stacy finally says.

"What?" I chuckle, cautiously.

"The first time you were in my house, you had a busted face and a fucked-up hand. Here you are, almost six years later, standing in my house, with a busted face and a fucked-up hand. I just think it's funny how things change but things stay the same, too." I'm still across the room, hand on the doorknob. I'd forgotten about my eye until he mentioned it. I look down at my hand, then use it to rub my eyebrow.

"I was starting to think you weren't coming," he continues, and inhales on his cigarette, the tip growing bright orange again. He's still not turning on the lights. What the fuck is going on here?

"Yeah, I had a stop to make in Sugar River." I'm stammering. "Took longer than I thought."

"You think?" Stacy snorts. "That was Sunday. It's Tuesday. I thought you bullshitted me."

"I get that," I agreed. "Total honesty, here?"

"Yeah, Jeremy. You can be fully honest. When it suits you."

It's not exactly hostility that hangs in the air between us but we're not trading pleasantries either.

"I went to Sugar River High School."

Stacy seems to consider this. He drags on his cigarette again. "They haven't torn that place down?" he asks suspiciously. "I thought I heard they knocked it down. How is that shooting gallery not a park yet?"

His tone is flat, indifferent. Steady.

"It's still there. I haven't been there since they took me out on a stretcher. I went inside. I looked around. It was crazy. It's still a crime scene in there, and seeing it all again hit me hard, bro. I passed out for, like, six fucking hours. I just woke up and drove to Madison. I got my hotel, and— swear to God—I killed the minibar and blacked out for thirty hours. I have no recollection of what happened. Second time something like that has happened to me in the past week." I'm shaking, sweating, over-explaining.

(the bartender hands me a letter with purple cursive and confusion and anger boils over)

I shake my head sharply enough to remind myself that my eye is still tender. "I lose time like that sometimes, but never this long and it's happening more. Six hours in the school, then thirty fucking hours in the hotel. I

288

woke up and drove here. I don't know why I didn't call first, just assumed you were going to be up because, well shit, man, you're always up all night."

My hands are trembling. I clasp them behind my back.

"That's quite a story, Jeremy." Does he believe me? His voice is flat, his demeanor impossible to read. I wish he'd turn on a light. I can't figure out what the hell is going on. Who are all these people? Where is Stevie? "Are you going to come all the way in or just stand at the door? I get it, hoss. I'd be worried if I was you, too. I told you I'd kill you if I saw you again. And here I am, seeing you again. I gotta admit, you got balls. I figured you said you'd come because you wanted your audience to think you're some badass, but the second you got off the air you'd back out. You being here? Shocks the fucking shit out of me."

I consider telling him that I want to make it up to him, that I'm honor-bound to a debt of gratitude I believe I still owe, that I promised, and even though I broke my word, I want to make it right in some fashion. I think about Stevie, and wonder what he looks like, and even contemplate revealing the truth.

Impulsively, I say instead, "I came because of Michelle. I came because you asked, but I'm here for her." Stacy has almost finished his cigarette. It's nearly impossible to see in the dark. He doesn't say anything. "Look, man, are you pissed because I missed the funeral? I didn't blow it off. I got super fucked up." I hold up my leather shaving bag with my good hand. "I brought what I've got left with me. But..." I swallow, hard. "I didn't miss her funeral, did I? Was it yesterday or today?"

"You didn't miss anything," he says. A wave of relief rolls over me. "Let's talk. Are you gonna stay, hoss, or you got some place to be?" I've not been forgiven. Nothing's been forgotten. Why am I here, really?

I move quietly across the trailer's small living room to the small kitchen—stepping carefully over the snoring stranger in the middle of the floor—and join Stacy at the kitchen table. He never takes his eyes off me, stabbing his cigarette into the top of an empty soda can, a sparkler of hot ashes pluming onto the table. He drops the butt into the can, picks it up, and spits a wad of saliva in after it.

I have a thousand questions about Stevie. "Who are all these fucking dudes?" I ask instead.

Stacy's answer is weird. "They've been here since New Year's Eve."

"But who are they? Do I know any of them? It's hard to see in the dark. Can we turn a light on?"

"The Indian is Louie Lightfoot. Just call him Big Lou. You know the other two. Guy on the couch is who you bought that car from. Brandon Bollinger. 'Soda.' And the other one on the floor is Jimmy Sullivan."

Some things change and some things stay the same.

"We've been at it since Friday." He called my radio show on Friday. Told me he was alone. He lied.

I have a thousand questions about Michelle. "You wanna get high?" I ask instead.

Stacy smiles at me. "I always say yes. You got enough in there for everybody?"

"I got enough in here for everybody in this fucking town," I brag.

"Well then, let's wake up the boys." Stacy gets up and flips on the kitchen light. There's trash everywhere. Piles of empty beer cans, pizza boxes, bottles. Chewed food has been smashed into the kitchen floor. Dishes are overflowing in the sink. The counter is a jumble of cans and empty liquor bottles. The trailer smells like stale beer and rotten garbage. How did things get this trashed, this fast?

With the kitchen light on, I can finally get a good look at Stacy. His hair is almost exactly the way I remember, still a snarl of curls, but now he has a receding hairline. Stacy's wearing glasses; the frames are trendier than they were in 1996. He's in a t-shirt and jeans—still too small for him—and I assume he's going to the gym because Stacy is stronger than I remember, veins popping in his forearms. The same waves of intensity roll off him, and his penetrating blue eyes are probing and turbulent.

"Wait, Stacy, don't get everybody up yet." I'm exasperated at how evasive he's being. but I'm also intimidated and off balance. "What happened to Michelle? I swear to Christ I haven't talked to her in years and I came all the way here from DC for the funeral because you said you don't have anybody to help you and you needed me, but there's a whole house full of people here. Where's Stevie at, bro? When's the funeral? Dude, I don't understand what's going on. Talk to me. Help me understand."

"Later. I know you've got questions. You and me, we got a lot of shit to talk about." Stacy watches me through the thick lenses in his glasses. "I've got a lot of questions for you, too, but now's not the time. You're here with your shit, and we ran out last night. Perfect timing." I want to talk to him about our friendship, and why I did the things that I did, and tell him I want to make things right in some way while I'm here. I want to tell him I'm willing to stay as long as I need to, that I'm not going back to DC.

"Bro. Five minutes first." I get up from the table and throw my hands up in frustration as Stacy ignores me and stomps into the living room, kicking at the person on the floor, ripping the jacket Soda used as a blanket off of him and snapping it like a wet towel at the others. He yanks on the cord that's dangling from the ceiling fan, bathing the room in soft light from the only working light bulb out of three.

"Wake up, motherfuckers," he bellows, playing a fake bugle. "Reinforcements have arrived. The cavalry's here. Daylight's wasting." Stacy looks at me. "Break out the shit, hoss. Let's get fucked up."

CHAPTER 29

All five of us peer into my unzipped brown leather shaving bag.

Two balloons of heroin, black tar in one, China White in the other. LSD. Amphetamines. Xanax. Almost an ounce of weed. Opium. Hash. The coke is almost gone, railed out in bathrooms across the Midwest.

"We're all dropping acid," Stacy orders.

I have no idea how many doses the Floyd Chicks had set me up with. I shake the tiny white paper chaffs into my palm and poke at them with my finger, counting.

Before I can answer, Big Lou snorts happily. "Five. Fucking fate, bro." Soda and Jimmy Sullivan both nod. I'm not so sure. Stacy is resolute, shaking his head yes and gesturing at my hand. Everyone reaches for one, from fingertips to tongues without further discussion. Stacy and I are the last to dose.

I'm compelled to ask an awkward question first. "Hey, man, this'll last, like, eight hours. Is the funeral today? We can't all be tripping around Stevie and talking to funeral directors and family and shit."

Big Lou, Soda, and Jim all look at me, startled and confused, and then back at Stacy. Stacy sets aside his bong, careful to avoid spilling the water. Did he already take his dose? I was distracted and didn't notice.

"The funeral's not today. Stevie's not here. Just take the fucking acid."
That same, monotone voice.

I have so many questions. Everyone stares. Time slows, again my enemy. "Fine. Fuck it."

I flatten my hand and lick the last tab of LSD off my palm. Stacy smiles. The others relax. I'm already paranoid, which doesn't bode well for my trip. Remarkably, I think I'd feel safer if Stacy and I were the only ones in the trailer. This houseful of *his* friends—two of whom I was acquainted with years ago, but who are now clearly much closer to Stacy—is disconcerting. Big Lou is gruff and looms over everything.

I have the urge to run. "I gotta take a piss," I say, and try to look down the hallway toward my old room, considering how I can at least glance into Stevie's bedroom, find some kind of clue—

"You know where it is. Use the one down there," Stacy gestures toward the bathroom near his and Michelle's room, and not the one adjacent to my old room, what I presume is now Stevie's room.

When I get into the hallway, I hear everyone talking in a low voice, someone laughs, but I can't make out who's saying what or who's laughing or what's going on. I want to turn around and ask what I missed; instead, I close the bathroom door behind me and turn the lock. The door is flimsy, a worthless deterrent if someone was committed to coming in after me, but the tension in my shoulders still releases. Privacy. Nothing about what's happening right now feels right. "I gotta get out of here."

The bathroom is a wrecked pit stop in Stacy's crash pad party trailer. The toilet is stained with textured flecks of brown and green from the water line to the lip. The tile floor is splattered with urine. There's trash everywhere, more cans and bottles, wads of bloody toilet paper, and half-cleaned puke on the sink. The shower curtain is missing; only the hooks remain on the tension rod with small plastic remnants still attached where the rest was torn away. The bathtub is rife with mildew and curly black hairs. I avert my gaze to avoid looking in the mirror, but not before seeing gobs of caked-on sputum.

I've only got moments until the LSD takes over. This trip has all the hallmarks of impending doom.

I slide my hand into the back pocket of my jeans. Michelle's letter is still there, damp from sweat, warm, creased, and unopened, right where I'd put it back at the hotel. I need another cigarette.

My fingers touch strange metal when I poke them into the front pocket of my jeans to fish for my lighter. I pull the mystery object from my pocket, needing a second to process what I'm holding: the blood-encrusted half of Sarah's Best Friends Forever necklace. It startles me, and I drop it in the sink, barely saving the chain before it snakes into the drain and disappears. I hold it up again, apoplectic.

What I thought I'd found it in a dream was actually *in my fucking pocket.*

Impossible.

How was it lying on the floor of the school, unclaimed, for seven years?

Why wasn't it in an evidence locker, or with Sarah's parents?

How do I have it?

A surge of heartache and gratitude builds to bursting as I dangle this memento of lost love, and friendship, in front of my eyes, swinging it gently from my bandaged hand. A remnant. A treasure.

I have to be hallucinating.

I need to stave off a bad trip, shift the trajectory as it hits, flip the switch. Think about my favorite day, when the possibilities were endless, Sarah had never looked more beautiful, when we were happy, before the disaster. See her as she truly was, and feel how I felt when I...

...awkwardly affixed a corsage to Sarah's dress, horribly self-conscious with her mom and dad scrutinizing every move. Fastening the safety pin while trying to keep from touching any skin or looking at her cleavage was

impossible. I was enthralled by her beauty. Sarah was perfect. I had trouble believing that she felt the same way about me and that we were actually going to prom together.

I tried not to stare, but I'd never seen her in a formal gown.

"The corsage is crooked." I admitted defeat.

Sarah tried to straighten it herself, and then her mom made an effort, before she got flustered and said, "It's OK. Leave it. We have to go soon. Time for pictures." I was familiar with her impatience masquerading as sweet-natured directives. Her dad had snapped candid shots on his 35 mm camera, but now we needed to pose, and I couldn't stage a smile without looking dorky.

Sarah was a radiant beauty, beaming without awkwardness, dimples, and a twinkle in her eyes.

The Class of 1992 had selected teal and black as our prom colors. My tuxedo was the cheapest one I could rent: plain black jacket and pants with a teal bowtie, pocket square, cummerbund and rented shoes that pinched my toes. I bought a teal band for my Swatch watch and swapped it out that morning so everything matched. I was a celebrity at the Academy Awards, a can of chewing tobacco tucked inside my jacket as I walked the red carpet in gas station sunglasses and posed for the parental paparazzi.

Sarah's teal dress was satin and tastefully revealing, showing a tiny hint of cleavage, freckled shoulders, and a hemline that ended just above the knee. She'd used enough hairspray to tease her hair, but not so much that it was brittle or would snarl in my hands. Sarah had borrowed a small black clutch from her older sister, and wore her Best Friends Forever necklace, despite her mom asking her repeatedly to take it off. I didn't understand why it was such a big deal and when we got in the car I told her I thought she'd made the right decision. She kissed my cheek. Her dad frowned, but Sarah's mom waved him off.

Sarah relaxed in the passenger seat. "Where are you taking me tonight, Mr. Peoples?"

She was beautiful. I kept thinking it over and over, sincerely amazed. I felt lucky and undeserving, and overcompensated with smart-ass innuendo. "How'd you like me to take you, Miss Brennan?"

She blushed. "I'd like to know where we're having dinner tonight, if I may." Sarah affected an amusingly formal way of speaking, undoubtedly brought on by our wardrobe. The Prom Planning Committee had picked what we thought was a mature establishment, where the Senior Class could all eat together.

"Red Lobster," I answered, relishing the thought of showing Sarah off, even if the idea of being in a crowd of people made my skin crawl.

Sarah waved one last time at her mom and dad.

I found first gear in my rusty 1984 Ford Tempo and pulled away from the curb, heading to Madison.

Conversation with Sarah was usually easy, but anxiety over wanting the perfect night stifled me.

"I know the official prom dinner is at Red Lobster." Sarah smiled. "But what if we skipped dinner with everyone and did our own thing before the dance?" she suggested. "Just us."

She knew I was uncomfortable in large groups. Inane conversation with people I barely liked and only tolerated held no appeal. I had assumed she wanted to be a part of the class dinner, even though I'd refused my nomination to Prom Court, so I could take an underclassman to the dance.

"What do you want to do instead?" I asked. "I mean, yes, obviously, I don't wanna go to Red Lobster."

Sarah laughed. "Let's go to a place we'll always remember. I mean, a place I'll always remember, too, since, like, you remember everything that ever happens." She laughed again. Her eyes were mischievous. We'd often talked about trying new things, daydream about skipping school, and taking spontaneous trips, but we never progressed past ideas. Tonight was different. Tonight we were actually going to do it.

"This might be stupid," I started to say, and Sarah immediately interrupted me.

"I LOVE STUPID!" she shouted. "It's, like, my favorite thing! Tell me more!" She giggled and grabbed my hand. I moved my hand from the stick shift to her knee, her hand resting on mine.

"There's a Greek Place on State Street. You eat on the roof and watch all the people walk by. Everyone would think we were cool in a tux and gown. They have great gyros and the roof is fucking awesome." I loved Madison, impatient for both of us to move there and attend the University of Wisconsin together.

"There's nowhere to park downtown," Sarah reminded me.

"I'll find a place by the lake. We'll walk. You said you like stupid. This is getting stupider by the second."

"Let's see when we get there. I only sort of like gyros, but I love State Street on Saturday. You haven't fully sold me yet, Mr. Peoples. I think maybe you can do better," she joked.

I moved my hand a little higher, from her knee to her thigh. I was a timid eighteen-year-old, but getting bolder.

Sarah slapped my hand. I didn't pull away, and she didn't slap me again; instead, she looked out the window with a bright smile on her face, dimples showing, then turned her face down, and put her other hand over her mouth. I noticed she hadn't covered her Cindy Crawford mole with concealer.

"You look...perfect," I stammered. "You're...so...beautiful. I'm waiting to wake up some days."

Tears began to rim in Sarah's eyes; she pulled a Kleenex from her clutch and dabbed at her mascara.

"Did I say something wrong? Why are you crying?" I felt myself freaking out. What had I done?

"There's nothing wrong. I'm just...happy when I'm with you. When you say things to me, I know you mean it. Kelly thinks you're an asshole because of how you act around Derrick and Aaron and them. No one would believe me if I told anyone that you say stuff like that when we're alone."

I didn't know what to say, so I moved my hand from her leg to the back of her neck, caressing her with my thumb and fingers. "Stop it, you're giving me goosebumps," she demanded, jokingly.

It took about fifty minutes from Sarah's house to downtown Madison, even with a few wrong turns. It seemed like it took another hour to find a place to park, but finally I managed to squeeze my car into a tight spot and we dashed toward State Street on foot, ridiculously overdressed, hand in hand.

As we pressed through the crowd, walking uphill toward the Capitol Square, some people glanced and smiled. State Street was a collage of students and yuppies, rednecks and hippies, families and beggars. Sarah insisted we duck into a thrift store. We spent ten minutes shopping for tweed jackets and bellbottoms, looking for the most ridiculous t-shirts we could find before I pointed at my Swatch watch.

"Alright, Miss Brennan. Gonna need a yes or a no vote on the gyros. We're running out of time."

"Let's do it," she decided. I held the door open for her and she sauntered through like a princess. I swiped my dip of chewing tobacco out on the sidewalk, spat twice, and continued to Zorba's Greek Restaurant.

The place was packed but they were efficient in getting people through the line. I grabbed a plastic tray, ordered two gyros without onions, add green peppers, two orders of fries, a Mountain Dew, and a Diet Pepsi. We had our food in five minutes, wrapped in foil and wax paper, fries greasy and steaming in cardboard, and wax cups brimming with ice. I pointed to the stairs in the back corner. People stared at our formal wear. I yelled "Mazel Tov!" for some reason and half the restaurant laughed.

She held the door for me this time.

Even in high heels, Sarah sprinted up the stairs, squeezing past me and onto the roof. I trudged after her, my feet increasingly uncomfortable in rented fucking shoes.

The rooftop dining area was nothing more than several concrete tables with umbrellas sprouting from the middle, and concrete benches. We managed to grab a spot closest to the edge. Sounds from the street murmured up to us: music, laughter, traffic. The whole thing felt inexplicably perfect.

"I'm going to wreck my makeup," Sarah told me. "I know it. How do you eat a gyro and not get it all over your face and hands? Can you get me a fork please?" she asked while pulling napkins from the metal dispenser on the table, one after another, five, six, seven of them.

"You can't eat a gyro with a fork," I replied. "Not gonna happen. Pick it up and be careful."

Right then, a glob of tzatziki sauce, mixed with lamb juice and green pepper, squirted out of the pita I was trying to shove into my mouth and plopped onto my rented shirt. "Fucking shit!" I bellowed.

Sarah tried to stop from laughing, failed, and spit a mouthful of Diet Pepsi in my face. Mortified, she jumped up with napkins and apologies. It took me a few seconds to gather myself, but when I realized what had happened, I couldn't contain it. Eyelids sticky, I laughed hysterically, and unabashedly.

"Stop laughing!" Sarah shouted. "I just spit in your face!" The rest of the rooftop customers were all watching us, amused. "Your shirt is all gyro-y! We have to go to prom! I spit pop on your shirt!" Each time she would add a description, I guffawed. I didn't care about my shirt, or the stupid dance.

She was about to cry.

And then she didn't because I finally choked out a few words. "Fuck the shirt."

A bashful smile passed across Sarah's face, but she kept trying to clean my shirt with the tiny napkins she pulled—one after another after another like a magic trick—from the metal dispenser on the table. She smeared soda *and spit and tzatziki sauce deeper into the ruffles of the tuxedo shirt, worsening the stain.*

"I'm not getting my deposit back!" I declared and set off a fresh set of giggles.

Sarah threw a balled-up handful of dirty napkins at me and sat down. "I'm getting a fork, Sloppy Joe."

"I have an idea. If you really feel bad, I could squirt some ketchup on your dress so we can match. I could even shoot some Mountain Dew on you out of my blowhole. This way it all balances out. I don't have to be the only one who looks like a horrible slob," I explained. "What do you think?"

"Zorba's was your idea. I was fine with Red Lobster," Sarah lied, and went off in search of silverware.

"I've got another idea," I told her when she returned with a plastic fork and began gingerly picking at her gyro, trying to take bites without eating her lipstick off. "This one is better, for sure."

"You're, like, oh for four when it comes to ideas tonight," Sarah sassed me.

"I think we should go back to the thrift store and I'll buy a new shirt." I played the violin with my straw and drink lid, squawking out an annoying version of "Mary Had a Little Lamb" while she thought it over.

"I don't have a better idea right now," she sighed. "We can't go like this."

We sat at the edge of the roof. Sarah finished her food. I watched people doing weird, people things.

I threw away our trash, tray and all, and again looked at my watch. "We should probably hurry."

We dashed down the stairs like we were eloping and returned to the secondhand store. I grabbed two shirts that I thought could work, one with amazing ruffles and oversized cuffs, and a vintage Led Zeppelin "Swan Song" t-shirt that was nearly the same age as me. Moments later we were back on State Street.

"This is way better than Prom Court Red Lobster and keeping my deposit," I whispered in her ear.

Sarah wasn't convinced. "Thanks for not being mad about it." Strange faces came at us from all sides, veering away at the last second when they realized we had no intention of moving. Always uncomfortable and uncertain in crowds, it was then I did something out of character for me.

I pulled Sarah into my arms and kissed her.

I opened my eyes as our lips parted. Hers were already wide open, blinking, surprised. There was a smattering of applause from somewhere, a whistle, some laughter. I looked around and noticed that people were watching us kissing on the street without a shred of self-consciousness. Sarah opened her mouth to say something and didn't. Was she embarrassed? I couldn't believe that I'd done it.

"You're blushing!" Sarah accused, playfully. "Why are you blushing?" She knew. She wanted me to say.

"I probably am," I agreed. "Everyone is staring at us. We need to go or we're going to be late."

Jesus. Had I really kissed her in public? In front of God and everyone on State Street in Madison?

"Why did you do that?" She grabbed hold of me as I tried to escape.

We were transfixed by a moment of our own making. Magic. Like a scene in a movie. "I don't know."

In the midst of the anonymous and annoyed masses jostling us, she grinned. "You're so weird. I liked it."

"I'm one for five on ideas, now, right? Sarah Brennan, will you go to prom with me?" I proposed.

"Not in that shirt. You're a big gross slob," she replied, throwing her arms around my neck, clasping her hands, and kissing me. Again, in front of everyone.

CHAPTER 30

"Get the fuck out of me!"

I tear the bandage off of my hand because there's a piece of glass under my skin. Some of my broken shower door is lodged in my arm. The shard is alive and moving on its own, cutting through veins and sinew on its way to bone. It is chewing its way into muscle. I throw open the filthy medicine cabinet, fumble for a pair of tweezers, and sink them a quarter inch into one of the wounds, picking at it in a desperate attempt to stop it from burrowing further, deeper, down into the soft marrow of my bone.

The glass is elusive. I think I have it, I don't, it scoots away. A plastic cup topples over, spilling a toothbrush and a plastic Bic razor into the sink. I must have done that. I didn't feel myself do it.

Dots of blood drip on the counter.

Could the glass get into my bloodstream and travel to my heart, or even my brain? What would happen then? Would I have a heart attack or a stroke? An aneurism? What if it pushes through my optic nerve and blinds me but not before it punctures my eye, stretching the membrane until it bursts open from the inside out? Or it slices open my throat, blood pouring into my lungs as I drown in my own fluids?

I have to get it the fuck out of me.

Starbursts of glittering gold and garish purple pop in front of my face, color and energy that distract me momentarily. It's emerald-green, the color of Michelle's eyes, descending across my field of vision like a waterfall, swallowing the vanity light in tint and darkening everything around me.

I hear a child's laughter.

"Stevie?" I ask. "Are you in here?" I turn around once, then again, in the tiny bathroom.

I'm alone.

Blood trickles out of the gash, a small and steady stream onto the floor.

I force the tweezers further into the oozing wound in my arm. The glass is hiding.

"GET THE FUCK OUT OF ME!" I finally yell, flinging my arms in desperation, the embedded tweezers clanging against the mirror, blood misting in every direction. The compulsion returns, so I dig into the wound with my fingernails, clawing out this parasitic piece of pain that has come to life inside of me.

I'm aware I dropped acid. But what I'm seeing and feeling is real. It can't be the drugs.

Right? Wrong. Wrong? Right. It's both. It's neither. My reality is a nightmare. My nightmares come true. All the acid did was open my mind to see both at the same time, separate but overlapping. A vivisection.

I hear the piece of glass cutting and chewing and tunneling. GET. THE FUCK. OUT. OF. ME. A sharp-edged hungry beetle clawing through tendons and meat. "Get the fuck out of me," I whimper. "Please stop."

I pull my fingers from the wound, pieces of scab and fresh blood embedded under my fingernails to the quick. I have to calm myself down. Gather my thoughts.

I close my eyes and try to will the glass piece from my body.

I'm meditating. I clear away each mental distraction. I descend down into myself.

Past the past. Into the metaphysical realms of power and distance, where soul and ego collide.

I open my eyes with renewed calm. "This isn't real."

The drops of blood swirl and mix with the filth in the sink, morphing into a mandala. I resist the need to blink. The laughter of a strange child returns. I feel heat emanating from a bonfire. Dozens of strange eyes glare their anger at me. Voices are coming into my mind from across the world, asking questions and lying to me, and all of my trust and safety and acceptance are snatched away by greedy hands and mouths that refuse what I'm offering and instead take tiny bites out of me as I vanish into nothing.

I have to hold back the bursting dam of memories.

"Of course this is real." Don't believe the lies I'm telling myself. I can see things as they truly are now.

My lips begin moving, mouthing a single phrase, fixated on one thought, demanding it, a panted mantra. "getthefuckoutofme getthefuckoutofme getthefuckoutofme GET. THE FUCK. OUT. OF ME."

Snatching the blue Bic razor from the sink, I snap the plastic head from the stem, recover the tweezers from the floor, and pull the razor blade free. The realization of what I'm going to do to myself sets in. "Oh my God, Oh my God, Oh my God." I know what I'm going to do but I don't want to do it but I can't stop myself but I need this piece of glass to GET THE FUCK OUT OF ME.

I press the razor blade into the cut and see my skin open wider, slashing and tearing.

My suicide attempt comes to mind. Slicing. Spurting. "Oh my God get the fuck out of me Oh my God."

Tears stream down my face. I keep cutting. I have to reach the glass before it gets into my bones or my brain, and rips and hides and damages and squirms and slices and murders and never stops.

Blood is running freely now. This is excruciating and terrifying, but the alternative is worse. The wound is now twice its original size; I can easily stick my index finger and thumbnail into the gash. The triangular piece of shower door is elusive, again twitching out of reach as it pricks my finger. Sweat pours off me.

My head is pounding.

I'm going to puke.

I gather myself to try again with the tweezers when I see the glass emerge from my arm, squeezing from the skin like a popped zit. It drops to the sink, trailing a bloody streak as it snails with deceptive speed toward… where is it going? At first I think it's about to drop into the drain, but now it's sliding up, unaffected by gravity. I'm transfixed, staring at this tiny piece of glass as it snails steadily toward its destination. My pants and shirt are covered in blood, the bathroom linoleum slick with viscera.

"This is real. This is fucking happening." This is NOT real. This is NOT happening.

The glass springs from the counter, startling me, and merges into the mirror, leaving only a tiny speck of blood where it was absorbed. "Did it just go into the mirror? How the hell did it do that?" I cautiously extend my index finger, hand trembling, and slowly move closer to the mirror, to touch the blood speck.

I put my finger to my tongue, tasting.

My tongue is suddenly leaden and lifeless. Spit gurgles in the back of my throat.

I'm struck by the terror that all of my teeth have fallen out. I try to talk, but can't. My lifelong defense mechanism—my mouth, my words, my weaponry—collapses under the weight of unsustainable inadequacy. I

305

push with my throat and gag, but still cannot speak. I can't look in the mirror. I'm terrified, but I have to see my face, my mouth. Are my teeth gone did I swallow them is there nothing but a jagged gumline and a withered tongue and a closed throat what happened to my voice why can't I make myself say the things that I'm thinking and instead I'm silent and choking? I finally look at my reflection.

The mirror talks. "What have you done with Jeremy Peoples?"

I jump backward, nearly tumbling into the bathtub.

I peer into the mirror, at the mirror, but I am nowhere to be seen. My surroundings are behind me, reversed as they should be, but I'm missing. In my place is a faceless Silhouette, an outline with three-dimensional depth, holding my attention as I look through the mirror and into an abyss. The Silhouette is alive, disguising its identity to protect me from its deeper secrets, mysteries that would bring about instant insanity if I'm unprepared. I squint, peering deeper into the Silhouette, where I discern a spiral galaxy at the far end of all existence, close enough for me touch and also trillions of light years away.

Unfolding before me, the millennial past, eons and epochs of time, an expansive universe endlessly vast, yet also infinitely tiny as it disappears into the quantum depths of microscopic particles. Each end of existence mirrors itself, stars and electrons, planets and protons, an exposed portal in Stacy's bathroom.

The Silhouette is a part of me, outside of me, brilliant beyond comprehension and innocent, ancient and current and distant and present and infinite and dying. Inside the palm of its hands are strands of DNA.

I don't know how I know, but the chromosomes and genes are obviously mine.

The Universe exposes itself to me with cosmic vulnerability. Mathematics and poetry and celestial perfection and humanity and the Creator and creation and predestined plans and our detours.

I see the effects of nature and nurture, cause and effect, fate and free will, life and death, unlimited possibilities that my choices and the Bend of the Universe collaborate to create. Nothing is isolated from anything else, despite the lying feeling of loneliness. The existence of everyone and everything is carefully woven together. I see it perfectly and how I'm part of all of it, but it's too complex to grasp.

"What have you done to Jeremy Peoples?" The Silhouette demands. "Where is Jeremy?"

"I'm Jeremy Peoples," I stammer, betraying my uncertainty, pointing at my chest with both hands. "I haven't done anything to him. He's me. I'm right here. You can see me. You know I'm me. Look."

The sounds I hear aren't synced with the movements in the mirror, and I'm not sure I'm hearing what is being said, or if I'm being exposed to it, like, radiation. Am I speaking or thinking my answers?

The Silhouette finds my answers unsatisfying. Purple vapor loops in the air, spelling my name in Michelle's unmistakable handwriting. "You cannot be Jeremy Peoples because he is not here. You are here, Jeremy Peoples."

The Silhouette is an enigma. I am Jeremy Peoples. Jeremy Peoples is me. What does it want me to say? My memories are my perfect proof, but The Silhouette ignores my past and my present consciousness.

"If I'm not Jeremy Peoples, then who am I?" I try.

"You are not Jeremy Peoples because you are Jeremy Peoples," The Silhouette explains.

"This doesn't make fucking sense! How can I be me, and not be me at the same time?" I explode. "I haven't done anything to me. I've tried and failed. With everything that everyone else has done to me, I should be gone, but I'm not. I should be dead, but I'm not. Is that what you mean? Am I supposed to do something? Am I another version of me, a mistake that needs to be fixed? Is something coming to get me? I shouldn't be here anymore, right? Is that it? God fucked up, didn't He?"

I'm euphoric, on the verge of an epiphany, a yogi ascending up from a pinnacle, higher, further still, into the clouds, a prophet channeling the Word of God. I need to understand what The Mirror is revealing.

I'm also inadequate. I want to know, but I'm not up to the challenge.

"I'm a failure. I'm a disgusting person. I'm not real. I'm a liar. I made Mason so afraid he thought he had to kill me. I'm a coward. I stood by and let him kill Sarah. I fucked my best friend's wife and abandoned my own son. I treat everyone like shit and keep getting rewarded. What can I do to undo all of it?"

Despite a keen awareness that The Silhouette is guiding me to the answer, that the journey is as important as the resolution, the frustration of being inadequate and impatient churns to the surface.

I want revelation, not education.

"Tell me!" I demand. "What do you mean? I want to understand. I want to do what you want me to do. How can I do what you want if you won't tell me? What can I do? Do you want me to kill myself?"

The mirror has stopped talking. The Silhouette stares into me, accusing but somehow sympathetic.

"I don't know who I am." I start again. "I want to be Jeremy Peoples, but I'm tired of being him."

"What have you done to Jeremy Peoples?" It asks again. "What have you done with you?"

It feels like a sauna in the bathroom. I turn on the faucet and slurp lukewarm water directly from the tap, splashing some on my face, further soaking my bloodstained shirt. I use my bandage to towel off.

"I don't know what's happened to me," I sigh, and pour out a torrent of confused honesty. "I don't know where I am. I'm almost gone. I'm used up. I'm here, but I'm not the me I wanted to be. My me is the secret me, the Sarah Jeremy, not the Mason Jeremy. That me is gone, I'm dying. I was almost back to life, but it's ending. I hate this me, but this is all the Jeremy that's left. I want to be gone, I want to see Sarah again, but I can't let go of this me and be the me that died. I can't go on, but I'm going on. It's like being on life support. The machines kept me alive artificially, and now I'm keeping me alive, artificially. I need to let go, but I'm afraid and want to keep what I've got. I am me, I'm just not me, me. Anymore."

The Silhouette seems to consider everything I've said.

"Because you hate yourself, you'll do what is required when the time is right. And if you do, you'll give up everything you don't want in order to get the thing you can't acquire." The Silhouette seems to repeat Mason Reynolds's prophesy, except it isn't. It's the voice of the Originator of the prophesy.

Booming yet stoic. Terrifyingly credible.

The Silhouette is no longer a dark splotch obscuring my reflection. For less than a second, I see myself, bloody streaks of fingerprints across my face, my good eye bloodshot, pupil dilated. My damaged right eye bruised, a pulsating chorus of colors. I have a full beard now. There's an Ash Wednesday Cross on my forehead. I try to rub it off, but it won't smudge. My hair is soaked. I'm surprised I still have my teeth.

Then my reflection rapidly fades, diminishes, disappears, and another shape replaces me in the mirror.

It's Mason Reynolds. With his rifle. CLICK. CLICK. CLICK. "Look what you made me do," he repeats. CLICK.

"Jesus Christ!" I fall into the tub this time, my head bouncing off of the chipped tile and crumbling grout.

Colors fill the room, like soundless fireworks.

Michelle Ramone and Jeremy Peoples eye color emerald-green.

Cursive handwriting purple.

Bonfire orange.

Unforgivable black.

Thirty pieces of silver.

Undeserved career success gold.

Prom dress teal.

Blood-soaked maroon.

Public humiliation yellow.

Gunsmoke blue-grey.

I am Mason's final fatality. Years later, he's still trying to kill me.

A child's laughter. Mason pulls the trigger again. But this time there's an explosion of fire and violence, and I watch in horror as the bullet moves in slow motion, out of the mirror, across the bathroom, on a trajectory to bore a hole through my forehead. I flinch, but I don't see darkness. I see Sarah, falling.

Dying. Then again, she dies. Then again, she dies.

Faster and faster and faster and over and over and over and I just fucking stand there and do nothing.

"STOP! What do I have to do to make it fucking stop?!" I force my eyes open, begging for mercy. At any moment, I'm sure the floor will burn away into a smoking crater as the demons of hell claim a refugee.

The mirror has one last thing to tell me.

Mason says, "Be The Jeremy Peoples, not This Jeremy Peoples. He will know what do to when Jeremy Peoples doesn't know. Jeremy Peoples will do what's right when Jeremy Peoples chooses not to."

CHAPTER 31

Someone's pounding on the bathroom door.

"Are you ever coming out, dude? Are you taking an epic shit or something? You've been in there for fucking ever, dude. Did you fall in?" WHAM WHAM WHAM!! "Come on, dude, did you pass out?"

I'm crossways in the tub, folded in half, head and neck leaning against the tile, feet dangling over the edge. "I did fall in," I confess. The weakness in my own voice surprises me. I barely get the words out.

Laughter. The person banging on the door isn't the only one in the hallway. How long have I been in here? It feels like it's only been a few minutes, but I can't be certain. I'm tripping my balls off right now.

I get up out of the tub, crawling across the floor on my hands and knees, careful to avoid being seen by the mirror. I unfurl a long strand of toilet paper. The freshly reopened gash has started scabbing over.

The door springs open. Big Lou and Stacy are standing over me.

"What the actual fuck?" Stacy says, laughing again. "You cut yourself shaving, hoss?"

"Looks like he can't hold his liquor to me, Stacy." Big Lou's lips pull back into a sneer as he picks me up and sets me on my feet like I'm a toddler. He's a brute, six feet tall, solidly built (his neck circumference is easily the same as my thigh) with jaundiced eyes, straight black hair pulled into a pony tail. With his skintight Wrangler jeans, boots, mother-of-pearl and turquoise belt buckle, and long sleeve, snap up flannel shirt with smiley-face arrows for pockets, Big Lou looks like he bought a cowboy outfit at K-Mart.

"I'm gonna clean this up," I promise, grabbing a dirty wash cloth off the floor and turning on the faucet.

"Leave it. No one cares. Wipe your face, get your bandage," Stacy orders. "Soda and Jimmy made a beer run." I follow them into the hall, winding the bandage over the wad of toilet paper I'm using as gauze.

I need stitches. I focus instead on getting a drink.

Before I leave the bathroom, I chance a short peek at the mirror. Just reflections. I shake my head.

I'm tripping. I can't trust what I see. I can't trust what I think. I can't trust myself, or anyone else here.

There's a swirling energy around me, a rainbow of darker colors and flavors. Violet, maroon, midnight blue, streaks of pitch black and emerald-green. I've never seen my aura before. It tastes swampy.

Big Lou moves through a piss-yellow mist that periodically obscures him from view. I gag when I gaze into it. It's putrid. I get the sense that Big Lou is fatally ill and unconcerned. Stacy seems to have no aura. There's a translucent bubble that surrounds him, clear and floating and liquid, impenetrable and protected with a tinge of charcoal that can only be seen when he makes eye contact with someone. Stacy's aura indicates he is hiding in plain sight. These are guesses. I'm floating in space.

"Here," Stacy abruptly says and hands me a glass. It's half-full of brown liquid and couple of ice cubes. I sniff it tentatively, nostrils assaulted by the unmistakable harshness of cheap whiskey. "Drink that. It'll help.

You're having a bad trip, hoss." I hear Stacy tell me I was in the bathroom for twenty minutes.

I down the glass in two strained swallows.

"Here," Stacy says again. "Smoke this," and hands me a joint that he's rolled from my stash. "I've got things I need to show you. We're going to go for a ride. I've got something you need to see."

I don't understand what he's talking about, but I nod in agreement. "Say when, bro. Let's do it." I'm desperate for answers, and I want Stacy to know that I'm finally trying to put things right between us.

Stacy holds out his hand and I grab hold with my good hand, clasping our arms together between us in a hug of sorts. I start to pull away but he tightens his grip. My face and his are only inches away from each other. His clear blue eyes are wild, like a cult leader's, penetrating, intimidating and influential. I smell the alcohol on his breath. He won't break eye contact, but neither do I. His mouth curls open in a humorless grin, jaw clenched, teeth bared. "I'm going to hold you to that, hoss. We'll do it together."

Big Lou snorts and bellows from the living room, "WORD IS BOND."

Stacy agrees. "Fuckin' A. Semper Fidelis, motherfucker. Always faithful. Well, most of the time faithful, right, Jeremy? You're more of a Sometimes Fidelis. But tonight, right here, this is your second chance."

He lets go, finally.

Big Lou guffaws, loud and ugly.

The door flies open. Soda and James Sullivan enter, each smoking a cigarette and carrying brown paper bags from Piggly Wiggly. Jim has two cases of Old Style; Soda has two cases of Miller Genuine Draft. "Brewski number twoski," Jim brays.

Everyone laughs but me.

James Sullivan reminds me of the comedian Gallagher, both his appearance and jokes. He's balding, but with enough hair to grow the black and grey mullet sticking out the back of his mesh trucker hat. Jim's probably in his late-forties. Back when I lived here, he toured the bar circuit with a guitar, harmonica, microphone, and amp, playing songs from the 1960s and '70s. He called it "Jimmy Sullivan's All That I Know Show." His head and neck are too small for his bushy mustache, bulbous nose, and oversized ears. Faded jeans hang loosely off his waist; a blue work shirt and cheap, unlaced high tops complete his look.

"Still got that car, dude?" Soda says. I can't help but smile, remembering how I bought my 1986 Dodge Charger from him. It's long gone, sold to a high school kid when I got my first talk show contract at the Madison radio station. "No, that's my black Mitsubishi out in the driveway. Loved that Charger, though."

"Fucking turbo, dude," he remembers. "Killer car. Hated to sell it to you."

Brandon Bollinger. I imagine only his mother calls him Brandon. Soda looks like a skater without a skateboard. It's been almost five years since I've seen him, and he dresses the same. His hair is twisted into brown mini-Coolio braids, sprouting and springing in every direction. Soda is gaunt, with bushy eyebrows and matching goatee. He's got on oversized, baggy red jeans, a thermal undershirt, an unbuttoned, padded flannel shirt, and a pair of checkerboard Vans. Poor hygiene has left him with a visible line of beige tartar across his gumline, acne, and bad breath. His tattoos are (still) unfinished.

"Good memories," I lie. "Hated to sell it, too."

(the bitter cold backseat, Michelle's hope for her child snapping into heartbreak as tears ran down her face and every right answer I knew to give was swallowed and replaced with lies and excuses and failure)

Soda is a blur of red and orange and white flares, spiking and interjecting themselves into everyone else's personal space, oblivious to boundaries and constraints. Jim is contained in an azure, pulsating aura of insincerity—concentric rings barely inches away from his legs, torso, arms, neck, and head.

The room ablaze with vapor trails and bursts of energy. My own aural presence shocks me.

It's the color and smell of decay, gangrenous and musty, abandoned-basement-black, infection-green, shit-brown, blood-poisoning-red. It hangs on me like detritus on burial clothes, weighty and corrupting. I hold my breath, afraid I'll pollute myself with it. It's a fog of despondency, a murky vomitous haze that recoils from the others, darkening and retracting when anyone draws closer to me. I need to look away.

"Hey, hoss, snap out of it." Stacy literally snaps his fingers in front of my eyes.

I exhale with a burst. "I'm here, I'm awake."

"That boy is tripping like a motherfucker," Big Lou judges.

"Yo, so am I," Soda agrees. "They got some ridiculous shit in DC, dude."

Stacy ignores Soda and points across the kitchen. "Earth to Jimbo, you with us, man? You haven't said shit since you got back. Have a beer. You're the only one who's gonna drink that fucking Old Style so get to work, hoss." Stacy seems almost *too* normal right now. He's clearly in control of his faculties.

Jim Sullivan is in outer space, smiling vacantly, and he cracks open a beer at Stacy's command.

"Ahhhhh," he jokes. "Still warm, just how I like them." Foam bubbles from the can and onto the floor.

Everyone laughs but me.

I guess I'm sitting down at the kitchen table now. It must have happened a few moments ago. Big Lou leans against the sink, arms folded. Soda has popped up on the counter, feet swinging back and forth, bumping the cupboard doors over and over, a hollow "thump … thump … thump …" that I wish would stop. Jim stands between me and the living room like a sentry.

Stacy sits across from me, shuffling a deck of cards, lit cigarette dangling from his mouth, eyes narrow.

"Boys," Stacy is holding court. "Jeremy Peoples went to Madison a few years ago, after he and I severed our business ties for personal reasons—" everyone nods "—and became a radio disk jockey. Then he started meeting famous people. Who'd you get on your last show in Madison, Jeremy? Chris Farley, right before he died? And Butch Vig—the producer who made that shitty Nirvana record? He got all the stars...athletes, actors, comedians, musicians. He really thought he was something. Then he got an offer to take his show to goddamn Washington DC. Our nation's FUCKING capitol! Don't know how that's going, can't listen back in here in little old shitty Stoughton. But you did good for yourself, Jeremy. Really managed to make that whole Sugar River Shooting survivor thing work for you."

He tosses the cards on the table, scattering them without regard, and starts clapping in a highly exaggerated fashion: slowly, loudly, arms extended, across the table, in my face. "Fucking famous."

I'm a trapped rat, surrounded by feral cats and hunting dogs.

The faces of Stacy's friends are melted and blurred and stoic. No one is smiling as they listen to Stacy's monologue, his slanted history of how my life has been after he held me at gunpoint and evicted me.

"C'mon, let's hear it for the Prodigal Son, home again," Stacy demands. "Clap, motherfuckers."

Everyone complies with joyless applause. It's a cacophony inside the small trailer, reverberating off the stacks of dirty dishes and piles of aluminum cans. Big Lou puts his fingers in his mouth and pierces my skull with an unending catcall whistle. My black eye throbs, a half-beat behind the thudding in my chest.

Is all of this just a bad fucking trip?

Stacy holds up a beer. Everyone does. Except me. I'm the only one without a drink.

"To Michelle," Stacy toasts. "Gone, but never forgotten. And Jeremy Peoples, forgotten but never gone. One will never be back. I told the other one never to come back, you fucking jackal. Drink up, boys."

Big Lou chugs his beer in seconds and crushes the can against his forehead. Soda takes a sip. Jim tries to chug his beer but gags and can't. Stacy tips an MGD to his lips, never breaking eye contact, and downs it.

"Oh, damn, Jeremy, didn't have a drink. Sorry about that, Jeremy. We'll get you next time, hoss."

I hoist the joint that I've been holding above my head and take a quick hit. Extending my arm again, I offer my own toast. "To Mary Jane. Like Spider-Man, I'm always looking for her when she's gone."

No one laughs but me.

"Hey, Jimmy, you got your guitar with you? Wanna play a few songs?" I inquire.

"Nope," is all he says.

"Stacy, you've got like a thousand tapes. Let's put some music on, man," I press.

"Oh look! The fucking disc jockey wants some music on. Sure, hoss, what you want to hear? Grunge?"

Everyone laughs but me.

"Something chill. Alan Parsons Project, Pink Floyd, The Eagles, Wishbone Ash, Rainbow? You pick."

Jim walks over to the stereo, running his finger over the tapes until he selects one for Stacy to approve.

Queensrÿche, "Operation: Mindcrime." The shirt Michelle wore on the day Stacy caught us together.

Does he remember? I'm on the verge of a full-blown panic attack when it finally hits me.

Stacy's not tripping. He must've ditched his dose when I went to the bathroom. Why would he do that? I have to stay cool. Stacy can't know that I know. No one can know. I have to say something. Anything.

"Solid choice, Jimbo." My voice quavers. Everyone has to hear it. "Although…'Empire' stands up better over time. 'Promised Land' was underrated, too. And 'Mindcrime' *is* a good record, no doubt, but has anyone ever been able to figure out that crazy storyline? Were Catholic priests actually turning runaways into prostitute caregivers for hitmen to help kill televangelists and support South American guerrilla warfare? I'm not sure that heroin injections lead to brainwashing, although I guess I can buy into that part of it. The story was too convoluted, but the music is killer." I'm rambling, filling the dead air.

Soda snickers. "You've really thought about this album more than anyone in the world, dude."

I want to distract everyone from whatever they're planning. My mouth is my only weapon.

"It's all based on true stories, I'm telling you, man. The Vatican has been hiding rumors of sex trafficking and priests for years. Iran Contra proved we fund revolutions in Central America by selling arms to terrorists because we hated communists. And evil televangelists aren't farfetched; after all the Jimmy Swaggart and Jim and Tammy Bakker shit was exposed. Ever wonder where all those girls on milk cartons go? Is it really that fucking crazy to believe that Queensrÿche was actually on to something?"

"It's a tape, bro," Big Lou says. "You talk a lot when you finally start talking."

Everybody laughs but me. Stacy turns sharply and snaps, "Shut the fuck up, Lou."

"What the fuck, bro?" Big Lou complains, but he looks down at the floor and obediently submits.

"Let him talk," Stacy demands. "Go ahead, Jeremy. What do you mean he was on to something?"

My mind is racing. I'm dehydrated, nervous, but Stacy switched sides and I'm eager to capitalize.

"There's any number of stories about how the government and the church disappear people. It happens all the time in other countries, across history. Hitler couldn't have done what he did to the Jews without the church in Germany giving him cover. The Killing Fields in Cambodia, the Great Leap Forward in China, Stalinist Russia, Pinochet in Chile. Governments and religion do all kinds of heinous shit. Why can't it happen here? And music is a perfect way to send a message. U2 used to be super political about the British government and Ireland. Remember 'Sunday Bloody Sunday'? So, fuck yeah, Geoff Tate could have been on to something back in 1988, and we won't find out until who-the-fuck-knows when."

I've never been more thankful that I literally remember everything I've ever read.

"He's doing his radio show in your kitchen," Soda laughs, and Jim Sullivan agrees. "Love it."

"Fucking know-it-all," Big Lou says.

"Look, you of anyone should agree with what I'm saying, Louie *Lightfoot.* Your whole fucking culture was nearly wiped out and your people live on reservations with token casino money thrown at your leadership to keep you quiet. The church and the government decided that they could tell everyone it was God's Will to move west and confiscate land, take your guns, break written treaties and promises, force-march millions of you to your death in mass relocation plans, kill all the buffalo, kill you off, men, women and children, and on and on. You didn't even get your own state. The fucking Mormons even got theirs in 1912. You don't think it can happen still? Manifest Destiny proves it already did happen in the United States of America with broad public support. Hell, read about what happened at Wounded Knee, or with Leonard Peltier. If I'm a know-it-all, maybe more people should be know-a-fucking-littles."

Stacy and Jim both shout with surprise. Soda makes a "can you believe what he just did?" face, mouth open. "Goddammit, Big Lou, good thing you're not on the radio with him right now or he'd have made you look like a fucking retard," Jim observes. "You don't want to argue with that motormouth."

"Not with his fucking perfect memory," Stacy says. "He reads shit once and never forgets. He can throw out names and facts like this all day. He's not as smart as he sounds. He's got a talent for cheating."

Big Lou glares and takes a step toward me. "We're not on the radio, you fucking smart ass."

"You really think this is happening right now, Jeremy?" Stacy asks softly.

It's difficult to concentrate, vacillating between reality and altered perceptions and I'm hanging on for dear life, certain that one misstep right now could bring on catastrophe. Colorful auras and cigarette smoke churn together in the air, a further nuisance. I can't resist starting at them and contemplating what they could possibly mean and the music suddenly seems really loud—

"Hey!" Stacy slaps his hand on the kitchen table. "Back to reality, hoss. You think kidnappings and white slavery cults exist? You believe it's happening right now, under our noses, all around us?"

"Hell, yes, I do."

Stacy stands up, bumping the table with his knee. He shoves his half-smoked cigarette into the empty Miller Genuine Draft bottle. I have no idea what's happening next, but I've seen Stacy like this before. He pulls himself up to his full height and orders, "All of you fuckers, OUT. Everyone bug out except Jeremy." He points at me. "You stay. Everyone else, it's time to hit the bricks and get the fuck out. Now."

"Bro, I'm fucking tripping balls. I go out again it's going to fuck up my peak," Soda bitches.

"We just got back, man," Jim complains.

Big Lou is still reeling from me making him look like a fool, and using his ethnicity to do it, and now he's abruptly being kicked out. Everyone bitches, but Stacy is resolute.

I'm nearly two hours into an acid trip, wondering if I'm still hallucinating in the bathroom.

No one says goodbye. Stacy escorts them to the door. He steps out on the porch, talking under his breath to Big Lou. The cool, early morning air is a refreshing change from the dry, stale heat of the past few hours. "Fucking today," I hear Stacy say to Big Lou, then another car starts, headlights flash, tires squeal, and it's quiet again. Stacy comes back inside, rubbing his hands. I grit my teeth.

"We're gonna take a drive, hoss. I need to show you what happened to Michelle and Stevie."

CHAPTER 32

October 9, 1996, was the first day I ever got to be on the radio.

Three weeks earlier, I'd gotten a part-time job working behind the scenes at a couple of radio stations in Madison: 1360AM WDCN "Dane County's News" and 92Q "Madison's New Rock Alternative."

At first, I was hesitant about pursuing Michelle's suggestion to become a DJ, certain I'd never get a job in radio without a degree. I'd almost gone to college, but I didn't. It didn't feel right without Sarah. But Michelle's pregnancy had shaken me into action, and awakened a long dormant sense of personal responsibility. I'd finally stopped sleeping in my car and got an apartment in Madison; I didn't have any decent furniture and bought my wardrobe at thrift stores and yard sales, but it didn't bother me. It was the start of something new. I could actually afford cigarettes, a tiny glimmer of optimism penetrating the shroud of bleak discouragement that mummified me. I hated myself a bit less than before.

On a whim—and feeling guilty about being happy the day I got the job in radio—I drove to St. Sebastian's Hospital and sat in the parking lot, debating whether to go in, contrive a reason to be there, and "accidentally" bump into Michelle, tell her about my new gig, ask how the pregnancy was going...

But I didn't.

Instead, I wrote her a short note, folded it until I couldn't fold it anymore, and scribbled "Michelle Ramone" on it. It said: "Hey, Shell! I got an apartment here in Madison and I work at a radio station now. I'm there all the time. Call me if you have time." I jotted both my work and home phone numbers on it and handed it off to the receptionist who sat at the information desk in the lobby.

Michelle never called.

I assumed the receptionist had thrown away my letter. But some days I decided maybe Michelle had read it and thrown it away herself. If she was holding a grudge, it was justified unforgiveness. And yet—before I'd completely let Michelle down—she had believed I could be on the radio. Her faith in me was enough to fuel my audacity. I was ignorant, foolish, and desperate. I was also finally ready to try.

I still thought often of Sarah. Some days I couldn't get out of bed, or in the shower, or out of my own way. I struggled to disregard the plans we had made together. Every recollection of gunfire and cowardice screamed at me with the same intensity it held in the original moment. It was difficult to leave my apartment, debilitated and lost in time. I found drug-induced amnesia made the pain from an unforgettable past tolerable. On those days, blissful inebriation was the best I could do.

Yet, just as often, I did go out. I was finding my way. Uncertain progress, directionless, but surviving.

So I filled out employment applications at all the radio stations in the city. Multiple times.

One company called me. I accepted their offer even before they told me how much I'd get paid.

I got my start plugging local commercials into the Green Bay Packer broadcasts that aired on 1360AM WDCN. I liked it as much as I hoped I would, skipping my restaurant job as often as I could in order to hang around the station. I begged to be on the air. My boss kept telling me my time would come, that I needed more experience, that I had to keep practicing and sooner or later I would get an opportunity.

So it was just when I was sure I'd overestimated my abilities and would never be an air talent, I got called in unexpectedly. I'd worked the breakfast shift at the restaurant, hadn't made shit for tips, and wanted to get high and watch a previously viewed copy of "The Basketball Diaries" I'd bought at Blockbuster.

I almost told them I couldn't make it.

I changed my mind when they told me the night DJ on 92Q was sick and no one else was available.

It was my break. I walked in the door grinning at 6:09 p.m. My boss was just leaving for the day.

"Jeremy, just do what I told you to do and don't fuck anything up. I mean it. Push the buttons, play the CDs, and read the promo cards and the commercial live reads," he reiterated. "Don't try to be a star."

"Odie," I corrected him. "I'm gonna be Odie on the air. Not Jeremy. I have to stay in character." Picking an air name was my first inept attempt at escaping the Old Me and embracing a New Me. "Odie" was an homage to one of my favorite records ("Odelay" by Beck) and the stupid dog in the Garfield comic strip. I thought it was cool. The Program Director was lecturing me about only talking twice an hour, and NOT saying anything unscripted, but I barely heard a word of it. I zoned out, lost in an adrenaline daydream.

He waved his hand in my face. "Fucking part-timers," he mumbled and headed out the door.

I'd grown to like the idea of maybe being famous for something other than surviving a school shooting. I suspected they gave me the job because of what happened in Sugar River; no one expressly told me that, but my name had been in the media for months while I recovered, and then later, when I testified. I was sure someone was waiting to capitalize on it at the right time, but tonight I was too excited to care.

"Fuckin' A," I said to myself. "I'm gonna be on the radio." I thought of people I wanted to tell, mainly to shove their insults back in their face and prove to them how they'd been wrong about me. People who should've been supportive and nurturing and caring but instead had beaten the dreams out of me.

Almost.

An unfamiliar emotion began to eclipse bitterness: Joy. I saw Sarah in my recollections, but not as I most often did, in our final fateful moments together. The small moments of quiet happiness that came to mind, the times we'd shared walking to school, arguing over baseball, riding around in my car, working on homework, planning for the future. What would Sarah think of me today? I never would have done this if she hadn't... I was certain she'd be happy for me. With me. Sarah would support me, tease me when I made mistakes on the air, and sometimes she'd even call in on the request line to talk to me.

God, I missed her.

Then I blinked and my memories turned to Michelle. I thought of her nearly as often as Sarah. I missed her, nearly as much as I missed Sarah. We hadn't spoken since April and I imagined what she looked like with a baby belly. Was she still lonely, or had pregnancy changed things? Did she wonder and worry about me, or had she hidden away our months together in her heart as a fading misstep? The lie must've taken root over the past five months and seven days. Did she believe her own deception, too, almost?

God, I missed her.

I'd begun to turn her irrational belief in me into something with potential, a hope that if I succeeded in radio—and validated her belief in me by getting my shit together—it might be an acceptable substitute for the other ways I'd failed her. I wondered why hadn't I told her the reason I was actually afraid of being a father. She might've understood and accepted it. I wish I'd shared my deepest secrets, found my courage, and given back to her what she gave me. The urge to call her was overwhelming. To thank her. To apologize.

To tell her I was finally trying to be a better man. To see if there were possibilities to explore.

I wanted to believe that she'd be proud of me, but I couldn't even be sure that she didn't hate me.

As I headed to the 92Q studio, I saw a pink "WHILE YOU WERE AWAY" message slip taped to the 92Q studio door with my name on it. No one ever called me here. I yanked the memo off the door.

The note had a message time of 5:45 p.m. and read simply: "Mish called. Her job interview at St. Sebastian's happened six weeks earlier than scheduled. In town until midnight." There was no phone number. At the bottom, the secretary had written a curt reminder: "No personal calls."

I instantly knew. Michelle had had her baby—our baby. Early. Today. Was she telling me I could visit but I only had until midnight? Did she go to the hospital without Stacy? I wouldn't be surprised if Michelle had decided to work up until her delivery date. Had she gone into labor during her shift and deliberately waited to call Stacy? Was she…was she waiting…on me? Was she giving me one more last chance?

It was an impossible decision.

In forty-three minutes I was going on the air for the first time, and if I walked out tonight they would fire me, right when things in my life were just starting to get a little better. Even if traffic was light and I got every light between here and St. Sebastian's…I'd be gone for an hour and a half. And that was only if nothing went wrong and I spent less than one minute with Michelle and our baby.

There was no way I could leave. There was no way I shouldn't go and see her. And our child.

I made a calculation. My five-hour shift ended at midnight; technically, my last talk break was at 11:50 p.m. The overnight girl would be here before that. I could tell her that I had an emergency, fly across town and even though I'd be late, there could still be time.

"That could work," I assured myself. I idealized the best-case scenario, convinced I could do both.

I slipped into the studio with a paper copy of the night's music log. I had to pull the CDs for my shift. The list called for Pearl Jam, Beck, Poe, The Pixies, Dandelion, PJ Harvey, REM, L7, Nirvana, Cypress Hill.

Michelle was in the hospital with our baby. I couldn't concentrate. What if Stacy saw me at the hospital?

He'd kill me.

I tried to clear my head.

92Q "Madison's New Rock Alternative." 92Q "Madison's New Rock Alternative." I practiced.

I tried using a DJ voice. I tried my regular voice. I had to project and articulate without sounding unnatural and pronounce everything perfectly and sound confident and cool while pressing all the buttons and keeping track of everything and talking over the intro music of the songs but finishing before the lyrics started.

Real DJs didn't call themselves DJs, they called themselves "jocks" and they didn't "talk over the intro" they "ramped the song and hit the post." I needed to use the right radio terminology. I was a jock now.

I made copies of the promo and commercial cards and instantly memorized them.

I smoked a cigarette.

I mentally mapped the fastest route to St. Sebastian's Hospital from the radio station.

Then it was time.

The 92Q "Madison's New Rock Alternative" Afternoon Jock went by the air name "Andrew Wood." It was an homage to Mother Love Bone, a band on the verge of stardom in 1990 when their lead singer overdosed on heroin. Half of Mother Love Bone hired Eddie Vedder and found immortality as Pearl

Jam; 92Q's Andrew Wood hated the idea that few people had ever heard of Mother Love Bone's Andrew Wood.

"You going by Jeremy on the air or something else?" he asked, right before his last talk break.

"Odie. I'm going to by Odie on the radio," I replied.

Andrew Wood nodded. "Odie. Like 'overdose. O.D.' Very cool. Deep. That jams, dude." He was super cool to promote that I was coming on the air after him, played the commercials and got out of the way, so I could settle in behind the sound board. He had his own headphones. I used the ones the station provided.

I cleared my throat and imitated every radio personality I'd every listened to when I was a teenager.

At 7:16 p.m., I opened the mic. The first song I talked out of was Soundgarden "Fell On Black Days."

"92Q Madison's New Rock Alternative, I'm Odie, with you until midnight filling in for Ace FreeBass. Be sure to join us this Saturday for a Badger Tailgate starting at 10:00 a.m., sponsored by Budweiser, The King of Beers, Mad City Harley Davidson, and Badger Bread Subs on East Washington. Then, stay for the game when U Dub takes on UNLV. Hope to see you there. Now, here's The Beastie Boys with 'Sabotage,' on 92Q Madison's New Rock Alternative!" I nervously stumbled my way through my first break on the radio, awkwardly pitching my voice up an octave because I forgot how to breathe in panicked enthusiasm.

I closed the mic.

Pumped my fist. Stopped. Looked around. A rush of excitement blew through my body. "HOLY. FUCKING. SHIT. I'm on the radio! I...am on the radio! Me. On 92Q. HOLY. FUCKING. SHIT. I can't believe it."

I froze. Did I turn the mic off? I was cursing and shouting. Was it going over the air? No. Relief.

That moment was better than any drugs I'd ever taken. The tragic past and the uncertain stress of the present had entirely disappeared into the background during those transcendent sixteen seconds.

I needed more.

Alone in the studio, tens of thousands of people across Madison, Wisconsin—a city I had placed on a pedestal of cool as a teenager growing up in a small farming town—had just heard my voice. There was a thrilling power in knowing I had an audience but I didn't have to look at them, and I felt no social anxiety while the mic was on. It was an only child's dream: everyone listening to me, but I didn't have to listen to them. It was like I just had thousands of one-on-one conversations simultaneously.

"Oh, shit, the CD!" Transfixed, I'd forgotten to start next song. That eleven seconds of dead air was the only mistake I made during my first hour on the radio. I never sat down.

The second hour was better. I finally sat down.

I got cocky in the third hour and took a listener phone call. She requested Cracker, "Low," and I knew that song was on our playlist. I recorded her, asked her "what's your favorite radio station?" and got her to say "92Q Madison's New Rock Alternative!" However, I didn't properly edit the audio and it sounded terrible on the air. I held my breath, waiting for the Program Director to fire me.

He didn't call.

The fourth hour was harder. I didn't want to read the copy. I had things to say about the songs, the bands, what they meant to me, things I knew about the singers and guitar players, and wanted to talk more and wanted the freedom to say what I wanted to say when I wanted to say it and move the songs around so I could talk up the ramp and hit the post of the ones I liked more than others. But I didn't.

I knew that night that being a jock was cool, but what I really wanted was to be the show. Playing music that others had picked out held only limited appeal. The thrill came when I opened the mic.

When I spoke, people responded. I wanted more of that. I finally felt free, if only momentarily.

Imagination had replaced memory for the first time in years. I could see my future, and it seemed possible. I didn't imagine myself on stage introducing bands in front of huge crowds like many of the DJs in the building bragged about doing. I wasn't even all that enthralled with the idea of meeting celebrities or making a lot of money. I envisioned myself alone in a studio atop a high rise in New York, sharing my opinions and creating audio art for millions of listeners.

Always behind the mic. And always taking calls.

A flashing strobe on the ceiling indicated when the studio line was ringing. I could push one button to start a recording and another button to talk to the caller through the mic but remain off-air. "92Q, this is Odie. What you calling about tonight?" I announced, trying hard to sound cooler than I was. Women called the studio line asking who I was, if they could meet me, would I play their request, what did they need to do for me to get a station t-shirt, if I had free concert tickets? The flirting was fun for a few calls, then uncomfortable as my mind would wander back to Sarah. Or Michelle. It felt like cheating.

By the final hour of my show, the newness had worn off and my enthusiasm waned as a feeling of impending doom took hold. Worried about Michelle. I went through the motions, ignoring the phone when it rang, and doing my promo reads without any zeal, fretfully chewing on my fingernails.

The overnight DJ was Alexis, she was only nineteen, and was super cool about letting me leave at 11:48 p.m. after I pulled her first two hours of music. I told her I had a family emergency.

I sprinted down the hall, burst through the door, and ran across the empty parking lot to my car. It started easily, which I never took for granted as the Charger aged and I neglected basic maintenance.

"THANK YOU!" I shouted to the gods for favoring me tonight, for a change, finally, and tore out of the parking lot and on to the Beltline. I pushed it as fast as I thought I could and not get pulled over.

Exited off the Beltline.

Surface streets. Ran the yellow lights, slammed on the brakes for the red ones.

I took corners too fast. I nearly struck a pedestrian. I didn't slow down or look back.

I blew through stop signs.

Shops and houses and bus stops and trees blurred by me as I hit sixty mph in a thirty-five-mph zone.

I never even turned on the radio. I raced in silence, aside from the wind that whistled through rusty doors and windows that no longer sealed tightly. It sounded like an adoring crowd, full-throated, cheering.

I kept looking from the speedometer to the windshield to the dashboard clock.

12:03 a.m.

12:04 a.m.

"Goddamn it, you stupid fucking clock, I'm going as fast as I can go!"

12:05 a.m.

Random thoughts leapt into my mind as I sped across Madison. I was just on the radio for the first time in my life and I sucked, but now knew I could do it. I was a father, and no one would ever know that I was a father. Would Sarah and I have ever had children? She'd still be in college. Probably not.

I saw the hospital, a dark outline against the night sky with a few windows lighted up. I tried to guess if Michelle's room was visible. I accelerated.

The Dodge Charger was barely up for the challenge. My rattletrap was sputtering and running hot by the time I pulled into St. Sebastian's parking lot at 12:22 a.m.

I easily found a parking spot close to the door, scrambled out of the car, slammed the door without locking back and ran. I was winded after only a dozen yards. Smoking had taken its toll on me already.

The automatic door wouldn't open. I jumped up and down, waving my arms at the sensor, before I saw the sign that said, "AFTER HOURS VISITORS MUST USE THE SOUTH ENTRANCE." I had no idea which was South so I guessed "left" and ran down the sidewalk. I was right. The gods continued to smile on me.

The door whisked open and I charged up to the same desk where I'd left a note only three weeks earlier.

Thankfully it was a different receptionist. "What room is Michelle Ramone in?" I demanded, panting.

"Are you family?" she asked. "Visiting hours ended a while ago."

Fuck you. "I'm…her brother," I lied. "I'm from…Florida, and I just got here. She had her baby tonight!"

"Young man, there's no need to be running then. Her baby isn't going anywhere. If she just had the baby, you won't be able to go in the room anyway." But she smiled. "Michelle Ramone is in Room 316. You can take the elevator right behind me to the third floor and check in with the desk up there."

I was off and running again, wheezing and sweating.

"No running! Sir! You can't run in here," the receptionist yelled and I ignored her.

I got to the elevator and mashed the button. Over, and over, and over.

For a few seconds I considered taking the stairs, but finally the elevator doors opened with a "DING!"

I stabbed the third-floor button with my thumb. Over, and over, and over. Finally, the doors slid shut.

"Fucking go," I urged the elevator. "C'mon, c'mon, c'mon." I was literally jumping up and down.

The elevator stopped on the second floor. Three people started to get on, but looked confused.

"Is this going down?" an elderly man asked me, holding the door open with a liver spotted hand.

"No. Up." I pointed up to further illustrate the direction I needed to go.

"Oh, I see," he mused, but didn't move his hand, and began to confer with a younger couple. "This one is going up," he informed them. "I don't know why it opened here then."

"Excuse me, but I'm in a fucking hurry," I interjected. "There's another elevator coming soon, OK? This one is only going to the third floor and then it'll be on its way back down in a second. I'm gonna need you to move your goddamn hand, though, because this is an emergency."

All three of them gasped. The old man let go of the door, startled.

"Thanks." I smiled insincerely. "You have a nice night, now. Bye!" I waved as the door closed.

When the elevator door opened again, this time it was on the third floor.

"Son of a bitch," I gasped. It was 12:27 a.m.

I glanced around, trying to get my bearings, squinted and saw signs above each archway. Rooms 300-319 were on the other side of the nurses' station. I dashed around the desk, skating on slippery linoleum.

Room 316.

I was cautious. I gathered myself. I couldn't just barge in. I had to know who was in there first.

I squatted down, and peeking through a sliver of an opening in the doorway I saw someone in a white lab coat, then glimpsed the briefest image of Michelle's strawberry-blonde hair and freckled face as she adjusted a pillow and slumped out of view again. Our baby was premature. Was everything OK?

I eavesdropped. A voice (the doctor?) was saying "—he's small but completely healthy. We'll keep them here until Wednesday, and then evaluate if mom and baby, or at least mom, can go home."

He's *small.* He.

A boy. I had a son.

We had a son.

I looked down the hallway in both directions, and seeing no one, I leaned in to listen again.

"—any other questions, Mr. Ramone? If not, we can leave the three of you alone for a while."

Mr. Ramone?

I couldn't see enough from this vantage, so I touched the door and nudged it open another half-inch, but remained frustratingly and tantalizingly blocked by the angles of the room.

Then I saw what I already knew.

Stacy had beaten me there.

I had missed the window Michelle had given me.

I tried to peek again, before the fear of what might happen gripped me. Could I see his little face, his tiny fingers or toes? Was he perfect and wrinkly and crying? Did he have green eyes and black hair? Were his tiny feet still blue from the footprints they'd put on his birth certificate? Were there already lies on that birth certificate, listing Stacy Ramone as the father?

How was Michelle?

What was my son's name?

I'd spent months in denial, uselessly trying to suppress the memories of my relationship with Michelle, and especially that last, ill-fated conversation in the backseat of my car. Tonight though, I saw my life reimagined as a pink note taped to a radio studio door, and had reconsidered the decision I had made. I never stopped caring for Michelle, or our child, but I was afraid—afraid that because of what had been done to me, and what I was capable of—it made me dangerous. Hope had crept in seven hours ago, but like me, its arrival was late and ineffectual. I let myself believe I might have the chance at a life with Michelle.

And end a generational curse.

It was fucking stupid and naïve. My son would always be Stacy's son.

I'd stayed too long and hadn't even made it in the room.

"I'm sorry, Michelle," I whispered. I kissed the first two fingers on my right hand, and touched the door. "I can't fix this. I love you and there's nothing I can do about it." It was the first time that I'd used that word to describe how I felt about Michelle Ramone, and I vowed to never use it again. She was just as lost to me as Sarah was, out of reach and unforgotten. "Take care of my son. Take care of yourself."

I walked out of their lives forever.

Hopelessness is deadly when it reappears after it seems defeated. The despair that overwhelmed me was stronger than anything I could have prepared for. Eager and optimistic after finding a hint of happiness in a radio studio only hours earlier, I was again shattered and burdened with merciless regrets. Every failure demanded to be revisited and I couldn't make it stop and all I wanted was for everything to stop.

I went home. I thought of Sarah. I thought of fatherless sons. I wallowed in it, alone in my apartment, and drank half a fifth of Jack Daniels to work up the courage to do what I wanted to do.

I played "Soma" by Smashing Pumpkins on my paint-spattered boom box, the song surging within me, encouraging me down the dark path, to sleep, to push into the pain, to make it worse for a second but then watch it drain away completely, to emptiness or reunion.

Either option—desolation or adulation—would be more satisfying than this life.

The first three punctures stung like jabs in the opening round of a fight. I pushed harder. Deeper.

The utility knife razor sliced easier and faster than I expected, a two-inch long, red sliver of freedom from wrist to forearm that emptied me of guilt and shame in a flood of bloody release.

It brought warmth without pain.

I wasn't afraid to die. Sugar River had permanently cured me of that fear. But I was afraid of the unknown. What if death was worse than life? What if a reunion with Sarah was just a delusion?

I would only find these answers through experience.

My hands and feet fell asleep, both heavy and numb and tingling with pinpricks.

Lightheaded. Nauseous.

The blood kept pouring out of me.

Suddenly, I was unsure.

Unexpectedly, there was a will to live.

I took a step toward the phone, slipped on bloody slickness, and fell in a heap, head throbbing and airy.

The familiarity of dying shook me. I swore I could see Sarah, gasping for breath, hopeless and just out of reach. Michelle screamed at me to wake up, but when I tried to speak, foam gurgled in my throat.

Why was I holding on? What was I holding on for? Who was I holding on for?

I was almost there. If I could just resist the urge to stay alive, I'd be at the end soon.

But a wordless power with soft tendrils of survival sunk itself deeply into my heart, like the gentle mouth of a rescue dog dragging a drowning victim to shore. I fought and thrashed. It held me. Tightly.

"Let me leave," I pleaded, my words barely a whisper. "Stop. Let me do it. Please. It's over..."

It wasn't over. Instead, the slowing silence of my apartment was filled with the sounds of a tragic future.

The universe gave me a vision of my son, a lonely child, an angry teenager, a damaged man.

I couldn't see his face, only an unhealthy soul through green, accusing eyes.

He was telling me everything and showing me his desperation and how he'd been traumatized and was demanding that I answer him: "Why. Did. You. Abandon. Me? Why. Didn't. You. Love. Me?"

I pulled on the phone dangling next to me and dialed 911. When the ambulance arrived, the EMTs dragged me out of my blood-soaked kitchen and took me back to St. Sebastian's. I had decided not to die that morning, postponing the inevitable. I hated my myself for not going through with it.

CHAPTER 33

It's been a long time since I've been in Stacy Ramone's 1972 Pontiac LeMans. One thousand four hundred thirty seven days to be exact.

I'm obsessively rubbing the scars on my left wrist, my recollections distorted through the lens of LSD.

What's a memory...

(skin tingles as Pink's mouth touches gunshot wound scars then guilt then shame then rage pushing her off I just want to forget what I've done just take me into the room just take me away just take me)

...and what's a hallucination?

("I need to show you what happened to Michelle and Stevie.")

I have to focus. Stacy's finally going to tell me—show me—what happened to Michelle and Stevie.

We've been in the car for a while and he hasn't said a word. The LeMans is perfectly clean: nothing on the floorboards, not a speck of dust on the dashboard, a sharp contrast to Stacy's trashed house trailer.

I have no idea how long we've been driving, where we are, or where we're going. I'm staring out the window. The LeMans rumbles with power as Stacy speeds along winding Wisconsin backroads. He's hunched over the steering wheel, cigarette in his mouth, neck vein twitching, hair and eyes wild.

I'm devastated by the revelation about Stevie and I'm barely holding it together.

(it burns it's burning I hold the lit cigarette against the back of my hand while Michelle drives away leaving me next to my frozen Dodge Charger and my skin scorches and a small dot of cauterized blood grows larger but I keep it there until finally that burn hurts more than the disgust I feel about myself)

Maybe I'm the ghost, and it's Sarah and Michelle (and Stevie) who are alive, moving on with their lives, as I'm slowly ushered into purgatory, forever observing my past with grief, a deserving penance.

I believed I'd meet my son this morning, that he'd toddle out of my old bedroom in a pair of *Star Wars: The Phantom Menace* pajamas, a child version of an undamaged Jeremy Peoples, rubbing his eyes, asking for a bowl of Cookie Crisp. I'd introduce myself as Uncle Jeremy, hoist him in the air. and have breakfast with him, but that is never, ever going to happen because somehow Stevie is gone, too.

"Where are we going, Stacy?" I ask again.

I lied when I told Stacy why I came home. I'm here because of Stevie, at least as much as I am for answers about Michelle, probably more about any misplaced loyalty to Stacy himself. I planned to hold his hand during the funeral. Stevie could sit next to me and I would sneak a look to see if he had the same emerald-green eyes that his mother has. Had. That I have. I'd tousle his hair and put him in a little man suit with a clip-on tie and tell him to brave, like his mom, for his mom.

For me, too.

"I'll tell you when we get there. You need to see what happened. Ten more minutes."

Streaks of grey snow against a backdrop of dark brown are a momentary distraction. The trees on both sides of the road are leafless and lifeless, the ground muddy, ditches filled with snowmelt and litter.

It's a monochromatic masterpiece in the morning sun.

I feel like I'm gliding along next to the car now, just outside the window.

My body remains in the seat, zoned out and vacant like an animated corpse, but my essence has become a traveling soul attached to the living in an attempt to avoid my final punishment.

(a slap and an insult and a closed fist take the wind out of me and doubles me over. Another one to my kidney and I'm sure I'll piss blood after that and will be covered in yellow-purple-green bruises and the terrible smiling angry looming drunken face is shouting, hysterical, "fight back you fucking pussy!")

Stacy startles me back to the present.

"You didn't just stab me in the back when you slept with Michelle," he begins. "You stabbed me in my fucking heart. You both did. I brought you into my home and I treated you like a brother."

His anger is just as fresh for him as memories are for me. He hasn't forgotten, and will never let it go.

Stacy's been thinking about this moment for years.

"We were business partners. That was me helping you. I knew what you went through in that school. I didn't ask for anything back. Just loyalty. But you took my money and you just kept taking and taking until you fucking took a bunch of shit that wasn't yours to take," he continues. "I should've killed you."

I'm in no shape for this conversation. My perceptions are altered. I'll answer questions and reveal too much. Stacy must've taken this into consideration. Is that why he had us all take LSD, then pocketed his? Are we driving to see what happened to Michelle and Stevie? Or is he taking me to an execution?

"You should've killed me," I agree. It's all I can say in order to withhold everything else. "I wanted you to. I remember it often, play it back perfectly. Michelle shouldn't have stopped you. I was pissed she did."

"Why'd you agree to come back when I called? Did you love her? At least tell me you loved her."

"It's complicated, Stacy." I'm trying to outthink him. "I love you both. I loved you like a brother, too. You pulled me out of the gutter, like, literally. And I loved her, yes, I guess, but it was more like I appreciate her. I don't know how to get my thoughts together to say what I wanna say. It was healing. Kindness."

Stacy corrects me. "You didn't love me. If you loved me like a brother, you never would have done what you did. You would've told me Michelle was lonely, so I could've tried to fixed things with her, hoss."

He's right. "I know. But I didn't. And now I can't change it. I don't know what else to say about it."

"How about you're fucking sorry?" Stacy shouts. "How about some shit like, 'I shouldn't have done that to you, Stacy, and if I got to do it all over again, I'd fucking do it differently?' How 'bout you start there?"

I'm going to be honest and I shouldn't be. It doesn't matter anyway. "But I'm not sorry."

"The fuck did you say?!" Stacy's face is red, eyes flashing with rage. "Tell me I just heard you wrong."

"I know I should be sorry. But I'm not. And if I told you I was I'd be lying and I guess I feel like I owe you more than that. I'm sorry we got caught. I'm sorry it fucked you all up, and our friendship, but I don't have any remorse about it. I'd probably do it again. No. I'm not sorry."

Stacy opens his mouth, closes it, then laughs derisively. "You're… fucking…sick."

"I am," I grant him. "But I also meant it when I said I love you, too. I know I did some shit that was horrible and ugly and I'm glad I did it because of how I felt about Michelle, but I also feel like the worst person who ever lived because I fucked you over to do it, and I changed everything forever."

I'm dangerously close to revealing parts of the story I know I shouldn't reveal, but the LSD has me pouring out my thoughts and heart and now it's nearly impossible for me to hide the truth from him.

"Brothers don't fuck their brother's wife." He spits the words, taking his eyes off the road to glare at me.

"I know. But it wasn't like that, Stacy."

"No! It absolutely was LIKE THAT. We had a pact. We swore an oath to each other. Do you remember?" Stacy snorts. "What the fuck am I saying? Of *course* you remember."

"I remember. That's part of the reason I'm here. Not just Michelle. I'm here for you, and I came here for Stevie, too. I came to honor what I told you I'd do if you ever needed me, even after you'd put a gun to my head and threw me out and told me you'd kill me if you ever saw me again. I thought you'd blow me away when I walked through the door this morning, but I came anyway. I'm here now because of what we promised each other." I offer half-truths convincingly, barely concealing devastating secrets.

"Maybe oaths mean more to Marines than they do to farm kid assholes."

"They probably do, bro. You're a better person than I am," I suggest.

"Don't patronize me, hoss. I don't need you to tell me what kind of a person I am," he orders.

I'm not going to get into a moral comparative. I'm the drugged-out, suicidal school shooting survivor who slept with his best friend's wife, and he's an ex-Marine drug dealer and loyal husband. It's messy.

(my open mouth on Michelle's neck, down to her shoulder, to her breasts and her hands are in my hair and her fingernails dig into my back and her breath comes in calming gasps as my hand finds her lower back and my other hand slips to her inner thigh her breathing quickens and she whispers my name)

"We promised each other that no matter where we were, no matter how long it had been since we talked, no matter what had come between us, if you needed me or I needed you, that we each had a 'Get Out of Jail Free Card' for the other. I'm here with yours," I recount. "You made me swear that we'd always be there for each other, no matter what. I swore, I'm here. What can I say?"

"We both swore," Stacy says. "But I meant it. You here now with that 'Get Out of Jail Free Card' doesn't make up for Michelle. You can't undo all your bad shit with a little bit of good shit. It doesn't mean you never did the bad shit you've done, and the bad shit doesn't release you from the promise you broke because it's still in effect. You owe me either way. You don't get a fucking cookie for showing up and doing the right thing. You do the right goddamn thing because it's the right goddamn thing."

I'm mentally incapacitated. I hear the words, I'm just not sure I understand what he means.

"Michelle was lonely. I should've told you. You're right. And I'm sorry I fucked you up, OK?" I say what he wants me to say, hoping to protect Michelle, and Stevie, even in death.

"But you'd do it the same way all over again if the situation was the same? That's not an apology."

"I can't expect you to understand this part, Stacy. And don't get pissed. I'm not being condescending. I'm not saying you aren't smart enough. I'm saying I can't explain it in a way that makes sense."

Sparkles and vapor trails skyrocket across my field of vision. A terrible mix of visions flicker through my mind. Michelle lies dead at Sugar River High School, Sarah is Stevie's mom, Stacy is holding Mason's gun, and I'm dancing with Pink at my prom. It's a mysterious jumble of commingled recollections.

Stacy turns and stares at me for an unnervingly long time while driving seventy-five mph. "Try me."

I swallow hard. Fuck it. "I had no hope. I came out of the hospital after the shooting with nothing to live for. Mason had come to the school to kill me. And instead of getting me, he murdered my girlfriend. And my best friend. And a bunch of others. That's all my fault. I have to live with that. Nothing helps. I would've done anything to stop that feeling. I was desperate. For meaning, for connection, for anything except guilt and pain. Michelle was my friend and she helped me live again. I forgot how to be a human being and she gave me a gift and I know I shouldn't have done it, but I don't care because I would've done anything to make the memories *FUCKING STOP*." Tears pour down my face. "I *am* sorry. And I'm *not* sorry. The few weeks I had with her was the only time in *seven fucking years* I didn't want to die."

Stacy says nothing. I'm rambling.

"Mason shot Sarah right in front of me. That memory never, *ever* fades. I see it every day, and feel it every day, dozens of times a day, like it just happened. And now I've got these new, terrible memories. Your phone call telling me Michelle is dead and now you telling me Stevie is gone, too. I'm in a prison of recollections. Time doesn't heal all wounds. Time heals small wounds. How can I heal and move on if I can't forget anything? Fading memories are a blessing. You have no idea. I can't live in peace."

Stacy mumbles something. When I start to ask him to repeat himself, he cuts me off.

"I said, you still shouldn't have done it. I know you're fucked up. But you still shouldn't have done it."

Stacy pulls over to the side of the road. Where are we? How long have we been driving? Fifteen minutes? An hour? Longer? Why are we stopping? Was this the scene of a car accident? How does it all fit together?

I've only gotten fragments from Stacy, like scattered, upside-down jigsaw puzzle pieces.

"And this time you're gonna keep your word to me. We're here."

"What do you mean? How? What do you need me to do?"

"You're going to help me get Michelle and Stevie back from the motherfuckers that took them."

CHAPTER 34

Everything I believed about the last five days is turning out to be a lie.

Michelle and Stevie aren't dead, they're missing? Is this just another lie? I drove eight hundred miles for a funeral that isn't happening. Because of a phone call. A FUCKING PHONE CALL. I just believed Stacy.

How could I be so stupid? What is going on? Why am I so easily manipulated?

What the hell have I gotten myself into? How the hell am I going to get myself out of this?

Why did I dose? Of all the things we could've done, I took the shit that lasts at least six hours. I've been in deep with drugs before, but I've never made an irrevocable mistake. Now, I'm sitting in Stacy's LeMans outside of a middle-class family's home with someone who might be plotting revenge and murder and is forcing me to be an accomplice. Is any of this real? Even if Stacy gives me his full explanation, I can't trust his version of reality. I shouldn't trust my own impaired judgment, either.

Through the gossamer of aural lights and hazy perception, I feel the sting of betrayal.

And my own obsequiousness. "What do you mean? Someone took Stevie and Michelle? Who?"

Stacy lights a cigarette, reminding me of my own sudden need for one.

"I'm pretty sure they're not in there anymore, but they were," Stacy explains. "When I realized I was on the radio when I called you, I knew I couldn't tell you what's really going on. They can't know that I know yet, and I needed to get you here. Me and Big Lou have been following this guy since Michelle and Stevie disappeared. It all comes back to this house, and the church. Now do you see what we're up against?"

I have no idea what he's talking about.

"Michelle...Stevie...they're not dead?" I finally stutter. "You gotta help me understand. I'm...I'm not thinking right. I'm trying to put the pieces together, but I'm not seeing what you're saying here, man."

Stacy is frustrated. "Listen to what I'm saying, hoss. Michelle is gone. Stevie is gone. These motherfuckers in this house *took them*. Lured them and trapped them somehow and took them and then who-the-fuck-knows? Chained them in the basement? Sold them into slavery? Carried out a cult murder? I don't know. I can't go to the cops because they're *a part of it*, man. They're using their *church*. Everyone is looking the other way because it's powerful people and everyone is getting rich. It's twisted shit, man. We have to get to these sick fucks and get Michelle and Stevie back before it's too late."

Stacy suddenly brandishes the .357 magnum revolver he'd once held to my head. The sight of it nauseates me. He puts the barrel to his head, then taps the driver's side window. "You owe me."

"Bro. Listen. I want to help, but I'm tripping major right now. We're going to run into this house with your gun, start shooting, and searching their basement and shit? I can't hardly see straight and I'm peaking and my mind is all confused in this story you're telling me right now."

Stacy's bright blue eyes burn with a seething rage. He takes off his glasses, wipes the lenses. "I'm not going in shooting. I want Michelle and Stevie back. They give me what I want, I'll be in and out. I don't want to kill anyone, but I can't let them get away with this. They took my *family*. I have to find them."

Is this conversation really happening, or is it in my mind?

"Look." I have a lump in my throat. "You told me *on the air* you needed me to come home because Michelle had *died* and you needed me at the funeral because you didn't have anybody. When I got here, you had a house full of people. Then you tell me Stevie's gone, too, but you're not telling me shit except you'll tell me later and then we go on this drive and you've got your gun and now you're saying Michelle isn't dead, Stevie isn't dead, they're kidnapped and this whole fucking town—wherever the hell we are—is in on some conspiracy and we can't call the cops and it's up to you and me and that Big Lou motherfucker? You lied to get me here, you've been lying to me the whole time I've been here."

Stacy is electric with intensity, but his hands are steady. He points the gun in my direction. Not *at me*, exactly, just lets his hand and wrist go limp and the barrel of the gun drops and bobs up and down.

"Sucks to have someone lie to you about something important, doesn't it? Fucking betrayal stings, fucks you all up, can't tell what side is up, what to believe. Yeah, I understand exactly how that feels."

My whole body is trembling. Stacy isn't shaking at all.

"I've got shit at the trailer that proves everything. Michelle wrote some stuff down, some of its about you. I need you to help me understand what it means. But I know I'm right. Michelle and Stevie went to that guy's church and they never came home." Stacy scratches his temple with the barrel of his gun.

"Who is *he*?" I carefully ask and put a cigarette to my lips, and after a half-dozen strikes, light my Zippo.

"This," Stacy announces as though he's the host of a true crime television docudrama, "is the home of the Reverend Seth Moseley, pastor of First United Methodist Church of Edgerton, where he lives with his wife and their two teenage sons, all of whom may or may not be aware of the heinous shit that he's doing. There are at least ten or fifteen people at the church that I've identified as being part of it," Stacy breathlessly informs me. "And the Edgerton Chief of Police goes to church there. I saw his cruiser in the parking lot on Sunday." He gestures with the revolver again. "The cops are in on it. At least a hundred people go to his church. No way something like this goes on in a town that small and not have everyone know about it and in on it."

Stacy looks at me expectantly.

"What about the FBI?" I try.

"Man, *what is wrong with you*, wanting to call the fucking cops or the Feds? What the fuck happened to you? You don't trust cops, the government. Even if the State Police or the Feds came in, they're gonna investigate and by then Michelle and Stevie could be gone forever. They'll just collect evidence and file reports and ask for my statement when they find their bodies in a quarry. You know. How good were the cops at stopping what happened at Sugar River? All they did was drag you out half-dead and make an arrest. We—" he pauses. "—you and me. We can STOP this."

Stacy knows I have no faith in law enforcement and he's playing on my latent paranoia from our drug-dealing days when I never would've called a cop for any reason, ever. "You're right. No cops. It's just…I don't know what do. It's different for you, bro. You're a Marine. This is fucking nuts," I blurted.

Stacy glares at me. "You *owe* me. I'm using my 'Get Out of Jail Free Card.' So get your mind right."

I take a longer look at the house, now that the sun's coming up. Thank God I have my sunglasses.

My pupils can't be dilating properly. The piercing glare of the rising sun is knifing through my eyes into my temples, magnifying the pain in my still swollen left eye. I'm fascinated by the way my Ray-Bans illuminate a prism being refracted through a small chip in Stacy's windshield. I can't help myself. I start to reach my finger out to touch it, to see if I can catch the light and put it in my pocket.

"Yo. Don't touch the windshield. What are you doing?" Stacy barks, running his hand through his hair, scratching his scalp with a quick back-and-forth motion.

"I want that rainbow for later," I explain. "I'm trying to save it before it goes away."

Stacy is again exasperated with me, but I can't help it. The chemical effects, the changing light, the reflection, and my proximity to it have all merged to distract me from a far more pressing matter. I've already spaced out on the reason we're here. All I can think of is pinching the tiny windshield-rainbow and saving it in my pocket, maybe asking The Mirror about it when I get back to Stacy's trailer...

"BRO!" Stacy yells. "You can't touch *light!* Get your shit together. You're fucking tripping." He's gotten so animated that the zippers and silver chains looped across his battered black leather jacket jingle and distract my attention away from the windshield. They're like amplified windchimes, clanging cymbals.

"What is that noise?" I want to know. "Is that your jacket? It's so LOUD." I crane my neck, stuffing my fingers into my ears. "They can totally hear that. Do *not* wear that coat on surveillance, dude."

"Oh my God. You are totally worthless."

Stacy drops the LeMans into drive and peels away from curb. Not a single car or truck passed us while we sat there and discussed the conspiracy that Stacy was certain had led to the abduction of his family.

"I'm good, I'm good. Where are we going?" My brain is short-circuiting. Mistaken memories, a flurry of images that overlap and juxtapose incorrectly. I'm holding a bottle of tequila and a burning branch over Stevie's head, taunting him at a bonfire while Syd begs me to stop. Michelle and I are dancing together in the gym at Sugar River, while U2's "Love Is

350

Blindness" blares over the loudspeakers. Wafer is pointing a rifle at Wendy the Waitress and shooting at her and I'm watching it all from the 92Q studio, describing it to the audience. Somewhere in the distance I hear myself suggest that I should call my therapist.

Stacy is pissed.

"You're too fucked up." He shoves the gun under the driver's seat. "We're going back to my place. We can talk more when you come down. I need you sharp, hoss. This is big. Bigger than anything we ever did back when you lived here. I need you right and ready. We're out of time. We need to go today."

Michelle and Stevie.

The trip is taking me in stranger than usual directions. The visual and auditory hallucinations are stronger than I remember from the last time I dosed with The Floyd Chicks. I'm peaking faster, though.

I glance at the side mirror, and I can see The Silhouette, peering back at me over the words "OBJECTS IN MIRROR ARE CLOSER THAN THEY APPEAR." He's saying something to me, but I can't hear over Stacy's haranguing and swearing. I start rolling down my window and a burst of cold, damp air floods in.

"Hey, hey! I'll turn the fucking heater down if you're hot," Stacy yells.

"That was a Meatloaf song. On that tape from that one day you went to jail." Disconnected events now belong together, separate timelines have a shared meaning. I reach into my pocket and pull out Sarah's Best Friends Forever necklace, crusty with blood and dirt. The clasp is broken. I hold it up, mesmerized.

"What's that?" he demands. "Put it away. It's shining right in my fucking eye while I'm driving, hoss."

"A Best Friends Forever necklace," I answer without elaborating or any sense of irony.

"Yeah, no shit, Sherlock. I mean, why do you have it? It's a kid's necklace."

When I look outside, The Silhouette in the side mirror is gone. "I found it."

Stacy is past the point of exasperation. "*Where?*"

"At a crime scene. It came to the present from back in time, so I took it before it disappeared again."

"Dude, are you peaking? You're talking crazy. I don't get what you're saying."

I'm talking crazy? I'm making perfect sense to me. He's the one expecting me to believe that Michelle and Stevie could still be alive but have been abducted by an Edgerton Methodist White Slavery Ring. I strain to see if The Silhouette is in the car and grab at the rearview mirror. I'm discouraged. I need more revelations, epiphanies, truths, and mysteries unraveled. Stacy shoves my hand away.

"Sit back!" he orders. "Stop fucking with my mirrors!"

"Best Friends Forever," I sigh with regret, then smirk. "And a 'Get Out of Jail Free Card.' Our lucky day."

CHAPTER 35

A few days after Michelle put me back together with popsicle sticks and frozen peas (along with Stacy's pain management program of Vicodin, Valium, Vodka, and marijuana), Stacy said I could stay with them. Michelle begrudgingly cleaned out their second bedroom. I'm sure there was an argument about it.

Because I didn't have a job, or any money, Stacy decided we'd sell weed and split the profit.

So I became a drug dealer without thinking much of it. I'd never considered selling drugs as a job, but I was open to new career opportunities. As a side benefit, I'd have all the pot, pills, and extras I wanted.

Stacy and Michelle had a straightforward plan, and mostly stuck to it: save money and buy out the Brew Haus (the owner who was ready to retire), then walk away from drug dealing and the hospital before it was too late. Michelle devised the perfect way to skim pills from different in-house pharmacies at the hospital. It was risky and lucrative, but she was cautious and smart, minimizing her exposure. The pills were easy money. Splitting up one-pound bricks of weed into baggies was time-consuming and less profitable. The supply chain was always in doubt, but we diversified our partnerships for a variety of options and cultivated strains. Stacy worked the bar at the Brew

Haus, selling pills on Fridays, Saturdays, holidays, and during big events. I sat around watching TV all day, waiting for our phone to ring.

When it did, I'd make a delivery.

Then I'd get high with the buyer.

Cops were always on our mind, but I kept things low-key. I rarely had more than a possession charge worth of pot on me, and we rarely dabbled in anything other than hash or opium. Stacy and Michelle agreed that crackheads and junkies were erratic and disloyal. Hippies had money, but wanted psychedelics that looped us into risky connections with unfamiliar suppliers. Tweakers needed meth or crank, and that forced us to work with bikers. Motorcycle gangs and their cooks were often tangled up in unexpected and sudden violence, bolstering their outlaw reputation, so we left that territory to others.

Mostly, I sold a shitload of weed and pills.

Stacy's customers called me "The Dude from That Shooting" and everyone knew what it meant. They loved me. I was the only stoner with a perfect memory and bullet holes in my stomach and chest. I was a celebrity, which made me uncomfortable, but people didn't fuck with me. I felt like I had climbed out of my grave into someone else's life, a ghoulish mooch hanging out for whatever happens next.

It was 8:08 p.m. on August 27, 1994.

By then I was comfortable enough to sprawl out on Stacy and Michelle's couch wearing only a pair of red and black swimming trunks because nothing else was clean. The air conditioning couldn't keep the trailer cool in the summer heat. I was watching TV when Stacy's LeMans rumbled into the driveway.

Surprised, I looked at the clock on the VCR. I had assumed he was already at the Brew Haus. Days blended together for me. I rarely asked Stacy about his work schedule because it was always changing. Michelle was at St. Sebastian's. I was stoned and didn't feel like doing anything for the rest of the night.

The moment Stacy flung open the flimsy front door I knew he'd been drinking. Stacy was an unpredictable drunk. It was a roll of the dice to see if he'd be fun, mean, impetuous, or melancholy.

He started fucking with me right away. "We gotta make a run, hoss!" he yelled. "Let's go!"

"Fuck, bro, I'm chilling. I'm watching this, man." I gestured at the TV with a dented and scorched Mountain Dew can I'd poked holes in to smoke weed with. "You're killing my buzz."

"You're watching Dr. Quinn, Medicine Woman?" Stacy laughed, incredulous.

"And COPS," I added. "I switch back and forth during the commercials. It's wholesome entertainment."

"You're baked, hoss. You could at least put in a movie. Fucking Dr. Quinn, Medicine Woman?" Laughing, Stacy snatched the remote out of my hand. My reflexes dulled, I barely reacted until he turned the TV off. "We gotta make a run. I don't have much time before work, I gotta take a shower, I gotta eat. We gotta go. I was at Jimmy's way longer than I planned to be. Come on, get the fuck up. Let's go."

I had no intention of going anywhere. I had melted into the couch. I waved him off, and lazily reached for the remote. "I don't feel like hurrying anywhere. I just got blazed, bro. I'm down for the night."

Stacy grabbed my arm. "Get up. We're rolling. I'm driving. I want to drive your car."

"The Ford? Why?" I asked.

"Did you get another car that I don't know about?" Stacy took my keys off the kitchen table and jingled them aggressively in my face. "We'll be gone for two minutes tops. I need you there, I want you to meet this guy, so next time I don't have to go. He doesn't know you, after today he will. You wanted this job, but I got a stack of applications and could start interviews for your replacement tomorrow."

Drunk people.

Stacy had his mind made up.

"OK bro, OK. I'm getting up." I held up my hands, surrendering. "Are you sure you're good to drive?"

"Better than you. Come on, hustle hustle hustle hustle!" Stacy clapped his hands at me like a gym coach. I looked around for my shirt, shoes, wallet. "Don't worry about it. It's still like eighty-five degrees."

"Dude, I need my shirt and my fucking wallet. And some shoes or some shit."

"Here. Heads up!" Stacy tossed a pair of green and yellow flipflops at me. "Put these on. You don't need your wallet. You're not driving. No time for a shirt. We're gone." I had no idea where my wallet was, and was so completely blazed from smoking dope that I spaced out I never went shirtless in public.

Ten minutes later we were out in the country, pulling up to a small farm in a cloud of dust.

"See," Stacy gestured. "Farmers. Your people. You'll love them. They'll love you. Talk about cows and manure and seeds and droughts or whatever. I'm going to buy a couple ounces, see if what they're growing out here is solid, and we're gone. Five minutes. You gotta be seen. Be cool. We need this."

My face burned and a lump formed in my throat. "They're NOT my fucking people, bro."

"You farmed. You're a farmer. Talk farmer shop with them. Teats and manure spreaders and silos and whatever-the-fuck." Stacy was oblivious to how pissed made me.

"Just because I lived on farm a doesn't mean farmers are my people, dude. I'm so NOT a farmer. If I was a farmer, I'd still be on a farm, which I am not." Usually I was good-natured when I got stoned, but Stacy calling me a farmer made me defensive. "My parents don't even farm anymore. I'm not even related to fucking farmers. I don't even want to think about it anymore."

Stacy continued to ignore me. "Ex-farmer is close enough. Just... be cool."

It took me a second to realize what was happening. "We're meeting in the fucking barn? I'm wearing flip flops, bro. Why didn't you tell me it was in a barn?" I hated how I'd do what Stacy told me to do without asking any questions. "I'm gonna get shit all over my feet, man." I threw my hands up in disgust.

"Hoss. Five minutes. They're supposed to be growing garbage bags of good shit out here. Let's go."

"I'm not even wearing a shirt. The flies are going to bite me, man. I have hay fever. I'll be sneezing and my eyes will get all red and shit. Can't we meet in the house? Or out in their field? Or a shed?"

Stacy's smile evaporated, replaced with sternness. "Quit bitching. Your eyes are already red, you pothead. Get out of the car. What's the big fucking deal?" It was an argument I was doomed to lose. I couldn't tell Stacy why being back on a farm was an oppressive force that filled me with anger and anxiety.

"Fine," I agreed. "Five minutes. Leave me the keys. When it's been six minutes, I'm leaving you here."

"Fuck you, hoss." Stacy's grin reappeared as he made a show of dangling my keys, taunting me.

When he jumped out of the car, I noticed for the first time how unsteady Stacy was on his feet.

He wasn't buzzed, he was really drunk. I still followed him like a scolded puppy at obedience training.

We chatted with Stacy's new connection for a couple of minutes. They were typical Southern Wisconsin farmers: ball caps, unshaven, blue jeans, tanned arms and neck, t-shirts, can of beer, can of chew, boots spattered with cow shit, amiable. I tried to strike up a conversation with a few guys who were eyeing me with bemused looks. Embarrassed and frustrated with myself that I hadn't made Stacy let me find a shirt, I was awkwardly trying to talk about the breeding charts of bull calf lineage wearing only swimming trunks, flipflops, a crucifix and a St. Jude medal, and nothing else.

I felt naked, my scars exposed, certain they were staring and would ask me how I'd been shot.

"I've been smoking all day," I jabbered disjointedly, with a matter-of-fact tone. "I don't even know what the fuck is going on. I'm with him." I tried to explain, pointing to where I thought Stacy was, but moments earlier he'd apparently left out another door. I spun around in a full circle, confused. "Well, I'm here with the guy who was just here." I stuck out my hand like I was meeting a banker. "I'm Jeremy."

I fucking waved, like a moron.

The smells of farm life tickled my hay fever and triggered memories of a childhood that I rarely encountered since escaping the family farm in the wake of the shooting. Manure, bales of hay, sour milk, and the damp sweetness of corn silage. Large flakes of peeling whitewash had fallen from the walls and remained where they landed. Milk cows mooed and swished their tails at biting flies. Dogs and barn cats darted after each other. An electric motor powering the milk pipeline was droning away. A muggy stink settled on me. It was hot, I was sweating, it was musty, my nose was itchy. Someone had shaken open a dusty straw bale. Anxiety built inside of me, everyone was looking at me, I had nothing to say.

But true to his word, Stacy was back in less than five minutes, reiterating to our new supplier that we'd be back for weight if we liked these first two ounces. Everyone nodded. I nodded so that I wasn't the only one not nodding. Stacy hollered across the barn, "We're out, hoss!" and then turned to the farmers again. "If we like it, we'll be back. Next time it'll just be him." He pointed at me. "We'll let you know."

Stacy led the way out of the barn, and I was on his heels, my sandals "flipflopping" with each step.

We ripped down the gravel driveway faster than we should have, kicking up a smokescreen, gravel pinging on the undercarriage. Stacy never hit the brakes; instead he popped the clutch and my Ford Tempo hopped up on to the county highway with a squeaking thunk.

He tossed the weed in my lap. "Sniff that," Stacy ordered. "Skunky. Resin, red hairs."

I unrolled the bag, stuck in my nose, and inhaled deeply. I got giddy. Sticky, kind buds. "Damn, bro."

Stacy rolled down the window, fired a cigarette, jammed the clutch, and hit fifth gear. It was a fifty-five-mph speed limit out there and he was mercilessly forcing the Ford to seventy-five mph. It was doing it, but I was worried a cop might pull us over with a bag of weed in the car and drunk driver behind the wheel.

I kept my mouth shut, all my objections screaming in my head.

There was a dubbed copy of Meatloaf, "Bat Out of Hell II: Back into Hell" in the cassette deck.

I pushed play and the tape started rolling about halfway into "Objects in the Rearview Mirror May Appear Closer Than They Are." Meatloaf was on our "Mutually Agreed Upon List of Singers and Bands" as a peaceful resolution to Stacy's hatred of grunge and my disdain for hair metal.

"One last thing. Then we're done," Stacy alerted me.

He downshifted and the tired engine whined as we sped into a gas station parking lot. The Ford screeched to a stop, bumping concrete. "Curb check. Still there. Need smokes," he announced and cranked the parking brake, leaving the car idling in neutral and was out before I could say anything.

After a few minutes alone I started bitching aloud. I didn't want to be in a parking lot, holding a fat bag of weed. "What the fuck is taking you so long, man? Why didn't you just get smokes at the Brew Haus?"

Jim Steinman's "Love and Death and an American Guitar" began to play, his booming confession to killing a boy with a Fender guitar, when a commotion broke out inside the store.

I could barely see through the full-length glass door. Stacy was at the register, a forty oz bottle in his hand. He looked pissed, waving it around. The store clerk was defiantly shaking his head "NO."

"What the fuck, bro?" I sighed. Why was he starting shit with a gas station attendant?

Stacy turned, grinned at me, and threw the beer at the glass door. It exploded in yellow and white foam, and the glass dropped in a sheet from top to bottom with a crash. I jumped in my seat. I yelled. "What the fuck, bro?!" Stacy kicked open the shattered door, hopped over the glass and beer, and got in the car.

I expected the clerk to chase him, but he didn't.

The clerk was on the phone. Probably calling the cops.

Stacy wrenched the old Ford into reverse and popped the clutch, killing it. The parking brake was still on. He forced the clutch again, restarted the engine, yanked the parking brake, whipped out backwards, grinding the transmission and squawking the tires.

"Can't let him see your plates, hoss!" he said, laughing as he hit second gear.

I said it for the third time. "WHAT THE FUCK, BRO?!"

"That asshole said I was overserved. I told him I was a bartender, I know when someone is overserved, I was fine, sell me the 40. He wouldn't do it, told me to leave, started bitching about his liquor license, I told him to take a fucking chill pill, I wasn't even going to drink it, I was buying it for you, then he wanted to see your ID and I got pissed. Fuck him. It's done and can't be undone."

This was the raging, recklessly drunk Stacy. I couldn't believe it. We were five minutes from the trailer. "What if he called the cops?! We have two

FUCKING ounces on us! That's possession with intent!!" I didn't want to go to fucking jail. Stoughton's a small town. We'd be easy to find. We didn't need cops coming by the trailer. "I don't want a 40, bro. What are you doing?"

"He didn't see the plates. I left too fast."

"You killed the car in front of the store. He got the plates. He could see what kind of car—"

"Fuck that guy!" Stacy screamed, interrupting me. "I'm a Marine. That little bitch can't tell me when I'm done drinking. I decide when I done. NOT HIM." His intense negativity had the instant capability of explosive rage, like bomb materials brewing in a pressure cooker. I shut down, looked out the window.

That's when I saw red, white, and blue lights in the side mirror, coming up on us. FAST.

"I'm going to run them!" Stacy declared, shifting and pushing the accelerator to the floor.

"This isn't the fucking LeMans!" I yelped. Panic surged through my body. Death didn't scare me, but the idea of being in prison or consciously trapped in a coma horrified me. "You can't outrun shit in this!"

Stacy yanked the steering wheel to the right, and we careened up a dimly lit side street. Houses and mailboxes whizzed by. For ten seconds, I thought our one, evasive maneuver was going to be enough.

It wasn't.

We made it one block further before two squad cars roared up behind us, sirens on, lights flashing.

I assumed that Stacy finally realized a 1984 Ford Tempo had no chance of outrunning two police cruisers, because instead of speeding up or trying another turn, he simply pulled over.

"I'm going to jail, Jeremy," Stacy imparted. "And probably you, too. Keep your fucking mouth shut. If you don't go to jail, call Michelle. She knows what to do. They can't find the weed or this—" he fished a Ziplock bag filled with at least fifty different kinds of pills out of his pocket "—or we're fucked."

I grabbed the pills and shoved them—along with the weed—under the seat, but in a moment of inspiration, I instead tucked it through the bristled slot in the plastic housing over the parking brake.

"Don't say shit to the cops. If they find the shit, tell them it's mine. They'll interrogate me and if they ask me about it I'll know they busted you. I won't let you go prison." I nodded. "Just promise me they won't find it." I had no idea how I could promise that, but I swallowed hard and nodded again.

Instantly there were officers on both sides of the car. I tried not to hyperventilate. A ruddy-faced cop tapped on the driver side glass and told Stacy to roll down the window. "I mean it," Stacy said to me. "Blame me." He flashed a smile, but his eyes darkened. He turned around and rolled the window down.

"Did I do something wrong, officer?" he slurred politely.

Officer Ruddy Cheeks slotted his flashlight into a loop on his belt, grabbed Stacy by the shirt with both hands and wrenched him through the open window out on to the street. My mouth dropped open. A second cop was suddenly there, too, twisting Stacy's arms behind his back and cuffing him.

I craned my neck to see what was happening.

Stacy laid his forehead on the asphalt.

A third cop yelled at me to turn and face the front. I spun around without saying a word.

Both cops grabbed an arm and hoisted him into the backseat cage of a squad car. I twisted around in my seat, trying to see. Stacy never said another word, never protested, never whimpered, never complained.

The cop on my side of the car told me to turn around and put my hands on the dash.

There was two ounces of weed and a bag of pills without bottles or prescriptions on me. It was my car. They'd call in a K9 unit and search it. They'd find it, then get a warrant to search the trailer.

My mind raced. What else did we have? More drugs. Thousands in cash. Guns. We were fucked.

I was going to prison. Stacy would go to prison. Michelle would go to prison.

I waited and tried to appear unconcerned. Minutes crawled by. What were they doing? What were they waiting for? Why hadn't they pulled me out of the car, too? I got up enough courage to look and the officer nearest me gestured for me to roll my window down. "Son, I'm gonna need to see your ID."

There was no way I was getting out of this. "I'm just the passenger, sir. I didn't do anything wrong."

"Son, how well do you know the driver?" he asked.

"He's my roommate, but we're not close friends, why?" I lied.

"Your roommate just blew a point two-two. That's more than twice the legal limit. He's going to jail on suspicion of DUI." The officer was deliberate and firm. He calmly asked, "Is this car registered to you?"

"It is. He was driving because—" I had to think quickly. "—I lost my wallet. I didn't realize how drunk he was until we were already in the car." The half-truth sounded weak. "I don't have my ID, officer."

"I'm going to need you to step out of the vehicle."

When I faced the officer, I was already considering what life would be like in jail. In the back of my mind, I recalled how I was flipping channels between Dr. Quinn Medicine Woman *and* COPS, *and here I was, a stereotypical suspect on the show: a shirtless white guy about to get arrested in public for drug possession. The only thing left was for a crowd of people to show up and cackle and point on camera.*

"What's your name, son?"

"I'm Jeremy Peoples. I haven't done anything wrong. I'm good to walk home."

The cop had a friendly face. He had me empty my pockets. I only had my Zippo lighter and a half a pack of cigarettes. He shined the flashlight in my eyes. I wondered why he hadn't asked to search the car yet.

"You're going to have to come with me. We need a witness to identify your chauffeur over there. And since you don't have your driver's license with you, I don't know that you are who you say you are."

It was then I had a moment of brilliance.

Stoned, I had momentarily forgotten that I never forget anything.

I recalled the day I renewed my driver's license on my birthday. March 16, 1994, four years to the day after I'd gotten my probationary Wisconsin license. I had looked closely at the photo to scrutinize my terrible tight-lipped grimace and whined at the DMV because my eyes were half-closed.

The driver's license was as clear in my mind as it was on the day I'd gotten it, months ago.

"I have my license number and social security number memorized," I blurted out. "You can call that in to your headquarters or whatever, right?" (Why did I say "headquarters?") "On the radio, the home office guy can tell you if what I'm saying is right, can't he? You tell him my description and it's on your computer mainframe thing, right?" (Why did I say "mainframe?")

The cop was incredulous. "You have your driver's license number memorized?"

I closed my eyes and saw the license again. "Yeah. It's B200-3407-8218-02. Expires 3/16/98."

I opened my eyes, and the cop said, suspiciously, "Say that one more time for me." I rattled it off again.

He'd written it in a small notepad. He reached up to the walkie-talkie mic clipped to the shoulder of his white uniform shirt and dutifully called it in, along with my physical description. "Yeah, just run that and then tell me what he looks like in the photo. I got a guy here with no ID telling me he has his driver's license number memorized. I just want to know if he's telling the truth. Suspect's name is Peoples. Yes, people with an s at the end, first name Jeremy." He clicked the mic closed.

"If you're lying to me, I will put you in jail for obstruction," Officer Friendly Face promised.

I held my breath. I realized I was doing it and tried to exhale quietly.

Even though I knew I said the license number exactly as I remembered it, I fretted over whether he'd written it down wrong or the dispatcher misheard. What if there was a computer error? One minor glitch and they'd drag me to jail and search the car and find the drugs and—

The cop had moved several feet away so I could no longer hear dispatch. But after a burst of squelch on the walkie-talkie, I did hear Officer Friendly Face's reply: "I shit you not. He had it memorized. Craziest thing I've ever seen. No. He just said it. Told me he knows his Social Security number too." Officer Friendly Face smiled and snorted. "Thanks, Tony."

He stopped smiling and pointed at me. "You. Stay right there."

I held up both hands, bent at the elbows.

Officer Friendly Face yelled over to Officer Ruddy Cheeks. "You're not gonna believe this shit!"

The two of them talked for a few minutes. I'd lost sight of the third officer, but assumed he was in the patrol car they'd forced Stacy into. At one point, Officer Ruddy Cheeks looked over at me and pointed. Officer Friendly Face kept shrugging. I heard one of them say, "Whaddaya wanna do with him?"

My incarceration, while still possible, seemed less likely that it had been just five minutes ago.

Officer Friendly Face walked back toward me, his expression relaxing. "You're gonna have to come with me. You were in the car when your buddy over there smashed out of a gas station door and the owner will probably press charges. I'm not gonna take you to jail, because other than being an idiot, there's nothing I can charge you with. Yet. But I can't just leave you here.

So, Jeremy Peoples-with-the-amazing-memory, you're gonna ride with me up the street to see what the clerk says about you and your pal."

He didn't cuff me. He did put me in the back seat of his squad car, then flipped a U-turn, heading back in the direction Stacy and I had come from twenty minutes earlier. I asked Officer Friendly Face if I could have my cigarettes and lighter back, but he said no, telling me I couldn't smoke in the squad car.

I needed a fucking cigarette.

Stacy was going to jail. The only thing in doubt was how many charges he would face, and when would Michelle and their lawyer be able to bond him out.

We pulled into the parking lot and I watched Officer Ruddy Cheeks walk into the store, stepping over the glass and pool of tepid beer, eyeing the shattered door and talking to the clerk. The conversation was brief. The clerk gestured at Stacy, and shook his head "no" when the cop pointed at me. Officer Ruddy Cheeks pointed again, and again the clerk nodded no. "Your lucky day, kid," Officer Friendly Face said.

"What's…next?" I asked tentatively as I felt the tension ease. "Can I go home? What about my car?"

"I can take you home. They'll tow your car. You can get it on Monday. I'll give you their number."

Towed? Searched. The pot and pills get found. They call the cops, or keep it for themselves.

Shit.

"Look, man—I mean, Officer—is there any way you could let me take my car home and not have it towed? I lost my job a few weeks ago and my money situation isn't right. I can't afford to get it out of impound," I tried to sound polite. Sincere. "I'm trying to find a new gig, but can't without wheels, man—sir. Do you have to let them tow it? I'm only like five minutes from my house."

Office Friendly Face didn't reply, and began to pull out of the gas station parking lot. I saw him eyeing me in the rearview mirror. I thought maybe I'd persuaded him. "No can do. No ID, you shouldn't be driving. I can drop you off, the car gets towed."

Desperate, I played my final card.

I hated myself for what I was about to do. "Please, can you just help me out? I don't know if you recognize my name, but I know you had to have seen the scars on my chest and stomach, right?"

"I was curious," Officer Friendly Face confirmed. "You don't have a criminal record."

I pimped out Sarah's death and the deaths and injuries and the trauma and the tragedy and the coma and the rehab and my parents' divorce and the bleak battles with depression and hours in court and every sacred memory I had about the Sugar River Shooting and its aftermath...for the chance to keep some fucking weed and pills. Filled with self-loathing and disgust, I was the worst type of sell-out: an intentional one with a cheap price. I thought of Lutheran Sunday School, Judas Iscariot, and silver coins.

"I was one of the survivors of the Sugar River Shooting."

Officer Friendly Face whistled. "Oh jeez, yeah, I do remember you. Oh my God."

I prepared to artfully mix in the right lie to get what I wanted. "The cops saved my life that day. They probably saved a lot of lives. I know that I shouldn't have been riding around with a drunk dude tonight, but shit has been hard for me, man. Really hard, OK? Can you just do me a solid here?"

I wanted to throw up. Officer Friendly Face sighed. He turned around to look at me with soft eyes.

"It says protect and serve on the side of my car. None of us in blue could have protected you that day, but one of us can serve you today. I'm gonna cut you a break, Jeremy Peoples. I'm gonna let you take your car home and not have it towed. I'll follow you to your place—you'd better go straight there—to make sure nothing happens. I'm sorry for what you've been through. My wife and I prayed for you and the families of all the kids who died. So yeah, I'll do you a solid tonight. It's the least I can do."

I was devastated inside. Ashamed. This cop was a genuinely good person. I was lying to his face.

"Thank you so much. You're really helping me out, sir."

We drove for the next minute in silence and then pulled up behind my old rusty Ford. Officer Friendly Face let me out, handing me my keys, lighter, and cigarettes. He put his hand on my bare shoulder, startling me, and noticed the silver crucifix and St. Jude medal around my neck. "I know what that cross is," Officer Friendly Face admitted. "But I'm not a Catholic. Who's St. Jude?"

"Patron Saint of Lost Causes, but I don't know much about it; it just looked cool and kind of spoke to me at the time," I remembered. "So I bought it. Yeah."

He seemed to consider what I'd just told him. "Lost causes, huh? Such a burden." He rubbed his forehead.

I was uncomfortable, but wasn't going to do anything to indicate I was in a hurry to get away from him. I suffered patiently. This seemed to be an incredibly significant moment for Officer Friendly Face.

"Can I pray for you?" he finally asked. "I know this might be wrong to do, but I really feel like God is asking me to pray for you before I get you where you're supposed to be tonight. Is that OK?"

Fuck, I'll let you do anything if it'll make you comfortable enough to leave me with my drugs.

"Sure," I whispered. "Thank you."

Officer Friendly Face left his hand on my shoulder and began to pray. "Father God, I thank you for sparing this young man's life years ago and I thank you for sparing his life tonight for his foolishness to go with a drunk driver. God, I ask you to provide a peace that surpasses all understanding as *he tries to put his life back together after such tragedy. I pray that you'll heal his body where it still needs healing—in the name of Jesus Christ—and that you'll heal his mind and soul, Father God. I claim the promise you made to us—that that which was intended to harm Jeremy would instead be used for good by you, God, to even save many lives in the future. And if this man doesn't know you as his Lord and Savior, I ask you to make yourself known to him, so that he might be saved when his heart is open to the truth, and the love you have for him. Help him understand that he's not a lost cause, that nothing is impossible for you. Thank you, God, for giving me the chance to help Jeremy tonight. I pray this in Jesus's name. Amen."*

"Amen," I repeated, and sighed. I couldn't stand to look Officer Friendly Face in the eye. "Thank you again," I told him, and began walking toward my car. "Really appreciate this. Super cool thing to do."

"Wait," he shouted after me, and I jumped. "You sure you haven't had anything to drink tonight?"

My heart rate doubled. "No. Just tired." My hands turned clammy.

"Put my mind at ease," Officer Friendly Face suggested. "Take a field sobriety test. I don't smell any alcohol on you, but your eyes look red and you're shaky. I want to give you the benefit of the doubt because you were just in a squad car and your buddy just went to jail, so it could be adrenaline, but still."

"I haven't been sleeping well," I offered. "But sure, I'll do it. What do I need to do?" I tried to laugh, but it came out like a gag and I coughed into my fist. "Excuse me. Never done one of these before."

The officer had me stand up straight, tilt my head back, extend my arms out in each direction, and try to touch my finger to my nose. I did it easily. He had me stand on one foot, then alternate. Done. He asked me to say the alphabet, which I also did without thinking. His final request nearly flummoxed me.

"Say the alphabet backward," Officer Friendly Face said.

"The alphabet, backward," I said, hoping he'd laugh with me.

Officer Friendly Face smiled, and clicked off his flashlight. "Alright, you're good. Just be careful. I'll be right behind you until you get to your place. And Jeremy? Stop riding around with drunk people."

"Yes, sir," I promised.

I got in the car, started it up, and with the shakes taking over my body, I pushed in the clutch, found first gear, and inched away from the curb. Meatloaf started singing again. I spun the volume knob down.

I drove the exact speed limit to Stacy's trailer.

When I pulled into the driveway, Officer Friendly Face waved, turned around at the end of the street, and headed out of the neighborhood. The second he was out of sight I puked in the front yard.

The next few hours were a whirlwind.

I finally got ahold of Michelle at St. Sebastian's Hospital.

She was pissed, and barked at me that she would call their lawyer and get Stacy out. "You stupid careless drunken fucking idiots. I always have to clean up your fucking messes," she snarled at me over the phone. Michelle rarely used the f-word. I tried to defend myself, but she hung up on me. I found a shirt and complained to myself, continuing the conversation Michelle had cut off. "Don't bitch at me! It wasn't my idea to go out and get the weed. Stacy was fucking drunk. I just wanted to watch Dr. Quinn..."

Stacy got home just after 2:00 a.m. "Tell me you've got our stuff," he said as he strutted through the door.

"I fucking got it," a smug grin concealing the shame I felt over what it took out of me to accomplish.

Stacy grabbed me in a huge bear hug. "Holy fucking shit, can you believe that shit?!" he exclaimed. When he let go, I pulled the bag of weed and pills out of the waistband of my swimming trunks. Stacy snatched them from my hand, tore it open, and smelled it again. "I almost don't want to smoke it."

"Oh, fuck you, we're smoking it," I cried and Stacy erupted in guffaws.

"I can't believe you didn't smoke it all while I was locked up, you fucking pothead," he teased.

"What did they charge you with? Are you gonna lose your license? How much did it cost to get out? How the fuck did the lawyer get you out of jail that fast? I thought you'd be in until tomorrow at least."

Stacy waved his hand in my face. "Lawyer shit. Let him fix it. Don't fucking sweat it, hoss." The answer didn't satisfy me, but Stacy kept talking. "And I don't want to hear it from you either. Michelle is going to be all over me when she gets home, and I'm gonna have to pay all this legal shit off. And work will have my ass for calling in like I did. Fuck it. Let's get high."

I started to press him and he cut me off again.

"I can't believe they didn't search the car and they let you drive it home," Stacy said, flicking his Bic lighter and taking the first hit. "The cop who drove home with you knows where we live now. Don't think he's got a reason to come back, do you?"

He handed the pipe to me, and I fired it, holding the smoke in my lungs for as long as I could, and exhaled with a couple of quick coughs. "I don't think so. I think he liked me. We're cool, I think."

"We're going to have to slow it down for a while. I'll talk to Michelle." Stacy caused this problem, and seemed ambivalent about the consequences. "How'd you do it, hoss?" Stacy fixed me with his piercing blue-eyed stare, his mood slightly suspicious. "Tell me everything."

"I bullshitted him," I summarized, and held up my shirt to remind him of my bullet wounds. Stacy nodded. I recounted everything I had told the cop and Stacy sat in rapt silence through the retelling of my part of our adventure. We cached the bowl. I felt normal again, pushing the shame over what I'd done aside.

"I'll never listen to that fucking Meatloaf tape again," I finished, and Stacy laughed. "Burn it. And you made me miss Dr. Quinn, you fucking asshole." I was uneasy, my tone not matching his, but I faked it.

Stacy started packing another bowl as I reflected on what he had said in the car before he was arrested. "Were you really going to take the fall for me if they found everything?" I asked.

He paused, looking me straight in the eye, suddenly serious. "Fuckin' A. You've been through the shit, hoss. I could do some jail time for you. I got your back. Glad I didn't have to. But yeah. I'd have done it."

No one, aside from Sarah, had ever tried to look out for me. I felt a response building inside me, before I could fully consider its implications. "Man, bro. I don't know what to say."

"You believe me, hoss?" Stacy never took his eyes off me.

I had no doubt he was telling the truth. "Yeah. I believe you, dude."

I took a deep breath, considering our bond of friendship. The sense of protection I got from Stacy was unlike anything I felt before I needed him to know. "No one ever looked out for me. You letting me live here, and now tonight, that's never happened for me before. Thank you." Stacy started to protest, but I looked down at the table and continued. "And I want you to know that if you ever need someone, even if I'm miles away or it's years from now, you call me and I'll be there. Big shit, little shit, anything. No questions asked. I'm your 'Get Out of Jail Free Card.' I swear to God. You can count on me, man."

"Semper Fi. Yeah." Stacy held out his hand, and I clenched it across the table. "We're in this together. You'll do what it takes. You proved that tonight. We're brothers now. I knew I could trust you, hoss."

CHAPTER 36

Stacy walks behind me to the bedroom, following me because he'll never trust me again.

I can't decide what's more confused: my mind—under the influence of psychedelics—or Stacy's. I drag my feet down the hallway, casting a sideways glance at the bathroom and wondering if The Silhouette is still in the mirror. The weakened floor thuds with every step I take, sagging over the dead space under the trailer. Stacy flips on the hall light and the bulb burns out with a fizz-POP.

I jump.

He doesn't.

I grapple for something that can ground me to reality, a fixed point to help me regain mental stability. I take a fresh cigarette from the pack and realize I'm already smoking one. Stacy wordlessly nudges me to the side and pulls a wad of keys from his front pocket. There's a padlock on his bedroom door.

I'm far too paranoid to ask why.

Stacy walks into his room—much darker than it should be this late in the morning—and turns on a desk lamp. A blackout shade is pulled over the window, newspaper articles taped to it, things are circled in red ink, but I'm too far away and the room is too dark for me to understand their significance.

As my eyes begin to adjust, I see more documents, more photos, more articles, tacked to the wall. I close my eyes and reopen them, trying to discern if I'm hallucinating. I don't seem to be. These pictures aren't original photos, they're copies from some sort of directory, each person posed for a formal studio sitting. Stacy's drawn an X across the face of a man in one of them, a red target over a woman's face, and he's apparently burned the eyes out of a third with a cigarette.

Pages of notebook paper covered with illegible scrawl are scattered on top of an unmade bed.

Two ashtrays are completely filled on the bedside table, heaping with butts and ash.

The room smells so sour, sweaty, and stale that it's hard to breathe.

I almost trip over a telecom technical manual on the floor.

An AR-15 is propped up in the corner, nearly invisible in the darkness. What does Stacy need with that kind of firepower? When did he get it? I never saw it when I lived here. A jolt of electricity shoots up my spine and into my shoulders. It's then that I realize, through LSD-induced vapor trails and dulled senses, that it's unlikely I'll make it out of here alive. Fear and relief wrestle for control inside me.

"Well?" Stacy breaks the silence. "Now do you understand what I was saying?"

"No, man. I don't. What am I supposed to be looking at?" I fail to contain my exasperation.

"Jesus. Evidence," he mutters, pulls the .357 from the waistband of his jeans and tosses it on the bed.

"Evidence of what?" I ask. I eye the handgun, consider grabbing it, but I'm a coward.

"Weren't you listening to *anything* I said? Or are you so fucked up right now you can't remember anything, even with your super genius memory? These are the people that took Michelle and Stevie." He waves his hand at the wall of photos and newspaper articles. "I fell on to them a few weeks ago, not long before my family disappeared. They made the mistake of calling the house and I got their number. They ran some kind of scam on her to earn her trust, got them to go to their church, and then two Sundays ago she and Stevie left and never came back. That fake preacher has them. I know it."

It's more scattershot logic and incongruent timelines. Stacy is inconsistently trying to bring order to chaos. How long has he been like this? Has the disappearance of Stevie and Michelle done this to him?

Or has he been this way for longer?

Stacy rattles on, the story he's telling is batshit crazy and yet…what if it's true? He clearly believes what he's saying. There is a passion and conviction in his eyes, mannerisms that can't be faked. His details seem confused and vague, but what if it's me? I'm going around in circles, giving him the benefit of the doubt, lost in a blur of hallucinations. He's a whirling narrative of names and locations.

It goes on, and on, for an hour. Maybe longer. None of it makes sense. Pastors, cops, guesses. Insanity.

Stacy gestures, points, waves his arms, snatches photos off of the wall and pokes at them, sharing what he believes are "facts," and then reaffixes them to their place on his conspiracy map. He snaps his fingers, either remembering a new detail, or inventing a new connection, and scribbles a quick note on a yellow legal pad that he scavenged from the bed amidst Xerox copies of even more documents. Stacy's eyes gleam with mania. Veins pop from his neck. Anger roils beneath the surface. He makes threats.

He believes with the fervor of a zealot.

"I need you to read Michelle's diary and tell me what this stuff means," Stacy demands. He thrusts a fistful of paper into my hands, shaking others in front of my face. There must be six or seven torn pages, in no discernable order, all in Michelle's distinctive, looped purple cursive, like the letter in my pocket.

"HERE," Stacy barks. "What does this mean?"

His voice again startles me. I'm suddenly cold. How does he have Michelle's diary? What did she confess in these pages? What has he already seen? What does it say about me, Stevie, all of it?

I scrutinize the pages, struggling to focus my eyes in the dim light.

"...I can't help but wonder what you'll think about me going to church and wonder who I'm turning into, a person even more disconnected from you than I was when Jeremy still lived with us. I need more..."

Even in the throes of an acid trip, it's perfectly clear. She still wasn't happy. I try to think what I could say to Stacy. I don't even get the chance to respond before Stacy foists another page at me.

"...I don't have anyone to talk to about this, it's so lonely and you don't understand. I can't be honest about everything, so I have to keep it all a secret to myself and it's harder than I thought it would be not having anyone to talk to. When Jeremy was here at least I wasn't by myself all the time..."

My name. In Michelle's diary. Is this what pushed him over the edge? Had Michelle figured out that Stacy was uncovering our lie? Did he threaten her? Michelle never would have put up with it, especially with Stevie. The past four years are a mystery. Stacy's changed, but how exactly? What does he know?

What has he done?

What is he not telling me? Is he testing me, watching my responses to what he's showing me?

"...I know I made a mistake not telling you everything after Jeremy left, but I want to make it work because I love you and I want us to be a family..."

There is no discernible order to what Stacy's showing me. He points at sentences, giving me just enough time to read what he wants me to see, and then yanks the pages from my hands and makes me review another entry. I struggle to keep my focus. This is going to be an interrogation.

"What didn't she tell me, after you left?"

"I don't know bro," I lie. "I have no idea."

Does he know I'm not telling him the truth? His paranoia is smothering and contagious.

He has one final page to show me.

"...Jeremy looked terrible. I expected it, but it still was hard to see how far gone he is. I don't know why I thought he'd do anything other than what he did. I feel trapped now. Even if I wanted to leave I can't..."

Why would she have been so careless, even in her diary? I need an explanation Stacy will believe. Memories ace through my mind, short-circuiting my ability to rationalize, imagine, justify, lie.

("...Fight back you fucking pussy...!") ("...What if I let Stacy think the baby is his...?")

("...You need to start making better choices...") ("...Semper Fi. Yeah. We're in this together...")

I'm frozen, shamefully holding Michelle's secrets under Stacy's watchful glare. "When did you see her? Why did she feel trapped? The two of you saw each other after I threw you out. Did you fuck her again?"

He's seething with doubt. I can't tell him about Stevie. He'll explode.

I have to say something or he'll know I'm a liar.

"Michelle came across me a few months after you found out about us. I was living in my car. I swear to God nothing happened. She said you were both going to counseling and she didn't know how it was going to turn out. I didn't want to get involved. Fuck, bro, you said you'd kill me if you saw me again. I was freaked out she was even there." The more I talk, the more I protest, the more dishonest it feels.

"I don't know what she was thinking when she wrote this. It's her diary. People write shit in there because a journal's supposed to be private. Helps you sort your thoughts and feelings and shit. How am I supposed to know what she's talking about? I can't make heads or tails of all this man. I'm still tripping. I mean, I want to help you understand everything, but *I don't even understand it myself.*"

There are times when I'm a terrible liar. I assume this must have been one of those times.

I'd fail a lie detector test. No jury would believe me if I was on the stand.

Stacy stares at me. Through me. "It doesn't matter now. She felt trapped and went looking for something and she should've just told me. It's what she does. She did it with you. She trusts the wrong people when she should trust me. And now these motherfuckers got her and Stevie. We have to stay frosty, hoss. I need your head screwed back on straight so we can do this right."

He slams the door behind us and clicks the padlock. I'm a few paces ahead as we get to the kitchen.

Stacy reaches into the Piggly Wiggly grocery bag on the counter and pulls out a can of Old Style. He hands me the beer, cracking the pop top in one motion with one hand. "Drink this down. I need to get you to come down off that acid trip, hoss. Quick as possible. You got any downers. anything that'll take the edge off?" He reaches for my bag. "Even better, Xanax? Xanax will pull you off the ledge fast."

I pull the leather shaving bag away from Stacy's grasp and snuggle it against my chest. "I'll look." First, I chug the beer. It's disgusting. I hate warm beer. I hate Old Style. I gag on the foam, but I push through. A loud belch rolls out of my empty stomach. Stacy laughs and hands me another beer.

"Kill another one. You gotta come down. Turn the corner on the trip. You know. Don't focus on the colors or the sounds, it just drags you back under. We've got time but you gotta start now, hoss."

I see my opening. "How long? When are we rolling? I got shit at my hotel and I should get it out of there if things go sideways. I can't just leave it if I have to run. I gotta check out and get my stuff."

Stacy lights a cigarette, allows a plume of smoke to nearly escape his mouth, then drags it back down into his lungs, before expelling it for good as a hiss between his teeth. "All of the players will be together tonight at 5:00 p.m. We'll move on those motherfuckers then. They won't expect it. Got it all planned out."

I sip the second Old Style, shake a Xanax into the palm of my hand, make a fist, and funnel it into the back of my throat, washing it down with another gulp of beer. I sit down at the table, and light my own cigarette. "How many Xanax you think I should take to come off the trip?"

"How many you got?"

"Like, eight more, I think." I look in the bag. I'm pretty sure I took Xanax. Pink did what I asked. She gave me a lot of everything. Xanax has become one of my best friends, taking the edge off anxiety and—when I took enough—dulling my mind and affecting my memory. I tried it with a prescription, but Dr. Darby had grown concerned that I was getting hooked. I tried to doctor shop, but The Floyd Chicks were faster.

Stacy snaps his fingers. "You listening? How many milligrams?"

I shrug. "How am I supposed to know? They work. I take them." Stacy laughs.

"Fuck it, take one more." I do. "Every hippie I know says a bad trip ends where Xanax begins."

"What's the plan, then?" I'm digging. I don't know what else to do. I gotta get outta here, though.

"We go in, we get them to tell us where Michelle and Stevie are at, we get them, we get out. Maybe we bloody a few noses, maybe we take an insurance policy with us, long enough to get down the highway."

I can't help but shake my head. I have no military background, but the cavalier way Stacy discusses the plan leads me to believe he's either not going to tell me everything because he doesn't trust me, or he's deranged. "That sounds like a Ready, Fire, Aim approach, dude," I challenge. "I thought you had a plan, intelligence, surveillance? You were a Marine. I have no idea what we're supposed to be doing."

"I *am* a United States Marine. Once a Marine, always a Marine. You just follow my lead and keep your fucking mouth shut. I know what we need to do. You don't have to worry about it." Stacy holds the cigarette with his thumb and index finger, the cherry pointed toward the palm of his hand. "They won't be able to keep it from me. I know *how* to ask the questions. One of them will fold. We're walking out of there with Stevie and Michelle, or none of us is walking out of there."

"Will any of them have guns?" I wonder.

"Have to assume some of them will. Some are cops. Besides, everyone around here has a gun."

"Do I get a gun? I haven't shot a gun since…before everything that happened with Mason Reynolds. I don't know how good I am anymore." The thought of holding a gun makes me queasy.

Stacy snaps. "NO, I'm not giving *you* a fucking *gun*! Are you nuts? You're gonna tie everyone up. I'll keep anyone from going anywhere. Then we just have a nice friendly talk and I get what I want, or I find the weak spot and push on it. But if you think I'm giving *you* a gun, you're out of your fucking mind."

This isn't a plan. This is a scene from a movie.

His eyes dart around the room, restless and blank.

I taste the remnants of my last slurp of Old Style in the mustache that's grown in while I've neglected shaving. I extend my hand, flexing it inside the bandage. My newly enlarged wound—freshly bloodied from my LSD-induced glass removal efforts—throbs.

When was the last time I ate?

Was my last meal the breakfast I ate with Wendy at Kay's South Side Café? That seems like a month ago.

My Last Meal. It's a death row thing to say.

I haven't eaten since Sunday. Or did I eat on Monday during my epic blackout?

I feel like I should be hungrier if I haven't eaten in two days. Shouldn't I?

"That's the plan, then? We both run in, you point your gun at everyone, I tie them all up one at a time, and then you interrogate them until someone talks? We're going to hope that no one tries to stop you, and they're going to tell us where Michelle and Stevie are, and we just drive away, leaving everyone all tied up, and then they just decide to stop abducting people because…you scared them? Do we have masks?" The Xanax is working. I'm clearer, but my words are coming out slower. "This plan is fucked up."

"I'm not going to explain the whole goddamn plan to you now and then have to retell it two or three more times because you're still all fucked up." Stacy's pissed again. "I got it all figured out."

"I've got a perfect memory. I remember everything forever," I remind him.

"When you're not tripping or drunk," Stacy counters and then changes the subject. "What do you need to get at your hotel, hoss?"

"Everything. All my stuff is still there. I thought I was coming over to talk and to find out when the funeral was." I point at myself. "I have to check out. I don't know what all I left behind in the room."

"Go get your shit and come back. We got time. I'll get the gear ready. We'll ride in the LeMans together." He drops his cigarette into one of my empty cans of Old Style, blows out his last lungful of smoke, and shoos me. "Go. We've got time, but not all day, hoss. You look better already. The hippies were right. Fucking Xanax and LSD." He laughs, short and surprised, then immediately grows determined again. "We'll go over everything when you get back."

Stacy's going to let me leave. It's all I can do to keep my relief from spilling into view.

.

CHAPTER 37

"You need to make better choices, Jeremy."

Sarah snatched the pint bottle of Peppermint Schnapps from my hand, took a drink, and coughed.

"I need to make better choices, too," she said. "In men, especially." She giggled. "Starting Monday, things are going to be different. You need to clean up your act if you wanna be with me, mister."

I held out my hand, expecting her to give me the bottle back. She slapped me five and took another sip.

We were parked behind "RJ's Kwik Stop Gas N Go" just a few blocks down Main Street Hill. Prom had started an hour ago, but we wanted to be alone together a little longer. Our teenage logic determined that arriving late, and drinking alcohol that smelled minty, would allow us to escape the chaperones' scrutiny. Our teenage logic felt definitive. Our teenage logic defied logic.

The bottle of Schnapps was almost gone. I finished half of it on the drive.

We'd held hands all the way from Madison back to Sugar River. I felt closer to Sarah than I ever had before, but I'd started brooding and she asked me a few times why I was so quiet, and I wouldn't tell her.

I obsessed over going off to college without her. It was a terrible misuse of my imagination, envisioning how my days, weeks, months—a year—would suck without seeing Sarah every day. The idea had gotten into my head as we drove past the UW campus on our way back and it drained my joy. I was worried.

"What's wrong, Jeremy? Is it the shirt? It looks...fabulous." Sarah poked at the ill-fitting replacement tux shirt that I had swapped out in a Burger King bathroom.

I tried to laugh. "It's not the shirt."

"Then what?" Sarah propped herself up on her knees, forgetting for a moment that she was wearing nylons and a formal dress and was sitting in the front seat of a car. She leaned over the gear shift, her face right next to mine, and gently asked, "Why won't you tell me? I hate it when you do this."

"I don't want to ruin the night," I lied.

"You're gonna ruin the night by getting all weird," she corrected me. "You disappear in your head."

"I'll tell you what's wrong on Monday, OK? I don't want to talk about it tonight, but I'll tell you," I promise. "It's prom. I don't want it all fucked up. I want to have fun. I swear to God I'll tell you."

Sarah fidgeted with her earring. "OK." She pecked my cheek. "Don't forget." I arched my eyebrow and she knew instantly what I meant. "Don't try to get out of it." Sarah stretched out her legs and sat back.

I nodded, and then reached into my tuxedo jacket and pulled out a book of matches and a joint I'd stolen from Derrick's older sister. Technically, Derrick and I each took a joint from her stash. It wasn't the first time I'd gotten high, and the idea of smoking weed with Sarah before prom delighted me.

Her eyes grew wide. "Is that pot? Why do you have pot?"

"Wait, is it? How'd that get in here? I thought this was a Camel Straight. The fuck?" I was clowning.

"Oh my God, Jeremy, where'd you get pot?" she slurred her words, buzzed from the Schnapps.

"You want to smoke this with me before we go in?" I tempted her.

"No way." Sarah crossed her arms. "This is a bad idea. They'll totally smell it."

"This from the girl singing 'Hits from the Bong' less than three hours ago on our way to State Street."

"That is so different, and you know it. That was a song. This is us going to prom smelling like marijuana."

The way she enunciated the word "marijuana," saying it so formally like she was delivering the responsibility lecture on the dangers of drugs and alcohol at the end of a Degrassi Junior High episode, broke my dark mood. "The marijuana is a gateway drug, Miss Brennan. Do not let peer pressure force you into something you don't feel comfortable doing. Leave all the marijuana for Jeremy. He's functionally incapable of making responsible decisions because his brain has turned into fried eggs like the commercial said it would. Dismiss yourself casually and call the police immediately."

"Shut up!" She giggled. "You don't talk for ages and then you just say all your words at once. Smart ass."

I knew she'd get high with me.

"And don't think I'll forget that you need to tell me why you think you're Dylan McKay all of sudden."

"It's probably my hairstyle." I licked two of my fingers and smoothed out the sideburns that extended nearly to the bottom of my earlobes. Sarah rolled her eyes; when she looked away, I saw her dimples.

I let the joint hang from my lower lip, struck a match—sulfur filled the car—and held up the flame. "You might as well smoke it," I told her, preparing to inhale. "You're going to smell like weed no matter what."

I was not prepared for how much harsher the smoke was compared to a cigarette and immediately exploded with coughing and choking as my throat and lungs closed spontaneously. I pounded my chest, hacking, face turning red. Lightheadedness made me swoon. It was fantastic.

"Oh, that looks appealing." Sarah said smugly. "I think I'll finish the Schnapps." She took a sip.

I couldn't catch my breath and had temporarily lost my voice, but it didn't stop me from continuing to convince her. "No, seriously," I wheezed. "Just try it with me," I pressed, hoarsely. "It's awesome."

I coughed again, and tried to suppress it. It was more of a cough-sneeze through my nose, and my ears popped. My rust bucket Ford filled with smoke. Sarah rolled the window down, but reached over and took the joint from me, holding it between her index finger and middle finger like she was Bette Davis. She looked around, satisfied that no one was watching, and put it to her lips. Her inhale was much smaller than mine; I watched a tiny puff try to escape her mouth, but another short inhale captured it, then she shot a small jet of smoke out the window. I finished the Schnapps. Sarah handed me the joint.

I took another hit, this time without coughing. I passed it back to her, holding in the smoke this time.

Sarah took a larger drag, squinting her eyes. "Track," she croaked, and I waited for an explanation that never came. I assumed she was fretting over what would happen if she got caught. I felt like I could hear her thoughts and knew she was worried that she'd get bounced from the team, leaving her friends and coaches disappointed in her and upset. Sarah was a dedicated athlete and an even better teammate.

"We should save the rest for after," I told her. "I don't have any more. I could only steal this."

Sarah started giggling. It was contagious. "I can't stop my face from smiling," she snorted.

"I can't either." I pressed on my cheeks to force my face into a frown and Sarah laughed harder.

"Stop! We can't go into the dance this stupid or they'll know. They'll, like, totally smell it and we'll have the giggles and be all thirsty and our eyes are red and our breath smells like Schnapps. Stop laughing!"

I rubbed the lit end of the joint in my ashtray, started the car, pulled up next to the gas station dumpster, and lobbed the empty Schnapps bottle out the window. It was dusk. It was a muggy evening; the air conditioner fogged the windshield. Oncoming cars appeared blurry as I sat, clutch pushed in, car idling, then I cautiously pulled out onto Main Street Hill, turning toward Sugar River High School.

"You know our whole class is doing karaoke tonight, don't you? Like, everyone voted and everything to rent this stupid machine. We're supposed to have a song picked out. There's no way I'm doing it. I can't sing." I was suddenly paranoid and gripped the steering wheel to keep my hands from shaking. My mouth was dry. It was as though the crushing reality of being in a crowd of people hit me all at once.

"We should totally do a duet!" Sarah exclaimed. "What about 'All My Life'?"

I was mortified. "Aaron Neville and Linda Ronstadt? That's the worst song ever! And I can't sing the Aaron Neville part—his voice is higher than hers and he's got that weird thing on his eyebrow. And you can't sing either! It would be the worst. I'm not getting up there in front of everyone. No. Way."

Sarah's eyes lit up.

"Do 'The Humpty Dance!' You even just changed your shirt in a Burger King bathroom. I've heard you do, like, every word to that song. You wouldn't even need the bouncing ball thing with the words."

"But I can't sing." I told her. "You can't sing. We're both terrible."

"That's the point of karaoke. No one can sing. It's supposed to suck. It's funny because it sucks."

"I'm not getting up in front of the whole school and sucking. Fuck that." She was talking me into it.

Sarah stuck out her bottom lip, exaggeratedly pretending to pout. "This was your chance to start making better choices," she warned me, but her eyes were twinkling. God, I loved being with her. "We agreed."

"You said Monday," I reminded her.

"I said I'd start making better choices on Monday. You should start ASAP as possible." When she added the extra "as possible" to "ASAP" we both fell out into hysterics again. "There's no way we can go in. They'll totally know we're high. I need some gum or something. Or Visine. Do you have Visine?"

"Why do you get to wait until Monday to make good choices, but I have to start tonight?" I pretended to whine. "I don't wanna make better choices! How this fair? You get a whole extra weekend of fuck-ups?"

"Because I'm mostly good, and you're mostly bad. You've got more work to do." Sarah was quick with her comeback. "I'm a good girl, you're a bad boy. I have time. You're not so lucky. Your time is up. If you don't change your ways right now, we're in for a disaster."

"I'm going to remember you said that," I lectured.

"You remember everything everyone says about everything forever. Big deal." She waved off my idle threat and immediately asked, "Do you have any gum? We can't go in there with Schnapps pot breath."

"I have Kodiak. Want a dip?" Sarah wrinkled her nose and shook her head back and forth.

I turned off Main Street. Every parking space in front of the school was taken. There was a rented limo; the Prom Court King and Queen had arrived. I downshifted and turned left, and then made another left and zipped into the student parking lot. When I turned off the car, we could hear music coming from the gym. The back entrance to the school was propped open with two teachers standing guard.

"We're going to get in trouble," Sarah said. The car engine pinged as it cooled. I ran my fingers through my hair again, smoothed my sideburns, and came up with the best reassurance I could think of.

"Just don't breathe on them when we go in. We'll be fine. It'll be dark in there. It's a dance."

Sarah rolled her eyes. "Darkness doesn't affect someone's sense of smell, Jeremy."

"I know that," I scoffed sarcastically and changed the subject. "How do I look?" It had been nearly impossible to tie my bowtie a second time, especially in a Burger King bathroom, but it held together, cockeyed and misshapen. The secondhand store tuxedo shirt fit terribly. It felt like I was suffocating.

"Like an international spy in a movie."

"C'mon…really? I feel like an idiot in this penguin suit and the wrong shirt. Do I look OK?"

Sarah finally got it. I was self-conscious and needed her validation to have enough self-esteem to go in.

"Hey," she said. I was still looking in the rearview mirror, tilting and holding the bowtie, believing it was going to stay in place. "Hey," she said again. I finally looked at her, and when I did, I knew I loved her.

"You look like the only person I wanted to go to prom with, Jeremy. Only you. You look great."

Sarah put her hand on my cheek, moving her whole body toward me, opening her mouth just enough, and kissed me. She took a small breath through her nose, and kept kissing me, deeply. She stopped, put up her hand, blinked her eyes about five or six times, and exhaled. "Woo. OK. We need to go in."

"You should fix your…" I pointed at her lips and spun my finger in a circle. "It's all smeared."

She winked. "Not it's not. It's all on your lips." She handed me a Zorba the Greek napkin.

"Did you just wink at me? When did you become a winker? You don't wink." God I was happy.

"I wink all the time. I can wink. I'm a winker." She then did the most ridiculous wink I've ever seen, widely opening her left eye, tilting her head toward me, squeezing her right eye closed, her mouth drooping and smiling at the same time. "See? That's my secret across-the-room-no-one-will-notice wink. I've been practicing it. I basically nailed it," Sarah rattled off her comeback and reached for the door handle.

"Don't get out yet," I ordered, threw open my door, slammed it shut, and slung myself around the front of the car to open her door for her. Sarah was touching up her lipstick and was doing that "SMOCK SMOCK!" noise that girls make when they've finished. She folded a stick of Double Mint in half, popped it into her mouth, took one last look at her hair in the visor mirror, and stepped out, one beautiful leg, then another. Sarah's ankles wobbled on feet unaccustomed to high heels after drinking Schnapps, but her knees didn't buckle, and she regained her balance with a giggle and a glance to see if I was watching.

I escorted her to the back entrance. One of the chaperones was the office secretary.

She flapped her hands, bent half over with excitement, and exclaimed. "You look all grown up!"

"Thank you, Mrs. Begley," Sarah replied politely. "I'll tell my mom you said hello."

I nodded, and we stepped from the darkness of the parking lot to the slightly brighter gymnasium. The Class of 1992 had spent hours of free time, study halls, before school and after practice—and a long Friday with understanding teachers—getting the teal and black decorations, tables and chairs and punch bowls and signs and DJ equipment and a karaoke machine and everything else in place that was incredibly important to our Student Council Leadership. I had ducked out each time I was asked to help.

In the center of activity, a massive gazebo had been erected, covered in teal and black streamers, tissue paper, and a sign that we had printed that said "LOVE IS ON THE WAY! Class of 1992 Senior Prom!" The DJ was playing "O.P.P." by Naughty By Nature, but no one was dancing. A few of the bleachers had been pulled out and everyone was sitting around talking. The girls were protecting their hair, dresses, makeup and nylons, resting their feet from uncomfortable shoes. The guys were backslapping each other, probably lying about their exploitative plans for later that night. Chaperones stood around the perimeter, eyeing us and likely debating when to intervene and when to let kids be kids.

There might've been a hundred and fifty students there, most from Sugar River High School, some from neighboring schools, and a handful of teachers, coaches, secretaries, a principal, and our guidance counselor.

Sarah saw her friend Kelly, squeaked, told me she'd be right back, and scurried across the gym.

I didn't know what to do with myself without her to talk to. I looked around, instantly on guard, edgy and awkward. Walls of arrogance went up as I feigned indifference. Aloofness was one of the defense mechanisms I'd learned to use when I felt anxious, my stomach churning with apprehension. If I couldn't sneak away and hide, I would do my best to act like I didn't give a fuck about anyone, or anything.

I spotted Aaron and stood next to him, but paid little attention until he asked if we were still doing the -post--rom bonfire. "Why wouldn't we?" I shot back. "I'm getting fucking shitfaced tonight, dude."

He said something else; I didn't reply, and he wandered off. I stared across the gym, watching Sarah.

I wasn't jealous that she and Kelly were such close friends. I didn't have any true friendships like theirs.

I resisted interfering, even though Kelly justifiably thought I was an asshole because of how I treated other people. Her distrust and dislike were both accurate and misguided. I could be horrible to people I didn't like and indifferent toward people I didn't know, ignoring anyone I had no interest in knowing.

However, it wasn't true that I couldn't be a trustworthy boyfriend. I craved a meaningful relationship. I didn't need a list of friends around me to feel popular. All I wanted was a partner. One person, thick or thin, lover and friend, same interests and dislikes, and fuck everyone else.

So in a sense, Kelly was right. I kept most people at arm's length with a quips and deflection. Sometimes I got in fights when I ran my mouth too much. Sometimes I ridiculed people who didn't want to fight. Derrick and Aaron thought it was funny. Everyone else thought I was a punk or a dick.

But from a different perspective, Kelly was completely wrong. Sarah had nothing to worry about. I cherished her far above myself. I wanted to know her. I was amazed by her. I looked across the room, fully captivated by Sarah Brennan. I was happy trying to make her happy.

She saw me watching from across the gym and waved, holding up her pointer and mouthing, "ONE MINUTE. SORRY!" She turned back to her group of friends and rejoined the chatter. I pretended as though I was talking to people I didn't care about, so she didn't feel the need to pull away from before she was ready. I said words to people, and they said words back. I ignored their replies completely.

It was the first few notes of Metallica's "Nothing Else Matters" that sent me striding confidently across the gym toward Sarah. It was my favorite song. I had memorized the lyrics, an aspiration, a message just for me, a piece of music that gave expression to emotions and hopes that I'd previously had no words for.

Kelly saw me coming before Sarah, poked her and pointed.

"Hi, Jeremy," she said with her usual tinge of disapproval. "We're almost done with our girl."

"Hey, Kel Can. Where's your date?" I thought using "Kal Kan Dog Food" as a nickname was funny. I didn't think she was ugly, it just worked. Kelly hated it. Sarah had asked me to stop doing it, but it slipped out.

"Around, I guess. I heard what you guys were doing," Kelly said, pinching her fingers together and holding them up to her lips, pretending to suck in, hold her breath and talk. "You stoners."

"I'll hook you up later. I need our girl," I said, and put my hand gently on Sarah's lower back.

"I don't smoke pot," Kelly judged. "Sarah shouldn't either."

"What, no concern for my brain cells, Kel Can? You're right. Sarah shouldn't smoke weed. And neither should I. But here we are, so like I said, I'll hook you up later. Right now, I'm taking our girl."

Sarah whispered firmly to me, "Please just be nice." I put my hands up in mock protest, as though I was offended by the suggestion that I was being anything other than a perfect gentleman. "Stop," she ordered.

"Will you dance with me?" I invited, and tugged at her arm. Sarah playfully waved at Kelly and the rest of her group. She let me drag her as far away from them as I could, too close to the speaker. Still clutching her tiny purse, Sarah tossed her arms over my shoulders and I slipped my hands around her waist, at the lowest part of her back, and interlocked my fingers. We didn't dance. It was unsteady, rhythmic swaying.

"Please be nicer to Kelly. Casey is ignoring her tonight and she's upset and you're using that nickname she hates. I want you guys to be friends. Please, try?" Sarah implored. "It's important to me."

"I'll try harder," I agreed, and I meant it. "I don't want to talk about Kelly and Casey anymore. Can we just dance? For just this one song? Then we can get our pictures and get the fuck out of here."

She nodded and placed her head on my shoulder. After only a few seconds, Sarah suddenly popped her head back up. "How long have we been going out?" she asked.

"Seven months, twenty-nine days. You said yes at 3:16 p.m. on Thursday, October 17."

"What was I wearing?" she pressed.

"Your volleyball uniform. You still had your knee pads on. Your hair was pulled back and braided."

"What were you were wearing?" she giggled.

"Track pants and an Air Jordan t-shirt."

"What was the weather like?" she was enthralled, testing my memory.

"It was warmer than usual for October. It was 77 degrees and had rained earlier in the day, but when I caught up with you before volleyball practice the sun was out again."

"What did you say when you asked me out?" Sarah loved doing this.

"I said, 'The only way to get me to stop asking you out is to say yes.' And you said, 'If I say yes once, you'll stop asking me out?' and I said, 'Yes, because then we'll just be going out, so I won't have to ask anymore.' I didn't know what else to say because the other times you just said no and that was it. I hadn't gotten that far before, so I didn't know what to do. When you said, 'OK, where are we going to go?' I just said 'Pizza Hut' because it was the first place that came to mind. It was pure luck that you—"

"—love Pizza Hut," Sarah finished. "What did they serve for lunch in the cafeteria that day?"

"I ate off-campus that day. I went to the gas station and had a micro-wave pizza with a can of Mountain Dew because school lunch was meatloaf, green beans, and pears. I didn't want any of that shit. I assume you took two milks, a white and a chocolate, like you always do, and probably licked the tray clean."

That night, with Sarah, my autobiographical memory was a blessing.

She was delighted and wanted to see how completely I had immortalized the Beginning of Us. She put a finger to the corner of her mouth and asked, "What was on TV that night?"

"Easy one. I normally watch 90210, but that night I watched the NLCS. Atlanta beat Pittsburgh. It was Game 7; John Smoltz pitched a 4-0 shutout and the Braves went to the World Series."

"How do you do that?" she demanded, joyful and thrilled. "I don't understand how you can just do that for any date someone picks. I mean, I remember our first day, too, but not like that."

I told her I didn't know. I stopped forgetting on my fifth birthday. No one could explain it.

"I hate it," I confessed. "I feel like a freak. Remembering good things is nice, but I can't forget the bad things and it makes it hard sometimes."

Her eyes softened. "You're not a freak, Jeremy. Don't hate it. You're special. It's like a magic trick, but it's real. You'll know everything we've ever done and never forget all of our moments together. I love it."

Sarah put her head on my shoulder again. The song was nearly over. I was overwhelmed with the closeness of the moment, our connection, my recollection of the start of our relationship, our kiss on State Street, her declaration to me in the car, her insistence I was special. I just said it, quietly.

"I think I love you."

The music was deafening near the speaker, the bass and guitar riffs from the Metallica ballad sending pulsating vibrations into our bodies, James Hetfield's vocals obscuring my weak and cautious voice.

Sarah lifted her head. "What did you say?" she asked. "Did I hear you say what it sounded like you said?"

I swallowed, gazed up at the ceiling, and then back into her eyes.

"I love you, Sarah. I'm pretty sure...I'm...in love. With you."

"You love me? You can't be pretty sure. You have to love me forever, or you can't love me at all. I don't want you to sort of love me. Can you do that, Jeremy Peoples?" She didn't break eye contact. She didn't smile. Sarah's brow furrowed slightly, lips pursed, brown eyes wanting and inquisitive. Hopeful. Her arms had tensed around me. "Can you love me forever? Will you love me like that?" We held each other.

The song ended but we didn't stop dancing. I nodded. "I will. Yes."

"Then I love you, too," she promised.

CHAPTER 38

I need to call Dr. Darby Grover.

My therapist. I need to talk to her. Right now.

It's almost 10:00 a.m. here, 11 o'clock back in DC. My appointment's in an hour. I don't have my cell phone. If I'm going to make my appointment, I have to call her from my hotel.

I need Dr. Darby so I can sort out what's happening. She can tell me what to do with Stacy, how to help him, how to keep this from escalating. I can't bring myself to call the police. What if I'm wrong and Stacy is just processing his grief? He needs help, someone who really cares enough to get him treatment.

Maybe I'm losing my mind.

Dr. Darby will know what to do.

The drive to Madison is a whirlwind of paranoid speculation and adrenaline, but I make it from Stacy's trailer to The Mansion Hill Inn by 10:54 a.m.

I can't wait for the elevator. I'm through the door to the stairs, up one flight, wheezing as I hit the landing for the second floor, sweating as I burst into the third-floor hallway, startling the cleaning crew. There's only a moment to catch my breath, and then I'm sprinting down the hall toward my room.

10:58 a.m.

Dialing. Ringing. Her office manager answers, pleasantly as always, and I breathlessly make my request.

"Hey, this is Jeremy Peoples, I had to leave town unexpectedly, and was hoping that Dr. Darby would be willing to do my session today over the phone. Normally I wouldn't ask, but I really feel like I need to keep my appointment this week. A lot—A WHOLE FREAKING LOT—has happened since last Tuesday. Please? Can you ask her for me? Thank you so much. How are *you*, by the way? Did you have a nice New Year's?" All of my questions are answered with a question.

"She's still with another client right now. It may be just a few minutes before I can get you an answer on your request for a telephone session. Can you hold the line for a few minutes, Jeremy?" She's always so patient and kind. I hate that I've never asked her name, or cared enough to learn it some other way.

"I can hold, sure. I'm calling long distance from a hotel, so please pass that along, too, if you could."

"I'll be sure to share that as well, Jeremy. Hold on please and when Dr. Darby is free, I'll speak with her."

My mind wanders while I wait. The LSD is loosening its grip on me. The Xanax must be working. I don't remember much of the drive from Stoughton to Madison; it's a blur of emotional outbursts at other drivers and worrying. I was on autopilot, and now I'm in a waking swoon. I spy the coffee maker across the room and the phone just reaches. I awkwardly get a pot brewing, half tangled in the phone cord.

"What the fuck is taking so long?" I complain. I look at my watch.

11:01 a.m. I've been on hold for less than two minutes.

I picture Dr. Darby. When I met with her for my first session, I thought her hair color was almost the same as Sarah's. She isn't stunningly beautiful in a traditional sense, but her intelligence, intuition, and education make her somehow transparently enigmatic. I try to imagine who she is in her personal life, but she has given me no hints; Dr. Darby is always—*always*—impeccably dressed, stylish but never too revealing. On more than one occasion, I've almost asked her to join me for a drink, or for dinner. She'd refuse, but I'm certain she'd minimize my embarrassment and we wouldn't discuss it again. Dr. Darby's kindness and empathy is my safety net. Someday, maybe, I'll start being completely honest with her.

She has to know I'm hiding things from her and trying to manipulate how she helps me.

"Tell me about Sarah," she'd said during one of our earliest visits. "What comes to mind first?"

"She forgave me," I had answered immediately, surprised that my response wasn't, "I love her."

CHAPTER 39

"Oh my God, Jeremy—stop! It's not funny! Stop!" The moment Sarah shrieked I came to my senses.

Illuminated by the firelight, Sarah's eyes pierced me with shame and regret. It was just a few short hours after I'd promised her I'd love her forever, and I now knew that she would never, ever see me as she had.

"What are you doing?!" Her shock was unmistakable and understandable, considering she had just witnessed me jousting a burning branch at a completely naked and bloodied Mason Reynolds.

The crowd of spectators had thinned out while my attack on Mason escalated from a typical high school fight to a vicious humiliation. Everyone wanted to retreat, create an alibi, escape responsibility. Car doors slammed, engines started, and headlights stabbed at the night sky as dozens of teenagers left beer cans and bottles behind and put distance between us. Of the few people who were still there, no one offered to help Mason. He looked around to see if any of his clothes had been spared from the bonfire.

The real world came rushing in to fill the hate space I created with my conscienceless bullying. I saw it immediately. The remorseless hostility and near-violence was sickening to Sarah, as it should have been to me. I hated Mason Reynolds for the tiniest of offenses: he'd been nice to me around the wrong people. My absurdly fragile ego had been threatened by the idea that my peers would learn I was friends with an outcast. It wasn't enough to humiliate him. I had to hurt him, and was one misstep away from burning him alive. I wanted revenge for what he had done to me. Desperate to hide, I carefully cultivated the lie that I was strong. Mason had upset that in front of everyone. The fear of being uncovered as a fraud, the need to deflect attention away from my weakness had overwhelmed me. I was a shallow degenerate.

My first instinct was to attack.

"You fucking pussy," I spat at Mason, the words I cursed him with had long since been ingrained in me.

"Jeremy! Let him go! What are you doing?" Sarah ran toward me, joining our semicircle on the fringes of the blazing bonfire. I tossed the burning branch back into the roaring bonfire with a swirl of sparks.

Derrick and Aaron brushed themselves off, ready to leave, probably worried that their participation would result in the cops getting called, or some other consequence none of us had drunkenly considered. It was as if I was their cult leader and they had only just realized I'd gleefully led them into destruction.

"What the fuck did he say to you, Peepholes? You went fucking OFF." Aaron seemed unsure about whether he should act like what we had just done to Mason was funny, or a tragedy seen by dozens.

There was no way I was going to tell them the secret I was hiding. "Nothing. He pisses me off."

"Jesus Christ, Jeremy," Derrick said. "What if you set him on fire?"

"I didn't. Fuck it. He's fine. He'll be fine." I shrugged, feigning indifference. "It's not that big of a deal."

Aaron disagreed. "I'm out of here."

Derrick grabbed his girlfriend's hand, and trotted off into the darkness without saying another word.

"We should go, too," I said to Sarah.

Sarah looked at Aaron, then at me, stunned. "You're just going to leave him out here?"

Mason was shivering and dirty, blood clotting in his nostrils, lip swollen, scratches on his chest and legs from where we ripped off his clothes. He tried to cover himself with his hands and stay warm, getting close—but not too close—to the fire. My empathy for him returned. I hated myself.

Aaron and his date receded into the night, nearly vanishing as they got further from the bonfire. "He's got his own car. We gotta go. I can't...I can't be out too much later. Curfew," he lied as he ran away.

"Where are his clothes?" Sarah demanded. I silently pointed at the fire. "What are we going to do?"

"I don't know. I can't..." my voice trailed off.

"We can't leave him here. Not like this." Sarah faced him. "Mason." Tears streamed down his face, cutting two clean lines through the bloody grime on his cheeks, reflecting the light of the bonfire. Earlier, I'd given Sarah my tuxedo jacket when she shivered in the evening air. It was then that she peeled it off and tried to hand it to Mason. He wouldn't look at her, refused to say anything, refused my jacket.

"Mason!" Finally, he glanced up. "Is your car here or did you ride with someone?" He bobbed his head in the direction of the only remaining vehicle, other than mine, parked about thirty yards away.

"Do you have your keys?" Sarah asked, but I knew he was stranded.

We could have given him a ride, but instead I chose ugly weakness. "We should go," I mumbled.

Sarah couldn't look at Mason. She wouldn't look at me, either.

"Mason, can you get home?" she offered, her voice cracking. "I don't want to leave you out here—"

"Just fucking go!" Mason screamed, sobbing. "I don't want your help. Leave me alone." When he looked at us, it wasn't fear I saw in his eyes. It was rage. "GO. BOTH OF YOU! LEAVE ME THE FUCK ALONE!"

401

Sarah was still hesitant. I took her hand and started leading her toward my car.

She pulled away and tried once more. "Mason, you can ride with us. Do you have any clothes you can put on?" The thought of letting Mason in my car made me sick to my stomach. I was relieved when he yelled, even more forcefully than before, "I DON'T NEED YOUR FUCKING HELP! I CAN TAKE CARE OF MYSELF!!"

Sarah took a step back. "I'm sorry, Mason," she whispered and started toward the car without me.

It should have been me apologizing, begging for forgiveness, but I couldn't. I wouldn't.

We left. Sarah kept looking back. I stared at the ground. We didn't hold hands. We didn't speak.

We walked through the field, feet soaked with dew, until we were next to Mason's car. My trigonometry textbook was on the passenger seat, wrapped in brown paper and covered in Sarah's doodles. I shamefully stole a glance back at Mason. The orange light of the bonfire obscured him completely.

I took the book. It felt like stealing, even though it was mine.

When I got in my car, I set my textbook in Sarah's teal and black satin lap. Her gaze fell on her scribbles of "I will love you forever, Jeremy!!" and "from me," clearly visible, even in the barely lit field. I thought she might soften, seeing her love note. Instead, she turned away, hiding her face from me.

I started my car and eased the clutch out, tires spinning in the wet grass. The tractor trail we had followed to get to the post-prom party was well worn and rutted, bouncing us around as I made my way quickly toward the road. On the way in, navigating the trail had felt like an adventure; we'd laughed as we approached the bonfire. The trip out was bruising as my car bottomed-out; we said nothing on the jostling return to the blacktop. I had dozens of things I wanted to say to her. It was beneath her to hear them. They were lies. Phony. They were excuses and I couldn't use them with her.

I left Mason behind, wishing my culpability would stay with him, in the emptiness, in the past.

The fire grew smaller, until we no longer saw it directly, only the evidence that it was still out there, a hue of illumination in the inky blackness of pasture, woods, and desolate farmland.

"I can't believe we're just leaving him here," Sarah sniffed.

I opened my mouth, closed it. I didn't know what to say. I feebly tried anyway. "You heard him. He told us to leave. We can't make him ride back with us. I mean...what could I do?"

Apologize. Show some compassion. Help him. Try harder to make it right. Anything but this.

"I don't really know you at all, Jeremy," Sarah said.

I wanted to tell her I felt the same way. I didn't really know me at all either.

CHAPTER 40

"Thank you for holding, Jeremy." Dr. Darby's voice brings me back from 1992.

Has it really been almost eight years? It seems like eight minutes. The past is constantly invading the present. Everything is now. I only remember or react. My memories are a monster.

"It's so good to hear your voice, Dr. Darby!" Tears well up in my eyes, spilling down my cheeks, dripping to the comforter spread tight across a freshly-made hotel mattress. I sob once, then catch my breath.

She's sympathetic and calm, exactly what I need. "Oh, Jeremy, where are you at right now?"

"Geographically or existentially?" I joke. I struggle to keep from breaking down, completely exhausted.

Dr. Darby laughs, a little, and replies, "I hear that you're out of town today, and quite a lot has happened since our last visit. Let's start with why you're out of town, if that's OK. Where are you?"

"It's kind of a long fucking story. I'm back in Wisconsin. Madison."

She pauses. "Why are you there, Jeremy? Are you visiting family? You don't sound like you're in a healthy place, but it's hard to tell on the phone. Why did you decide to go to Wisconsin?"

Fuck my family. She's always nudging me to talk about my parents because I never want to. I should've made up a believably saccharine story about my childhood and lied to her.

"I guess you didn't hear the radio show on New Year's Eve?" I'm deflecting her questions because recounting everything that's happened since Friday night seems impossible. We only have an hour and I'm going to need enough time to tell her about Stacy and get her diagnosis of what's wrong with him.

"I'm sorry, Jeremy, but I wasn't able to listen. You know what my objections have been to your interview with Mason Reynolds. Did something happen while you were speaking with him? Is that why you've left town so suddenly? You made no mention of a trip to Madison last Tuesday."

One of my great struggles is over-describing the vivid events that circulate in my brain. I can't separate a vital piece of information from the incidental. It *all* feels important to me. I swing between hyper-descriptive anecdotes and inconsequential summaries, rarely finding a middle ground. Dr. Darby knows this about me, and she prompts me accordingly. "How about you give me the highlights?"

I detail my New Year's Eve show, including Stacy's call and Mason's supernatural message.

Dr. Darby pauses so long that I fear we lost our connection. "Are you still there?" I question.

"Yes, I'm sorry, Jeremy, that's a lot to absorb. I'm so very sorry to hear about your friend Michelle. Our previous conversations have indicated you still have a strong connection with her, even if you've not seen her for several years." I haven't revealed to Dr. Darby that I'm secretly a parent. I don't have time now. "I wonder how you've chosen to process these strong emotions and the painful memories that are coming to the surface simultaneously, both of Michelle and the tragedy at your high school. You've demonstrated remarkable resilience in spite of your self-destructive behavior, and we've collaborated on visualizing a healthier you with more effective habits, but I wonder if you've stayed disciplined."

I consider lying. I shouldn't lie to her as often as I do. I trust her, but only to a point.

"No. I sort of relapsed a little. A lot. Bad."

"I thought that might be the case. It's OK. Let's talk about that later. You've just had two very different traumatic events converge in a confusing and intense manner. A woman you've cared deeply about for years has passed away and you conversed with the man who nearly killed you *and* he used the occasion to try and inflict further harm on you. It's what I was worried about. You built these unhealthy barriers of protection around yourself, and developed coping mechanisms for pain management, but then you let the wrong people through your walls, violating your own internal boundaries, and focus on the painful events, leading to the spiral of depression we've been trying to get a handle on. Together."

I'm calmer.

"Has there been any other unhealthy behavior?"

The Floyd Chicks. Snorting heroin. Taking LSD and then Xanax to come down. Binge drinking.

"Some."

"Would you be willing to elaborate?"

"There's lots more. I've lost a lot of time. Like, these waking blackouts. Also...Michelle left a letter for me at a club I've never been to but somehow she knew I'd be there and hand delivered it."

Dr. Darby gently interrupts me. "What did the letter say, Jeremy? Do you mind sharing it with me?"

"I haven't opened it yet," I tell her.

"Why haven't you read it yet?" This is the first time I've heard her sound surprised.

"I can explain why, but I know it's not time. I feel like I'll know when I should. I can't bring myself to look at it yet. I'm nervous about what it says. I want to know, but I don't want to know." The letter, with its loopy purple cursive writing on a stationary envelope, is the only thing I have left of Michelle Ramone.

"Would you like to open it now, together, in a more structured circumstance?" Dr. Darby presses.

"No, thank you, no. I'm not ready to see. I can't. I won't. I'm sorry."

"Jeremy, remember, you don't need to constantly make a value judgement on your feelings. It's perfectly acceptable that you don't want to read the letter today. There's nothing right or wrong about that emotion. It simply is how you feel about it," Dr. Darby cautions.

"I remember everything. Remember?" I'm condescending. Therapy makes me defensive at times.

"Yes, you are the single most remarkably adept person I've ever met in that area of cognition, maybe who has ever lived. Yet at the same time, you're just like everyone else. While you remember everything perfectly, you still struggle to understand the meaning of those events in your life and then apply what you've learned to change your behavior to find positive outcomes in your relationships."

Darby is always *so fucking right*. It's both a comfort and maddening. She makes me want to argue.

"I don't disagree. But there's more to this. I'm..." I start over. "Look. Mason told me on the phone that I'd get an invitation to come to Wisconsin because it was God's will or whatever. That was minutes after Stacy called the show and asked me to come back for Michelle's funeral. He didn't know Stacy called in. Then I met Wendy, and I went back the school and found the necklace. It all seems like it's building toward something, but I can't see what it's supposed to be. I need you to help me figure this out."

"Who's Wendy?"

"Never mind, it doesn't matter. She's just…it's nothing…" I fall silent again. Wendy was so gentle and kind and calm. I was rude and ugly and mean. I wish I'd just stayed in that booth at Kay's South Side Café for the last three days instead of driving the rest of the "home." I wonder what Wendy's doing right now. What if she was praying for me? Was she wondering if I'd found God after our talk? How can I be expected to find God? Why can't He just find *me*? How hard can it be for an omniscient, omnipresent, omnipotent Father to find one more lost boy like me? Why was it up to me to find Him and try to salvage this disaster He created me to be?

I can hear Dr. Darby shifting in her seat. "What school did you go to, Jeremy? Did you visit Sugar River?"

The explosive memory of that visit causes a shudder to run through my entire body. "I did."

"You went to your high school? I thought you said it was condemned, that it had been torn down? We've talked about possibly revisiting this in the future, but had agreed you are too fragile right now for an action step of this magnitude. The substance abuse, insomnia, and your ongoing difficulty in managing your memories so that you can function effectively in your day-to-day life have left you in a weakened state emotionally, physically, and psychologically. We had collaboratively agreed that you need to be further along in your recovery before visiting the site and releasing some of those unresolved emotions. What made you decide to go against our therapy strategy, Jeremy?" Dr. Darby challenged.

Drugs. Stupidity. Opportunity. A compulsion for self-harm. A need to be satisfied. Guilt. Impatience.

"I wasn't planning to go. I went to the park where Sarah and I had been together on prom night. I drove into town to use the phone and just wanted to see it again. It made me come inside. I couldn't help it. I tried to talk myself out of it, but I needed to see if she was still in there," I recount. "It wasn't good."

"You went inside? To the scene of the shooting? Do you want to tell me what you experienced?"

"I thought I was dreaming. The town couldn't have left the building in that condition. Dried blood everywhere. Smashed windows, boarded up doors, vandalized. It had to be some kind of memory overlay with reality. But I found the Best Friends Forever necklace that Sarah and her friend Kelly always wore together. I took it. I have it. Then I passed out on the floor. I thought maybe I was finally dying from heartbreak. It felt…relaxing." I omit the part about sleeping in Sarah's tape outline, the only way that I could be inside her again. "But the really crazy shit didn't happen until after I left the school."

"Were you under the influence when you exposed yourself to this trauma?"

I've been under the influence of something since Friday. Yes. I'm under the influence right now. But the drugs aren't the problem. Stacy is. I need to know what what's wrong with him and how to deal with it.

"I need you to help me understand something that happened. There's so much that doesn't make sense, but there's so much that fits together, and then there's other stuff that seems like it could fit but I'm not sure how. I need you to help with something though, that's not about me, I need your expertise about someone else. I don't understand what I'm involved in." I breathe deep. "How can you tell when someone is truly mentally deranged? I mean, I know you don't believe I should be institutionalized, that I should be in rehab, that I've got disorders and sicknesses, but how do you know when it progresses past what can be dealt with on the outside? Like, when the person might be a danger to others?"

"Jeremy, are you planning to harm yourself?" she gently inquires, again steering the conversation back.

Yes, of course, if I wasn't a fucking coward, I'd hang up the phone and take all the pills that are in my shaving bag and wash them down with the contents of my freshly restocked minibar. Let's fucking go.

"No. I'm struggling, but I think I'm OK. This trip has been hard—really fucking hard—but this isn't about me. I mean, how can you tell when someone is just crazy like, 'I'm sitting in my house watching too many Oliver Stone movies and reading *The Turner Diaries*,' crazy or when someone is crazy like, 'I'm going to go out and blow up a building or assassinate the president to impress Jodi Foster' crazy?"

"The difference between you and—for example—Mason Reynolds?"

Her answer frustrates me. "I swear to fucking Christ this isn't about me and Mason! Just help me out here. How do you know the difference between harmless crazy and dangerously deranged?"

"That's a complicated and important question. You have to be careful not to draw a distinction because such a diagnosis, if improperly applied, can alter someone's life for many, many years. May I ask why you are so agitated about this? Who are you concerned about?" Dr. Darby always makes adept adjustments. "I'm willing to listen to your concerns, but I caution you against using the word 'crazy' to describe this person. I don't care for the term and urge you to resist it as well." She's tapping her fingernails; I can hear it through the handset. Dr. Darby does that when I'm being particularly unhelpful.

I deliver a radio monologue with all of my inflections and theatrics.

"Fine. Here's the scenario. I told you how Stacy called my radio show and told me his wife, Michelle, had died, and that I needed to come home for her funeral. He did it live on the air. Based on that, I drove back to Wisconsin to be there for him, despite our shared history with her. I feel like I owe him, that I need to make things right with him, and since I thought Michelle was…no long with us…I could fix things between us. When I got to his house, he's super weird, vague about giving me details about the funeral, and then tells me not only is Michelle gone, but…" I collect myself. "Their son Stevie is *also* gone. He keeps saying gone, not dead. Then he takes me on a drive to someone's house and tells me a crazy—I'm sorry, but it is what it is—a crazy story about how Michelle and Stevie have been abducted by some church cult and how the cops are in on it and that he expects me to help him get them back."

The fresh memory of my morning with Stacy shudders through me. I'd been lying in bed, staring at the ceiling, twirling the phone cord with my good hand. Agitated, I sit up, waiting for Dr. Darby to respond. She's likely taking notes, but has to find it hard to keep up with the confusing events I've outlined.

"Michelle *hasn't* passed away?" Dr. Darby asks cautiously. "There's no funeral to go to?" I can almost hear her frowning over the connection. I visualize her face, soft, brow furrowed, forehead lines a washboard, crow's feet barely discernible through her foundation, uncrossing her legs again.

"No funeral. It was a lie. He said that to get me to come home and help him perform what I first thought was some kind of rescue mission, but then he showed me all of this shit he's been saving and reading and now I don't know what he's going to do." I can't seem to make it sound as serious as it all feels.

"I apologize, but I'm having difficulty putting this all together. What do you think Stacy is going to do?"

"I think Stacy has lost his mind and is planning to break up this cult that he believes has Michelle and Stevie, and rescue them, maybe? An assault, I guess? He has a plan and he's doing it tonight. His bedroom is like some kind of military command center. He's taped newspapers over the windows and drawn the curtains and has maps and photos he's found somewhere and tacked to the walls. He's written notes and ideas and random shit on them with markers, Dr. Darby. I've never seen anything like it. He's a Marine. He's got guns. Technical manuals for I don't know what. People could get badly hurt."

Dr. Darby's voice is firm over the phone. "Jeremy, I want you to listen to me very carefully."

I ready myself. Finally, something I can use to stop what I've gotten sucked into.

"I think you should pack your bag and come home immediately." What the fuck? "I think it would be best if we had another session together, this week, in my office. I am concerned that your memories, your trauma, and your drug use are creating a manic dissociative episode."

I start to interrupt, protesting. "This is really happening!" I yell. Now I'm really pissed. I'm pissed *at her*.

"Jeremy," she patiently and calmly stops me. "Listen to me. Listen to your reality. You're the victim of a mass shooting that you repeatedly insist you are responsible for. You believe it and will not be dissuaded. You've just returned to the scene of your trauma for the first time since that incident. A day or so before that, on your radio show, you spoke to the shooter. That conversation in and of itself is an act of psychological violence against yourself. You've admitted to relapsing, and the drugs you have used in the past are known to distort perception. Your memories are so vivid, so realistic, that you've said you have to forcibly think yourself back into the present—"

I interrupt her again. "You don't understand. I was there. I saw the house, his room. Dr. Darby, please, I need you to believe me. I know what I saw." But do I really know? I dropped acid. What if she's right?

"Please, let me finish. I want you to hear this, internalize it, and consider it. Your friend, the first friend you really made after the shooting, who held you at gunpoint because of your affair with his wife, calls you and tells you she's died. That alone, apart from any of the other things I've just said, would be difficult news to hear. It could be that you are coping with the news of her death—and the memories of the loss of Sarah—by creating a scenario in your mind about another shooting. One that—this time—you can do something about. Where you can be the hero. I looked back on our notes from the past several months and you keep returning to this theme of forgiveness, needing it, expecting that everyone will offer it to you for causing the shooting in Sugar River because of how you bullied Mason. Maybe you believe if you stop this mass shooting it will be a type of penance, a grand good deed to undo the terrible events in your past. Guilt and shame are powerful emotions, and some of your recent choices may have set back your therapy somewhat, but it's nothing that we can't work through together. I believe you're subconsciously overlaying memories into your present and struggling to distinguish between what is really happening and your new, alternatively perceived reality."

I wait for her to finish. She continues. "I simply need you to consider the idea that this could be true."

The living shard of glass that I sliced free from my own arm.

The conversation with the mirror in Stacy's bathroom.

Arriving at Club Insomnia with no recollection of how I got there.

Losing an entire day, sleeping fully clothed in a hotel room and no memory of front desk conversations.

What if I got a concussion in my fight with the bartender?

Hoping that Pink would fuck me and use me and leave me for dead.

The feeling of me being the fake me, co-existing with the real me at the same time.

Passing out at a crime scene and sleeping for hours in the exact spot where Sarah's body fell.

Punching my own shower door while remembering a phone call I never made.

I've taken ecstasy, heroin, cocaine, amphetamines, LSD, Xanax. I'm drinking heavily.

Spiritual coincidences and seeing auras and feeling connections between things and timelines.

"You think I'm imaging all of this? That it's all a delusion?" I'm crying again. My nose is running.

Dr. Darby is rational. "You have been avoiding the difficult and painful work of processing deep grief, coping with the depression and post-traumatic stress that led to your arrested development. You've relapsed and your memory is unlike anyone else's. I won't call it a delusion. Your mind has been severely injured by the things that have happened to you, and it continues to revisit these events in such a vivid way that you're trying to find a way to escape. It's understandable. This is your way of fighting back, fighting to protect yourself. You've created a villain out of Stacy so it no longer needs to be you."

Did I hallucinate everything Stacy said? Was the trip to the pastor's house just misfiring synapses?

Both realities seem like they could be true.

Dr. Darby is so certain, so convincing. She's so intelligent and experienced. I mostly trust her.

I also know what I've experienced these past few days. I don't trust myself, and yet…something about what I'm in the middle of—right now—is *significant* and confirms the idea that even though something appears irrational doesn't mean it's false. *There's no way this is a fucking delusion.*

Michelle's letter and Sarah's necklace are on the bed in front of me. Both are physical evidence that I didn't hallucinate certain parts of the story. They're real. I'm looking at them. Right?

"I guess," I finally say.

"Jeremy, the human mind is incredibly powerful. It can create poetry and discern the mathematical and scientific underpinnings of our natural world. It retains vast amounts of information in all different forms, while simultaneously operating the body's functions, twenty-four hours a day, seven days a week, for as long as you remain alive. It imagines things that don't exist and is the centerpiece of our identity and our emotions. However, all of this power is also dramatically shaped by nature and nurture. You were born with a gift of autobiographical memory, and that memory has been distorted by traumatic events. This is something we can continue to work on, in a structured environment, but I want you to come home." Darby is extremely deliberate with her language. "Please, don't drive. Do you need me to make arrangements for you to be cared for, so that you can return home safely?"

I am home. Wisconsin is home. This is where I'm from.

Washington DC is not home. It was an escape from my home.

(*"I think you should go. And if you can somehow not come back, you should try to, like, stay gone."*)

What if I my conversation with Syd never happened? Was her warning another invention for the elaborate fantasy Dr. Darby believes I've created? Did anything after Club Insomnia really happen?

I have a bag of drugs. Where else would I have gotten them?

"But it *feels* real. I looked in the paper. There's no obituary for Michelle, and she's not at the house."

"I'm certain it does 'feel real.' Elements are undoubtedly true. Everything that affirms what you want to believe garners greater significance, and anything that contradicts it becomes proof that there are forces at work stopping you from achieving what you believe you need to achieve. The event that you've entered into is a construct of your mind, and that construct is self-sustaining because its goal is to preserve itself, and protect you from you."

"But I have the letter," I object. "I'm holding it."

"Why won't you read it?" Dr. Darby asks. "What will happen if you open it? Why can't you?"

"It's not time?" I suggest. I suddenly feel exhausted, like I've lost a debate. "I don't want to yet."

"Might I offer a different thought? The letter represents hope. And possibility. I can't be certain that Michelle didn't actually leave that letter for you somehow, but I also can't be certain that *you* didn't create the letter during these—" Dr. Darby pauses again, probably looking at her notes "—'waking blackouts,' as you call them, to carry with you on this difficult trip to Wisconsin. The unopened letter from the woman you've said helped you live again could be your mind's way of preserving itself. As long as you are in possession of the letter, contents unknown, there is hope for your future after all." Dr. Darby offers me solutions and diagnoses instead of her normal tactic of guiding me to the decisions that would be best for me. She's rarely this definitive.

"But it's her handwriting. It was the rainbow pen. She wrote my name in purple ink," I whisper.

"There are case studies of people who have labored in the same manner you are, who were able to perfectly duplicate handwriting and even create works of art that they otherwise could not. I'm not accusing you of anything. Again, it's just as likely that Michelle was indeed in Washington and left it for you. I'm not sure how she found you in the manner you describe, but I'm willing to acknowledge that it's possible, or we don't have all the information. I think it would be beneficial for you to read the note to me, since we're together. I'm curious to hear why she chose to reach out to you after all this time."

This is all a fantasy? "I'm holding the necklace I found at the high school. *Sarah's* necklace. Right now." I wish I could show her. "I fucking HAVE it. In my hand. It's covered in dirt and Sarah's own blood!"

"I understand that you believe you have Sarah's necklace. Does it make sense to you, honestly, that seven-and-a-half years after the shooting the school is still standing—open and untouched—and that her necklace was just lying on the floor for you to find at your convenience? Or is it possible that you bought another Best Friends Forever necklace, a similar one, somewhere, maybe during a blackout, as you've tried to deal with the grief and shame matrix that you've built around the girl you loved, who used to wear one? You've also been spending time with your own, former best friend, Stacy, who you've admittedly wronged and could never explain yourself to in a proper, constructive way. I am not surprised that you've intertwined these timelines as part of the event you're building. Hope, relationships, and loss are at the heart of the human condition. I guess what I'm saying is: it's…psychologically predictable that you have found yourself in the position you are presently in."

The way that Darby talks, soothing and confident, educated and formal, is convincing.

And yet.

What if she's wrong? What if this conversation is a manifestation and everything else is real?

What if?

What if this conversation is real, but the things Dr. Darby believes are mental metaphors are real?

I now doubt everything.

"I don't know. You're not here," I try once more. How could I be doing all of this to myself?

Dr. Darby Grover agrees with me. "You're right, I'm not there. It's why I want you to come home. My assistant can book your flight, and we can just invoice you for the airfare when you get back, if you think you can fly. Valet-check your bag at the hotel if you don't feel like bringing anything home with you. It's important to me that you come back as soon as you can and give yourself separation between this unsupervised journey you've put yourself on. Some good can come from this. My concern, right now, is that you immediately get yourself back into a safer, structured environment, so we can begin to sort out what is real, and what is actually part of a scenario you've subconsciously chosen to place yourself in."

I think of another angle. I'm persistent.

"How about a thought exercise? Would you be willing to do this for me, just for a minute? I think it could really help me understand what you're saying. I'm open to coming home, Dr. Darby."

"It depends on what it is, I suppose. I won't make any promises, but I *will* listen to what you're asking."

My elbow has started to ache from being on the phone for so long. I shift the phone from my right hand to left, stretching my arm. There's a knock on the door, and a muffled voice says, "Housekeeping" from the hallway. I'd forgotten to put the DO NOT DISTURB sign on the door.

"Come back later. I'm fucking busy!" I shout toward the door. Dr. Darby must be grimacing at the rudeness I can demonstrate when I'm tangled in anxiety. I've been the same way with Wafer and Sammie, with Wendy the Waitress, with Mason Reynolds. "Sorry. It's just, this is private. I'm on the phone. Please come back later. I'm sorry. I didn't mean to swear at you," I call out, overcompensating.

"Go ahead, Jeremy," Darby prompts. "I have another patient immediately after our session today and I want to be sensitive to both of you, regarding the schedule, and what I believe you're going through. What do you want me to consider with you, your thought exercise?"

"You said a few minutes ago that I've constructed Stacy into a villain, that my imagination is making him into something that he's not. Right?" My inartful summary forces Dr. Darby to offer a gentle correction.

"I think it's possible that you've turned Stacy into a Jungian archetype and you're wrestling with amygdala-based decisions that you've made in your past, where—when confronted with a fight or flight response—you've consistently chosen flight, and now you believe you're forcing yourself to fight. Stacy may be manifesting questionable behavior, but you're incorporating it into your perception of things."

I pretend to understand what she just told and press on. "Exactly. Indulge me. This version of Stacy that I've manifested, what is wrong with him? What would your diagnosis of him be? Is he psychotic or a sociopath

418

or what? If this is coming from within me, what does that say about what I'm dealing with?" I'm trying to carefully get the answer I want, and Dr. Darby is too experienced and too intelligent to be easily manipulated. I'm letting her see the surface manipulation, while getting her to offer enough for me to understand what I'm confronting—either in reality or fantasy.

"I don't know that I feel comfortable with this, Jeremy."

"What does this say about me? Is this version of Stacy a part of me?"

Dr. Darby is typing on her computer for a second. She's put me on speaker phone. "This is very, very difficult to discuss on the phone, in an unstructured environment. You're asking me to diagnose someone I don't know, who is manifesting behaviors that may or may not be real. I can't do that. I'm sorry. I understand why you want to know. This is a very delicate, important time for you."

"Am I making Stacy out to be a paranoid schizophrenic to you, Dr. Darby?" I push. "Just, please answer the question the best way you can, and I swear to God I'll get on an airplane and come home tonight."

"It's possible, yes, that you've decided in your mind to give Stacy the characteristics of someone who suffers from paranoid delusions, similar to what someone with adult-onset schizophrenia might exhibit, but it's highly unlikely that you have enough clinical understanding to do that on your own. And from what I know of you, in our time together in therapy, and even with the concerns I have about your mental state right now, you seem lucid enough, even under the influence of chemicals and alcohol, that I do not believe that you yourself are suffering from schizophrenia and projecting that on to Stacy. I'm not certain where his descriptions of delusional plans, in your construct, are coming from, exactly, but there are several explanations." She pauses. "I guess you're hoping for something more definitive."

I take Darby's small acknowledgement that I could be right as validation, and throw everything else out.

"I need to stay here and see this through to the end, Dr. Darby. I'm sorry I lied to you."

"Jeremy, listen to me, right now. You need to come back to Washington. I mean it. Because of your history, you're a self-harm risk. You've relapsed and are demonstrating some concerning behavior. Please, do what I'm asking you to do." Dr. Darby is as stern with me as I have ever heard her.

"I'm sorry. I can't. You don't understand. I know you think you're right, but I don't know that you are."

Dr. Darby tries another tactic. "Then call the police. Give them Stacy's address and tell them his plans. They'll stop him if you're right, and if you're wrong it will expose your suspicions as a delusion."

I hesitate. I consider it. "But what if Stacy is right? And I call the cops and Michelle and Stevie really were abducted and the police know all about it? One call to the cops and they're lost forever. Everything I tell you is confidential, right? You can't testify about shit I say to you in our sessions?"

"Within reason. If I think you're going to commit an act of violence and put others at risk, then no. But otherwise, yes, the things you tell me during our talks are considered privileged and confidential."

"I have a lot of drugs on me. Like, thousands of dollars' worth. If somehow the call comes back to me, Stacy and his friends can turn me in. They've seen the drugs. I could go to prison for a long time. I've driven across state lines. It's a federal offense. A felony. I can't call the police."

Have I constructed a fantasy this elaborate to operate within? I have a flimsy excuse for every exit strategy Dr. Darby presents. My reasoning doesn't hold up when I follow it to its logical conclusion.

I don't care. I'm not getting on any fucking airplane and I'm sure as hell not driving back to DC today.

"Flush the drugs. Normally I wouldn't advise a complete, white-knuckle detox in a hotel room, but if you're driving around with narcotics on you, and they're keeping you from coming home, and they're keeping you from calling the police to stop an act of violence you believe is in the planning stages for tonight…flush them, Jeremy. Then it's Stacy's word against yours and there's no proof. You need to get some mental clarity. Continuing the addiction cycle, the self-medication, this pain avoidance, anesthetizing your emotional duress has to end anyway. Nothing bad can come from you dumping everything in the toilet right now." Dr. Darby has taken the phone back off of speaker and is talking with a level of urgency and passion that surprises me.

"You're a good person, Dr. Darby. You've really helped me."

"Jeremy. What hotel are you staying in? Just tell me that much, and I can send someone, a colleague, to come by and help you. You don't have to come back tonight. We can slow things down."

She already has too much information about where I am.

"No, I think I'm doing much, much better now. I really feel relieved after talking to you."

"Have you stopped taking the antidepressants, Jeremy? Are you completely off your medication?"

I never refilled my last prescription.

I have to stop what's about to happen.

"Because you hate yourself, He knows you'll do what is required when the time is right. And if you do, you'll give up everything you don't want in order to get the thing you can't acquire," I repeat.

"I don't know that means, Jeremy. What is that from?" Dr. Darby has to realize that she has made a few missteps with my treatment over the past few months, underestimating the challenges, and she didn't effectively control the narrative today, either. Her concern is genuine. I don't doubt her heart. She doesn't have the capacity to understand the intricacy of the puzzle I'm assembling.

"Mason told me that if I accepted an invitation to come back to Wisconsin, I'd get what I want. I want forgiveness. I want to make amends for what I started, what I did to Sarah, to her family, to all the people who died, my friends, their families, my classmates, the teachers, to Mason, to everyone. To all the people I've fucked over. Stacy. I want relief from it all, Dr. Darby. I'm reliving the most painful events of my life, over and over, every day, all day, seconds, minutes, hours of time replaying all the time, and I can't keep it up. I need it to be over. I have to see if Mason was right. There's no explanation for how he knew that Stacy was deceiving me into coming home. That happened. That's not my imagination. Hundreds of thousands of people in my audience heard him say that to me. It's not a coincidence."

"You're right. You have the ability to stop what is happening. Visualize what I'm telling you. You have convinced yourself that this alternate reality you're living in is real. It's not. You're in distress, and there are absolutely unexplainable things that are happening. I am certain this is the result of post-traumatic stress, your hyper-realistic recall, your drug use, your obsessive behavior, and the convergence of multiple events in your life at a very fragile time for you. But you haven't taken any actions that have permanent ramifications. You can stop, today, and return to recovery," Darby reiterates.

She's run out of new things to say.

I almost pity her.

I know she feels responsible, but she's not. I can relate to her plight on a certain level. I wonder if she's able to recognize the irony in the situation. I could use her own words against her now. I choose not to.

She sees this as a failure. She's failed me. She hasn't.

I'm failing her. I'm incapable of helping her understand the situation.

"Darby, I've wanted to ask you out for a drink or dinner since the first day I walked into your office."

The sudden left turn leaves Dr. Darby Grover speechless for a moment. "Oh. Jeremy, to accept would be inappropriate and unethical. I'm flattered, I…can we return to the other discussion for a moment?"

"I just wanted you to know. None of this is your fault. I hope you don't feel like it is." I'm trying to release her from any responsibility, but the words I'm using, and the tone of the conversation is only making everything feel darkly fatalistic. I have the sense that there's not much left for me to do.

"Jeremy, wait—"

"I have to try and stop him."

I hang up the phone. I need a cigarette.

I don't know what I should do next.

I pick up Michelle's letter from its place on the bed next to Sarah's necklace.

My name, written in purple with a child's pen, is faded and smeared to illegibility.

I didn't write this. It's not a delusion. I never imagined receiving this at Club Insomnia, right? I arrived there in the middle of a moment, like a dream, no beginning to how I arrived, no memory of what happened after screaming and speeding down the road, and then I was just there drinking and The Floyd Chicks were suddenly there without explanation. But I remember leaving and I never woke up unless I've been in Madison for a while and I woke up in this hotel room earlier tonight fully dressed after dreaming everything that happened in DC and now I'm awake and this is actually reality, but a version of reality where Stacy is insane, and I'm a hero, but really I'm insane and Stacy is Stacy.

I can't decide what the truth is. I can't discern reality. The past and present are merged into confusion.

The unopened letter, Dr. Darby had told me, was my way of holding on to hope for my future.

I tear open the letter and finally start reading.

CHAPTER 41

Jeremy,

I'm not surprised you didn't come—you sounded really out of it on the phone. I'm just disappointed. Again. I wanted you to meet Stevie before we left. It seemed like I owed it to you, but now I just feel stupid and I guess it was another mistake like all the others I keep making. It was a big mistake trying to hide this from Stacy. I should've just left him years ago. My mom is with us in DC. She and my dad know about you now. They're helping us get away. There's so much I needed to tell you. Do not believe anything Stacy says. If you talk to him DO NOT COME BACK TO STOUGHTON. We are not going back there from here and I do not want him to know where we are. Today was the only day we could be here. I'm sorry it didn't work out. Our timing was always terrible.

You were right when you played that song our first night together. Love is blindness.

I looked the other way too often when it came to the people in my life I thought I loved. Not anymore. From now on

I'm doing whatever it takes for Stevie and me to be safe and happy. I thought a lot about maybe trying to find a way to make things work for you and me and Stevie here in DC somehow, but safe and happy aren't words I use when I think of you. Our son needs a real chance and I think I can give that to him but not with you in the picture. He's a good boy. He has our eyes. I hope he's like me.

I miss you, but only the good stuff. I don't miss the rest at all. I hope you find peace. You deserve it.

Goodbye, Jer. I think of you often and always will.

Michelle

CHAPTER 42

Sarah said nothing.

We'd been driving in silence for fifteen minutes. I turned on the radio, then snapped it off. The music was an intruder, an attempted cover-up. The quiet was painful but honest. I knew I had to say something.

"Do you want to go home?" I asked tentatively.

"Maybe," Sarah whispered. "I don't know what to do. I don't know what to say."

"I don't either," I admitted. "I'm sorry."

I wasn't driving anywhere in particular. We were on backroads to nowhere. I hadn't thought about the night much beyond the bonfire and didn't know what else to do. We pulled up to a four-way stop, and I noticed a white and brown sign indicating Pec Park was only six miles away.

I was suddenly fueled with a compulsion to get out of the car as fast as possible. Sarah normally objected when I drove recklessly, but instead she leaned back against the headrest and closed her eyes, only opening them when she felt me braking when the entrance to the park appeared.

I coasted in through the open gate, drove partway down the incline toward the river, almost to the pavilion, and stopped. I wrenched the parking brake and let the clutch out to kill the car in first gear.

We were surrounded by thick, lush greenery. The grass had been mowed, and several yards of gravel had recently been added at the entrance and at each trailhead. Picnic tables had been moved under the pavilion, presumably in anticipation of a public gathering now that the weather had gotten warmer.

I'd never been there at night. Frogs sang to each other, crickets harmonized. It was peaceful.

A crescent moon hung low in the night sky, just above the tree line, reflected in the river's dark waters.

I looked over at Sarah and was surprised to see her looking at me.

"I've never been here at night," she confessed, coincidentally. "It's so peaceful."

I started to tell her I'd been thinking the exact same thing but instead I nodded and said, "It is. It's nice."

Regret and adrenaline had taken the edge off my buzz, and I was thinking more clearly, yet I still had no idea how I could make this situation right with Sarah. We sat in silence for two or three minutes.

Sarah spoke up first. "I'm trying to figure out...which Jeremy is the real Jeremy," she said. "Is it the one who doesn't even get a tiny bit angry when I spit pop in his face and says he loves me, or is it the one who did all of the horrible things to Mason? The one Kelly told me to stay away from?"

My emotional walls of silence went up. "I don't know," was all I could muster. I'd have to do better; Sarah could not have known that squeezing out that one small ambivalent phrase took a massive amount of effort on my part. It wasn't anger that I saw in her brown eyes. It was confusion.

"Kelly told me you're an asshole to people but everybody does stuff like that sometimes. What you did to Mason wasn't just mean. Like, you could've really hurt him! What did he do to you? Did he start it?"

"He didn't start it. Something happened and I snapped and all I wanted to do was make him look stupid and then I guess we got carried away and everyone was laughing and then...I don't know why I did what I did." I couldn't bring myself to say it. My head hung down, chin on my chest, eyes clenched shut.

"But why?" Sarah demanded.

"I don't know. I just...hated him when he was making me look different than I wanted to look. I didn't want anyone to know I'd been at his house and told him to keep his mouth shut about it and he just came up and started talking about how I left my fucking trig book at his house and it pissed me off."

Sarah's mouth dropped open. "When did you go to his house? I didn't know you hung out with Mason!"

"When we were sophomores, we were both into football and baseball cards. You were at track practice, Derrick is obsessed with getting valedictorian and Aaron is all into baseball, and I couldn't...didn't want to go home. I just asked Mason if he was still into cards and he said yeah. I sold all mine to buy this fucking car but I'm still kind of into it, too, so I went over to his house and looked at his card collection. I guess I left my trig book over there. I didn't want Derrick and Aaron to know," I confessed.

"You never said a word to me." Sarah was bewildered.

"I didn't want you to know either."

Sarah fell silent again, trying to put it all together. She was smarter than the average seventeen-year-old, but lacking the life experience and education to analyze the triggers and responses she witnessed.

I didn't understand them either. I needed to keep secrets, protect myself. From everything. Real and imagined. I felt terrorized. Protect everything. Tell lies to feel safe. Threats surrounded me on all sides.

"I wouldn't have cared," Sarah reminded me. "You're always good to me. I don't get it."

Anything I would have said in response to that would have been the wrong thing.

She continued. "You can't think of single reason why you'd act like that? I want to believe you'll never do anything like that to me—or anyone else— ever again. Can't you just promise me that?"

How could I answer her question? The real Jeremy was who I was when I was with her, and obviously that's what she expected me to say. The truth was the truth. It was also the predictable response from someone convincing someone else that the terrible things they do would never, ever happen again. That promise would ring hollow. I'd say anything to keep Sarah from leaving me. The truth had the appearance of a lie, and even I couldn't trust it, because I couldn't trust myself. I wanted to promise her. But I couldn't. I wanted to be honest and I wanted to promise I'd change and I couldn't do both. I found that I was different—no, better—with Sarah, and that was in conflict with the Jeremy everyone else knew. These past few months I was less likely to ridicule someone, start a fight I knew I could win, or disrupt a classroom by creating a confrontation with a teacher. When Sarah and I weren't together, that vulnerability left me feeling even more off-balance. I hated the act I felt forced to maintain.

Where had the desire—this need—for this other version of Jeremy come from?

I imagined everyone could see through me. Could they glimpse the sensitivity that I reserved exclusively for Sarah? Did I look weak? Walls began to crumble and the real Jeremy was now exposed and I couldn't stop it from happening. I needed people to believe I was impenetrable, armed with an acid tongue, mean-spirited humor, and a crazy willingness to fight. Impossible to wound, keeping everyone at arm's length. I resented the jocular harassment Aaron and Derrick dished out over my devotion to Sarah, but they were the closest thing I had to friends so I tolerated it, barely. I also further distanced myself from them. If they laughed at me, I shut down and said nothing or hit back with unnecessarily vicious insults.

I couldn't recall a particular moment in my past when I'd decided that the public and private Jeremy should, and would, become different people. It simply evolved. It affected how I dressed, the movies I watched in groups and when I was alone, the books I read, the music I listened to. I was protecting myself from the possibility of humiliation, anticipating and shutting it down before it could get started. There were threats everywhere. I was constantly in fear. Where did all of this fucking come from?

I thought all of these things in the span of a few seconds, but even still Sarah pressed me once more.

"Say something. Please."

"What can I do to fix this?" There was a barrier in my heart and mind, blocking me from opening up and telling her everything. I wanted to share my fears of being humiliated, that I needed to protect myself at all costs, even if it meant sacrificing people like Mason Reynolds. It was wrong, but I was desperate. That level of vulnerability, despite the trust and love I had for her, was still too big for anyone to know about.

"I don't know. You have to go to Mason and apologize. Maybe in front of everyone. I don't know. That probably won't be good enough. But you totally have to do that." I nodded, but I was thinking of how I could fix things between me and Sarah, not me and Mason. She was typically solutions-focused, where I was hyper-emotional. It brought me some comfort to see her fight for us, in her own way.

"I can do that. I'll do that. I'll do it at Skip Day. Our whole class will be together, last time before graduation. No teachers, so I won't get in trouble unless Mason called the cops on me. I'll do it. I swear to fucking God, I'll do it. I'm so sorry, Sarah. Please," I promised, repeatedly. "Please." I was sincere.

"Jeremy, I don't know how I can be with someone who does things like this. It's, like, so ugly and horrible, you know?" Sarah had a right to be scared after tonight. She'd seen me when I was at my very worst.

430

Why did I do these things to myself, let people in, then push them away with the very actions that repulse them the most? And self-sabotage my happiness? And wall myself off from any real friendships? Or react with unjustifiable hatred at the very hint that my self-created security might be in jeopardy?

Why couldn't I open up with the few people I knew I could probably trust, withholding myself from them?

Sarah's eyes filled with tears. "Why won't you talk to me?"

"I don't know." *I shrugged. I didn't know how to answer.*

"How can you not know? Why did you attack Mason like that? Just because you don't like him?"

Fuck him. Fight back, you fucking pussy. You're nothing. You'll never be anything. You fucking faggot.

Thoughts in my head, my voice, not my words. This rage, it wasn't just mine. I was having the best night of my life and then I'd exploded with furious humiliation over something insignificant. Still, I blamed him.

"I just...he pisses me off. He didn't need to let everyone know I hang out with him. I didn't want anyone to know and he knew that! I shouldn't have done what I did. I know I overreacted. But he shouldn't have brought that book out there. He was fucking trying to make me look stupid in front of everyone."

Sarah face grew flushed. "He wasn't trying to make you look stupid! But even if he was, you can't attack people like that. What if I said something that embarrassed you? Would you scream at me? Hit me?"

"NEVER."

"But how can I know that? Until tonight I never thought you could ever hurt me. Now I don't know."

"I swear to God I would never, ever hit you or yell at you or do anything to hurt you. EVER. I'm better when we're together." *I was flailing, attempting to save the only good thing in my life. I knew she shouldn't accept my answer, but I needed her to believe me. I wanted to believe me, too.*

431

But how could I swear that she'd never trigger my anger if I didn't understand it myself?

"I don't know. I don't know what to say," I repeated. "I just want you to believe me. Kelly doesn't know. She's not around us. I know I pick on her and I pick on other people but...I don't hate her. I don't know."

"You keep saying 'I don't know,' but I don't understand how you can't know why you do it. Are you lying to me? Do you think it's funny? Do you really know but don't want to say?"

"I'm not...I'm not lying. It's not funny. I really don't know." I hunkered down behind my protective walls. I felt the fear and anger roiling beneath the surface. I needed the rising panic inside of me to subside. Questions led to accusations led to insults led to terror led to punishments led to beatings led to helplessness led to rage..."There's just this...thing that happens."

Sarah must have seen something on my face because she said the one thing I needed to hear from the one person I would have believed while they were saying it. "It's OK, Jeremy. You're safe. You can tell me anything. I just want to know. I want to believe you. What is happening inside you?"

I'd never put everything together until that moment. Why was I exhausted and defensive and angry and in self-preservation mode all the time? Why was I isolated and afraid, lashing out and hiding my vulnerabilities and the things I truly loved? Why did I feel like I was going to be randomly attacked or ridiculed and needed to show I wasn't weak and defenseless? Why did I feel like two different people?

Why didn't I know why...when I remembered everything else? "I don't want to say it."

Sarah relaxed. "I won't tell anyone. I promise. I'll listen. You can tell me." I was aware that she was giving me a real chance and would listen. She wanted honesty and I had faith that I could trust her.

"It's been...years. And I can't make it stop and I can't tell anyone."

"Something's happening to you? Is someone doing something to you, Jeremy? What are they doing? Have you told your mom and dad?" Sarah sat up straight in the passenger seat, turned slightly at the waist so she could face me, eyes wide open, nervously chewing her lower lip. "What is it? I'm here."

She was trying to drag it out of me. It was a secret. No one could know that I was such…a fucking pussy.

Sarah's love and patience and persistence had carefully gotten through. Maybe because I was buzzed. Maybe because I loved her and she was the only person that I wanted to know. The secrets, the pain, the humiliation. I desperately wanted to be right, that I could trust her, that she'd help me, that she'd understand, that she'd forgive me. Somewhere I found the lost bravery I didn't believe I had and told her my secret truth. To save our relationship. For us, I finally heard myself say the words out loud.

"My dad beats the fucking shit out of me, OK?!"

CHAPTER 43

I've read Michelle's letter fifteen times. I read it again. And again.

"How absolutely fucking perfect." Michelle had called. Michelle and I had made plans to meet. I know when it happened The timeline finally makes sense. I'm not surprised that a nurse could get my phone number and address with a plausible story. She routed her escape from Stacy to meet with me, to let me see Stevie, to give me one more, one last chance to redeem myself. And we missed each other.

No. *I* missed *her*.

She did everything she could do, again. She made every effort, again. She did everything right, again.

We didn't miss each other. *I* fucked it up. Again.

I reread the letter for the eighteenth time, but can't look any further than the first sentence: *"I'm not surprised you didn't come. You sounded really out of it on the phone."*

My memory is perfect, but I'm not infallible. I realize now exactly what happened.

Nine days ago. The day after Christmas. I was with the Floyd Chicks, at their house in DC.

Syd was next to me on the couch, animated. Piper was on the other side of me, unenthused as usual.

I'd been drunk and high for almost forty hours and needed to reload. After buying an ounce of weed and some coke, Syd and I had spent the last ten minutes getting high. I was flopped out on the couch waiting to talk to Pink privately and thinking about what I'd say when she got off the goddamn phone.

"How do you not now about this? A Boston DJ figured this out! It's the height of cool radio shit and you've never even heard of it before?" Syd was incredulous, arms crossed. "Are you fucking kidding me?" Syd was wearing flannel pajamas, stripping a Fruit Roll Up from its wax paper with her teeth.

Piper yawned. Pink was down the hall, arguing with someone about something. I strained to overhear.

"We are doing this tonight. I have the movie and the CD. You need to experience this. There's no logical explanation for it. It has to be some supernatural fluke or something," Syd continued.

"This is, like, all she talks about when someone doesn't know about it." Piper rolled her eyes. I nodded distractedly, still trying to eavesdrop on Pink's private conversation. At first it had seemed like she was having an argument, but now she was smiling and twirling the curlicue phone cord with her finger.

Piper had on dark blue bib shorts, a vintage Moody Blues t-shirt, and a look of disgust over Syd and the Fruit Roll Up. I thought about asking for a bite. It had been years since I'd had a Fruit Roll Up. I lit a cigarette instead. There were half a dozen ashtrays, all of which needed to be emptied. This fit with the rest of the haphazard décor. Posters tacked to the wall, laundry strewn on the floor. Empty baggies. Crumbs ground into the carpeting. Coffee table stacked with dented soda cans, some that had been turned into makeshift pipes and had been scorched by butane lighters and blackened with resin.

"I need something to drink. Do you have any Orange Crush?" I begged. "Anything? Water? A beer? Jesus, I'm fucking dying here. Mind if I look around for something?" I needed a reason to snoop on Pink's call.

"No. We don't have anything. Suffer," Piper smirked at me. She didn't get up and neither did Syd.

I had been buying from Piper, Syd, and Pink for five months and eleven days, and had been over to their place twenty-three times, but had never gone any further than the living room. I never asked about their supplier. I didn't care. I only wanted the drugs I needed to keep flowing to me.

"How long is she going to go on about Dark Side of the Rainbow?" I asked. "Not a very creative name."

"How can you talk shit about something you've never even heard of? It's only the single greatest moment of artist synchronicity in the history of humanity, dude. Like, The Wizard of Oz was made in 1939. Dark Side of the Moon came out in 1973. The songs totally fit each of the scenes of the movie. There's no way that just happens." Syd litigated her position with a television lawyer's passion.

Piper wasn't as impressed. "Some of the songs work. But the movie is, like, an hour longer than the album. And not every song fits. There's like two or three trippy scenes. Syd, you're a fucking stoner."

"Wait. So, what happens exactly?" I had only been half-listening when Syd explained it the first time, distracted by Pink strolling around the house in tight jeans, a t-shirt, and no bra. I was also high as hell and braindead after almost two straight days of sitting in bars and getting high in bathrooms. "I spaced out. Are you sure they didn't record it to work out this way on purpose? Some secret practical joke?"

Piper points at me, nodding. "See."

I point back at her with my cigarette. "Yeah. Like, see."

Syd was ready with an answer. "Nick Mason was asked about it on MTV. He totally denied it. But when you first see the Yellow Brick Road the song 'Money' starts playing. 'Brain Damage' comes on when Dorothy finds the Scarecrow. When Dorothy is on the poppy field fence, you can TOTALLY hear the lyrics about being balanced on the biggest wave clear as fuck. They didn't plan it, and it is all right there, man, I want to hear you sit down with Alan Parsons and Roger and everyone and just ask them about it on your show."

"Who figures this shit out?" I wondered aloud. And who knows this much about Pink Floyd?

Piper shrugged.

I looked back in Pink's direction. She was still on the phone. "You don't have anything to drink? At all? Some sink water and a fucking cup? A Diet Coke? How can you not have any liquid in your entire house?"

Piper shrugged again.

Syd was really into convincing me. "If you start Dark Side on the second roar of the MGM Lion, it works perfectly. Most people think it's the third roar, but I tried it both ways and it's tighter when you do it on the second one. How can you not think this is cool? This seems perfect for your talk show!!"

"Alright, it's cool, it's super fucking cool," I deadpanned. Piper snorted. Syd glared. I laughed.

"We're watching it. Tonight. There's no way you can't not watch this." Syd got up from the couch, sprinted five steps across the room to their TV and held up a VHS copy of The Wizard of Oz. She started rummaging through a box of CDs next to the television and finally snatched a scratched case from the pile. Countless lines of heroin and cocaine and meth had to have been snorted off of it. "Voila!" she yelled. "We are doing this. We are TOTALLY fucking doing this, Jeremy! And then you can, like, talk about it on your radio show and ask listeners to decide if it's some crazy stoner coincidence or not."

"You're geeking out, Syd. I'm not watching this tonight. I got shit to do."

I had nothing planned other than staying high, which I already was, and spending as much time around Pink as I could, if only she would just get off the goddamn phone so I could—"There's really only one way to watch Dark Side of the Rainbow, Jeremy," Pink said, suddenly right behind me on the couch. I hadn't heard her come back into the room. Pink began pinching

437

painfully at the tension in my shoulders. She had to know it hurt. "Comfortably numb, baby. Wanna drop a little on some brown and stay a while?"

I handed her a wad of bills. She peeled off an amount. I had no idea how much. She gave me the rest back, and I tucked it into the front pocket of my jeans. I lit another cigarette, forgetting I still had one burning in the overflowing ashtray. I handed the freshly lit one to Piper, who took it but looked irritated.

Pink disappeared up the stairs, thumping two feet per step, the floor creaking as she strode across the room above our heads; it creaked again on her return journey, then more stair thumping, and she reappeared with a wicked grin on her face. She held up the corner of a baggie, packed tight with brown heroin, twisted into a plastic knot. Pink grinned. "Habit, tying it off. We doing this here?"

I reached for the baggie, and snatched another CD case off the coffee table.

"Oh, baby, no. You can't rail this out. We need the kit." Pink shifted from one bare foot to the other.

The needle. The lighter. The cotton balls. The spoon. Drops of water. Rubber tubing. The vein.

I was afraid of the needle. AIDS terrified me. I put every chemical into my body during my time at Stacy and Michelle's, and that continued in DC. I snorted, smoked, and drank. I had never touched a needle. I partied. I had issues. I drank all the time. I was a druggie. But I wasn't a junkie. I couldn't do it.

I was not crossing that line. I rolled up my sleeve.

"Fuck it, I always say yes," I announced. A moment later Pink scrounged a small, blue kit from somewhere. She unzipped it: a bent, scorched spoon, cotton balls, three clean needles, one used.

Pink took the dirty needle and the spoon, palmed a lighter, and sat down next to me on the couch.

"You want to tie yourself off?" Pink purred. Piper was no longer lounging. She was up and watching. Syd had moved away from the TV, rejoining the group, still holding the CD and VHS tape.

I unthreaded my belt from the loops and fashioned a tourniquet on my left arm. Have I lost all self-respect? Am I really going to let her put a dirty needle in my arm? I wanted the clean needle. I had no strength left to try and protect myself. Why do I let people do things to me that hurt me?

Why couldn't I stop her, even when I was on the brink of a breakthrough?

I was less than a week from confessing to Mason Reynolds, finding forgiveness, turning my life around. But I couldn't stop getting high. I didn't want to stop. I wasn't sure what would happen, especially with the pressure mounting as the show with Mason drew closer. Doesn't degradation always come before redemption? But if redemption never comes, temporary relief would still be worth the price I paid.

So, even as I was on the verge of my own, orchestrated redemption with Mason Reynolds, I held out my arm. The thought of a disease-ridden needle poking viruses and infections into me filled me with dread.

"You with us, baby?" Pink asked. "You look a little zoned out. Your face is all peaked."

I tapped the blue veins in my forearm with two fingers. "Just waiting on you."

Pink pinched some brown into the spoon. Piper had gotten a glass of water. Syd checked her own veins. Pink stuck the bloodstained needle into the glass and drew a few CCs of water into the syringe. Piper leaned back on the couch again, her bare arm brushing against mine, giving me goosebumps. Syd tapped her arm a few times. Pink dripped a few beads of water around the small mound of heroin on the spoon, flicked the lighter, holding it under the spoon until everything bubbled and melted. Piper handed her a cotton ball. Syd set an empty soda can in front of Pink so she could prop the spoon, let it cool, and draw the mixture into the syringe. Pink flicked the syringe twice and squirted a tiny jet from the needle. Syd turned the TV and VCR on, pushing the tape in and sliding the CD into the open carousel of their stereo.

I looked away, involuntarily closed my eyes.

Her fingers were cold, touching the vein. She crisscrossed it with her index finger.

"X marks the spot," she breathed.

"Finding the G spot is better," Piper corrected. Everyone laughed but me. I held my breath.

I felt the sting of a crusty needle. I imagined rust and bacteria and filth injected into me.

The stinging sensation was like an injured funny bone in the bend of my arm.

An ocean of pleasure washed over me, from within me, it rushed through me, my nerve endings and internal organ wrapped in warmth, drowning me. It felt like the hair on my arms was standing on end. I could not open my eyes. Each heartbeat seemed to be followed by thirty seconds of silence. There were a thousand thoughts and a million memories stirred together, each existing for only a fleeting second.

It was an orgasm in my brain.

Vaguely, I was aware someone was saying my name. "Jeremy. JEREMY. Jeremy!"

It was Pink. She brushed her lips on mine, and I opened my eyes. "Now you get it, baby. Now you see." Piper was wrapping a rubber tube around her arm. "You bought enough for all of us," she informed me.

"Dark Side of the Rainbow," Syd said eagerly. "Once you see it, you can't unsee it. You'll fucking love it!"

The MGM Lion roared once, twice—Syd started the CD—three times, and Pink pulled out the needle. A pounding drum and the ticking clock and voices murmuring and paper tearing and the cash register and hysterical laughter and a lunatic screaming and SCREAMING and the black and white

Dorothy and Toto and the tornado and ruby slippers and a Wicked Witch of the West and never had I felt anything like it.

I thought I might vomit, but I don't remember if I did or if the feeling went away.

Suddenly, The Wizard of Oz and The Dark Side of the Moon were both over. Had I slept through it?

"Wasn't. It. Amazing. Jeremy? What. Did. I. Tell. You?" Syd was talking to me through a tunnel.

I nodded. "Huh. Yeah. Yes." I looked around the room. I hadn't moved in...two hours?

"What. Are. You. Doing. For. New. Year's. Eve. After. Your. Radio. Show?" Syd asked.

Pink was gone. Piper was passed out on the couch. Syd was too close to my face. I held up my hand.

"You. Should. Meet. Us. At. This. Club. Downtown. Club Insomnia. Pink. Wants. To. Go. So. We're. All. Going. You. Should. Totally. Fucking. Come!" She told me the address. I nodded again. I couldn't keep my eyes open. The outside world seemed distant and fading away. "You're. Not. Going. To. Come. Are. You?"

"Maybe," I mumbled. "Mason show. Can't know. Thank you." Syd giggled. "Need to leave."

"Are. You. Good. To. Drive?"

I nodded and about ten minutes later I got up from the couch.

My belt uncoiled from my arm and fell to floor.

"Where's the door?" I asked, and Syd pointed to the door, directly in front of me.

"Where's my keys?" I asked, and Syd pointed to my hand.

"Why don't you have drinks here?" I asked, and Syd laughed loudly.

"Where's Pink?" I asked. Syd answered, but I didn't listen.

And then suddenly, I was in my car, engine running, a cigarette smoldering in the ashtray. How long had I been sitting there? Had I even gone anywhere? No, I was still in the Floyd Chicks' driveway. I put the car in reverse and creeped backward into traffic. I sped up and slowed down and stopped at traffic signals and stayed in the right lane and just when I thought I couldn't keep my eyes open, that I'd lost complete awareness of the road and other cars, I saw my street and turned into my condominium parking lot.

When I again looked at the clock on my dashboard radio, I realized I'd fallen asleep in my car for almost an hour while I sat outside. I started to rub my eyes and saw Syd had written the address to Club Insomnia on my hand. I got out of the car and my pants nearly fell down, my belt in the passenger seat. I held my pants up by the waistband as I walked to the elevator, then stumbled through my front door.

I couldn't be bothered to turn on the lights.

I kicked off my shoes and nearly fell down.

I fell onto the couch. I wanted to enjoy the nothingness. Guiltless emptiness. Sliding away.

"Dark Side of the fucking Rainbow," I said. "That's some trippy fucking shit, man. Syd was right."

Suddenly, I was awake again. I was facedown, half-smothered in couch cushions.

The phone was ringing. No one ever called me here.

"No one calls me," I said. "Who is it?" I shouted at the phone from across the room.

My answering machine greeting was from Jim Morrison's "American Prayer" poetry album.

"Is everybody in? Is everybody in? Is everybody in? The ceremony is about to begin. The entertainment for this evening is not new, you've seen this entertainment through and through. You have seen your birth, your life, your death...you may recall all the rest. Did you

442

have a good world when you died? Enough to base a movie on?" *The BEEEEEEEEEEEEEEEEEEEEEEEEEP felt like something piercing my skull.*

I couldn't move, so I listened to my machine echo in the loneliness of an empty room. Whoever it was hung up without leaving a message. The phone rang again. I still couldn't move. It went to the machine again, only this time there was five seconds of silence, a loud, exasperated sigh, a click, and a dial tone.

Then the phone immediately rang again.

"WHAT THE FUCK?!" I groaned and fell off the couch. I pulled myself up onto all fours, crawled to the bar, reached up, caught hold of the counter-top, hoisted myself up and answered the phone before the machine picked up for a third time. I couldn't talk. I just breathed, slowly and heavily, into the receiver.

"Hello? Is anyone there? Jer? Is this you? Do I have the right number? Is this Jeremy Peoples?"

I must've been dreaming. The person on the other end of the line sounded exactly like Michelle Ramone.

"Who the fuck is this?" I demanded, slurring my words, fixated on the needle mark in my arm.

"Oh my God, Jer. It's Michelle." I wobbled on my feet, unsteady in the darkness. "Jer?? Are you OK?"

"Yeah. I mean no. I'm...a little fucked up right now. I...I was asleep. You woke me up. I'm sorry."

Michelle sighed loudly into the phone. "It's really good to hear your voice."

I patted myself down for my pack of cigarettes. I had no idea where they were. "Shell. How'd you get this number? I didn't even know you knew that I moved out here. You're a spy or some shit."

Laughter. "It doesn't matter. Listen, I can't talk very long. I'm...I'm coming to DC this week. I'm going to have Stevie with me. I have a lot of things I need to tell you, I just can't do it right now. Is there someplace we can meet? Can I come to your place? Or to the radio station?" She hesitated. "I don't know where anything is in DC, but I won't be there long. Can we…can I see you?"

"I can't find my cigarettes," I told her, rubbing the tiny scab where Pink had jabbed me.

"You don't sound like you just woke up, Jer. You sound like you're totally out of it."

"I just need something to drink. Some Kool-Aid or something." I refocused. "You're coming to DC? This week? Why? For work? What day will you be here?"

"I can't talk now. I'll be there Wednesday. With Stevie. Where do you live? Where can we meet?"

"Shell, it's so good to hear from you, I think about you all the time, I just never call because I'm afraid of what Stacy will do if he finds out I'm trying to call you."

Michelle's voice softened. "I know. It's better you haven't called. I need you to tell me where we can meet. Any time before four in the afternoon. I have to get off the phone. Just give me your address."

I looked down at my hand. I don't know why it seemed like a good idea. I was completely fried. "Let's meet at this new place." I read her the address for Club Insomnia, written on my palm. "I won't be at the radio station that early in the day." Where did I find my cigarettes? I put one in my mouth and lit it.

"Jer, why can't we just come by your house? I don't understand—" Michelle stopped abruptly. "I have to go. I'll meet you at 2 o'clock. I really can't wait to see you, Jeremy. So much is happening. I gotta go."

She hung up before I could say goodbye.

And then I was waking up in my bedroom, it was Monday afternoon, and the weekend was a blur of bars and Seagram's and the Floyd Chicks and heroin and The Wizard of Oz and a faint recollection of what must have been a dream about Michelle, and the more I tried to remember it the more elusive it became, until I stopped trying and I let it go in the way that average people do with their memories every day.

There's nothing else there. The rest is a blank space. Vertigo hits me as I deduce the most plausible explanation for what had eluded me for days. "Son. Of. A. BITCH!" I shout. "I fucking *FORGOT?!*"

Why didn't she come to my condo when I didn't show up at Club Insomnia in the middle of the day? I never gave her my address. Even still, why would she? She said it herself. I had disappointed her again.

Why didn't she call? I haven't checked my home answering machine in weeks. She probably called.

Her voice might be on my machine right now. When I stood her up, she must have written the letter, maybe tried to call, maybe not, maybe debated whether to find my condo, maybe not. Her plans for a new life with Stevie didn't include me anyway, so why go even further out of her way for a fuck-up?

I want to tear the letter into a thousand pieces. Her words are an acid burn of heartbreak.

Instead, I read it again, put it back into the grimy, sweat-stained, purple-smudged envelope, fold it along its well-worn crease, and slip it into my blazer pocket.

I'm devastated but relieved. Michelle is gone. But she's safe, and alive, and has Stevie, somewhere out of state, with her mom and dad. She saw what I saw and got away from Stacy.

Her resilience is one of the things I adore about her the most.

I'm still fighting my way to the surface; the grief from knowing that I've lost Michelle feels identical to the shock that tore through me when I thought she'd died. It's selfishness. It's the despondency that settled in when I woke up in the hospital and couldn't stop the flood of memories of Sarah's death. Sorrow. Regret. The ache of what will never be overlaps the shock of watching it end. I've gotten used to being alone, but always had a lingering hope that maybe, someday, there'd be a maybe with Michelle.

Her letter killed that hope forever.

I'm angry, but now I'm also fully convinced I know what the truth is.

Dr. Darby is wrong. Stacy is wrong. I'm the only one who's right and no one believes me.

Deep breath. Think. Slow it down for a second.

(*I'm awakened by the door and a burst of cold air and Stacy's rage and I'm shocked he sees us together*)

What am I going to do about Stacy? What can I do?

(*I'm staring through a crack in the hospital door to catch a glimpse of Michelle holding our child, our son*)

I don't think I can run from this.

(*I'm trembling with self-hatred as I grasp the utility knife and plunge the razor into my arm*)

Every moment that I failed Sarah, Mason, Michelle, Stevie, and even Stacy is roaring in my head, reminding me of my cowardice, inadequacy, inaction, and self-centeredness. The list unspools. I want to stop it, but I also want it to cut me. I need to feel the pain, the reminder that it's real.

What am I going to do?

Stacy is planning to save Michelle and Stevie. In his delusion, the people he believes have them will have no idea what he's talking about. What will he do then? Take hostages? Open fire? Turn the gun on himself? How many did he say he thought were involved? Was there a church service tonight? Do people go to church on Tuesday? I don't know. What if there's an event at the church? Could there be even more people there than usual? Is that why he's going today? Because there are going to be more strange faces in a crowd than a normal service, so he won't stand out? What if there are children?

Should I go to the police? I have to go to the police.

What evidence do I have? A handwritten letter of unprovable origins saying vague things from someone I claim is his wife who is calling Stevie my son in the same letter? There's nothing in the letter about the church. The only evidence that exists is inside Stacy's trailer. He's probably destroying all of it right now.

I've got nothing. My own therapist doesn't even believe me.

Could I make an anonymous call and claim there were gunshots in his neighborhood?

That might work. But what if they drive through and don't see anything, or knock on some doors and his neighbors confirm that there haven't been any shots fired? The cops will assume it's a prank.

Could I call in an anonymous tip that there's a possible mass shooting happening at...where? The parsonage? The church building? Some other location? Both places? Stacy never expressly told me where he was planning to "recover" Stevie and Michelle, or how. He was clear only with his objective. His research was comprehensive but incoherent. He hadn't revealed the details of his plan to me yet.

What if I call in a bomb threat?

What if I went to the house, or the church, or wherever these people were going to be, and got them to believe they were in danger, and had them call their friends at the sheriff's office? I could refuse to leave, which would unnerve them, and maybe they'd call the cops. Do they even know Michelle and Stevie? Or has Stacy just invented this completely, from nothing? There's too much unreliable information spiraling around inside my head, making it impossible to eliminate variables. I'm desperate for sobriety, something I haven't craved in years. The lucidity that comes with a detoxed mind is just beyond my grasp. I'm blunted, incapable of effectiveness.

I can't let another tragedy happen. I could never have predicted what Mason Reynolds would do on May 23, 1992. That failure of my imagination cannot be repeated today. I have to believe the worst is not only possible but also happening. Right now. Stopping this feels like a lost cause, but I have to try anyway.

Instinctively, I touch the St. Jude medal around my neck. The Patron Saint of Lost Causes. I say the prayer that came with my pendant; I memorized the few, simple lines on the day I bought it. As I pray, I wonder vaguely what Officer Friendly Face and Wendy the Waitress would think of me now, how I'm just superstitious enough, just desperate enough, to have faith in almost anything if it will help.

"The Saint Jude Prayer is a very powerful prayer. Pray to Saint Jude when you are in dire need of help from God: May the Sacred Heart of Jesus be adored, glorified, loved, and preserved now and forever. Sacred heart of Jesus, have mercy on us. Saint Jude, worker of Miracles, pray for us. Saint Jude, helper and keeper of the hopeless and lost causes, pray for us. Thank you, Saint Jude."

I take Sarah's Best Friends Forever necklace in my hand. The clasp is broken, the gold chain caked with Sarah's dried blood. Eyes closed, I let the half-heart pendant fall free of the chain and clench it in my fist.

Then I open my eyes. I open my hand.

I half-expect to see an empty hand, knowing that Dr. Darby had actually been right all along, the necklace was an illusion, a dissociation, a figment of my psychotic break, part of my contrived narrative to be the redeemed hero, running to save an imaginary world from an invented villain.

But here it is, in my hand, impossibly real. Best Friends Forever.

I unclasp the necklace that holds my silver crucifix and slide Sarah's pendant onto the chain so that it's side by side with the Cross. I fasten the necklace around my neck and tuck Sarah's chain in my pocket.

Fuck lost causes. This is my second chance.

"Why did I wait so long to open the goddamn letter?" I lament. "She told me not to come back." I'm sorting it out like I would when I prepare for a radio show. When I verbalize it, the answer always comes. "But then I would've stayed and what if Syd was right? What shit storm would I be in right now? And if I never came, would Stacy even go today? Or maybe he's only doing it because I came, and if I'd never shown up, he wouldn't do it at all. Maybe he still won't? Would I have come even after reading the letter? Mason told me I needed to come home if I was asked. I probably still would've come."

If I believed in fate, I'd say that everything that's transpired has happened for a reason, and if anything different had happened, I'd still be in the exact same spot. I feel silly even thinking it, yet I wonder if the universe was forcing this confrontation. It was too grandiose: what if my life was trying to correct itself? Was this God... *fixing shit?*

I dismiss the thought.

There's never been a point to any of this. It's been hope, loss, sadness, and failure, on repeat.

My dad beating the shit out of me for years, filling me with shame while I unknowingly became him?

My hideous secret and its random rage creating a monster in Mason Reynolds that took seven lives?

My love for Sarah, made meaningless as Mason savagely ripped her from me and the world forever?

My time with Michelle, finding hope in our loneliness while betraying Stacy, then abandoning Stevie?

My career, on the verge of stardom, unwanted because it had never really been my dream at all?

My life, devoid of family or real friendship, filled instead with manipulative drug dealers?

I feel like an abandoned house. The frame is here but barely standing. The foundation is cracked, crumbling, and crooked. There are leaks everywhere, and I'm empty inside. There are only memories haunting me, photos of the dead on the walls, and bloodstains on the carpeting. The love that makes a house a home has receded and vanished. Any thought of renovation is daunting and beyond hope: too much work, too time-consuming, too costly, too far gone. Perhaps I could be salvaged, but isn't demolition a more merciful move for a forgotten hazard? It would be the wiser choice, for the house, and for others, so they won't stumble inside and fall victim to its snares. Burn me to the ground.

There isn't any goddamn meaning. I'm just the only one out here who knows what's going on.

There isn't anybody else. I don't know what I'm going to do, but whatever it is, I have to do it now.

But maybe—if I can get this right—my whole stupid fucking life will finally be worth something.

CHAPTER 44

Sarah's eyes filled with tears. Her hands went to her mouth, then to her lap, then she tried to reach for me, but stopped. "Oh my God, Jeremy. Why didn't you tell me? Why'd you keep it a secret? Why didn't you tell anyone?" Why hadn't I told? Fear? Guilt? I hated my dad, but he was my dad and I wanted him to love me and I wanted to love him. It was humiliating. Shame and embarrassment burned in me. A shudder ripped through my body like an electric shock, one moment of honesty had released decades of pressure. As soon as the last spasm escaped through my fingertips, I broke down sobbing uncontrollably.

I hated my dad.

It was an explosive confession, letting go of the terrible secret I'd hidden from everyone. I repeatedly tried to stop the abuse, and when I couldn't, I suppressed everything, forcibly forgetting the truth. I believed I was responsible. It was ALWAYS my fault. I fucked up somehow, said the wrong thing, didn't say the right thing, did the wrong thing, didn't do the right thing, did or said the right thing at the wrong time, had the wrong look on my face, didn't respond fast enough. I never knew when it was coming.

As soon as I told Sarah, the dam broke. Thirteen years of suppressed memories poured from a dark and secret place and unspooled like an evil home movie.

I slammed my head against the steering wheel until Sarah stopped me. The embarrassment and secrecy that I had hidden in my heart and behind walls of bullying and smart-ass remarks or stoic silence gushed out in a torrent of tears and snot. I starting slapped myself, unable to control the outbursts. All the lies, the deflections, the rage, and self-hatred came out at once, wreaking havoc as it exited like a tantrum.

I was suddenly exposed. I felt weak. I was at risk, suffocating and claustrophobic.

I flung open the door and ran toward the river.

I stumbled. I fell.

Tumbled headlong. I tried to catch my breath. I got up and kept going.

Sarah was behind me, running in nylon feet and yelling for me to stop. I didn't stop.

I was heading for the river.

Memories screamed at me and pummeled me like reckless fists, filled with vengeance.

(Four years old, couldn't tie my shoes, laces tripped me, fell on the driveway, ripped my pants, Dad yelled, grabbed me by the arm, yanked me inside, pulled his belt out of the loops in one fluid motion, wrenched my pants down, underpants down, whipped me once, twice, three times, too many times to count over and over clouding my mind with pain and confusion what did I do wrong why won't he STOP)

I was off the bank and knee deep in the river before I realized it.

(My seventh birthday , my new BB gun, all real men had a gun, and I learned how to use it and was so excited that I pumped it and loaded a pellet and pointed without aiming and pulled the trigger and heard a TING from the front fender of the work truck and turned to see my dad watching and his pride turned to rage over shooting his truck and he snatched the gun from hands and held it by the barrel and swung it like a baseball bat and hit me in the stomach and knocked the wind out of me and when I tried to get up he brought the gun down across my shoulders and drove me to the ground)

Sarah splashed into the freezing water after me, without hesitating. "I'm here, don't go in, it's too deep!"

(I faced off with him in the barn the smell of manure and hay was thick in my nose and I was thirteen and finally had enough and said FUCK YOU there's no way I'm going to let you hit me again not this time and I stood my ground and I balled my fists and he smiled that violent gleeful smile and came at me and my adrenaline spiked and I flinched and he punched me in the ribs and the pain and the embarrassment of losing so quickly and he kept yelling at me "FIGHT BACK YOU FUCKING PUSSY!!")

Sarah. The sight of her stopped me, stopped the memories, stopped everything, brought me back from the past, drew me back into our present. "Your dress is ruined," I pointed out, dejected and shivering.

"I don't care, just come back up here, let's get out of the water, please, OK? I'm freezing." Sarah and I stood knee-deep in the Pecatonica River, her nylons soaked, her teal dress stained and mud-spattered.

Floating away. It felt like an answer. A solution.

Sarah gripped my hand. "If you go further, I'm going, too, but please don't make me."

A sliver of moonlight refracted across the surface of the water in the darkness, reflections of a reflection, haunting and alluring. I wanted to go in, freezing, sinking, numbing, drowning. I tugged lightly against Sarah's grip. It was the first time I considered what it would feel like to take my own life, to be missed.

It felt perfect.

I wanted it to be over. I wanted to stop being who I was becoming. I didn't know another way to escape.

"Jeremy, stop. Don't take me with you. I love you. Let me take you back."

I wanted her more than I wanted to let go. I surrendered to her love. I turned back.

The icy water had shocked me and fleetingly stopped the flow of tears, but the relief from plunging into the water began to fade as we scrambled through mud and silt, out of the river, and onto the grass. There was no sound aside from the bubbling current and our clumsy splashing. I sprawled out on my back, breathless, teeth chattering, staring vacantly into the night sky. Sarah joined me flat on her back, hands crossed on her tummy, chest rising and falling. I could've stayed there, alone with her, forever.

"What does he do to you? Can you tell me?" Sarah finally asked after we'd laid there for at least five minutes. I wouldn't have gotten up or spoken if she hadn't done it first. "You don't have to if you don't want to. We can just stay here and be quiet." She was shivering without complaint. "It's OK."

I didn't want to confess. But then, I just did. I told her about the vicious beatings and incessant verbal cruelty that started when I was four and never ended.

That my dad punched me and beat me with a belt and sneered at me and called me a pussy when I would run or cry and mocked me when I tried to hide and he caught me and twisted my arm and laughed in my face and it happened week after week after week and no one would stop it, not even my mom.

Sarah listened. And cried. Sarah was the only person I ever told.

I talked for over an hour before I was exhausted and ran out of words.

I opened up to her about everything. Everything I tried to forget. I relived it. It was excruciating, but the honesty and closeness I experienced with Sarah was the first time I ever believed I could be OK.

As long as we stayed together.

"I'm so sorry. Please don't leave me." I begged her. "I'm so, so sorry. I am. Please."

"I forgive you. I do. It's why I went in after you. I'm not leaving you, Jeremy."

Confession and forgiveness.

I started crying again, but this time it wasn't bitterness. It was relief, a taste of what healing could be.

"We'll make it OK! We'll tell someone. We'll do it together. You don't have to face your dad alone, Jeremy. We'll get help. They'll make him stop. I'll be with you. I promise. I'll always be here. I forgive you. I do. You don't have to worry. I won't leave you." Sarah was resolute, brave, loyal. Her self-lessness and commitment to the truth and restoration brought a glimpse of abandoned hope.

I was emotionally bloodied, but the noose of shame and secrecy had loosened, and I wasn't alone.

Visions of a future—to graduate and escape, to take Sarah with me, wherever that was—appeared before me. She couldn't have known the significance of her hearing my secrets and forgiving me.

This was the first time I'd felt safe in fourteen years.

"Jeremy," she whispered. "Can we get up now? I'm soaked. I'm freezing. We don't have to leave, I just want to sit on the picnic tables or get in the car. If you don't feel like it, it's OK, too. I just thought I'd ask."

I leapt up and offered her my hand, helping her to her feet. After she steadied herself, she tried to hide her dismay over her prom dress, muddy and ruined. The look was only a flash, but I saw it and it stung. This wasn't the Prom Night she had dreamed about. I let go of her hand, my arm sagging limply, but she squeezed. I clasped her hand again, tighter this time, and we squished our way toward the pavilion.

"I have a blanket in my trunk. I think it's clean. You want it?"

She nodded. "Please. Can you get my shoes, too? They're in the front seat." Sarah scooted herself on to the top of the nearest picnic table, knees together, biting her lower lip, shivering. I ran to the car, fumbled with the keys, opened the trunk, and grabbed my red Wisconsin Badgers stadium blanket. I was back by her side in seconds, draping the blanket over her shoulders like a cape. Sarah took her shoes from me, grabbed a corner of the blanket and flapped it open like a tent entrance, inviting me to cuddle.

"Are you sure you don't want to leave?" I asked. "We can go. I can take you home. Or we can sit in the car and turn the heater on. We don't have to sit out here anymore. You're freezing."

"I don't want to leave. I want to stay. With you. I don't care that I'm freezing." She cozied in even tighter, teeth chattering, her head on my shoulder. I put my arm around her under the blanket, rubbing her back.

We didn't talk for a long time, but it could've only been moments. I savored everything. I'd remember tonight perfectly, the terrible parts, but also this moment, forever.

"I can't believe you spit pop on me," I said finally, hoping to ease the tension.

"It was your fault. You made me laugh!" She fussed with her corsage, crooked all night.

"And you made me sing karaoke. The fucking Humpty Dance." I smiled, mortified that I'd done it.

"It was awesome. Terrible, and awesome. Where did you find the nose and glasses?! I forgot to ask you. You had the same ones Humpty wears!" Sarah laughed and lifted her head off my shoulder, mischievous, seeming to forget about Mason and the bonfire and everything else.

"Groucho Marx glasses," I told her. "Mr. Severson has a pair in his classroom for some reason, and I remembered they were in there, so I got them. If I was going to do it, I wanted to do it right."

"Of course you remembered," Sarah nodded. She pecked me on the cheek.

"And you're a stoner. You smoked pot. I can't believe you gave into the peer pressure so easily." I teased her. "Like, man, you're through the gateway now, man. Like, totally."

Sarah shoved me back and set the record straight. "That was your weed. And the alcohol was yours, too. You're the bad influence. I would never have done anything like that if you hadn't made me."

"Made you?" I feigned shock, complete with fake stammering and wide eyes. "And it wasn't my pot. I stole it from Derrick's sister." Sarah didn't have to fake her surprise. "You stole it from her?"

It was wonderfully cathartic to laugh.

The giggles subsided. We grew quiet again.

It felt like we had run out of other things to talk about. That was odd for us and it made me uneasy. It was possible that our relationship had grown stronger; it was just as likely that I'd broken us beyond repair. Sarah said she had forgiven me, but spontaneous forgiveness could be fickle and superficial. I wondered if she could ever trust me after seeing what I was capable of. I wondered if she'd want a burden like this and would soon seek out less complicated relationships. The seeds of doubt that were germinating within me were the offspring of what I imagined had taken root within Sarah, somewhere.

She'd forgiven. But could she forget? I was close to her now, terrified this was the best it would ever be.

"You're doing that thing again. Do you get quiet like that because of... what you're going through?"

Her intuition, though slightly off, validated my concern. "Sometimes. Sometimes I'm just lost in thought and my memories are so strong and clear that it's hard for me to focus on anything else. It's like watching a TV show of your life in your head. But sometimes I just go somewhere else so it doesn't hurt."

Sarah put her arms around me, draping from my left shoulder, fingers interlocked over my right arm.

"What were you thinking about just then?" she pushed tenderly.

I wanted to say—You. Me. Us. This is the best moment in our relationship and it's the beginning of the end. I'm scared and trying not to let that fear become a self-fulfilling prophecy. I'm desperate to keep time stopped because it's all going to change soon. You'll change, I'll change, how we feel about each other will change, and we'll look back on tonight for years to come but separately and with different feelings and it will fade away for you but will replay with painful vividness for me as I compare every girl I meet to you and every meaningful occasion to this one and we'll be apart but I'll still love you forever and you will have long since moved on and mostly forgotten about me—

"There's going to be a really big fucking mess on Monday with Mason," I blurted out instead. "He probably called the cops. I would've. I could get arrested. Derrick and Aaron will probably get busted, too. They may not let us graduate. I'm really fucked. I'm not gonna get away with this."

Sarah shushed me. "I don't want to talk about it anymore."

"You asked," I reminded her.

"I changed my mind. I'm a girl. We can do that." She snuggled back in next to me. She was warmer now; she'd stopped shivering and the goosebumps on her arms had disappeared.

My thoughts were obsessively focused on our future. "Will you promise me something?" I decided to ask.

Sarah shifted so she could look me in the eye. "Maybe," she admitted. "I'll try."

"Can you not treat me weird at school on Monday? Like, even though you know what you know about what I told you, could you just act normal and shit? I don't want it to be weird. Can you try to, I don't know, sort of forget like you know about my dad and we can have things stay the way they are?"

Sarah looked away. The frogs and crickets had resumed their serenade.

"We can't pretend like this didn't happen." She shook her head. "We can't ignore it, Jeremy."

"I know, I don't mean ignore it. I mean, I don't want it to be the only thing we talk about. I like that we have fun together and talk about other stuff. Maybe like, the first time we see each other again next week, could you act like you don't know any of the bad things that happened? I know it sounds stupid."

"I can try. But we can't not ever talk about it again. You have to talk to someone about what happened. Like, a counselor or a teacher or someone. And we have to talk to Mason. You promised you would."

"I will. We'll talk to someone. I'll talk to Mason, too. I swear. I want it to go back to like it was, too."

It didn't seem unreasonable to ask. Sarah had the awareness to know why I was asking and what I wanted, but seemed unconvinced she'd be able to do it, or if it was actually the right thing to do.

"I'm sorry," I mumbled.

"You don't have to keep saying sorry. It's going to be OK. It is OK. Do you believe me?"

I reached out and held her Best Friends Forever charm between my thumb and index finger, only a breath away from her skin. Sarah tried to see what I was doing. "What are you looking at? Is it broken?"

"No, it's fine. I was just thinking about something."

"Want to tell me, too?" She plucked the necklace from my fingertip grasp and rested it against her chest.

"Kelly is your best friend, and you're Kelly's best friend, but Sarah, you're my best and only real friend."

Sarah's brown eyes softened, growing bigger. "You can have more than one best friend."

It felt silly to say it out loud. "Best means best. Nothing beats it. If you're the best, you're number one. You can't have more than one best friend. It's

OK, you've been friends with Kelly since kindergarten. But you're my best friend. I don't really have any friend friends. You're the only one I talk to about anything."

"You can TOO have more than one best friend." Sarah debated the point, missing the meaning of what I was saying. "You're my boyfriend and you can be my best friend and Kelly can be a different best friend. People can have all kinds of best friends. That's just how it works. You can't order me to not have as many best friends as I want and I have two. Kelly's my best friend friend and you're my best boyfriend."

There simply weren't the right words in my teenage vocabulary to say it any other way than I did.

"You're not just my best friend. You're my only friend. I don't have anyone else but you."

I shifted stiffly on the picnic table and placed my trembling right hand on her cheek. I moved my fingers into her hair. My thumb rested just behind her ear, caressing her neck. I pulled her into a kiss that we both knew was coming, kissing my only friend, the only person I'd opened up my entire life to.

Loving her.

She lay back on the table, the blanket beneath her. Our teeth bumped with a click. Embarrassed, we giggled. My hands were carefully uncertain, inexperienced, curious and eager. My mouth was on her neck; her breath came in tiny gasps, airy sounds escaping her lips. Her hands gripped my shoulders.

We'd come close before, more than once, but this pace was faster, inevitable. I couldn't decide where to draw the line with her tonight. I wanted her, but even more than that I wanted her to feel safe. When I hesitated, she put her mouth on my neck, wet and hot, and then I wasn't thinking about stopping any longer. I pulled her dress up, then even further, kissing and caressing and wondering and anticipating.

I felt her wiggling, saw she'd slipped something black and lacy down to her ankles.

"Stop," I warned her. "Don't do that if we're going to stop. I don't want to go more and then stop."

She smiled, dimples and youth and decisiveness.

"I want you to," she promised.

"Are you sure?" I asked again. This was too important for us. So much was happening in this one night, it was a lifetime unfolding in hours, joy and sorrow, laughter and pain, failure and forgiveness.

"I'm sure. I am."

"It's your first time. I don't want to…I don't want to fuck it up for you," I stammered. I wanted to make love to her, but I couldn't unless I knew this was the right moment for her, too. "I need you to be sure."

She bobbed her head, bit her lower lip. "I want it to be with you. Stop asking. I'm sure."

And then we were one, breathless and comforted, exposed to each other, filled with a shared and unspoken belief that this was the beginning of our life together.

"I love you, Sarah," I breathed into her ear, wrapped in the blanket, going as far as we wanted, together.

She opened her eyes, filled with a look I'd never seen before. "I love you, too, Jeremy."

I was grateful we had never gone too far until now, when it wasn't too far, when it was just right.

It was my first time, too.

CHAPTER 45

It's 12:28 p.m. and I've got a big problem.

Stacy took me to a house on the outskirts of Edgerton, Wisconsin. We were parked along the street as he told me his delusional theories and I have every detail about the house memorized.

All but one thing.

I was too *tripped out* to notice street signs, landmarks, or anything else I could use to find my way back.

My perfect memory is useless. I'll never find the house. I have to go to the church. I have no other move.

I don't even wait for the valet to get out of the car before I'm slinging my bags into the backseat. The moment I feel privacy, I let out my frustration. "Why did I leave my fucking cell phone in DC?!"

Deep breath.

First United Methodist Church of Edgerton. Pastor Seth Moseley. There are numbers I can call.

I can find a payphone, I can call information, I can get the number to the church. Do people work at churches during the week? I have no idea, but I scan the street for the nearest gas station.

I have time to call. I don't have time to guess wrong.

What will I tell Pastor Seth Moseley if he answers the phone? My thoughts are a jumbled mess. Should I tell him who I am? Would he remember me from seven years ago? He'd undoubtedly remember the shooting. It's seared into the national consciousness and it happened less than an hour from Edgerton. Could I invent a story and turn the conversation to what Stacy is planning to do?

Or should I just rush in and scare them into calling 911?

I see a gas station with a payphone affixed to the brick façade, so I whip the car into the parking lot and slam on the brakes. I'm out of the car, searching for more change in my pockets, but I have to go inside.

People ahead of me in line are asking questions, scratching lottery tickets, writing checks, chitchatting with the clerk because they're regular customers and I'm about to lose my cool when it's finally my turn.

I swear to God it has taken an hour for this idiot behind the glass to ring up three people. It's 12:37 p.m.

I slide a dollar bill into the slot between the glass and the counter. "Can I get four quarters, bro?"

"Hey man, sorry, but policy is no change. Gotta buy something."

"Look. It's for *your* payphone. On the wall of *your* gas station. I'm going to be a customer in fifteen fucking seconds if you give me four quarters, so I can make an urgent telephone call. Literally a matter of life or death." I try to fake a smile. I can't. "Think that conforms to the goddamn policy?"

The clerk is apathetic. "No. It doesn't. You have to buy something in the store. We don't own the payphone. I can't open the register unless I'm ringing up an item you buy here or you get gas."

I hadn't really looked at the clerk until now. He's likely a college student, white kid, scrubby beard, Che Guevarra t-shirt, green and white flannel shirt sloppily pulled on over top of it, unbuttoned and flapping, with a

Jamaican Rastafarian hat and a clear awareness of the power that he holds over me right now.

"Fine. Pack of Marlboro Lights in a box. Sorry. Thanks." I shove the dollar bill back into my wallet and instead grab a five. "I'm sure you know, but I'll need one of the dollars back in quarters. Thanks again."

I'm back out at the phone, dialing 1-608-555-1212 for directory assistance. An operator is on with me after one ring, but I immediately strike out. There's no Seth Moseley in the phone book. He must be unlisted, or that isn't even the name of the person I'm supposed to be looking for. I got the name from Stacy and I have no idea how much of the information he's given me is accurate or truthful.

There *is* a number for First United Methodist of Edgerton. She connects me and I pump two quarters into the slot at her prompting. I still have no idea what I'm going to say as the phone starts ringing.

An elderly woman answers. I calm my voice, a technique I silently thank radio for forcing me to learn.

"Hello, ma'am, I'm trying to reach Pastor Seth Moseley. Is he available by chance, or is he at lunch like everyone else probably is?" I'm trying to be charming. It's not something I'm very good at and today it's just as awkward as it usually is. My laugh sounds fake. "Hope I'm not bothering you? Is this a good time or should I try to call back a little later if that's maybe more convenient for you? Or him."

"Are you a telemarketer?" she asks flatly.

"No, ma'am, I'm not. I used to live in the area, and I'm back for just a short amount of time, and my parents used to go to church here when I was a little kid. I'm just taking a quick stroll down memory lane today and wondered if I could maybe meet the pastor and see about taking a little look around?" I lie.

"Well, I'm not sure how old you are, but Pastor Moseley has only been assigned to us for the past seven years. Before that it was Pastor

Jack McElduff, and he was probably the one you'd remember, if I was to guess." This church secretary is giving me a history lesson on Southern Wisconsin Methodism.

"Yes, of course, Pastor McElduff. That sounds right. I was a little kid when my parents moved away. Is Pastor Moseley in this afternoon, or is there another number I could call to reach him by chance?"

The woman is kind and generous with information. "He should be back in about an hour. We have a lot going on at the church today because of the meeting, so he'll be here all afternoon, if you'd like to come by. I'm certain he would be honored to hear how the church had been a blessing to your family."

I pry just a little more. "May I ask what the meeting is tonight? I don't want to be a disruption if you have important church business to attend to."

"It's our annual business meeting where we present the church finances. Most of our parishioners will be here to vote on the budget. It's something our board members must do every year," she explains.

"Has the church grown a lot since my parents went there?" I need to get a sense of the crowd size.

"We have a hundred and twenty-two members and we're expecting nearly everyone tonight. The meeting takes about an hour, but we have a wonderful dinner planned beforehand and that really draws them in." She laughs slyly, their secret food bribery a righteous deception to get people in for a discussion about church finances.

One hundred and twenty-two people. Oh my God. This could turn into a bloodbath.

I swallow hard, barely keeping my voice from cracking. "What time does that meeting start?"

"Oh," she says, "we'll have dinner ready for everyone in the fellowship hall at 5 o'clock, and then the meeting should start right after we've finished eating. You could stay for dinner if you like, but I don't think you could attend the meeting since you're not a tithing member of our church body."

"Well, I understand that. Thank you for all your help and your time. Please tell Pastor Moseley that I called and I hope to see him soon. Have a nice day, ma'am, and I look forward to meeting you, too, when I get there. Buh-bye." I slam the phone down before she can say another word.

Mosely will be at the church in an hour. I can get there in an hour. Timing is going to be everything. Stacy must have picked tonight because of the meeting. Standing here now, I still can't completely piece together the details of his conspiracy, but it doesn't matter. Whatever he's planned HAS to be going down at the church. I have to do something. Stacy believes they have Michelle and Stevie. He's coming.

CHAPTER 46

The sixty-six-minute drive from Madison to Edgerton is exactly the time I need to record everything I want to say to my audience about what's happened since I left the show.

I pull the cassette tape out of my portable recorder and rush into the Post Office, which is conveniently situated directly across the street from the First United Methodist Church of Edgerton.

I write Wafer a note. I can't bring myself to call him again.

Play this tape on the air when you get it. It's only an hour, so figure it out. Do whatever you have to do, but do not let the cops know you have it, don't ask for permission, lock the studio door, fight people. I don't care. THIS MUST AIR! And if you play it on Thursday, you'll win the $435 in the office pool for staying my producer for six months. Congrats. See, I do listen. HaHa. I never thought you were going to make it. Sorry, I left you hanging. Too much to say on the phone but this will explain everything. Trust me, if you find a way to play this tape on the radio and tell people you were my producer, you'll get a job anywhere. Good luck. — Jeremy

The Edgerton Post Master General sells me a padded envelope, ink stamps MEDIA across the front of it, stands by silently while I scribble the address across the front, and watches me lick and stick a bunch of

467

thirty-two-cent stamps in the right-hand corner. The glue tastes stale, like dusty chemicals. I hand the precious package over to him. He nods an odd little salute at me, and tosses it in a wire-cage mail bin.

"Make sure it gets there," I warn. I'm smiling, but I'm deadly serious. My show was my life. This is the last one. I'm placing my goodbye show in the hands of the United States Post Office. It has to arrive on time.

"It always gets there," he replies with what's likely his well-worn postal joke. "Except when it don't."

I roll my eye at him and slide on my sunglasses, lighting a cigarette as I jog across the street. I hesitate at the door of the church and finish my smoke, trying to get my thoughts together and relax.

The church looks ancient, the original limestone building must be at least a hundred and fifty years old, with newer additions extending like wings from each side. The main door is open, there's no security of any kind. There's no one in the small lobby, but there are two more doors that I assume lead into the sanctuary.

I pass by several people carrying tables and chairs. Kitchen noises come at me from somewhere. It smells like a cafeteria in here. I try to approximate where the kitchen might be, where the dinner and meeting will take place, but can't get a sense of things. No one pays attention to me, strolling down the halls in a pair of jeans, a black tee, and a black leather blazer. My sunglasses effectively hide my black eye, and the sleeve of my blazer extends far enough to obscure most of the bandage on my right hand.

A bead of sweat trickles down my temple to my jawline. Another one chases the first.

I want to appear relaxed and confident, roaming the halls uninvited, looking at office doors as if I belong.

How am I going to find this Pastor Moseley? I don't even know what he looks like.

I rehearse what I'll say if confronted. I practice my introduction to the pastor. *Where is this fucking guy?* What if he's not back yet? What if I can't connect with him in time?

At the end of a hallway, I spot "Seth Moseley, Senior Pastor" posted on one of the doors.

I simultaneously knock and go in unannounced.

There are floor-to-ceiling book shelves, a massive oak desk, a couple of matching accent chairs. The room is dimly lit, with beige carpeting and a blue and white area rug that disappears under the desk. It's the office of a scholar, with several diplomas on the wall, dust-free books, and a desk that's covered with neatly arranged stacks of papers and more books. He has what I assume is a photo of his wife and children on the desk, turned so I can barely see their faces. In the far back corner, there's a couch and another chair, with a coffee table between them. The walls are covered with photos of church events and the faces of people I couldn't know, along with a handful of posed photos that show a family in varying stages of growing up, and growing older, together. Seth Moseley's office feels like the rest of the church, frozen in time, a relic of religiosity and quaint, meaningful associations.

There's nothing that hints at the conspiracy Stacy unraveled for me in his convoluted rantings.

Pastor Seth Moseley is seated behind the desk, a pen in his ear, and a shuffle of papers in his hand. My arrival isn't an interruption. His look of perplexed consternation dissolves. Maybe I'm a welcome distraction from whatever budget spreadsheets he has to review for tonight. That feeling won't last.

"Hey, sorry to bother you. I assume you're Pastor Moseley?" I walk over to the desk, extending my hand.

He stands up, and we shake hands cordially.

Pastor Seth Moseley is middle-aged with a neatly trimmed beard that's almost entirely grey, and swirling dark brown hair—parted on the left, combed-over to the right—will soon follow. Either he's spent a fair amount of time in restaurants or at potlucks because he appears to be about a hundred pounds overweight. At about five feet seven inches he isn't an imposing figure, rather he's the type of man you'd ask to play Santa Claus for an elementary school play. Pastor Moseley is wearing a brown collared shirt, a brown and mustard sweater vest, and a pair of khakis that are belted below his ample waist.

"What can I do for you, young man?" he asks, looking over the rims of his bifocals "Looking for someone?" Pastor Moseley has a preacher's voice, solemn and quiet, but a vibrato bass rumble in his throat that indicates he can get loud when he needs to.

I don't trust him. Is he smiling to put me at ease? Is he smiling because he's nice? I don't trust anyone.

I peel off my sunglasses and Pastor Moseley's face indicates he's taking note of the purple-green puffiness of my right eye, and the burst blood vessel that hasn't cleared up. "Actually, you're just the man I'm here to see. I don't suppose you've got a few minutes? I see you have a lot going on here this afternoon, so I could come back at a better time if this is an inconvenience." I'm not going to leave.

"Well, most certainly, son. Looks like you've had a rough day or two there," Pastor Moseley agrees.

"Oh, right, the eye." Instinctively, I put my fingers to my face, exposing my bandaged hand, dried blood visible through the gauze. "Yeah. My hand," I add, sheepishly. "I...uh...was in a car accident a few days ago. Banged up a little but painkillers help!" I'm trying too hard, offering too much false information.

"And you are..." he leads me to the introduction I should've already made. He's avuncular.

"I'm Jeremy. Jeremy Peoples. I used to live not far from here. I grew up on a farm outside of Sugar River, went to high school there, but I do radio in Washington DC now. Feels good to be back home."

After years of introducing myself, I know exactly what he's going to ask me next.

"If I might ask, were you one of the shooting spree survivors over there back in 1992? Are you *that* Jeremy Peoples from Sugar River?" He's warm and inviting, even asking a difficult question.

I nod my answer. He looks at the floor, shuffles his feet a step or two, then looks at me with wet eyes. "I'm sorry, son, for everything you've been through. I can't even imagine what it's been like. You should know that you've been prayed for, quite often, by a good many people in this town. Maybe not as much as we used to, but every now and then something comes up in the local news and I pray right then."

"Thank you," I manage to choke out. His sincerity moves me, even if it's misplaced.

"Glad you're home. You're a long way from Washington, though. What brings you through our doors?" Pastor Moseley pronounces it *"Warshington."*

Here we go.

"I know there's no way you could have heard my radio show last week, but I interviewed the man who shot me. A few other things happened that night, too, and that's the reason I'm back."

Pastor Moseley moves out from behind his desk and gestures toward his couch, chair, and coffee table.

"I don't think I follow," he replies. "Of course I didn't hear your radio show all the way out here in Wisconsin but the *State Journal* had a write-up in the Monday edition. You made national news, which I guess is the name of the game in your profession. It sounds like some unexpected things transpired," he explains, adding, "during the interview, and before it." He puts his glasses on, then immediately takes them off again. It's the first indication I have that Pastor Moseley might be nervous.

"I made the news out here?" I asked, incapable of hiding my surprise. I hadn't turned on a TV or read a newspaper, other than to check for Michelle's obituary. There was something in the way he said what he said. What was he implying? Does he know that Stacy called me? Mason Reynold's cryptic message?

"You did. Newspaper said it was Mason Reynolds's first and only interview since the shooting."

Of course. I continue. "There were some things that Mason said to me on the show, and my callers and I spent most of the hour before that confessing things we'd kept secret, and hoping for forgiveness." I briefly tell him what the New Year's Eve show was supposed to accomplish, and Mason's unwillingness to forgive me. I carefully avoid mentioning his prophecy. "There's a lot I don't understand," I conclude, "but right now I'm back, and trying to sort out everything that went on. It's…it's complicated."

"Confession and forgiveness," Pastor Moseley nods. "The cornerstone of Christianity. Do you know if Mason Reynolds found Christ in prison? I haven't read much about him. Did you talk about his faith?" He paused. "Or yours, if I may ask? I'm at a disadvantage, not having heard this interview myself."

My fucking faith? I don't have faith in much of anything other than the fact that my psychotic former friend is about to come into your church and forcibly start interrogating you and anyone he thinks is responsible for his family's disappearance. I have faith in the fact that his paranoia is due in part to my betrayal of him and he's coming up with wrong answers for the blanks created by lies and secrets.

"No, we didn't discuss anything about faith or God or whatever until the end. My goal in bringing Mason on the show was to confess to the audience, ask him to forgive me, and help him. He wouldn't accept my apology or my help. I've wrestled with that for days, pastor." A little truth mixed in with the lies.

"That was either a very brave and noble thing to do or the most terribly morbid and tabloid effort to get ratings I've ever heard of," Pastor Moseley contemplates, and continues. "I don't know you well enough to judge, so how about I give you the benefit of the doubt?" He sits down on the chair. I perch on the edge of the couch across from him, knees bent, elbows resting on my knees, chin in my left hand.

"Totally get that. I'm not sure which was which yet either," I admit. "Probably both." I haven't figured out how to start this conversation with him. I languish in hesitation, unable to overcome my cowardice.

Absentmindedly, Pastor Moseley interrupts the brief silence, musing and reminiscing.

"You know, I used to do a little radio back when I was a younger man, on a small AM radio station up in Door County. I would put our church services on the air every Sunday on a tape-delayed broadcast for our members who were shut-ins. Still appreciate the trade," he gushes proudly. "It wasn't exactly a talk show in Washington DC, that much is for certain, but I'd be a guest sometimes during their morning program if they needed a pastor's perspective on current events. I guess I got bit by the radio bug, too. I suppose you understand exactly what I'm saying. Once it's in your blood you always love it."

I can't believe my luck. We talk radio for a few minutes. I indulge him, and can tell he's flattered but I can't put this off any longer now that the ice is broken. I set my jaw. My shoulders sag and I sit back on the couch. I lick my lips, brow furrowed, and sigh through my nose, wishing I could smoke.

"Everything alright, Jeremy?" Pastor Moseley probes.

I swallow hard and blurt it out. "Do you know Michelle and Stevie Ramone?"

The color drains from Pastor Moseley's face, his eyes harden, narrow, and his relaxed, inviting posture stiffens into defensiveness. "What has this been about, really? Why are you here?" Pastor Moseley flashes righteous anger at me. He clears his throat. "This isn't about a radio show, is it?"

I shake my head. "I'm out of time. I need you to listen to me."

"I'm not listening to a word you've got to say to me, young man. I want you to leave. Right now!" he thunders, standing up and puffing out his chest. It's for effect. I can see Pastor Mosely is afraid.

I remain seated. "Look. I'm not going to leave. You have no idea what's happening right now, but I need some answers. Do you know Michelle Ramone? Maybe her parents? I'm here to give you information about something terrible I think is about to happen because you know them somehow. Did you help them escape from her husband, Stacy? You don't have to tell me where they went, in fact I don't want to know, but I need to know why Stacy thinks you have something to do with it." I'm calm. So far.

"I'm not telling you anything. If you don't leave, I'm calling the police. I know—"

"The chief. Yes, you know the Chief of Police. He goes to church here. He might be the one to call."

Pastor Moseley affixes me with a stare of stunned uncertainty. "I don't…you need to go. Now."

"I'm not going to go. And you can call the police if you want. Hell, I've almost called them fifty fucking times, but I can't bring myself to do it. If I'm wrong about all this, I don't want anything to happen to Stacy. I wish I knew what to do, but I have this feeling that if I call the police things will not go the way they're supposed to go. So maybe *you* should call them. Maybe we should call them later. Or maybe it's too late. Stacy says he's planning to come up here. I believe he's going to do something. He thinks you have his family; he believes you've kidnapped them and you're holding them against their will."

Pastor Moseley stammers, stops, stammers more, stops, and stares at me.

"I appreciate that you aren't going to give me anything. You shouldn't. Not about them, anyway. But, pastor, I need you to believe me. I'm not here to find them, or hurt them, or you. I'm trying to help."

Silence.

I offer him more. "I know you know them. That much is obvious. I don't know how, or what you've done to help them, but you're in trouble because you did. Your whole church is in trouble. Michelle wouldn't have told you my name, but she might have told you that Stacy isn't Stevie's father, even though Stacy thinks he is." I take a deep breath. I've never told anyone what I'm about to say. "Stevie's my son."

Pastor Moseley gathers himself. "*You're* the father? The one she was going to see?"

"Michelle came to DC last week to see me, but we missed each other. She left me a letter, I just didn't open it until it was too late. She tried to warn me to stay away, but I came anyway. Stacy called the radio show and lied to get me to come back. He said Michelle was dead. People don't just do that, make up a story like that and go live on the air during a radio show and just...lie. I've never heard of anyone doing anything that brazen, that bizarre. I just...I believed him. I drove here, and he had this story, this plan—"

"I don't know where they are, or how to find them, or how to reach them. You can do whatever you want to do to me, but I can't tell you anything," Pastor Mosely cuts me off. He holds his hands up.

"I'm not here to find them. I'm not here to hurt you. *Will you just listen to me for a second*?"

"So many lies," Pastor Moseley sighs. "All of us." He slumps back down, takes his glasses off, rubs his face, clenches his jaw until his molars squeak, and looks off into the distance, shaking his head slowly back and forth. "What have we done? Lord, have mercy, I only wanted to help."

"Why would Stacy think you have something to do with Michelle and Stevie leaving him? Give me something I can use to convince him that you're not who he thinks you are." Panic fills me again. I want to protect Michelle and Stevie, save Stacy from himself, prevent tragedy, stay alive.

"I'm not telling you anything further."

"Was he beating her? Was he hurting Stevie? What happened that made her leave? It had to be bad. Give me something. I need to stop this. I can't let it happen again." I was desperate. "I can stop this."

"What do mean you 'can't let it happen again?' What is going to happen, Jeremy? Another shooting?"

"Stacy's not the kind of guy to call the cops, or hire a lawyer, but something is really wrong with him. Maybe it's schizophrenia or paranoia or psychosis. I don't know. I'm not a psychiatrist, but Stacy *is* planning something terrible. He showed me everything he has. None of it makes any sense, but he believes it's all evidence of some conspiracy and you're at the center of it. He's coming here and I think he is planning to try and rescue them and stop you. He's mentally ill. He needs help."

"I don't understand why you didn't just call the police," Pastor Moseley revisits, trying to follow the unfathomable narrative I'm recounting. He can't understand it because none of it makes sense.

I try again. "Every time I start to call them, I get this resistance, this overwhelming feeling that it's not the right thing to do, not yet. Maybe it's because I don't have any evidence other than what he told me. I can't stop you from calling the cops and maybe they'll do more since you're friends with them. But…"

Why is he doing this now?

Why did he tell me what he's planning to do?

I continue. "I feel responsible for this, too, like I can stop it. If Stacy can hear the truth, he won't hurt anyone. I know I can do it. I just don't know how yet. I need to get to him before he comes through those doors with evidence he can't explain away. I can show him Michelle's letter. I owe him. He called us brothers. I fucked him over—more than once—in the worst ways a person can do to someone else. I need to help him, too." I'd forgotten I was in a church, talking to a pastor. I apologize. "Sorry about the f-words." Midwestern manners prevail, even in a crisis. "I need your help. Please. I can talk him out of it."

"Jeremy, that's not a plan. You're hoping you can talk him out of it? That's absurdly naive. You're going to get people killed." Pastor Moseley is incredulous, using air quotes around "talk him out of it."

"I need to try," is all I can offer.

"I can't put my faith in that, risk the safety of a hundred people. I have to call everyone. Tell them to stay home. Evacuate everyone who's already here. I'll lock the church down, call the police, you tell them everything you know, I tell them everything I know, and have them send the State Police to Stoughton."

He's right. There's no chance I can stop Stacy on my own, armed only with the letter and my mouth.

But something else is buzzing in the back of my mind.

Why had Stacy let me go? He wanted to kill me the last time I'd seen him. Now I'm his partner?

It didn't feel right at the time, but I was relieved that I'd gotten away after being in his room, surrounded by his demented displays. I was overwhelmed, terrified, obsessed with calling Dr. Darby. I never stopped to think about it until now. What if he let me go to use me? What if he expected me to betray him? What if he let me go because he predicted what I'd do? What if he wanted me to come to the church?

"But why did he take me to your home?" I mumbled, lost in the memory, forgetting I wasn't alone.

"You went to *my home*? How long have you been following me…?" Pastor Moseley continues to accuse me, but his voice fades into the background as I struggle with the puzzle pieces. I can see everything now, but I cannot make it fit together the way it needs to. I keep expecting it to click, but the exhaustion, the lingering effects of the LSD, the Xanax, the urgent pulsing tension of the immediate moment distorts the bigger picture. I'm on the verge of solving a riddle, but can't quite get there.

The diary pages. Why were they torn out? Stacy didn't show me the diary. He showed me the pages he wanted me to see. There had to have been others. Stacy caught me lying. He tested me and I failed.

I'm part of his plot.

Suddenly, and finally, it starts to come together in my mind. "Who all are here, right now?" I demand.

"What do you mean? Who all are at the church, now?" Pastor Moseley responds sharply.

"Yes!" I shout. "I saw and heard a bunch of people when I first came in. Who are they?"

Pastor Moseley considers the question for a moment, then answers. "Our board of directors, their wives, some of their children. There are a few others, volunteers, church leadership, my associate pastor. Maybe thirty people. Why?" His face is red, eyes squinted. He's still unsure of me.

I've been swallowed up by memories and grief, drugs and alcohol, remorse and justifications. Nothing I've done these past five days has made any sense. I panicked, responded illogically. I've been trying to find a way to restore a friendship with Stacy, not because I wanted him in my life, or as a debt of honor, but because of the unresolved shame I feel over my betrayal of him and years of lying about Stevie.

He's cunningly used it against me. "I think I was wrong. I should've called the police."

"My family's here, too," Pastor Moseley whispers. "Something terrible is going to happen, isn't it?"

"Yes. Call the police. Where is everyone, right now?" I ask.

"Kitchen, fellowship hall, maybe in some of the offices or classrooms."

"Is there another way out, aside from the front door?"

"Yes, but it's not easy to get to from the fellowship hall. There's only one door in there. Why?!"

Memories are supposed to stay where they belong. But they don't. History harmonizes. This is exactly where I'm supposed to be. I know why everything happened the way it did. I know why I'm here.

"Stacy's already here."

CHAPTER 47

Sarah gripped my arm. "Jeremy, no. Don't go."

Seconds ago—wearing my sunglasses, letterman jacket and Cubs hat—she was being silly, a carefree teenager doing what I asked her to do after I exposed my suppressed secret. She was acting like everything was normal, unchanged by what I had done to Mason Reynolds. Sarah was committing to her promise to forgive me, even if she didn't fully understand the maturity of that simple act of silliness. Coming to school on Skip Day, for a few, fleeting moments, had been the best decision I could've made.

"No one's stupid enough to shoot off a gun in here," I reassured her.

There were a handful of students in the hallway; the teachers had disappeared around the corner. We both looked at each other as we heard a chorus of screams echoing toward us. There was no laughter.

It was 7:53 a.m. The tardy bell was going to ring. I thought this would all be over once people realized what time it was. Camera in hand, I didn't want to miss out on something we'd talk about for years.

"It's not cherry bombs," Sarah insisted. "Why are people screaming?" She pointed toward the side door. "Let's just go. Something's wrong. I want to go. I don't wanna go without you. Please. Come with me!"

I stood next to my locker, door open, Sarah—on the verge of tears—tugging on me, pleading with me.

What was I waiting for? Why wasn't I afraid? Why couldn't I move?

I heard the noise again, much closer this time, and I knew then it was a gun, and now it was too late.

Everything slowed down. I turned toward the escape route Sarah begged me to use and realized it would do no good. The locks for the side entrance had been broken for months; the janitor secured both doors with a sturdy chain and combination lock to keep vandals out and sneaky students in. Both the lock and chain were still in place. Someone had forgotten to remove it before the start of the school day.

There was no escape from whatever was coming.

"Oh my God." I began to feel what Sarah had sensed only moments earlier. Dread. "Oh my God."

The sprinkler system suddenly let loose, a torrent of water burst from the ceiling, drenching us. Instinctively we stopped and looked up, shielding our eyes to see. Cascades splashed off the tops of the lockers, the white noise obscuring all but the loudest shouts coming from the common area and cafeteria. And sporadic gunfire. There was nowhere for us to go.

The first shot I heard in the hallway struck a sophomore that I'd never met, standing only fifteen feet from us. She went down in a heap, bloody, crying and anguished. What was her name? I didn't know.

Was this really happening? Someone was killing students at Sugar River High School.

I barely made out a thin silhouette at the end of the hall, clad in a blaze orange vest, the unmistakable outline of a deer rifle in his hands. Who was it? It was impossible to see clearly through the sprinklers.

"JESUS CHRIST, JEREMY! COME ON!" Sarah screamed. I had to see who it was. I needed to see.

Sarah turned to run without me, her sneakers slipping on the wet tile, and she dropped to her knees with a yelp of surprise and pain. She was staggering back to her feet when the next shot exploded down the corridor. Sarah screamed as she got up and covered her ears with both hands, forcing her eyes shut.

I never flinched as the third shot was fired down the hallway. The bullet struck another sophomore in the pelvis, blood blossoming on his jeans and shirt, spinning him like a pirouette to the ground with a splash and a gurgle. Immediately, he grabbed at his crotch, yelling and begging for help, mortally injured.

A fourth shot blasted indiscriminately, seemingly aimed at nothing, and ricocheted into the ceiling.

Light ballasts popped and burst with a dazzling and disorienting shower of sparks in the falling water. Electricity arced as a second ballast snapped loose and dropped before getting tangled in its own wiring.

The shooter was finally close enough for me to see who it was through the vents in my locker door.

The sprinklers ran out of water.

I yelled in disbelief. "Jesus NO!" yet somehow I knew who the executioner would be.

It was Mason Reynolds.

His stringy, dirty blond mullet was drenched and dripping. His eyes were wild, but I didn't think he'd seen me yet. Mason reached into the pocket of his hunting vest and shoved one, two, three, four more bullets into his rifle and shouldered the weapon. His footfalls sent plumes of water into the air.

Mason was gaunt; soaked to the skin, he approached like an emaciated phantom, pale and murderous.

And unrelenting. "Last four, motherfucker!" Mason howled as he racked the bolt action on his .30-30.

Sarah had stopped trying to run, pressing her back against the lockers across the hall from me, palms flat against the wet, brown metal in a futile effort to disappear. She was silently crying. My ears rang in the aftermath of the last gunshot. Sarah's eyes begged me TO DO SOMETHING. No one was going to stop Mason. There were no police, no teachers, no parents, no athletes, no one coming to save us. No heroes.

"No one gonna fuck me with me EVER AGAIN!" Mason screamed down the hall.

I knew I was going to die. I knew Mason Reynolds was getting his revenge. He'd come here to kill me.

Sarah's auburn hair was stuck to her face and neck, wet strands glued to her neck and forehead.

I had left her alone. Sarah stretched out her hand toward me.

Instinctively, I reached back. We were too far away to touch one another.

"Jeremy, help me," she begged, she screamed. "Please! Do something! Jeremy! Wake up!!"

I was transfixed, sliding into the safe mental place I would go when my dad attacked. I disappeared inside myself, hiding, running toward a sliver of light in my mind, covering my ears, closing my eyes.

Sarah's brown eyes filled with terror, then resignation. She knew what was going to happen before it did.

Mason sneered, "Your fucking boyfriend, you stupid bitch." Two gunshots came in rapid succession.

It was horror unfolding in slow motion, forever unforgettable. Mason's first shot struck Sarah at her hairline. She was beyond saving before her body slumped to the tiled floor, her outstretched hand flailing and then falling limp, her body jerking as the second shot struck her in the chest. She caromed off the locker and collapsed soundlessly forward. Her right cheek splashed to the floor, mouth opening and closing in short, tiny gasps, bubbles forming at her nostril and lips, brown eyes vacant and searching. Life bled from her body in an expanding red pool on the ground between us.

I couldn't look away.

Sarah drew her last gasp, her final breath, an involuntary and hopeless act. Her beautiful, promising existence wrenched from her body. Her fingers twitched and for a moment I thought she might miraculously still be alive, but the movement was fleeting and ceased. The chain on her Best Friends Forever necklace had broken, the pendant had skittered on the wet floor, floating a few feet from her body. Every dream and joy she'd created and envisioned, her essence, her soul, her friendship, her love, her life, vanished in that last instant, replaced with the lasting image of fading grey dead eyes.

She was gone.

I wanted more than anything to follow her into darkness. "I'm sorry," I whispered. "I did this to you."

I screamed, and then a storm of memories hit me. Volleyball practice. Pizza Hut. Walking to school. A Gin Blossoms concert. Gyros. A crooked corsage. A kiss in the crowd. I love you forever. Her ruined teal dress.

Confessions. Forgiveness.

Sharing our first time together.

Her life, our life together, ended.

I was still behind my locker door, and just as I moved to step out from behind it, Mason fired at me from ten feet away. The bullet tore through the thin metal, hit me in the stomach, and punched out through my back. I felt nothing. The final shot came and struck higher, again through the flapping locker door, blowing through my chest and into the wall of lockers. I choked, tried to breathe, tried to speak, couldn't.

Sudden, vicious pain, clawed at me from inside, burning and pounding.

I staggered, tried to take a step forward. My legs wouldn't work. I fell backward into a pool of water.

I aspirated my own blood, wheezing and coughing, a shuddering agony with each spasm.

I looked to Sarah's body. Why wasn't anyone coming to save her? Where was the ambulance?

She was dead. But they could bring her back. I'm dead. I don't care. I deserved this. She doesn't.

Mason was still trying to shoot me but he was out of bullets, pulling the trigger over and over. I was suffocating, losing consciousness. I couldn't let myself black out. The slightest movement caused spearing pain. Was I paralyzed? I exhaled sobs. I couldn't inhale. A blood bubble formed on my lips.

Was that my blood? Had I been shot? I was at school. How did I get shot? What happened?

I tried to pray.

God, if you're real, keep her alive. Leave me. Help her. I failed. Let her live. Please.

Do a miracle. Save her. Let her be alive. Or let me die. Please.

Amen.

Mason dropped his gun and sat down in the water next to me. Why was Mason here? Did he get shot, too? Was he OK? Who was shooting people? What the fuck was going on? I couldn't breathe. My vision was darkening. My ears were ringing, a sharp and incessant whistle. I tasted metal, smelled gunpowder.

Mason stared at me, disappointed, as though he'd failed at something. Why were we at school? Wasn't today Skip Day? I was supposed to do something today. Apologize? What had Sarah wanted me to do?

Where was Sarah?

I let my head flop in the opposite direction and saw Sarah's body, just out of reach. My fingers danced in the water as I tried to touch her and couldn't. Her mouth gaped, her eyes had rolled back in her head.

"I love you, Sarah," I gurgled. "I'm getting help." I tried to get up. I couldn't. I tried again.

Where were the fucking cops? The fire alarm was blaring. The pain was excruciating. My chest was being crushed in a vice. Why can't I breathe? I coughed, a fresh eruption of agony in my head.

Am I dying?

Did my dad finally kill me? Had he fucked me up so bad I was dying? Where was he?

Mason pointed his thumb and finger at me, making a gun. What was he doing?

"Look what you made me do!" he screamed at me. "LOOK WHAT YOU MADE ME DO."

I didn't understand. What did I do? What did he do? Sarah would know.

It took all of my effort to roll on my side. I wretched up a curdled black-red mix that was both meaty and bitter. Where was it all coming from? The throbbing wouldn't stop. What was wrong?

Oh my God. I'm covered in blood. I'm all fucked up. Was I in an accident? Were those sirens outside?

I tried to sit up but fell back and cracked my head on the tile floor.

I pulled at my shirt, startled to see it was soaked in carnage as more of the black-red blood squirted out of a hole in my shirt. I poked my fingers into the hole and they disappeared up to the first knuckle. I jerked them out with a sick sucking sound and fell back, unable to find the strength to do anything more.

"Mason, what happened? Are you hurt?" Every gasp was impossible. "I think I'm dying. I think I'm dead."

The class bell went off. Mason looked up. "First bell," I said. "7:54." I spit blood.

Turning my head to again, I looked to Sarah Brennan, hoping against hope to see her as I had only minutes earlier, running playfully toward me with joy and a forgiving heart.

I wanted to gaze into her eyes and see the same welcoming softness just before we made love.

Instead, my dying eyes locked with Sarah's dead eyes, a wordless accusation, her haunting white face, lips painted with blood that drooled from her open mouth, body broken and lifeless, a twisted ghoulish heap in a pool of water, clumps of wet hair plastered across her forehead, framing the fatal wound.

Every perfect thing she had been was now gone.

My eyes fluttered shut. Darkness, no light. No fear, only warmth. The pain, easing. Peace. I was done.

I knew Sarah would be there when I woke up, so I let go.

CHAPTER 48

Snowflakes the size of quarters are falling, silently and rapidly making the dirty world a virgin again.

Pastor Moseley is on the phone with Edgerton's Chief of Police, tethered to his desk by the phone cord.

"He needs to fucking take this seriously," I urge him. "He needs to send someone, everyone, *now*. We need to get everyone out of here now. I'll go. Just tell him what I said. Stacy could do anything. He could be anywhere. Did I mention he's a Marine and I saw two guns in his house trailer in Stoughton? You need to send everyone here now and you need to send someone to his trailer. The address is—"

Pastor Moseley tucks the phone into his chest. "Jeremy. Please. Just— shut up. I'm sorry, but I can't hear with you yelling." He puts the phone back to his ear, plugging his other ear with his index finger.

"How long can it take for cops to get here in this town? Thirty seconds? Jesus Christ, tell him whatever you have to tell him to get everyone here. What does he think we should do? Evacuate or stay put?"

"Jeremy. Enough," Pastor Mosely rebukes me. He puts the phone back to his ear. "What do you want us to do, Dwight? Yes, I think he's serious. Yes, I believe him. No, I've never met the husband, I only heard about what he was doing. Yes. No, she and the boy aren't here—"

I can't stand not knowing what Dwight is saying. I interrupt again. "Put him on speaker phone."

"—Dwight, can you just come over? Or send someone now? We've got about thirty people in the building. No, I haven't seen anyone or anything suspicious, except Jeremy. I don't know, but he's telling the truth. Well, he believes what he's saying is true, I think. I don't know if the husband will come, but Jeremy said he has a pistol and a rifle, and the wife told us about his behavior the past few months…Right, yes, drug trafficking too. Dwight, please…just send a car. For my peace of mind."

One fucking car?

Peace of mind?

Why is this a debate?

"Listen, *Dwight*," I shout over Pastor Moseley's urgent inadequacy. "Fucking send everyone!"

Pastor Moseley glares at me. "I can stay on the line, yes."

"No, he can't, *Dwight*," I yell, reach over and disconnect the phone. "Now you'll come, won't you?"

"Jeremy, what are you doing?!" Pastor Moseley's face is red. "He wanted me to stay on the phone!"

I hold up my bandaged hand. "We need to get the people in the kitchen and that fellowship hall place and get them out of here. Right now. You know this building. I don't. Show me. You have to find anyone else and take them out a back door. We can't leave them down there not knowing what is going on." I can feel myself sweating, hear my voice quavering. "If we wait until the cops decide if they're coming because of whatever circle jerk they want to have with each other, it'll be too late. Trust me, I've been through this. It happens too fast, people freeze, you can't think. Please. We have to get everyone out."

The cops had better be coming after I hung up on Dwight.

Dark patches of moisture have formed under Pastor Moseley's arms, sweat soaking through his shirt.

"You need to take care of your people. We just need to get to them, get them to safety. That's it."

"What if he's outside and just starts shooting people when we walk out the door?" Pastor Moseley asks. "We should all just get together in one place and wait for the police to arrive."

"I don't think so. He knows you had something to do with Michelle and Stevie's disappearance. He wants them back, and doesn't know what you did with them. He needs answers. Stacy's not going to come in fucking blasting and kill everyone indiscriminately..."

Probably.

"...He's going to make you tell him where his family is. If you don't know and you can't tell him, he's not just going to surrender and drive away. You understand? He's going to *make* you tell him, any way he can. Once he has you, no one's walking out of here. Your people aren't safe. We can't keep going round and round, arguing about this. I'm going with or without you. I need your help, but I can't wait for it."

"OK." Pastor Moseley begins to nod, almost imperceptibly at first, but then in full agreement. "OK."

"Show me where everyone is. I'll run outside, see if I see anything, and meet you back there. I only need to see how to get there one time. Trust me, I'll remember."

"Jeremy, no, I don't think going outside is a good idea. We should get everyone together first, stay together—" he gestures like he's waving a group of friends into his office "—and leave together."

This argument is going to get people killed. "I'm the only one who knows what his car looks like. I'll stick my head out, see what I see. By then the cops should be here anyway, right?" Before Pastor Moseley can argue

490

further, I step into the hallway with the bravado that comes with thinking I'm right. God, I hope I am. "C'mon. We gotta go."

We've gone a few paces when Pastor Moseley passes me, opens a door, leads me down another, shorter hallway, then opens one more door on the left and barges into a large, rectangular, windowless room. I stand in the doorway, nervously sneaking glances up and down the corridor, then up and down again, before peering into the room. There's about twenty people, some talking with each other, others at work setting up folding chairs and tables. I hear kitchen clatter and laughter coming from somewhere.

"What is this room?" I ask.

"The Fellowship Hall," Pastor Moseley explains, and points to the far end of the room. "Behind that passthrough counter is the kitchen. There's about four or five more people in there now, cooking."

"Is there a back door in the kitchen? Out into an alley or something?"

Pastor Moseley shakes his head. "Not from here. We have to go back out this same way, and then go through the sanctuary to get to the rear entrance." This place feels like a maze with no exits.

"Do you remember how to get to the entrance from here?" Pastor Moseley continues.

"I remember everything," I reply and lower my voice further. "Tell them only what they need to know or they'll panic. Keep them here until I get back. If he's not here, we'll go. If he's here, then…well, you're a pastor. Start fucking praying. And I hope Dwight and your cop friends hurry up and get their asses here."

This has to be the right decision. Right? Stacy said it was going down at 5:00 p.m. There's time. Right?

I pull the door closed behind me, and I'm back at the front entrance in less than thirty seconds.

Fucking *Dwight*. Where the hell are you?

I look at my watch, surprised at how dark it is already. It's 2:23 p.m. Looming clouds have filled the Wisconsin sky, their white and grey heaviness bringing colder, damp air and snow.

Lots and lots of snow.

White in every direction, a blank curtain falling across my stage. I marvel at how less than two inches of pure snow can make everything seem fresh and new. It's transformed Edgerton from a colony of lifeless buildings, dead grass, and fading asphalt into a quaint winter village.

It is silent the way it is in a heavy, windless snowfall. The few cars in the parking lot are covered. None of them appears to be a 1972 LeMans. Stacy wouldn't be that stupid—or brazen—would he? I shiver as the chill cuts through my sweaty clothes. I'm not dressed warmly enough. Slipping on the slushy pavement, I jog a couple of paces away from the building to get a better vantage of the street in each direction. There's no one on foot. I don't see any Edgerton Cops yet, either.

What the fuck are these stupid cops waiting for?

What am I going to do if Stacy shows up before the cops?

I flick open my Zippo, poke a cigarette in my mouth, and try to light it. Over and over. The Zippo won't fire. Three, four, five, six times. I hold it upside down. Seven, eight, nine times. I shake it. Still nothing.

It's the first time my Jack of Clubs Zippo has failed to light.

Disgusted, I throw the cigarette on the ground and poke the lighter in my front pocket.

I stamp my feet to stay warm. Two cars and a truck creep by, slowed by slippery conditions. Neither of them is Stacy's car. Could he be in another, less recognizable vehicle? I search my memory, back to when I arrived at Stacy's and found three cars in his driveway. Any one of them could have been Big Lou.

Dr. Darby's words come back to haunt me.

Did I invent everything in my mind in an effort to reconcile my life, my guilt, my loss?

Did I hallucinate everything that happened in Stacy's trailer, the trip to Pastor Moseley's house, The Silhouette in the bathroom mirror? What if I'm the one who's lost his mind, disappearing into dissociation? I can't tell the past from the present sometimes. I'm blacking out, sometimes a full day at a time. Did years of abuse, trauma, and my vivid recollections merge into a fantasy that only I can resolve? I grab the door handle, and am nearly inside when I catch my reflection in a pane of glass in the door.

I look like shit.

The eye the bartender shattered has improved, but it's still haloed with discoloration. A full beard has grown in, graced with melting snowflakes, patchy at my cheekbones and down my neck, thicker across my jawline and chin. I've lost even more weight since New Year's Day. I haven't been this thin in years, since high school. Dressed in black, my hair slick with sweat, I look like a pallbearer in a winter funeral.

If I'm a hero, I'm a broken-hearted, reluctant one, eager to hand my assignment to any replacement.

We're in danger. Not the indiscriminate danger of Mason Reynolds, afraid and unhinged. This is deliberate, unrelenting danger. The kind that won't stop. The kind that's grounded in conviction. Mason demonstrated his evil bravery by facing his abuser—me—in a way that I never did with my dad, but he was unfocused and thoughtless, claiming innocent lives while failing to tally the guilty. Mason acted emotionally, out of a need for revenge, fear-driven that he had to act or I would hurt him even worse.

Stacy is acting out of belief. Moral certainty. Blind faith born in a demented mind that he's doing the right thing by coming here to rescue Michelle and Stevie, to bring them home, to save their lives, to stop this from happening to others. He's a Marine. This is his mission. He won't stop until he can't go on.

This is a lost cause, but I have to stop him. Somehow.

Where are the cops? How is there not a goddamn SWAT team and negotiator here, right now?

I'd settle for one, trigger-happy *Dwight*.

I throw one final glance over my shoulder. Stacy's not out here.

A cold wind from the East whips the last vestiges of warmth from my body. Foreboding hangs over me like a poised predator, unseen but with an unmistakable and palpable presence. My resolve is failing me at the moment I need it more than ever. Help is not coming. Just like last time. Prayers are going unanswered. Just like last time. I'm about to be overtaken by the evil I've managed to outrun until now.

I could leave. I *should* leave.

My car is still sitting in front of the post office, hidden under freshly fallen snow.

I could skid out of town and never look back. I've done my part. I warned Pastor Moseley.

I don't even know these people. The cops have been called. What more can I do?

If I'd read Michelle's letter before today, I wouldn't even be here.

It's not up to me to save anyone. I'd just be one more hostage for the cops to worry about.

My hand is still on the door handle. I've been outside for two minutes. It must seem like an eternity to Pastor Moseley, waiting for me to come back, like I said I would.

"You can't hide. You can't run anymore," I order myself. "You fucking pussy. You baby. Go back inside and get these people out. Do something right for once in your life." It's my voice but my dad's words, motivating me from within, cruel but honest. I can't let him be right about me this time. I can't be a coward who runs or cowers and disappears within myself instead of finding a way to do the right thing.

(*"You need to start making better choices, Jeremy..." Sarah says*)

I yank open the door and for the second time today, and the second time in over eight years, I enter a church. My heart is thumping, the snow on my hair is melting in a cold trickle down my scalp and neck. I shake off my jacket, pop the collar and sleeves, and resist the urge to run down the hallway. The earlier activity I could hear throughout the church when I first arrived has ceased.

First Methodist Church of Edgerton is completely still.

Retracing my steps, I'm at the closed door to the Fellowship Hall in less than thirty seconds. Sensing this is our moment, I fling open the door. "OK, Moseley, we gotta go. Now." The small group I'd seen earlier, along with Pastor Moseley, has huddled quietly in the far corner of the room, nearest the kitchen.

These people are going to get themselves killed. "What're you doing? C'mon, let's go. I didn't see any—"

The door slams behind me. Startled, I spin around.

I'm face to face with Stacy Ramone holding an AR-15, his .357 Magnum revolver tucked into the waistband of his jeans. His hair is wild, glasses and leather jacket beaded with melted snow. He's only been inside for a minute or less, somehow through the back entrance, easily outsmarting me.

Stacy's eyes burn with confirmed suspicion. "I knew you were part of it, you motherfucker."

I learned my lesson from Michelle, years earlier. Say nothing. Respond carefully. Don't initiate.

"Get over there, traitor. With them." He gestures with the barrel of his rifle.

I obey, joining the cowering mass of whimpering humanity in the corner.

Stacy pulls a cell phone from his jacket pocket, puts the extendable antenna in his mouth, pulls it out, and dials three digits. "It's me again. Tell them to stay back, like I said, or I'll shoot three people right now and throw their fucking bodies out the front door. Don't call me, or I'll shoot three people right now and throw their fucking bodies out the front door. And if any cops try to come in here, I'll kill every fucking person in this room before they even get to me. I've got someone watching the entrances. I'll call you when I have the proof I need. I'm exposing these motherfuckers and getting my family back."

Of course the cops never came. Stacy probably called them immediately after I disconnected Pastor Moseley's call. The telecom manual. He could've been listening to the phone conversation with Dwight. All the details were laid out in front of me and I've been a step behind, drunk and strung out on drugs.

Everyone in the room—aside from me and Pastor Moseley—seems utterly bewildered and petrified.

Stacy stands, legs straddled, AR-15 on his hip, barrel pointed at us, and says nothing. Minutes tick by.

I'd seen him fall silent like this, burning with betrayal and anger but also uncertain. When he came home to find Michelle and me together, I was repeatedly wrong each time I predicted what he would do. It's the same today. I know this can go any number of different directions; it's our responses that will determine his actions, not any strict adherence he has to a plan. His emotions will override his discipline.

"Say something," Pastor Moseley whispers to me out of the corner of his mouth. "You said you could talk him out of this. You need to do something or he's going to shoot someone. Maybe all of us."

I don't even acknowledge that he's nudging me to act. A woman and two teenage boys are behind Pastor Moseley, each clutching at his shirt. His family. The boys are stoic. His wife seems equally scared, but less adept at hiding it. No one else dares to speak to anyone else.

The enormity of what could happen at any moment is a living, breathing entity.

Were there others in the room who helped get Michelle and Stevie to freedom? What was the church's connection to them? Pastor Moseley didn't trust me enough to fill in the gaps. Stacy's eyes dart from face to face, his lips moving silently as he thinks. What is he waiting for? Why isn't he asking questions?

The room is humid, thick with sweat and tears and the hot breath of people facing their own mortality.

When Stacy finally speaks, it's with conviction. "I know all of you," he declares. Grandiose. "I know what you've done. I know what you're doing." He starts listing names he's memorized, poking the barrel of the AR-15 at each person when he identifies them, calling them "co-conspirators." People begin openly crying. "You fooled everyone else, but I figured it out. I want. My wife. And son. Back. Where are they?"

No one answers.

Stacy unzips his leather jacket, the silver chains swing and jingle. He's wearing a red Marine Corps t-shirt, the words "SEMPER FI" emblazoned over a yellow Marine Corps emblem.

"I'm not leaving until I have them. I swear to God I will put fucking bodies in bags until I get to someone who will tell me what I want to know. Where's Michelle Ramone?! Where is Steven Ramone?! I know you know, goddamn it! *What have you done with my fucking wife and son!?*" He paces while he rages.

Stacy looks directly at me.

"Fucking lying little bitch. Reading her diary and lying to me in my own home. You fucking idiot. I knew you'd show up here. Where is she? Has she been with you this whole time? You fucking her again?"

I don't even know how to lie.

"I have pictures of him with her," he explains to the room full of people. "Just like I have of all of you. Did you think you could get away with it? You did, didn't you? You thought you could do what you wanted. But you can't. I've got all of you now, and one of you *IS GOING TO FUCKING TALK!*"

He'll never believe the truth.

I have two weapons. The truth and my mouth. Michelle's letter is still safely tucked in my inside blazer pocket, written in her purple ink in her unmistakable handwriting. If I can focus his attention on me, and get him to argue with me, I can give the cops a chance to come up with a plan. I just need an opening.

Stacy drags a metal folding chair across the floor, whipping it in a wide circle, and stops it next to his leg. He leans his AR-15 in the corner behind him, pulls the revolver from his belt, and gestures at us with it.

"You. Seth Moseley. Sit. Right here. You've got fucking answers, hoss. We start with you."

Pastor Moseley doesn't move. Out of the corner of my eye, I see his wife squeeze his hand and his two sons tense into a defensive posture. "It's not a request, Seth Moseley. It's an order. Come. Sit. *NOW.*"

There isn't going to be a standoff. Stacy doesn't care about hostages. He only has one, simple demand. Stacy isn't going to negotiate with the cops. He wants his wife and son or no one is leaving alive.

I realize how deep into darkness Stacy has descended. If he doesn't find Michelle and Stevie alive—here AND now—I'm afraid his delusional worldview will shatter and he'll lure the police into killing him.

"MOSELEY! Get your fat ass into this fucking chair!" Stacy shouts. Pastor Moseley relents, pulls his hand away from his wife's grip and reassures his boys, and steps out from the small crowd. As he reaches the folding chair, Stacy cocks the hammer on the revolver and points it at the back of his head. The room comes alive with gasps, crying, and appeals. Stacy glares, blue eyes demonically wild. "SHUT UP!"

Mrs. Moseley begins to cry, openly.

"Where are they? Are they with Jeremy?" Stacy peppers him with questions. He grabs Pastor Moseley by the hair, yanking his head back at a severe angle, puts the gun to his temple, his nose a fraction of an inch from Moseley's face. "Where are they? Where are they? Where are they? Tell me, goddamn it!"

"I don't know, Stacy," Pastor Moseley replies calmly.

"You don't know what?" Stacy demands. "You don't know what I'm talking about? You don't know where they are? You know me. You know *him*. You know Michelle. You know something, you fat fuck."

"I don't know anything."

Stacy pushes the gun barrel into Pastor Moseley's mouth. "LIES. You and your cult of lying fucking liars, and Jeremy the King of the Liars, all of you, stealing people and using people and lying to everyone. All of you. Twisted fucking sickos. I see you. I see all of you. You can't fool everyone. You didn't fool me."

Pastor Seth Moseley narrows his eyes and—gagging on the gun— wordlessly stares back at his assailant.

"Fine. Don't talk." Stacy yanks the revolver free from Moseley's mouth, grabs it by the barrel and bludgeons him across the face with a sickening wet thunk. Pastor Moseley topples from the chair, blood spurting from a gash across the bridge of his nose, glasses broken. "You wanna talk now, you piece of shit? This isn't going to stop. I know you know." Stacy turns to the group. "I have pictures of all of you!"

I'm hiding in the crowd, watching. Just like I did on May 23, 1992, at 7:53 a.m.

It's then that Pastor Moseley's wife overcomes her paralyzing fear and runs to the side of her bleeding husband, comforting him. The entire room falls silent, all eyes darting from Mrs. Moseley back to Stacy.

I don't even know her first name.

Stacy points his pistol at Mrs. Mosely and I envision her as the first of a dozen victims. But then I see Stacy's eyes darting from side to side as he conjures a new idea. He snorts, grabs Mrs. Moseley by the hair, and drags her over to the chair. She screams at him to let go; her teenage boys both object and push through me. Pastor Moseley props himself up with his right hand, waving at them to stay back.

"No, boys, no! He'll kill you!! It's OK."

Buoyed by his new plan, Stacy is flushed, feverish, with piercing blue eyes and a wicked grin. He effortlessly lifts Mrs. Moseley off the ground and on to the chair and turns the revolver on her.

"You take my wife, I take yours. And when I'm done, I take your son like you took mine," he taunts. "I'll let you decide which one you want to keep and which one you can live without. You have the power. Tell me where my family is and all of this stops." Stacy puts the barrel of the .357 to her forehead.

I'll take your son like you took mine.

What had Pastor Moseley told me in his office? *"I don't know where they are, or how to find them, or how to reach them. You can do whatever you want to do to me, but I can't tell you anything."*

I'm about to witness another murder, another innocent person dying because of me.

What can I do? This is going to end in a bloodbath.

I don't know where Stevie is. I can't give Stacy what he wants. No one can.

"This isn't a movie, hoss! I'm not counting to ten. You tell me, right now, where Michelle and Stevie are, or I put bullets in her fucking brain." Stacy's gleefully deranged expression reminds me of Mason Reynolds. I know when someone has resolved to kill; Stacy would've done it in 1996 if Michelle hadn't acted when she did. Mason and Stacy. Mayhem and premeditation, linked by fateful violence.

It's then that Seth Moseley surrenders. His wife is about to die and he's facing the prospect of his children's murder. "Alright. Don't hurt her, please, I'll tell you where they are. Just, please, don't."

I hold my breath, stunned. Pastor Moseley lied to me? He knows where they are? If he's lying now, he's only bought his family a few extra seconds of life. I want to stop him from talking, but I can't.

"Last chance, old man. Where. The fuck. Are they?"

Pastor Moseley sighs, blood dripping onto his shirt and sweater vest. As he opens his mouth, I know he's going to give up Michelle and Stevie. I'm in a standoff with myself as seconds tick away.

Once Stacy has a clue, he'll take hostages, he'll get away, he'll find Michelle and Stevie and he'll...

An icy tremor penetrates me from my spine through my chest.

For the first time in two thousand seven hundred and eighty-three days I'm afraid to die, petrified of what I'm now certain will happen next.

"This is what I heard the voice tell me to tell you. 'Because you hate yourself, He knows you'll do what is required when the time is right. And if you do, you'll give up everything you don't want in order to get a thing you can't seem to acquire.' You're gonna die, Jeremy," Mason Reynolds promises me.

I know Stacy's going to kill me when I tell him, when I prove to him that his son is my son.

I feel my eyes close and the darkness fills with images of the random and sudden rage of my father.

His breath smells like cheap beer and chewing tobacco. He leers at me while I lay in the gravel driveway gasping for air as my mother turns away from the window where she's watched the whole thing and she sees me see her and shuts the blinds and he lifts his steel toed boot and rears back and kicks me in the side and I cry out and beg and he only curses "you fucking pussy get up stop crying you little faggot!"

Temptation draws me to descend into the safety of my mind. I refuse. *When I do, Mason Reynolds is bearing down on us with his rifle pointed at Sarah and he's angrily screaming "Your fucking boyfriend, you stupid bitch" and the gun goes off and I close my eyes but somehow can still see everything happen.*

I don't want to be afraid of everything anymore. I don't want to let the people I love get hurt anymore. I don't want to hurt the people that love me anymore. I don't want to let anyone hurt me anymore.

Sarah's pleading eyes are begging me to move, to do something, anything.

Michelle's hope for her unborn child convicts me while her belief that I have courage proves false.

I can't find freedom from these memories, this life of failure.

"Stacy." I give up trying to save my own life, my own way. "Stop."

I step out from the crowd of terrorized parishioners. "Moseley doesn't know shit. But you're right about one thing: Michelle came to see me in DC," I begin. "We hadn't spoken in years, but she took Stevie and she came to see me when she knew it was time to go. No one kidnapped your family. Michelle left you."

He blinks repeatedly. "She didn't leave me. You fucking TOOK her!" Rage gives way to confusion.

"No. She left. She took Stevie. She left you. She was afraid of you. Michelle wanted a better life."

Stacy is mystified, but he's finally turned the gun on me and away from Pastor Moseley's wife. I'm not choosing my words; the truth is revealing itself. My sins have found me out, cannot hold them back, I cannot keep the secrets any longer. I feel as though I'm reading a script filled with long overdue truths.

"She wasn't afraid of me. She…she didn't leave me. You…you're lying."

"I'm not. I have proof. I can show you. You can read it. Her words, her handwriting. A letter." I hold open my blazer, the top of the white stationary envelope barely visible in the pocket. "Take it. Read it. See for yourself. I'm not lying, Stacy." There's nothing left to hide now. Nowhere to run. It's all just spilling out of me, somehow both prepared and spontaneous. I have no fucking idea what's going to happen next.

Stacy grabs me by the throat and places the revolver flush against my bruised eye. "I should've fucking killed you. None of this would've happened."

Gasping for air, I manage to choke out a reply. "Take it. Just read what she wrote."

He yanks the folded, stained envelope from my pocket. My name is still visible in purple cursive.

Stacy never takes his eyes off me, furiously fumbling to open the letter without letting his gun drop.

He takes a few steps back from me.

His eyes dart across the page.

It takes him seconds to digest it. He finishes, flips the short, definitive note over to see if there's more, turns it back over, and scans it again. Stacy's face burns red as he reads it a third time. A fourth. A fifth.

She lied. We lied. For years.

"This is a fucking LIE! Stevie's my son!" Stacy bellows, jabbing the revolver at me. "You. You made this somehow. What did you do with them? Where are they?"

The recollection of Sarah, reaching across the hallway, desperate for my help, reverberates through time with perfect clarity, echoing as a part of me. It is again how it always is: I don't go to her. I can't protect her from Mason, I can't save her, I don't even try, I lose her, she loses everything. Not again.

"Look. He's my son. We shouldn't have lied. But we did. He's mine, and they're gone, and no one is going to tell you where they are, ever. You can keep us in here for a fucking week. We don't know where they are. She left me the letter and I never saw her. They're gone, and I'm glad she left.

Michelle deserves more, and Stevie—my son—deserves better than anything you or I could do for him."

I'm not done. I feel tears streaming down my face.

Even if I knew where they were, I've finally found my resolve. I'm protecting Michelle. And my son.

"So fuck you. You'll have to fucking kill me. I'm never telling you a goddamn thing."

Raw fury explodes out of Stacy, the product of years of suspicion, suppressed paranoia, drug abuse, imbalance, and hatred. He brings the gun handle down on top of my head with a crushing blow, and then cracks me across the face with the back of his free hand. The bang-bang assault staggers me. I almost regain my balance but collapse to the floor, woozy. Flashes of light distort my vision. My head is ringing. I'm nauseous. I will myself to stay conscious. Before my vision returns, I roll over on my stomach and prop myself up on all fours, grappling with my fear and disorientation, mustering whatever strength and courage I have left to get back on my feet. It's pure willpower that keeps me from passing out.

But I cannot get up.

"GET UP, YOU FUCKING PUSSY!" Stacy screams, like my dad. "I'll kill you! I swear to God I'll kill you if you don't tell me where they are!"

My head sags, I can't even look up, but I can sense it in his voice. Stacy has lost his grip on the situation, but even worse: he feels it, too. He knows it's almost over, and he's wildly, recklessly, unpredictable.

I know I'm a dead man. I don't care, as long as I can somehow keep him from hurting anyone else.

Pastor Moseley drags himself across the floor, cowering just out of the line of fire, and shields his wife.

Stacy crumples Michelle's letter in his left hand, balls it up, and throws it at me. It bounces off my face and falls to the floor, unfurling and dabbed in blood, open so I can see my name where Michelle had begun her final goodbye to me, and her old life.

Jeremy.

I understand now.

Apologies aren't enough to repair devastation and erase regret.

I'll never be able to undo Sarah's death. I'll never be able to go back and stand up to my dad, or tell someone, anyone, and make the beatings stop. I'll never be able to undo my grotesque bullying of Mason Reynolds. I'll never be able to make up for abandoning Michelle to lie to Stacy about Stevie.

Something has to change.

Stacy tucks the revolver back into the waistband of his pants, picks up the AR-15, and holds it to his shoulder. Only, he's not pointing it at me, and he's not pointing it at Pastor Moseley and his wife. He's aiming at the flinching crowd, who begin crying out and begging for their lives.

I have to stand up. He's a one-man firing squad. I get to my feet, swaying and staggered.

"Stacy...don't do this! They don't know anything. They're not a part of this. You don't have to hurt anyone else." I hold both hands in the air, surrendering. "I'm sorry, I'm sorry. It's my fault. Shoot me."

"You and Moseley can tell me how to find them." His finger's on the trigger. He's in a hypnotic state, oblivious to what I'm saying to him. "One of you knows." I see he's defeated.

"I'm sorry, Stacy, for everything. For lying about Stevie, for taking Michelle from you. You're right, we were brothers and I fucked you over and you never did anything but help me. You helped me the first night we met. You let me live with you. You kept me out of jail. Just...just don't shoot. Please."

My eyes never leave his trigger finger. It tenses. This is the end.

He's not going to stop. He's going to kill everyone in this room.

I can't let it happen again. I only have a split second to act, and I take my opening the moment I see it.

The clock on the wall reads 3:16 p.m. I finally lunge at him.

Stacy's military training takes over. He adjusts his aim, turns the rifle from the group, levels it at me.

I'm almost on him, closing the gap in a second. I'm going to get to him before he can pull the trigger.

Almost. The realization is like a bomb blast in my skull. I needed one more step. I wish I'd been better.

Stacy fires once, twice, three times. I see the muzzle flash. Someone shrieks. I don't feel anything aside from a thudding impact that would have spun me completely off course if I'd been further away.

I'm shredded. Blood everywhere. Searing and debilitating agony.

But Stacy can't fucking stop me now, even as the bullets rip through me. I take all three shots as my momentum carries me into him. Stacy is stronger and has trained for combat, but he also believes shooting me will end it. He's wrong. We tumble to the ground in a twisted bloody pile. Stacy claws at my face, gouging at my bad eye, bucking and kicking at the wounds in my chest with an animal's ferocity.

All I can do is hold on, squeezing him in a slippery hug.

My grip weakens. He's getting free. We're face to face.

If I let go, he's going to murder someone else. I dig my fingernails in and hold.

He stops. We make eye contact.

There's nothing I recognize behind his desperate, clear blue eyes. He's wild, gone, emptied of humanity.

Stacy will never recognize it's over. If he pulls away from me, everyone's dead. Stevie and Michelle are safely hidden away, but if I can't hold on… thirty innocent bystanders will lose their lives, complicit only in

Stacy's delusions. The last vestiges of strength gush from my body, covering Stacy as he struggles, and spreading across the floor. He's shrieking from betrayal and dismay that I'm thwarting his plan. He throws me aside, grabbing for the pistol he dropped when I tackled him.

He slips on my blood, skids, reaches, misses.

The AR-15 is too unwieldly to use as a gun, but instinctively I try for it anyway. I'm losing consciousness.

"I'll fucking kill you!" Stacy is screaming. He's inches from the pistol. "I'll kill all of you!"

It takes everything in me, but I fling the AR-15 away from the fight, toward Pastor Moseley.

I have to stop Stacy from getting the pistol. I can't. My mind tells my body to get up. It doesn't move.

I see Sarah's last moments of life, the certainty of our fate in her soft brown eyes, holding out hope.

I see Michelle in the backseat of my car, resolute, mournful eyes, disappointed and tearful.

I see Syd, fighting with me, laboring under the memory of her stepsister, to save me from me.

I see Wendy, reluctantly evangelizing that some Fathers are good, faithful, loving, and content.

I no longer see today, only yesterdays. My brain is shutting down. I can't…give up…until…it's done.

Finally, the room acts.

First, it's Pastor Moseley, then his boys, then others, women and men, all rushing in to pile on top of Stacy at the last second before he can get his hands on the revolver. Someone grabs the rifle, doesn't know what to do with it, and runs out of the room, away from the turmoil, to keep it from being used.

Words aren't coming out clearly.

"Jesus," I gurgle. I'm trying to say, "Help. I'm...fucking...I'm shot. Help."

Stacy thrashes under a pile of humanity. He lands some blows, a few hard enough that they knock a couple of his attackers free of the melee, but not enough for him to get loose. It's almost over now.

I'm on my back. I stop trying to see. I lay my head back on the floor. Staring at the ceiling.

My circle of vision is closing. Soft darkness outlined by gentle white creeps in, a welcome intruder.

I'm alone. Everyone else is dedicated to the assailant.

Are there sirens? Are the police coming? I think to ask for a doctor, but I say something else.

"Sarah. I'm sorry," I tell her. I see her face, dimples and downward smile, covering her mouth, auburn hair, tangled but untainted by blood. Sarah's eyes are filled with an inviting love. She's a short distance away, waving me over. Beckoning me. Is she wearing a Gin Blossoms t-shirt? A Cubs hat? Is this real?

She hasn't changed in seven years, young and delighted, hopeful and forgiving. Sarah. Sarah.

I'm sorry. "I fixed it. I kept my promise. I'm sorry it took me so long."

Commotion explodes into the room. Police officers yelling. Civilians dispersing from the pile that had held Stacy until their arrival. It's happening a few feet from me, but I can't even turn my head. Shapes and faces and several someones are now asking me how badly I'm hurt.

I can't answer. It doesn't feel like I'm hurt that bad. I don't feel any pain. I'm just paralyzed. I'm OK.

"You did it, Shell. You saved yourself. And our son." Michelle is a strong and amazing woman and mother. It is the thing I adore about her the most. "I'm sorry I wasn't there; you didn't need me. Free of it," I

508

apologize. Someone asks me what I'm saying, but I can't repeat it. I don't have the strength. I don't need it. Michelle has enough strength for both of us. Maybe she'll be there when I wake up. I want to have someone to fight for. Maybe she'll come back. Maybe she'll bring Stevie with her. Maybe not.

I don't want to die alone.

I don't want to die.

I don't want.

I don't.

Pastor Moseley is suddenly by my side. "The snow. Jeremy, the ambulance is here. You'll be…"

Stacy screams obscenities at everyone, and especially at me.

I smile. I didn't get him killed. And he won't get to Stevie or Shell.

I visualize the entirety of the last week and a half now, the perfection of it all. The timing was like a masterful orchestration, incomprehensibly organized around my poor decisions and my mistakes.

The last piece fit naturally. I shake my head no.

"What is it, Jeremy?" Pastor Moseley is holding my hand, but I can't feel it, only see it as he raises our clasped and interlocked fingers into my field of vision. "They're almost here. You're OK. You're OK."

I cough up blood, a spray that descends across my face. Pastor Moseley is crying.

"You saved my family. You saved everyone, Jeremy. You saved Michelle and Stevie. You did it. I would've told. You stopped it. Jeremy, you can't save yourself. Not from this, not from what might come next. Can you understand me? Please, Jeremy. I am so sorry." Tears fall on my face.

He's stopped making promises he has to know aren't true, shifting to ones he believes are.

"Jeremy, I'm going to tell you something right now, the most important thing you'll ever hear. I only have a few seconds. Listen to me. When

Jesus Christ died on the Cross for our sins, He was crucified between two criminals. Before they died, one of them asked Jesus to remember him, a simple act of contrition. Jesus said they'd be together in Paradise. He was forgiven. Jeremy, you only have to ask God to forgive you, for everything, and He will. Even now. I know you want to be forgiven. You can be. I promise you. Just ask Him, in your mind. If you can't talk, just think it. He will hear you. He will."

Forgiveness.

My necklaces have fallen free of my shirt, dangling to the side. Pastor Moseley reaches down, gingerly touching each of my three pendants. St. Jude, The Patron Saint of Lost Causes. Best Friends Forever. A crucifix. "Where is the ambulance? He's bleeding to death!" he shouts, looking toward the door again.

Where's Michelle's letter? I can't lose it. I reach out, but no one knows why or for what.

Her note becomes nothing more than evidence to be collected in a crime scene.

I gasp for breath, drowning on dry land. There's a stretcher now. I'm being lifted up.

Glimpses of faces, moments in time.

Sarah, dying. My dad, screaming. Stacy, shooting. Pink, using me. Jeremy, self-destructing.

I always feared happiness because it's fleeting. The joy that others find consistently isn't destined for me. It is an affliction of apprehension. Why seek something that will end unexpectedly and terribly? At least my relationship with melancholy was consistent and familiar. Sadness is a faithful companion, certain to stay as long as I'm grieving, never abandoning me, always outlasting everything else. The second I let myself dream of brighter days, my cynical heart and doubting mind conspired to create a self-fulfilling prophecy. I'd never be happy, because I knew I never would be, because I knew I never could be, because I knew I never should be. Disappointment was always lurking and waiting, ready to affirm me with the welcoming promise of isolation and intoxication, comforting me and nursing my injuries and the broken heart I received while foolishly daring to be open to impossibilities. Love and hope are for fools and romantics. I am both, and I am neither. I'm a survivor, but I can't take this type of punishment any longer. The world I inhabit isn't meant for me. I send risk away, push despair to the fringe, and invite numbness to overstay its welcome now that my part in fate's design is complete.

Pastor Moseley is still by my side, rushing along with me. We must be moving. I can't feel anything.

"Do you believe, Jeremy!? Can you hear me? Do you already believe? Jeremy!"

There's an oxygen mask over my face, but I can't inhale. Hands. Distant twinges of pain. Bandages, a needle. Questions. Flashing lights. Crying. Is that Stacy, screaming from somewhere? It's still snowing.

Play the fucking tape, Wafer. I'm sorry, bro.

My eyes widen on their own. I scrape the mask from my face. The EMTs try to force it back on. Only Pastor Moseley seems to understand what's happening. "He wants to say something!"

Tell Michelle I'm sorry. I was terrified I'd be my dad to my son. I love him. I didn't want to hurt him.

His face is near mine again. "Jeremy. God loves all of us so much that He sent His son to die in our place, so that all we have to do is believe He did that, for us, and we can be forgiven for all the things we've done to ourselves and others. He loves you just as you are. He's a good Father, ready to bring you home and take care of you. He'll love you forever. He'll forgive you. I promise. I swear. Everything. All of it. Do you believe that Jesus Christ did that for you? The pain will be over soon. It's almost too late. Please."

A good father. Wendy was right. I want a good dad. I need one now right now. I'm scared.

I've been trying to fix everything on my own, balance the scales, compensate for the wicked things I've done and save myself, but I repeatedly stumble and fail in a cycle of spectacular failures. I needed to change but didn't until it was too late. Time couldn't heal my wounds. My recollections wouldn't let me live. I suffered brutality and humiliation at home. I sought revenge, but hurt Mason. I gave my damaged heart away to Sarah, but she's gone. I love my son, but I abused him with neglect the way my father had ruined me with his cruelty. I left Michelle when she needed me. I'm ready to go. I've wanted it for years. I want the pain to be over. I'm lost. I want someone to find me, finally.

I don't want to stay here anymore. Save me from all of this. Save me from myself. Save them from me.

"Do you believe, son? Can you say it? Squeeze my hand, say anything, let me know you understand!"

Pastor Moseley is yelling from far away, across a great divide, on the other side of a snow-covered canyon. I close my eyes, the din of activity fading into background noise. I understand, and I want to tell Pastor Moseley that everything will be OK, so he can tell Michelle, but the distance is too vast.

Sarah. I see her now, exactly as I remember her. Perfect. There's Someone Else here, too. But she's here.

"Let me bring you back," she seems to whisper. "Stay. I'll love you forever, Jeremy. I promise."

She reaches out her hand. This time, when I reach back across the expanse, I find my hand in hers.

Contentment.

I believe.

And it's over.

I'll be happy here.

I'm eternally grateful for the support of so many along this journey, but I expressly could not have done it without my friends on Kickstarter: Jason N, Rebecca E, Rachael K, Chris G, Lisa B, Lisa H, Ann B, Jodee Z, Joel G, Jim S, Jake B, Steve O, Joni G, Shauna, Jimmy W Jr., Joyce W, Lori P, Anna, Michael M, Mary S, Kate B, Craig W, Brandon M, Linda M, Steve F, Lori, Sarah Z, Janet M, Tara B, Eric G, Susan M, Todd C, Jason P, Michelle W, my Dad, Chad M, Kim G, Erin M, Tommy N, Carrie V.A., Jennifer C, Adam A, Ross G, Susan L, Stephanie A, Justin K, Seena, Dave S, Dale R, Teresa E, Danelle S, Mark P, Philip H, Dawn B, Ruth W, Andy W, Joe G Melanie H, Melissa P, Brian S, CJ, Jackie D, Joy R, Melissa C, Mark H, Peter B, Maureen D, Karen R, Alex B, Annette A, Anne E, Samantha B, Alyssa S, Mike W, Rick S, Tracy D, Stacy N, Andrew A, Valerie H, Lindsey M, David H, Dawn, Summer S, Dan G, Chris G, Caz B, Valarie B, Matthew D, Amy E, Jennifer H, Regina M, Tim S, Carol R, Carrie P, Natasha O, Mati S, Marty P, Rusti M, Brittny C, Natalie S, Brian M, Eric W, Heather W, Kanada D, Ted L, David A D, Jackie L, Jason L, Andrea J, Jessie G, Phil D, Justin, Sheila S, Matt F, Heather, Craig N, Melody T, Tonya W, Abigail B, Dwayne T, Teka B, Michelle R, Linda B, my Mom, Brenda H, Trevor W, Cassie F, Chuck K, Bernie R, Matthew S, Melissa C, Matthew B, Lynette B, Christine T, Jordan C, Adam B, Rachelle M, Julie, and Jo C. You made a childhood dream come true!!

And to my editor Joelle, who was invaluable in smoothing a first draft into a novel: thank you.

If you enjoyed my debut novel
(and want more stories like this one reach publication)
would you consider telling a friend and writing
an honest review on Amazon or Goodreads? Thank you!